BLOOD LOSS

Alex Barclay lives in County Cork, Ireland. She is the best-selling author of *Darkhouse*, *The Caller*, *Blood Runs Cold*, *Time of Death*, *Blood Loss*, *Harm's Reach* and *Killing Ways*.

For more information about Alex Barclay and her books, please visit her website, www.alexbarclay.co.uk

Praise for Alex Barclay:

'The rising star of the hard-boiled crime fiction world, combining wild characters, surprising plots and massive back-drops with a touch of dry humour'   *Mirror*

'Tense, no-punches-pulled thriller that will have you on the edge of your deckchair'   *Woman and Home*

'Explosive'   *Company*

'*Darkhouse* is a terrific debut by an exciting new writer'
                    Independent on Sunday

'Compelling'   *Glamour*

'Excellent summer reading . . . Barclay has the confidence to move her story along slowly, and deftly explores the relationships between her characters'   *Sunday Telegraph*

'The thriller of the summer'   *Irish Independent*

'If you ha   ump on
the band   *agazine*

Also by Alex Barclay

Darkhouse
The Caller
Blood Runs Cold
Time of Death
Blood Loss
Harm's Reach
Killing Ways

ALEX BARCLAY

Blood Loss

HARPER

This novel is entirely a work of fiction.
The names, characters and incidents portrayed in it are
the work of the author's imagination. Any resemblance to
actual persons, living or dead, events or localities is
entirely coincidental.

Harper
An imprint of HarperCollins*Publishers*
1 London Bridge Street,
London, SE1 9GF

www.harpercollins.co.uk

This paperback edition 2012
10

First published in Great Britain by HarperCollins*Publishers* in 2012

Copyright © Alex Barclay 2012

Alex Barclay asserts the moral right to
be identified as the author of this work

ISBN: 978 0 00 738343 6

Set in Meridien by Palimpsest Book Production Limited,
Falkirk, Stirlingshire

Printed and bound in Great Britain by
Clays Ltd, St Ives plc

Find out more about HarperCollins and the environment at
www.harpercollins.co.uk/green

To Grainne and to Melanie

PROLOGUE

It was an imprisonment, twice over. Minds captured first by insanity were captured a second time by Kennington Asylum for the Insane. Built in 1904, it was a dignified structure on a salvaged tract of Denver city parkland; mental wellness forged from red bricks and green grass. In appearance, it stood for its promises. But until it became the hollow shell it is today, it never truly reflected them.

In contrast, the grounds were overrun, choked by nature untended, as if the twisted roots of madness, ignored for over a century, were finally unbound.

People had been sent to Kennington to be healed, but when they were captured a third time – by a camera's lens – they stood in doomed herds, their faces blank, their brains looted. It was clear that the asylum was not a pitstop on a journey to wellness, it was the endpoint of a descent. Their clothes were soiled, their limbs atrophied, their bodies swept into corners like dirt, like something to be thrown away.

*   *   *

CONDEMNED. Even the sign was. The boy stared at it. The Kennington photographs had been taken in 1950, but they had resurfaced sixty years on to be laid bare across eight pages of a Sunday supplement. They had made grown men cry. But the not-so-grown, the high-schoolers . . . well, the photos made them want to go to that fucked-up place and party with ghosts.

The boy climbed onto the perimeter wall and took a thick black marker from his coat pocket. He gripped the sign with a gloved hand, crossed out the C-O-N and drew an A through the E. DAMNED. Just like a century's parade of lunatic patients . . . just like the people inside the building that he had come for tonight. He was yet to know that he would leave without seeing them. And his inadvertent victim, laughing and throwing back shots, dancing through the abandoned wards this Hallowe'en night, was yet to know that her bright ethanol eyes would be haunted hollows by the time the music died.

The boy made his way through the woods that bordered the drive. It was a tangled mess of trees and bushes, and he moved blindly until his boots hit stone. He looked down. There they were – the signs painted onto the ground to lead the way: small, yellow lightning strikes. He followed them around to the back entrance where a huge timber door had hung until its hinges had been unscrewed, until it had been thrown to one side.

Somewhere in the dark distant heart of the building, voices and music pulsed. He paused in the empty doorway. Up ahead, more lightning strikes were drawn on the ground and he began to follow them, moving toward the sound and to where the final symbol was drawn outside the door of the old electroshock therapy room.

He stepped inside. The room seemed filled with giant

eyes. He blinked. There was a swamp of people in front of him. He blinked again. They were moving like a mass of maggots. He blinked again. This was not his world. He was sober. They were all drunk, or wild or weakened by illegal drugs. He moved through the crowd, and it swelled against him. A door led off into another room. He was about to go in. Then he saw someone. A girl, standing against a wall, talking to a guy. But her eyes were boring into *him*, he could feel it like heat. She left the other guy, and walked toward him, and when she got past him, she glanced back, and her smile was like the answer yes. He followed her. She was wearing a black top that was slashed all the way down the back. Her skirt was *so* short, plaid and pleated. She had black leggings underneath, and boots like his, the tongues out, the laces undone. Her hair was black and shiny and cut into a short bob like a doll's. A small tattoo was growing like a vine up the center of her neck.

She picked up speed down the hallway, down another, disappearing when she reached the last room. He felt his heart surge. She slid on top of the table at the furthest corner of the room, and her knees were apart. She was smiling at him. His whole body was pounding, not just his head anymore. She opened her mouth to speak, but as he pressed himself against her, he could feel that her whole body was exactly the same way, and he knew that no-one should talk.

It was his first time. He had no idea sex could make you so angry. So, so fucking angry. *This is insane.* He laughed. *This is insane.*

He lay there when it was over, staring at the ceiling. They had wound up on the floor. Her hair had come off. It must have been a wig. It was in his hand.

He got up and started to fix his clothes. 'I gotta go,' he said.

When he put his hands in his pockets, he could feel the paper. He didn't need the drawing any more. This had made up for it. She could have it. He crouched down beside her and placed it by her head.

'Thank you,' he said. 'That was awesome.'

As his mouth pressed against her cheek, a small bloody bubble of saliva grew between her lips, and burst.

1

Taber Grace had a slim file on the passenger seat of his car and a cigarette burning down in the ash tray. He was sitting back against the head rest, his bloodshot eyes staring into the dark. He had often thought about sitting in the same position, in his garage, breathing in exhaust fumes through a hose pipe.

Taber Grace was forty-two years old, short and slight. He liked to dress in straight-leg jeans and plain, washed-out shirts, always buttoned to the neck. His hair, thick and brown, fell across one eye. Someone in a bar once joked that it was his private eye. The Private Eye with the private eye. Taber Grace mostly had the sense not to go into bars to listen to drunk talk. He was not a competent drunk. He would recognize the early signs of his drunkenness – the softness around the edge of his vision, the longer search for words – and it was too hard these days to resist being drawn to the dissolution.

After an hour waiting in the dark, watching the snow fall over Denver, Taber Grace knew that his client was not going to show. November 14, evening: it was to have been their second meeting – to see how the client wanted to proceed, based on Taber Grace's preliminary findings. These meetings were always the same. The client would sit like a prisoner in the electric chair. But the current came from within – the spark of dueling fears as their suspicions were about to be confirmed or dismissed. There was no comfort in either. And there was no comfort for Taber Grace. He had intimate knowledge of his clients, their lives, the lives of those close to them. He was the stranger-witness to their darkest betrayals. They needed this knowledge, they paid him for it, yet they didn't want him to have it. Each time he delivered it, he could see in their eyes how quickly he became repellent.

Taber Grace had been the bearer of bad news before. It had been part of his first job. Then, like now, it never touched him. It was a practical delivery of information, uncomplicated by emotion. In that job, he had been bound by propriety. He was on time, he spoke politely, he never swore. When he was fired, it became easy to believe that he was what he had always feared he was – just a small-town boy, shoulder to shoulder with his blue-collar buddies, no taller. The problem was that he had never fit into that small-town world and he had run from it as soon as he could.

Taber Grace had liked the mannerly man he became when he left his home town. He liked his new life in Denver. But what he had loved at the start became what he hated at the end, like a failed relationship. The life that came with his job was like a smart overcoat he had carefully put on, that fit perfectly, but gradually began to slip from his shoulders. And he only realized it was gone when the world got very, very cold. And later, when his home did.

Melissa Grace, his sweetheart wife, had also liked the mannerly man, and couldn't understand why, despite the early end to one career, her husband appeared to have thrown it all away. But Taber Grace, fired and depressed, slowly convinced himself that his job had been the first thing his wife had seen, the part that impressed her, and promised her so much. It turned out that Taber Grace never believed that his wife loved him for who he was. For his heart . . . or for how it used to be.

The Graces had one son. He had blond hair to his shoulders and an exceptionally pretty face: his mother's face, with his father's long eyelashes. He was christened Taber Grace Jr, but his father, as his own life unraveled, began to call him TJ. He had given him the nickname he swore he never would, because maybe being called Taber Grace would just be bad luck.

Taber Grace knew that he had neglected his marriage to death. Even now, at times, he felt that the life he thought he would have ran parallel to this new, empty one. At times, he felt that back at his house, Taber Grace 1.0, proud, loving husband and father, was having pancakes with his wife and son.

Yet, here he was. He had walked from his marriage not into bars and strip clubs, but down into the sewage pipes that ran under other lives. A client might heft the manhole cover aside; Taber Grace made the descent.

And Taber Grace was the one who came back up covered in shit.

2

Summer was hiker and biker season in Breckenridge, Colorado, but winter was when the pretty little town really came to life. It was then that its true beauty shone – in the glow of the white peaks, in the sparkle of the fairy lights down Main Street, in the headlights of the groomers, in the bright, after-ski faces.

In winter, the population of Breck could go from three-and-a-half thousand to more than ten times that, yet its magic was how it held its ground and its charm. There were plenty of hotels, inns and condos to accommodate Breck's visitors, and the newest was The Merlin Lodge & Spa. It was a small hotel in a small town with a big heart, and it had a mid-sized problem: it had opened too early.

'That's my opinion, anyway,' said the desk clerk. His name, Jared Labati, was printed on a gold badge on his white shirt. The shirt was a size too small, his black pants a size too big. He was only in his late teens, yet strikingly at odds with the healthy image of the country's skinniest state. His shaggy brown hair curled out at the ends and was combed forward and sideways across most of his wide face.

It was a style for a slimmer kid. A tiny diamond ring shone in a right ear that was prominent enough to poke through his mass of hair.

Erica Whaley was standing at the check-in desk with her husband, Mark. 'It didn't say anywhere on the website that the hotel was brand new,' she said. 'Lucky us.' She smiled.

Mark Whaley was holding his credit card paused in mid-air. He glanced at his wife. They laughed. 'OK – go ahead,' said Mark.

'Did you have far to come?' said Jared.

'No – Denver,' said Mark.

'The rooms are completely finished – don't get me wrong,' said Jared, 'and any extra work that needs to be done won't happen on weekends, so it will be quiet during your stay. The major work is done . . . except for the Spa. Sorry.' He directed this at Erica. But she had turned to see her three-year-old son, Leo, hanging upside down from the back of a brown leather sofa, his face red with the rush of blood.

Mark spoke to Jared. 'Our son tests all surfaces and objects for suitability to climb or swing from.' He paused. 'Then climbs or swings from them, regardless of his findings.'

Erica sprinted for Leo, grabbing him under his arm and swinging him into the air.

Mark raised his eyebrows at Jared. 'That was close. His Spidey sense is weak.'

Jared smiled.

'OK, be honest,' said Mark, leaning in to him, speaking quietly. 'Will this be a comfortable stay? My little girl isn't feeling too good.' Mark's eleven-year-old daughter from his first marriage, Laurie, was on the sofa reading a book, oblivious to her Spiderbrother.

'You bet,' said Jared. 'They're just doing some things like wiring, and putting fancy room numbers on the doors, etc.'

'Hmm . . .' said Mark. 'No room numbers? That could be interesting.'

'The doors are numbered with laser print-outs for now, don't worry,' said Jared.

'OK,' said Mark. 'I just wanted to make sure that if the Parkers are coming back to reclaim Leo that they know which room to go to.'

Jared paused for a moment, then smiled. 'Peter Parker is Spiderman, right?'

'Yes, he is,' said Mark, 'just so we're clear . . .' He smiled, and turned around to see his wife struggling back to the reception desk with her bucking son jammed onto her hip and shouting at her to let him go.

'Take him,' said Erica to Mark. She almost dropped Leo at Mark's feet. The little boy sprang up.

Erica shook her head. 'He's like those indestructible, I don't know, *zombies* that you can't kill – they keep coming back to life.'

Mark looked at Jared. 'We don't want to kill him,' he said. 'Honestly. Or return him to the Parkers.'

Erica had clearly heard the Parker reference before. She called, 'Laurie, sweetie?'

Laurie closed her book and came over.

'Just like that,' said Erica, squeezing Laurie against her, and kissing the top of her head. 'How are you feeling, sweetheart?'

'I'm fine now,' said Laurie. 'I don't know what happened, but the pain's gone.'

Erica held the back of her hand to Laurie's forehead. 'No fever. And you've got good color in your cheeks. I pronounce you fit and well.'

Laurie smiled. 'Why, thank you.'

Leo was swinging out from the reception desk, his feet

working hard to climb to the top. He dropped to the floor and ran away.

'Your turn,' said Erica.

Laurie ran after him.

Jared went into the back office.

'Loving the loose cannon desk clerk,' said Mark.

'I know,' said Erica. She wrapped her arms around Mark, and kissed his neck. Then she moved up to his ear.

'Is this about hotel sex?' said Mark, leaning back.

Erica smiled. 'That goes without saying,' she said. 'This is about dinner.'

'What about Laurie . . . is she feeling better?' said Mark. 'Is she OK to be left with a sitter?'

'Oh, she's fine,' said Erica. 'I think it might have been a little attention seeking?'

'Or she wanted to make sure we wouldn't leave her to go to dinner,' said Mark.

'No,' said Erica. 'I was just talking to her, she said she was absolutely fine. So?'

Mark hooked his arm around Erica's waist, and pulled her close. 'I promised the kids I'd watch *Toy Story 3*.'

'Well, I promised myself I wouldn't lose my mind,' said Erica. 'So, you watch the movie, I'll go down to the bar and pick up a snowboarder.'

'Mrs Whaley,' said Mark, 'the kids and I can watch the movie while you take a bath, slip into something less comfortable, and by the time you have done the makeup I don't think you need to wear, yet apply so beautifully, I'll be ready to accompany you to the bar to oversee your choice of snowboarder.'

'Deal,' said Erica.

Jared came back to the desk. 'Alrighty,' he said, setting two keys on the desk.

'Old-fashioned keys,' said Erica. 'Nice touch.'

'You'll be in Room 304,' said Jared. 'That's on the third floor. Elevator is that way. You'll be staying in a family suite – two inter-connecting rooms. Do you need help with your bags?'

'No, thank you,' said Mark.

'Well, OK then. Enjoy your stay.'

'Oh, we will,' said Erica.

'We'd like to arrange for a sitter to look after the kids for a couple hours, while we go down to dinner,' said Mark.

'Not a problem,' said Jared. 'For what time?'

'Eight thirty for the sitter?' said Mark. 'Nine for dinner?' He turned to Erica. 'That'll leave us some time to check her out before we entrust our prized possessions to her.'

3

Agent Ren Bryce sat at her desk in The Rocky Mountain Safe Streets Task Force, a violent-crime squad of eleven based in Denver. It was Saturday night, and everyone had gone to the bar, except the boss, Special Supervisory Agent Gary Dettling, and Cliff James, Ren's big-bear buddy. Cliff was ex-Jefferson County Sheriff's Department. At fifty-three, he was the eldest of the team, and at two-hundred pounds, the most huggable. Cliff and Ren, along with blond, kind, grandma-friendly Robbie Truax and arrogant, short-ass numbers-guy Colin Grabien, had become a mini-squad of movable parts. The arrangement of their desks and the maneuvering of two filing cabinets could create a subtle break in the squad's bullpen that was more psychological than visible. Otherwise, their boss would have done something about it. If he could have only thrown Colin Grabien out into the general population, that would have worked for Ren. The book was *The Three Musketeers*. Not *The Three Musketeers and the Dickhead*.

Ren's cell phone rang, and the screen flashed with a photo of her older brother Matt – her best friend, therapist, and moral conscience rolled into one. He was thirty-nine – two years older than Ren – and lived in Manhattan with his wife, Lauren, and their three-month-old son, Ethan.

'Finally,' said Matt when Ren answered.

Silence.

'You're alive,' said Matt.

'Yes, I am,' said Ren.

'Just, you didn't text back,' said Matt. 'And . . . did you get my voicemails?'

'Sorry, yes,' said Ren.

'Are you OK?' said Matt.

'Yes!' said Ren. 'Why wouldn't I be?'

Pause. 'Um . . . maybe because last month, you could barely make it from the bed to the sofa? And you phoned me several times bawling your eyes out. In the middle of the night—'

'I'm so sorry,' said Ren. 'I know that's hard with Ethan and everything . . .'

'You can call me any time, you know that,' said Matt. 'I'm always here, but . . . that's not the point. You dropped off the face of the earth.'

'I'm sorry,' said Ren. 'I didn't mean to worry you.'

'You never do,' said Matt.

'What's that supposed to mean?' said Ren.

'Exactly that. You never *mean* to. Next time, keep me posted, that's all.'

'Fine.' *Jesus.*

'So . . . what have you been doing?' said Matt. 'Are you OK? What changed? I was so worried. Ever since Helen . . .'

Ren was bipolar, unmedicated, and shrink-free. Her beloved psychiatrist of two years, Helen Wheeler, had been murdered four months earlier, and Ren and her FBI undercover past had been painfully entangled in her death.

'Positive thinking!' said Ren. 'Talking to you really helped that last time, Matt. You cheered me up. And when I got off the phone, I just said, OK, what can I do? So I went online, looked at positive thinking websites, ordered some positive thinking books on Amazon. I looked up psychiatrists in Denver, printed off a few names . . . and I just told myself, get a grip.'

'And did you find a psychiatrist?' said Matt.

'No . . .'

'Ren . . . you've been very down for . . . months.'

'I'm OK now,' said Ren. 'I'm feeling much better.'

'Well, I'm glad to hear that,' said Matt. 'I really am.'

'And,' said Ren. 'I met this amazing guy.'

Silence.

'Matt?' said Ren. 'Are you there?'

'Yes,' said Matt. 'When did this happen?'

'Two weeks ago—'

'Which might explain the radio silence . . .'

Ugh. 'Anyway, I went out with work, then the guys all went home, I stayed on with Colin Grabien's girlfriend, Naomi. The woman is nuts. Anyway, next thing, I met this really cute guy—'

'And off the radar you go.' His tone was flat.

'I wasn't off the radar,' said Ren. 'I was in work.'

'I got one text from you weeks ago, then nothing,' said Matt.

'You sound like mom . . .'

'Your worst nightmare. We've been through this before, Ren. This is not an on/off thing: you can't call me all upset, then drop off the face of the earth when everything is OK. *I* didn't know everything was OK.'

'Well, I would have called you if I was going to jump off a cliff . . .' Ren laughed.

Silence.

'So . . . how're things with you?' said Ren.

'Exhausting,' said Matt.

'You don't sound yourself,' said Ren. She could hear him sigh.

'So,' said Matt, 'are you going to call one of the psychiatrists?'

'Yes . . .' said Ren.

'Once more with feeling.'

'I will. It's Saturday night . . .'

'Ren . . . Monday morning, please do.'

'Yes, OK. Jesus.'

'Enjoy the rest of your weekend.'

'You too.'

Ren put down the phone.

Well, that was depressing.

Ren turned to Cliff.

'I'm taking advantage of Colin's absence,' she said. 'To ask you this question – is he serious about crazy Naomi?'

'I think he has found The One,' said Cliff, smiling.

'Hmm,' said Ren. 'I'm not sure she feels the same way. I really like the woman. I do. But . . . remember I ended up staying out with her a couple of weeks back? We had a lot to drink, but she was . . . behaving like a single lady. All the single ladies.'

'All the single ladies,' said Cliff. He put his hand up.

'She zoned in on this guy at the bar, like it was her mission to bag him,' said Ren.

'And did she?' said Cliff.

'No, but . . . I was right there – she was hardly going to disappear with him.'

'Maybe she's just insecure,' said Cliff, 'or competitive, or . . .'

16

'Hmm,' said Ren. 'She's like those women who other women love . . . until they see them around their man. She's a girl's girl, and a man's girl, but . . . you get the feeling she's distracting you with her high-larity, while she's got her hand on your boyfriend's ass.' Ren paused. 'I'm safe for girlfriends and wives. I'll laugh or joke with yo' man, but I don't want him, he's all yours. I think I make that clear. I've never taken someone's man. Naomi . . . I think . . . she *does* want to take other men.'

'And I thought you didn't care about Colin . . .' said Cliff.

Ren smiled. 'And don't mention this to him, by the way.'

'No,' said Cliff.

'It would be quite the irony,' said Ren, 'a manwhore hanging up his riding boots for a womanwhore.'

'Ren, that sentence is wrong "on so many levels",' said Cliff.

'I'll get you coffee for that,' said Ren.

Cliff's phone rang. He picked up. 'Glenn? Shoot,' he said. Glenn Buddy was a Denver PD detective, and Cliff's closest friend.

'Really?' said Cliff. 'No. Nothing. I'm here with Ms Ren. Let me put you on speaker.'

'Hey, Ren,' said Glenn. 'We've got a second rape. Victim's parents found her in her bedroom when they got back from the movie theater. She is hanging by a thread. We think it's the Kennington guy . . .'

'Shit,' said Ren.

'That's bad news,' said Cliff.

'How old is she?' said Ren.

Glenn let out a breath. 'She's fourteen.'

4

From the windows of The Merlin Lodge & Spa, the peaks of the Tenmile Range over Breckenridge glowed against the black sky. Snow was falling, more than was forecast, a white powdery gift for the next day's competitors. The town was hosting a snowboarding championship two weeks ahead of the world-famous Winter Dew Festival, when up to one hundred thousand visitors would hit Breck.

Mark and Erica Whaley sat at a table against the wall half way down the restaurant.

'OK,' said Mark, looking at his watch. 'It's eleven thirty. I told the sitter I'd go check on the kids half an hour ago.'

Erica pulled the bottle of champagne from the ice bucket beside the table and held it over her glass.

'I think you'll find that's empty,' said Mark, smiling.

Erica leaned back in her chair. 'Oh, well . . .'

There was a moment of silence between them.

'Honey, are you OK?' said Erica, reaching out for Mark's hand.

'Yes,' he said. His jaw clenched. 'Why? I'm fine. You'd be the first to know if I wasn't.'

'Exactly,' said Erica. 'I *am* the first to know . . .'

'What's that supposed to mean?' said Mark.

'It means that most of the time I know before you do that something is up,' said Erica.

'That's ridiculous,' said Mark. 'Nothing is up.'

'Calm down,' said Erica.

'I'm just tired of being asked,' said Mark.

'So, I won't ask, then,' said Erica.

'Thank you,' said Mark.

'I won't care any more if you're OK,' said Erica.

'Honey . . .'

'I'll be one of those wives who lets her husband come and go, tends to her children, sleeps with the pool guy and plays bridge with her lady friends.'

'We're never getting a pool,' said Mark.

Erica smiled.

'I only ask because I care,' she said.

'Yeah, I get that,' said Mark.

'Don't be like that.'

'Honey, we're on vacation,' said Mark.

'Away from things,' said Erica. 'Isn't that a good time to talk?'

'Sure it is,' said Mark. 'But let's not get into the "are you OK" thing.'

Erica gestured to the waiter walking past.

'Could we get another bottle of champagne, please?' she said.

'You bet,' said the waiter.

'Thank you,' said Erica. She looked at Mark's face. 'Oh, come on. I'm fine.'

'I didn't say a word,' said Mark.

Erica made an expression to mimic his.

'But two bottles – really?' said Mark. 'We've got snow-boarding tomorrow, the championships, the kids . . .'

'You don't have to worry about me,' said Erica.

'Emphasis on the "me",' said Mark.

Erica rolled her eyes.

'From the lady with the horror of eye-rolling,' said Mark. 'There *was* an emphasis,' he said. 'Subconscious or not . . .'

'That is not fair,' said Erica. 'You know I'm not like that.'

'Do you know something?' said Mark. 'Being mean when you're drunk is a drink problem too . . .'

'Wow,' said Erica. Mark wasn't looking at her. 'What has gotten into you?' She waited. 'Mark, look at me.'

He did.

'Are you OK?' she said.

'You're seriously asking me that,' said Mark, 'after everything I just said . . .'

Erica's eyes were alight. 'Oh my God, I have put up with so much shit from you. For months! Have you *any* clue? You work late, or you're locked away in the den—'

'It's been really busy. You know that—'

'We have sex once a month—' said Erica.

Mark looked at her like she was nuts.

'Trust me,' said Erica. She paused. 'Once a month . . . I feel hideous.'

'Hideous?' said Mark. 'What the . . .?' His face was stricken.

'I'm thirty-nine years old and I feel like a hag,' she said. 'My husband barely comes near me. So forgive me for asking if everything is all right. And it's not just about sex. It's about you being distant. From all of us. Sure, here we are in a beautiful hotel, but what's the point? I've tried tonight, and no, I'm still getting nothing from you. So, forgive me for trying to get something from a bottle of champagne.'

Mark said nothing.

'I'm your wife,' said Erica. 'I know you. I'm not asking if

you're OK for the hell of it. I'm asking because I know that everything is not OK. I'm asking a question I know the answer to, whether you do or not, whether you're lying to me or not. I'm giving you an out, Mark. I'm giving you a chance to tell me the truth. Because I *know* you. And, therefore, I know that something is not right.' Her chest was heaving. 'Do you even know the significance of this weekend?'

'What?' said Mark. 'Of course I do. I'm the one who's spent years trying to get a judge to let me have my daughter overnight—'

'You're not the only one,' said Erica. 'I was there too. I was the one who helped to change that judge's mind, who gave you the stability to—'

'I gave *myself* the stability,' said Mark. 'I'm the one who went for treatment, I'm the—'

'Anyway, I'm not talking about Laurie,' said Erica. 'I'm talking about us.'

Mark paused. 'Our anniversary is Tuesday. Not tonight. Not this weekend. Seriously, Erica. Did you think I'd forgotten?'

Erica looked away. 'I . . . yes. I did. I'm sorry.'

Mark shook his head. 'Why would you think I'd forget that?'

'Because of everything I just said to you. And because . . .'

'Because what?' said Mark.

Erica looked him in the eye. 'Mark, are you seeing someone else?'

He stared at her. He took a deep breath. Then he threw his napkin onto the table. 'I'm going to check on the kids.'

*   *   *

Ren and Cliff waited as Glenn Buddy held his hand over the phone to talk to a nurse.

He came back on the line. 'The vic won't be ready to talk any time soon.'

'Were there any signs of forced entry at the house?' said Cliff.

'Yup,' said Glenn. 'He broke in the back door. She was alone; her parents were at the movies.'

'And you think it's the same guy . . .?' said Cliff.

Even though it's forced entry in the victim's own home.

Ren glanced at Cliff, but he missed it.

'Yes,' said Glenn. 'Similar build, frenzied, same unwashed smell, terrible breath, stab wounds in all the same places.'

Ren knew where those places were and it was horrific.

'Anything left at the scene this time?' said Cliff.

'Nothing that hopped out,' said Glenn. 'Our Evidence Response Team's going through it. And we're still trying to round up kids from the Kennington party. It's The Silent Order of the Teenage Freaks . . .'

'What do you need from us?' said Cliff. 'Shoot.'

Mark Whaley rode the elevator to the third floor of The Merlin Lodge and Spa. He jogged down the dark hallway. He turned the key in the door of Room 304. The sitter – blonde, curvy, sixteen years old – was standing in front of him . . . naked.

5

The restaurant at The Merlin had emptied, apart from Erica Whaley. She sat scrolling through her cell phone, glancing up when her husband appeared in the restaurant doorway, then turning her eyes back to the screen. Mark sat down. His heart was pounding. Sweat dampened the hair at his temples.

For minutes, they sat in silence. Erica had put away her phone and was staring at the floor.

She spoke quietly. 'I don't want to be this couple,' she said.

'What couple?' said Mark.

'I don't want to be two people staring across a table trying to find the person they fell in love with.' Tears slid down her face.

For a long time, Mark Whaley said nothing. Then he reached out and squeezed her hand. Pulling her with him, he stood up and took her in his arms. 'I'm so sorry,' he said. 'I . . . you're right. I've been . . . I am so sorry. I love you more than I have ever loved anyone in my whole life. I am not seeing anyone else. I am so hurt that you asked. You are my world, Erica Whaley. And anything I have ever said or done that may have made you think otherwise is wrong. I can't bear it. I can't bear any of this.'

Erica pulled back. 'Any of what?' she said, squeezing his arms.

'Just . . . conflict,' he said. 'Life.'

'Life?' said Erica. 'Life is wonderful.'

He hugged her tight. 'Life is wonderful,' he said over her shoulder, out to the world.

'How are the kids?' said Erica.

'Asleep,' said Mark. 'Let's stay a while longer – the sitter was in the middle of watching something on the television. I'm sure she won't mind.'

Ren Bryce pulled out the top drawer of her desk to get some gum. The list of new psychiatrists she had so enthusiastically printed out at five a.m. the previous month was folded there, as likely to be used as the throat lozenges, the broken watch, and the birthday candles. After all, she was fine.

Shit – Gary's email.

Ren grabbed her mouse and went to her flagged emails. Gary Dettling had sent her one two weeks earlier that had a vague resonance.

She clicked on it.

Ren,
I've set this up:
Monday, November 16, 1 p.m. Dr Leonard Lone.

Recommendation from a friend . . .

This Monday.

Ren sat back in her chair, and stared up at the ceiling.
I'm fucking fine, people.

24

Gary Dettling was the only one in the office who knew Ren was bipolar. Before he had hired her for Safe Streets, he had trained her as an undercover agent, and then became her case agent on one of the most well-known undercover assignments in the Bureau – it had proved Ren's talents, and almost destroyed her. Not long afterwards, she had been diagnosed. The arrangement with Gary was that she always had to be under a psychiatrist's care, but he allowed her to use an outside psychiatrist, because she had never clicked with an Agency one.

She read the reply she had sent him.

Thanks so much, Gary. I'll be there.

In the meantime, please, someone, give me a plausible reason not to be.

Gary walked into the bullpen as Ren was closing his mail. He was hard to miss – tall, dark and athletic, he was the perfect front man for Safe Streets, and a boss that no-one could or would argue with.

'Guys, this is SA Ben Rader,' said Gary.

A short guy stepped forward from behind Gary and gave a small nod. He was five foot eight, with tanned skin and black hair. He had green, smiling eyes. He was dressed in black jeans, with a military shirt hanging open over a black t-shirt. He had a wide silver band on the middle finger of his right hand. He was shifting from one foot to the other, and had jammed his hands into his pockets. He looked about eighteen.

The Young and the Restless.

'Ben is one of our finest UC graduates,' said Gary.

'Yup,' said Ben. 'Strictly deep cover in retirement homes . . .'

Ren laughed. He flashed a big smile her way.

'I'm just passing through,' said Ben. 'I thought I'd catch up with Gary, say hi.'

'Please, excuse me,' said Ren, standing up, and moving around her desk. She pointed out the door. 'I was on my way to the ladies room.' She moved to walk past Ben and Gary.

'This is SA Ren Bryce,' said Gary.

Ren shook Ben's hand. 'Nice to meet you,' she said.

Ben beamed. 'You too,' he said, keeping her hand in his grip.

Oh my God. Stop.

Ren glanced, panicked, toward Gary, but he had turned toward the hallway. Ren pulled Ben a little closer, and as she moved by his left ear, whispered. 'I found your skull ring . . . it was in the shower tray.' She slid her hand out of his. She walked to the ladies room.

Ben texted, All that soap . . . ☺

She texted back:

Slippery . . .

He texted back:

When Wet . . . ☺

6

Ren stood in the ladies room, sliding her belt out of her work pants. She stepped out of them and pulled on her jeans, tight and low-riding, cutting into the hip bones that had newly resurfaced.

She was aware that her brother, Matt, had fired something at her, and that it was trying to pierce some part of her. But she was too far away.

Go away, Matt. Go away.

She pulled off her white work shirt and skin-toned bra, and pushed them onto the pile in her locker. She grabbed the pink bra that matched her low-cut boy shorts, hooked it at the front, adjusted the contents, adjusted the straps. She pulled on a scoop-necked gray tank with black leather strips and small silver buckles on each shoulder. Her arms were leaner, the long muscles defined again. She could see veins. She applied more makeup: light base on sallow skin, extra liner, extra mascara, tan blush on cheeks that had hollowed under the bone.

Bones and veins, coming through. The surface.

Ren thought of the men who had gotten to know more. Paul Louderback, her former physical training instructor at Quantico. Her only unfinished business. It had been seventeen years since he first got inside her head. She was twenty years old, standing in boxing gloves in the gym at the Academy, knees bent, punching the focus pads he was holding up. His eyes were extraordinarily blue, sharp, intense. She missed a beat. He struck her hard on the side of the head.

'Focus pads!' he roared, 'are for guess what?'

'For focusing on,' Ren had shouted back.

'Then focus!'

'Yes, sir.' She punched. One, two.

'And when you punch, you need to follow through! Punch like you're aiming to go through the focus pads, or through the punchbag, or through the dirtbag!'

His eyes.

'Follow through,' he had roared. 'You need to follow through!'

'Yes, sir.' One, two.

His eyes. Shit.

'Focus pads!' he roared again, 'are for guess what?'

'For focusing on,' Ren had shouted back.

'Then focus!'

'Hard to do,' Ren had told him months later. 'When the instructor looks like—'

'He wants to kiss you?' said Paul.

But she had found out that Paul Louderback was married, and she wanted to grab those boxing gloves and use them on him again for not wearing a wedding band. So she had treated the 'wants to kiss you' like it had never been said. It was the first time, in words, he had made his feelings clear. For the seventeen years since it was hinted at in emails, and gifts, and rare phone calls that she knew were a secret from his wife. This simple contact meant that no matter who Ren was with, at times she would imagine what it would be like to walk down a beach or an aisle with Paul Louderback. But he had already done both with someone else, and Ren was no homewrecker, and no-one's second best.

Just once they had dared to say more about what might have been, eighteen months earlier, in the shadow of Quandary Peak outside Breckenridge, in the aftermath of a murder investigation. Since then, there had been no contact. Paul Louderback had a life in D.C. with his wife and two daughters, and she had a life in Denver.

Then there were the men Ren had been with in the past ten years, since her mind was stamped with crazy: Vincent, everloving until she broke under the weight of his knowledge of her; Billy Waites, confidential informant, bright and brave, deep and tattooed, quietly concerned, secret. Then from the sawdust of the National Stock Show, came the extreme rider, riding fast toward her manic high, and roping her. Then a few more, scattered and grim, drawn to the same empty flame. *Come to crazy*: when Ren, fresh from sorrow, could feel her eyes dancing like fire, and her chest bursting with roving love, her glass and her wallet overflowing, her flesh showing, her smiles killing her jaw. *Come to crazy. I'll keep you up all night.*

It would last for days, or weeks, or longer. If she was *lucky* – she thought – it would last for months. Her trickster mind would tell her that the high would never end: this time I promise, this time I promise. And then came the certain, slow, quicksand low: the knockdown, turnaround low. It would sidle up to her like a street-corner mime with an upright middle finger, rocking with silent laughter at the ridiculousness that it could still surprise. It would bring terrible things, silently. It carried thoughts with claws and teeth – thoughts that she may have fought before, and beaten. But her trickster mind would tell her that this low would never end: this time I promise, this time I promise.

'Surpri-ise!' it would mouth. 'You fucking sucker.' Rocking shoulders, silent laugh. 'I. Always. Win.'

Ren leaned into the mirror, sliding red gloss across her lips with an upright middle finger.

Not this time, motherfucker. Not this time.

Erica Whaley leaned in and kissed her husband hard on the mouth, knocking his head back against the mirrored wall of the elevator. When it stopped on the third floor, she made a dash for the room. She went the wrong way, then spun around and, laughing, went back the right way. Mark moved slowly after her. He could not bear to be in the room with the sitter. As he came closer, he heard a terrible, agonizing scream. He ran through the open door.

'Laurie,' Erica was screaming. 'Laurie!'

Little Leo was standing in the middle of the bedroom floor. He had wet his Spiderman pajamas.

'What do you mean, Laurie?' said Mark. 'Where is she?' He dashed past Erica into the kids' bedroom. She followed him in. Her face was white.

'She's not here!' screamed Erica. 'Laurie's gone.'

Mark Whaley shouted out his daughter's name, pulling back the wardrobe doors, throwing himself onto the floor to check under the bed, running to the curtains, swinging them back and forth, as if his daughter would play a hiding game as her stepmother screamed. Maybe this is for attention, he thought. He ran back into Erica.

'Where's the sitter?' he said.

Leo was now wailing, copying his parents. He plunged toward his father's leg, and clung to it. In a trance, Mark bent down and picked him up, started patting his back, not even aware that Leo's wet pajamas were soaking into his shirt. And still, Leo bawled.

'I'm trying to think,' Mark shouted. 'Stop crying, Leo. For crying out loud!'

Leo cried harder, alarmed by the scene he had woken up to. 'Laurie,' he sobbed. 'Laurie.'

'Give him to me,' said Erica.

Mark grabbed for the phone. He called reception. As he waited for them to pick up, he turned to Erica. 'Call 911 from your cell phone,' he shouted. 'Call 911. And call Laurie's cell.'

Jared Labati picked up the phone in reception. 'Hey,' he said, long and slow, as if he was talking to one of his best friends.

'This is Mark Whaley, Room 304. My daughter is missing. My daughter's gone. Call 911. Call the police. Where's the sitter? Did you see the sitter leave?'

Jared stammered, 'Uh . . . your daughter's gone? Where?'

'Yes!' shouted Mark. 'She's gone! She's taken my daughter. I don't *know* where.'

'Who?' said Jared. 'Who's taken your daughter?'

'Jesus Christ, I don't care, my daughter's gone. Shut down the hotel. Now. And get the police here. Now.' He slammed the phone down. 'What a fucking idiot.'

Erica was still on the phone to 911. Mark started answering the dispatcher's questions along with her. She held her hand over the receiver. 'Stop,' she said. 'Stop! You're confusing me.'

'You're too slow!' he said.

He got his cell phone and dialed Laurie's number.

'It's ringing,' he said. 'It's ringing. OK. It's ringing. That's good. Come on, Laurie, pick up, pick up.'

He became aware of a song playing in the room next door, a song he vaguely knew, one that Laurie had loaded onto Erica's iPod, but he knew it wasn't the iPod, it was the phone, and as he walked into the bedroom, there it was, flashing on the floor of the bedroom: Laurie's little pink cell phone. He ended his call, picked up her phone and brought it into Erica.

'I'm going to check the other rooms, I'll check the other rooms, stay here, in case she . . .' He ran from the room and down the hallway, hammering on every door, shouting for Laurie.

'My daughter's missing!' he shouted. 'My daughter's gone! She's eleven years old, blonde hair, blue eyes, seventy pounds, wearing . . . wearing . . . pajamas! Pajamas with . . . pink pajamas . . . with Jesus . . . just pink!'

Doors started to open along the hallway.

'Anyone!' said Mark. 'Anyone! Has anyone seen her? Everyone, my daughter's missing! She was here just a half hour ago. I just checked on her. On the sitter. There was a sitter. Blonde hair. Five two . . . sixteen years old.'

Jesus, she was sixteen years old, he thought.

7

Ren Bryce woke up with Ben Rader behind her, his thick arm wrapped around her waist. He pulled her closer to him, and kissed her shoulder, then her neck. He leaned into her ear, and spoke very quietly, telling her what he was guessing she wanted. As she backed up against him, his hand moved up her body, stayed longer than she could handle, then slid all the way down. She was barely awake as she moved on top of him. He sat up to meet her. He slid them both to the edge of the bed. Every movement he made was rock solid. Ren was looking into the mirrored wardrobe door, where she could watch him, and his bare muscular torso, and his white-knuckle grip on her hips.

And the award for outstanding performance by a male in a leading role goes to . . .

Her cell phone rang. *No. No.*

'No,' said Ben.

'No,' said Ren.

Ren glanced down at the screen. *Shit.*

'I have to,' she said. 'Don't move.' She grabbed the phone. *Remove the sex from your voice.* 'Well, hi, High Sheriff.'

'Special greetings, Special Agent.' Sheriff Bob Gage was the Summit County Sheriff, two counties west of Denver.

'It's late, it's early,' said Ren, 'and there is a grim tone to your voice.'

'There are grim happenings in Breckenridge,' said Bob. 'I'm just about to call your boss to get your Safe Street asses over here.'

'What's going down?' said Ren.

'Missing child, missing sitter,' said Bob.

'Missing from where?' said Ren.

Ben lifted Ren onto the bed beside him. She wrapped a sheet around herself.

'They disappeared from their room in a brand-spanking new hotel,' said Bob. 'The Merlin Lodge & Spa. Or maybe the sitter took the little girl. Or maybe they were both abducted. The sitter is sixteen years old, and the girl is eleven. The parents were down in the restaurant, the stepmother was drunk, got through a couple bottles of champagne on her own. They were seen arguing at the table.'

'And the father?' said Ren.

'He's a mess. This was the first time he was allowed overnight parenting time. I can't get a handle on him, though.'

'Allowed by whom?' said Ren.

'A judge,' said Bob. 'Don't you hate that legal bullshit "parenting time"? Isn't the whole time "parenting time"? It bugs me. Anyway, he's got two kids. The girl, from his first marriage, and a three-year-old boy with his current wife – the drunk one. The ex-wife is the primary care parent, she wanted him nowhere near his daughter, but eventually a judge over-rode her wishes, had sympathy for the guy – he had turned his life around. His "parenting time" increased. And the latest development was that he could take her overnight.'

Ren sucked in a breath. 'What do you mean "turned his life around"? What kind of guy are we talking about here?'

'He's a recovering alcoholic,' said Bob. 'He's no low-life. He's a big shot in a pharmaceuticals company in Denver. The CFO. What's that – Chief Financial Officer?'

'Yup,' said Ren. 'What about the ex-wife? Have you spoken with her? Could she have taken her daughter to get back at him, to prove a point?' She paused. 'But, then, where did the sitter come into it?'

'I don't know,' said Bob. 'We haven't spoken to the ex-wife yet. The sitter's a local kid, pretty blonde, good-girl type. She's with an agency that's on call at the hotel. The hotel's only open a couple weeks. Just get your ass here, we'll talk more.'

'I'm on my way.' Ren hung up.

Ben Rader was in the bathroom.

'Do not reveal yourself until I'm gone,' Ren shouted. She started to gather up her clothes. 'I won't be responsible . . . or professional . . . or . . .'

The door opened and Ben Rader walked in, naked and smiling, toward her. 'Seriously . . .' he said.

You wonderful man.

I-70 was eerily quiet, stretching out in front of Ren like a road to nowhere. She turned on the radio, turned it off, picked up her iPod, threw it down, looked at herself in the mirror, thought of Ben Rader, smiled, then reached for her cell phone. Her hand hovered over speed dial number three – Janine Hooks, her friend of four months, and the entire workforce of the Jefferson County Cold Case Unit, based in Golden, fifteen miles outside Denver. Janine had short brown hair, a wide mouth with full lips, and prominent, pretty teeth. She was small and boyish, and weighed no more than one hundred pounds. Ren worried that she was anorexic.

Ren and Janine had met over a cold case linked to Helen Wheeler's murder, and came to blows over it when Billy Waites, Ren's confidential-informant ex, broke into Janine's office to steal a file. Yet, from this betrayal came a close, fast friendship, and the understanding that it had all been for the greater good. Ren's only regret was that she hadn't met Janine Hooks years ago.

Ren hit three on speed dial.

'Wow,' said Janine, 'three thirty a.m. is always such a good time for me.'

'I'm driving by yo' house,' said Ren. 'And test-driving my new hands-free. You can still like a guy who makes a Bon Jovi reference . . . right?'

'You can like him even more,' said Janine. 'What was the reference?' Ren knew the facial expression Janine would now have – frowny, chin out, head a little tilted. When Janine Hooks listened, she listened.

'*Slippery When Wet*,' said Ren.

'Album number three, 1986,' said Janine.

'I love Bon Jovi fans!' said Ren.

'Who is this man?' said Janine. 'I was wondering where you had disappeared to.'

'Special – very special – Agent Ben Rader. Michael J. Fox gene, goes undercover with the underage. A man with a Major in minors . . .'

'And . . .' said Janine.

'Well . . . he is . . . amazing,' said Ren.

'Oh, God,' said Janine. 'I just got the *Slippery When Wet*. No more details. Please.'

'Oh my God, I didn't mean it like that,' said Ren. 'It was soap.'

'Aren't you guys not meant to date other agents?' said Janine.

They both laughed.

'Gary *would* go apeshit, though,' said Ren.

'He sure would,' said Janine.

'In defense of myself and hot agent, neither of us knew we were FBI Agents at the time of meeting,' said Ren.

'What?' said Janine.

'That's the funny thing,' said Ren. 'We met in Gaffney's because Gary had recommended it to him. I was there because that's where Safe Streets goes. I don't like men liking me for my job, Ben doesn't like women liking him for his job. So a lot of agents lie when they go out. And, he does *not* look like an agent, and he didn't think I did. And, part of undercover training is literally to go into a bar, and get as much information as you can out of someone—'

'Therefore, would you not be immune to someone doing it to you?' said Janine.

'That was the other funny thing,' said Ren. 'We *are*. So neither of us really got anywhere. We kind of bonded over the fact that we were both being shady. I mean, I made up a pretty decent background, and so did he, but our hearts weren't really in it.'

'So, the foundation for this *amazing* new relationship is your shared gift for lying?' said Janine.

Pause. 'You don't have to put it like that.'

'Even if that's the way it is,' said Janine.

'He's got other gifts . . .' said Ren.

'So I gathered,' said Janine. 'Let's take that as a given from now on.'

'I'm just excited,' said Ren.

'Maybe it's just me, but how could you trust a man like that?' said Janine.

'I don't need to trust him,' said Ren. 'I just need to trust that he'll show up for . . . dates. Which he has. And hey, I'm trustworthy. Just because I lie for work sometimes . . . '

'True. I didn't mean it like that,' said Janine. 'So where are you going at this hour of the night? Or where are you coming from?'

'Two girls have gone missing from a resort in Breck. Sixteen and eleven. The sitter and the girl she was looking after.'

'That's terrible,' said Janine.

'And there's been another rape in Denver – a fourteen-year-old girl. Did you hear about the rape at Kennington?'

'Yes,' said Janine. 'Is it the same guy?'

'Possibly,' said Ren.

'I have a case from 1978,' said Janine. 'A children's choir from a Catholic school was brought in to perform for the patients at Kennington. Including – wait for it – the male dangerous sex offender posse.'

'What the—?'

'Yes,' said Janine. 'Several male patients had to be removed from the audience for . . . well, you can guess.'

'That is vile.'

'So, anyway, the kids leave after the performance, they get back on the school bus and when they arrive back at the school, one little girl is missing. Nine years old. Gina Orsak. Her body was never found.'

'That is heartbreaking,' said Ren. 'Any leads?'

'No, nothing,' said Janine. She paused. 'So, is Misty with you?' Misty was Ren's black and white border collie cadaver dog.

'Aw, you always look out for my girl,' said Ren. 'And no, she is not with me – I had to run straight from hot agent's place. But could you go to my house in the morning and pick her up for me? Hot agent is on his way there now, bless his heart, but can you relieve him – please? It's just . . . you know Misty so well. He could be clueless.'

'Well, he can't be amazing at *everything*,' said Janine.

Ren laughed, but as soon as the call was over, the laughter died, and the Jeep was quiet. Golden was behind her and she was heading for Breckenridge, a route she knew so well – every beautiful straight and turn. Ren knew that it would lead her to a place she loved, but one that trailed poignant memories like smoke. The previous year, she had investigated the murder of a fellow FBI Agent. Jean Transom's body had been found not far from Breckenridge. The case had brought Ren together with terrible scenes, with death and secrets and unprofessional risks. But it had also brought her together with Janine Hooks and with Bob Gage, and with Salem Swade, a wonderful, damaged Vietnam Vet – Misty's first owner. It had also brought her together with Billy Waites. And it had brought her closer to being fired than she had ever been before.

8

The Summit County Sheriff's Office was off Highway 9 on the edge of Breckenridge – a single-story, pale brick building that the Sheriff was kind enough to share with the county jail and courthouse.

Ren walked across the parking lot through thick flakes of falling snow that were being swept around her in the wind. She stopped inside the door and popped some Wintergreen gum in her mouth. She sprayed some perfume, and brought a citrus cloud through security.

Goodbye eau de tramp.

Sheriff Bob Gage was leaning against the reception desk with a mug of coffee in his hand. He was six foot tall with neat side-parted fair hair, a warm face, and a belly larger than he would have liked. His arms were muscular, not from gym time, but from hauling and hammering and chopping things.

'You give the best hugs,' said Ren. She could smell sporty shower gel and detergent. He had a good old-fashioned wife who laid his clothes out on the bed for him in the morning.

'You're not so bad yourself for a skinny gal,' said Bob.

'I'm far from skinny,' said Ren. She started to pull off her coat.

'Are you kidding me?' said Bob. 'I'm surprised you made it across the parking lot without the wind cracking your head off a wall.'

'Getting up after your phone call made me feel like I had cracked my head off a wall.'

'So, not from being over-served at a bar last night . . .' said Bob.

'Absolutely not,' said Ren. She smiled.

Bob took her coat and hung it up for her.

Ren felt a hand on her lower back. 'Hey, Ren, welcome back.' She turned to see Undersheriff Mike Delaney, his big smile, and his blond hat hair.

'Hey, there,' said Ren, hugging him lightly. 'You always look fresh from the slopes.'

'That's because he usually is,' said Bob.

'Not now, I'm not,' said Mike. 'It's crazy over there at the hotel. And bad news is ten thousand people have hit town this weekend for the snowboarding championships.'

'So, fill me in . . .' said Ren.

'The missing girls are Laurie Whaley, eleven years old, and the sitter, Shelby Royce, sixteen years old,' said Bob. 'The Whaleys came back from the restaurant, the two girls were gone. The three-year-old son, his name is Leo, was there alone. Mike and I have taken statements from the Whaleys, from the guy on the front desk, any servers in the restaurant who were still there. The statements are in my office. We're talking to the rest of the staff, the guests – there are twenty rooms, eighteen were occupied – and any other diners who were at hotel. The Royces – the sitter's parents – are at the hotel too.'

'Were you with the Whaley family the whole time since they reported it?' said Ren.

'I was,' said Bob. 'They were in the hotel reception with their three-year-old when I arrived. Poor kid had wet himself. I went back up to the room with all three of them, so they could change his clothes. The father had to change his shirt too, because he'd been carrying the kid.'

'And you were with them the entire time . . .?' said Ren.

'If "entire" and "whole" mean the same thing, then yes,' said Bob.

Mike smiled.

'Sorry,' said Ren. 'I'm still asleep.'

'And yes, I have the father's shirt in an evidence bag,' said Bob. 'And both kids' clothes. Here's a photo of the eleven-year-old, Laurie Whaley,' said Bob.

Ren took it. 'Oh, God, she's beautiful.'

Bob nodded. 'I know. It was taken tonight in the hotel room on the step-mom's cell phone. So, it's what she was wearing.'

Pink pajamas.

'Were any of her other clothes gone?' said Ren. 'A coat? Shoes?'

'Not according to the parents, no.'

Ren looked out the window. 'It's freezing out there. And what about the sitter?' said Ren.

'No,' said Bob. 'Nothing of hers in the room. Here's her photo.'

'The blonde ponytail, the perfect skin, the perfect smile . . .' said Ren. 'These are two very pretty girls.'

'I know,' said Bob.

'So, what's your thinking – is this an abduction?' said Ren. 'Did the sitter take her? If not – who was the target? Laurie Whaley or Shelby Royce? Both of them? But I can't see how that would work – different ages, strangers to each other . . . or were they?'

'Until we know differently, they were strangers,' said Bob.

'Do the Whaleys' stories add up?' said Ren.

'Like I said, the wife's been drinking, the husband hasn't,' said Bob. 'Witnesses saw them in a "heated" discussion, the husband left the restaurant, says he checked on the kids, the kids were apparently fine . . . he comes back to the restaurant for half an hour, then they both go back to the room, and the kids are gone . . .'

'And how long was he gone when he went to check on the kids?' said Ren.

'He says twenty minutes.'

'Do we have video?' said Ren.

'There's a working camera in the foyer,' said Bob. 'That's it.'

'What?' said Ren.

'They opened the hotel before it was ready is the general feeling,' said Bob. 'The electricians are still working on it. They're disarming things, forgetting to turn them back on, etc.'

'So, we have a bunch of contractors we need to look into as well,' said Ren.

'Yup,' said Bob. 'It's Holder Electrical Contractors, a local firm; same firm that's doing work here in the office.'

'Do you have a good relationship with them?'

'When they're not not showing up,' said Bob.

'Could you call in employment records from the boss?' said Ren.

'Not a problem,' said Bob.

'I'm presuming his men are all on the books or he wouldn't risk working under the watchful eye of High Sheriff Gage . . .' said Ren.

'I put the fear of God into these people,' said Bob.

Ren smiled.

'It's a local family-run business, Holders,' said Bob. 'He employs part-timers, but it's all above board from what I can tell.'

Ren nodded. 'So, just the Whaleys are here.'

'Yup – with their son,' said Bob. 'They're all in separate rooms.'

'Who's with the son?' said Ren.

'One of our lady detectives,' said Bob.

'But she's not interviewing him—' said Ren.

'No,' said Bob. 'Relax. They're playing with blocks.'

'Yes – step away from the child,' said Ren.

'At least you can laugh about it,' said Bob. 'You won't believe it, but apparently there are some uptight Feds . . .'

Ren smiled. 'Well, we are armed and dangerous on the child forensic interview front—'

'And I'm glad we don't have to be,' said Bob.

'Me too,' said Ren. 'Two of our finest are based in Denver. My guess is that Gary's already called one in. OK – let me go read these.'

She sat down in an armchair by a small table in the corner and began to read through the statements. Bob left her alone. When he came back into the room with coffee, Ren was on her feet.

'OK,' she said, 'let's go talk to the father.'

9

Bob led Ren down the hallway to the meeting room where Mark Whaley was waiting. He was startled by the opening door. He stood up and shook hands with Ren.

'I know you've already spoken with the Undersheriff,' said Ren. 'But I'm going to have to ask some more questions, and go over some of the same ground again.'

'Sure,' he said, nodding, shifting forward in his seat. His hands were clasped in front of him.

'Could you talk me through your evening?' said Ren.

'My wife and I went for dinner at nine p.m.—'

'Let's start with when you checked in,' said Ren.

'OK, sorry,' said Mark. 'We checked in at seven p.m., and Erica . . . my wife . . . really wanted to go to the restaurant for dinner later on, so we asked at reception for a sitter for eight thirty.'

Ren nodded. 'Who was on reception?'

'A guy called Jared.'

'Did anyone take your bags?' said Ren.

'No, we took our own bags to the room. We watched *Toy*

Story with the kids . . . well, I did. Erica was getting ready at the same time.'

'Did you see anyone else in the foyer?' said Ren.

'No.'

'Did you meet anyone in the elevator?' said Ren.

'No.'

'Did anyone pass you in the hallway?' said Ren.

'No,' said Mark.

'What can you tell me about the sitter?' said Ren.

'She was . . . sixteen, she told us. Short, maybe five three, blonde . . .' He shrugged. 'Long blonde hair . . . well, to her shoulders. Wearing sweats . . .'

'Was there anything unusual in her demeanor, or in her behavior when she first showed up?' said Ren.

'No,' said Mark. 'She seemed like a good kid . . . normal . . . we weren't concerned about her, if that's what you mean.'

'Did you have a conversation with her?' said Ren.

'Yes,' said Mark.

'What did you talk about?'

'High school, living in Breck, the kids, what to do . . .'

'Did you notice anything else about her that you think might help?' said Ren.

'Nothing I can think of,' said Mark.

'So, you went down to dinner,' said Ren.

'Yes. A little after nine.'

'And you were there for how long?' said Ren.

'Well, until a little after midnight, I guess,' said Mark. 'But I went up to check on the kids . . .'

'And what time was that at?' said Ren.

'I guess . . . eleven thirty? And then I came back down to Erica. We didn't stay much longer. We went back to the room.'

Ren looked up. 'Sorry . . . let's go back to when you got to the room.'

'Yes, sorry . . . uh, when I got to the room . . . the sitter was on the bed in her sweats, watching television. I asked her how the kids were, and she said they'd been really well-behaved . . .' Tears welled in his eyes. 'They were asleep. So . . . I went to their door, and stuck my head in, and they were fast asleep.'

'They were in an adjoining room,' said Ren.

'Yes,' said Mark. 'The kids had twin beds, we had a double bed. That was where the sitter was. In the main room. Where Erica and I would be sleeping.'

'OK,' said Ren. 'So when you checked on the children, they were sleeping. Was there any sign of a disturbance, anything out of place in their room?'

Mark shook his head. 'Absolutely not. Nothing.'

'Did anything happen while you were in the room?' said Ren.

'What do you mean?' said Mark.

'Did you have a conversation with Shelby Royce?' said Ren.

'Chit-chat,' said Mark. 'Hope they behaved for you, what time did they go to sleep, are you bored, that kind of thing.'

'And what was her demeanor at this point?'

He shrugged. 'Fine. She seemed a little bored.'

'Did she seem at ease?' said Ren.

'Yes.'

'Did you get the sense that she was eager to finish up?' said Ren.

'No more eager than most sitters at that age, I guess . . .'

'Did she mention that she was going anywhere, or planning to meet up with anyone afterward?'

'No,' said Mark.

'You understand I'm asking all these questions because you are the last person to have seen Shelby before she disappeared . . .'

'Yes, I'm sorry if I seem a little . . . I suppose I want the attention focused on Laurie. I . . . know that sounds terrible.'

'It's understandable,' said Ren. 'But Shelby Royce, and her state of mind, and her actions, are crucial to us working out what happened here. Right now, we can't call this an abduction, because we have no evidence that it is.'

'What?' said Mark. 'But . . . what else do you think happened?'

'That's what we're trying to establish,' said Ren. 'They may have left voluntarily.'

'There is no way that Laurie would do that,' said Mark. 'No way.'

'I'll put that in my notes, so everyone is aware of how you feel about that,' said Ren.

He nodded.

'OK,' said Ren, 'after you had checked on them, what did you do?'

'I went back down to my wife.'

'Did you tell the sitter what time you intended to come back to the room?' said Ren.

'No, no . . . I . . . left. I went back to the restaurant.'

'How long did all of that take?' said Ren.

'How long to get back to the restaurant?' said Mark.

'No,' said Ren. 'From when you left the table to when you returned to the table.'

'Oh . . .' he rubbed his chin. 'Fifteen minutes?' He paused. 'Twenty?'

'And how long did you spend in the restaurant before you went back up to the room and discovered that your daughter was missing?'

'Twenty minutes, maybe thirty,' said Mark. He paused. 'Closer to thirty.'

Ren nodded. 'Mr Whaley, do you have any reason to believe that someone would want to harm you or your family?'

'No,' said Mark. 'No . . . why would someone . . .?' The words caught in his throat. 'Please, please, find her,' he said. 'Let me get out there and look for her. Please. I can't stay here. This is . . . it's been hours now,' he said. 'Please, I can't just sit around here doing nothing . . .'

'All the Sheriff's Office detectives are on this,' said Ren. 'And more of my colleagues are on their way. I'm sorry that you have to stay here, but these answers could help us to find your daughter.'

'Laurie . . .' said Mark. He took in a breath.

'Mr Whaley,' said Ren, 'who knew that you were coming to Breckenridge this weekend?'

'Some of our friends, I guess. Erica probably mentioned it to some of hers. It's . . . it's our wedding anniversary this Tuesday; that's why she pressed for going to dinner I think, even though we had Laurie. I wasn't thinking that way, but she was.'

'Mr Whaley, several witnesses have said that you and your wife had a heated discussion over dinner . . .'

He blinked. 'I wouldn't have called it heated . . .'

Ren waited. He didn't fill the silence.

'Can you tell me what the discussion was about?' said Ren.

'Couple stuff. It wasn't about Laurie.'

'It doesn't have to be about Laurie to be relevant to the investigation,' said Ren.

'I know . . . it's just . . . it was a private conversation that I didn't think I'd have to share with anyone. Especially the FBI. My head is . . . please. Let me get my head around this.

I'm thrown.' He took a breath. 'Erica thinks I've been distant. I disagree.'

Ren waited.

'That was the crux of it.'

'Your wife thinks you've been distant – is there any reason for that?' said Ren.

'I work hard,' said Mark. 'Long hours. And I take work home. If that makes me distant . . .' He shrugged. 'I'm doing it for my family. So, I guess, yes, it makes me mad . . . not mad . . . just . . . frustrated when she accuses me of being distant.'

'She's accused you of this before,' said Ren.

'No, not like that . . . just she asks me if I'm OK a lot.'

'And are you?' said Ren. 'How are things going for you?'

He frowned. 'They're going well. Why do you ask?'

'I'm trying to get a handle on everything,' said Ren. 'That's all. Is everything going OK in your work?'

'Absolutely.'

'You work for,' she checked her notes, 'MeesterBrandt Pharmaceuticals.'

'Yes,' said Mark. 'I'm the CFO.'

A flicker of something crossed his face.

Annoyance?

'How long have you worked with them?'

'Since 1989.'

'And what do you do there exactly?' said Ren.

'I'm head of the Finance and Administration Department.'

'And how are the finances of MeesterBrandt?'

Mark Whaley gave a wry smile. 'Well, have you heard of the drug Ellerol?'

'It's new, isn't it?' said Ren. 'I've seen the TV commercials.'

Eighteen seconds of dazzlingly positive effects, and twenty-two seconds of rapid-fire side-effect warnings. Guarantee: no guarantees.

'It's been on the market one year,' said Mark. 'And it's already one of the top five revenue-producing drugs in the country.'

'But . . . it's an antipsychotic,' said Ren. 'In the top five?'

'All of the top five are antipsychotics,' said Mark.

Oh. My. God.

He looked like he had shocked people before with this information.

'So,' said Mark. 'You can understand that success on that scale would create a lot of work.'

And misery, clearly.

'And, obviously, it's not our only drug,' said Mark.

Ren nodded. 'Are you happy at MeesterBrandt?'

'Yes,' said Mark. 'Why are you asking these things?'

Ren didn't reply. She stared.

'I'm sorry if I'm sounding a little short,' said Mark. 'I just don't see how this is relevant.'

'I understand that,' said Ren. 'You want to get out there, you want to find your daughter. But I'm not wasting your time. Like I said, the more we know—'

There was a knock on the door, and Bob Gage leaned his head in. Ren followed him outside.

'Beating a confession out of him?' said Bob.

'Only a matter of time,' said Ren.

'The ex-wife is outside,' said Bob. 'Laurie's mother – Cathy Merritt. She was going crazy at security. I told them to let her through.'

'We'll take him out to meet her,' said Ren. 'Let the magic happen.'

'You're a twisted one,' said Bob.

'This could be a ransom situation,' said Ren. 'MeesterBrandt's worth big bucks. Then – would they choose the CFO's kid over the CEO's?'

'Does the CEO have kids?' said Bob.

'We shall find out,' said Ren. 'Did you know that the top five drugs in our fair land are antipsychotics?'

'What?' said Bob. 'There are that many psychos out there?'

'Keeping us in a job,' said Ren.

'We just need them to stop taking their meds,' said Bob.

10

As Bob and Ren walked with Mark Whaley into the reception area, Cathy Merritt burst through the door from the foyer. She was a round, heavy-set woman with thick black hair that was still dotted with snowflakes. She had a full face and cheeks that were beaming their high color through a thick layer of foundation. She was dressed in a low-cut green velvet dress that had shunted her large breasts down to her waist and left a pale, flat expanse of chest behind. Her legs were plump, and covered in black panty-hose. Her feet were squeezed into a pair of black shiny Mary Janes.

Bob and Ren exchanged 'nutjob' glances.

Cathy Merritt lunged for Mark, slapping him hard on the chest and pushing against him. Despite her bulk, he didn't move.

'I knew it,' she screamed. 'I knew it. What have you done? That judge! What have you done to Laurie? I heard this from a hotel receptionist!' she said. 'That's how I heard my daughter had gone missing. I tried your cell, I tried Laurie's, I got nothing, I called the hotel, and they told me all hell has broken loose, a child has gone missing. My child! That's how I hear it! What have you done to her?'

'What have I *done* to her?' said Mark. 'Are you insane? Nothing! We came back from dinner . . . she was gone. I had checked on her!'

'You went for dinner?' said Cathy. 'You left her in the room alone?'

'Don't be ridiculous,' said Mark. 'She was not alone. Leo was there. And we had a sitter.'

'Oh, you left her with a three-year-old and a stranger!' said Cathy. 'Well, then!'

'As if you've never left her with a sitter,' said Mark.

'Sitters I know!' said Cathy. 'Not strangers. Who was this person?'

'She works for the hotel. She's a high school student . . .'

'Why were you even getting a sitter?' said Cathy. 'You were taking Laurie away for the first time in years!'

'I . . . I . . . we watched a movie together, she was going to bed in a little while . . . I didn't think going to dinner . . . we're in Breck, for crying out loud, it's not like we're in a war zone. We were going downstairs for a couple of hours. We could just as easily have been doing that at home.'

'So, strangers can just walk in and out of your house, no problem?' said Cathy. 'And was it a couple of hours? Really?' She pushed him again. 'You know what? On the drive here, I'm thinking "once a worthless piece of shit, always a worthless piece of shit". You haven't changed one bit.'

She turned to Bob and Ren, and stabbed a finger at them, then at her ex-husband. 'Watch this guy,' she said. 'He is a liar, an alcoholic, and . . .' she turned to Mark, 'you're a loser!' Her eyes darted back to Bob to Ren. 'A loser. Save yourself the time it took me to figure that out.'

*   *   *

Erica Whaley appeared from the hallway where the rest rooms were. The female detective alongside her was reaching out to stop her from getting any closer to Cathy Merritt. But Erica shouted from where she stood, 'Mark is *not* a liar. You don't know him! You haven't known him for years. He has a new life now.'

'God help you,' said Cathy. 'You seem like a good person, Erica. And Laurie adores you, but . . . how, *how* can you be with this . . .' She looked at Mark with years-long disgust.

'He is a wonderful husband, and a wonderful father,' said Erica.

Mark shook his head. 'Don't Erica . . .'

'No,' said Erica. 'I can't listen to this. I can't, honey. And I'm not having the FBI, and the Sheriff, and everyone else listening to it either. From the day I met you, you have loved me, cared for me, provided for me and the children, not done one thing to hurt us. Not one thing.' She turned to Cathy. 'I'm sorry, Cathy, but he is not the man you married.'

'Well, you know something?' said Cathy. 'I'm not the woman he married! Because he wore me down. Your *wonderful* husband nearly destroyed me and he nearly destroyed our daughter—'

'Destroyed?' said Mark.

'We were driving around in the middle of the night dragging you out of dives. Laurie was only a baby!' She turned to Erica. 'There's your wonderful husband! The man, hanging over the toilet bowl, after a night of hard drinking? Wetting the bed? There's your wonderful husband!'

Who'd have thought?

Ren watched, mute, as the conversation unfolded. *You nasty, nasty woman*. Ren had pressed her elbow against Bob to keep him from intervening.

Wait for those wonderful things that are revealed in anger.

The door had opened behind Cathy Merritt, and Gary Dettling walked in with Robbie, Cliff and Colin. They stopped at 'wetting the bed'.

Ren gave the briefest acknowledgment of their arrival, but quickly turned back to Cathy Merritt, whose voice was riding high on hysteria.

She was shouting, 'Oh, puh-lease, the "people change" bullshit. Look where it's gotten you. Seriously. Look!' She poked a finger toward Ren and Bob. 'What happened to my baby? I knew this was going to happen. I knew it.'

Mark snapped. 'You knew this would happen? Don't be ridiculous! You knew this would happen? You're trying to tell me you were so worried about tonight that you – what? Where were *you* tonight?'

'What the hell is that supposed to mean?' said Cathy.

'Just answer the question,' said Mark.

'We were at dinner, at home, with Jonathan,' said Cathy. 'So shoot me.'

'And what?' said Mark. 'You were waiting by the phone the whole time for a call from the cops?'

'Well, it would have been a damn sight better than hearing this from a desk clerk a hundred miles away . . .' said Cathy.

'Right,' said Mark. 'You thought your daughter would disappear, so you . . .' he looked at her, '"dress up" . . .?'

'What the hell?' said Cathy. 'I put on a dress and stay home for dinner and that means I wasn't worried? You bet your ass I was worried. And, clearly, I had every reason to be.'

11

Gary Dettling stepped forward and introduced himself to Cathy Merritt.

'Your daughter's missing, Mrs Merritt,' he said. 'We need to focus on that.'

'I want my husband,' she said, trying to walk by him. A man stepped out of the corner. No-one had noticed him come in, even though he was well over six feet tall, and far from slim. He had thick, graying hair and a full beard. He went to his wife and put an arm around her shoulder.

'I'm Dale Merritt,' he said, shaking Gary's hand. 'Cathy's husband. I'm sorry about all this.'

He glanced toward Cathy. She looked up at him, a small flash of anger in her eyes.

Gary nodded. 'Let's just take you somewhere to sit down.'

He guided the Merritts to one side.

'Would it be possible to make a call to my son to let him know what's going on?' said Dale.

Gary nodded. 'That's not a problem. How old is your son?'

'He's sixteen,' said Dale. 'Joshua.'

'And who is the Jonathan you mentioned?' said Gary, turning to Cathy.

'Jonathan Meester,' she said. 'He's a friend of ours.'

'The Meester in MeesterBrandt?' said Gary.

Cathy nodded. 'Yes.' She paused. 'Jonathan and Mark are college friends, but Jonathan stayed close to both of us after the split. He's Laurie's godfather.'

'Is he still at your house with Joshua?' said Gary.

'Yes,' said Dale.

'He was kind enough to stay,' said Cathy.

Gary nodded. 'Excuse me for one moment.' He walked over to Bob and Ren.

'Bob, how you doing?' said Gary.

'Good,' said Bob, shaking his hand. 'Good to see you again. How are—'

'Can we get someone to take the Merritts to a room?' said Gary.

Bob nodded.

'I've called in a CARD team,' said Gary. 'Our Child Abduction Rapid Deployment Team. We've got four members en route from Denver right now. They'll be here within the hour. They'll coordinate the search. We expect to do that first thing in the morning.'

Bob nodded again.

'Are we taking over the same room as the last time?' said Gary.

'Yes,' said Bob.

'That's great, thank you,' said Gary, already walking past, and down the familiar hallway to the room that they would all squeeze in to for as long as it took.

Ren leaned in to Bob. 'Gary has a form of Tourette's. It's, like, the involuntary vocalization of what he is going to do in an investigation.' She paused. 'All anyone else needs to do is not to succumb to regular Tourette's in response . . .'

'I hear you,' said Bob.

'Consider this an apology on his behalf.'

'No need,' said Bob. 'Gary is . . . well, he's a Fed . . .'

'Textbook,' said Ren.

'You're more . . . Facebook.'

'I don't know where you're going with that,' said Ren.

'Nowhere, it just sounded kind of catchy. What next?'

'I'm going to read through more of the guests' statements, and then I'd like to talk to the stepmother. We can all go to the hotel, then back here for the press conference.'

Bob raised an eyebrow. 'That Tourette's is catching . . .'

Ren followed Bob into the small interview room where Erica Whaley had been taken. The furniture was the result of checks in boxes on the order forms of an office supply catalog. A long fluorescent strip light glared down on the cheap glossy veneer of the oval table. There was a strong smell of alcohol in the air. A young female detective stood up and left the room when Bob gave her the nod.

Erica Whaley sat at the end of the table with a glass of water in front of her. She was dressed in a heavy silk silver halter-neck that crossed over just under the neck. Ren could see gray pants legs and silver sandals. Her blonde hair was pinned up, but had fallen loose around her face. Her cheeks were red, the foundation washed away with tears and rubbed away with Kleenex, her mascara smudged under her eyes.

She looked up, blinking with panic . . . then hope. Ren had seen the reaction a thousand times, when a door opening took on an unimaginable significance.

You thought your night would end so differently.

Ren reached out her hand. 'I'm Ren Bryce, I'm with the

FBI; the Rocky Mountain Safe Streets Task Force in Denver. We'll be working alongside the Sheriff's Department on this.'

'Thank God,' said Erica, standing up, shaking Ren's hand. She glanced at Bob. 'I didn't mean that the Sheriff's Office isn't . . .' She trailed off.

'The Sheriff's Office knows Breckenridge and the surrounding area inside out,' said Ren. 'As you know, their officers are already out there looking for your daughter. My colleagues from Denver will be processing the scene, seeing if we can get any information from that, interviewing staff members and guests, looking at CCTV footage, we'll canvass the town, carry out road-side canvasses. And Sheriff Gage here has already emailed Laurie's photo to every law enforcement agency in the country, and to the media.'

Erica nodded at almost every word.

'OK . . . OK . . . thank you,' she said.

'Let's sit down, Mrs Whaley. I've read through the statement you gave to Undersheriff Delaney. I'd just like you to go through everything with me again.'

'I mean, it's a regular thing to do, going to a hotel, getting a sitter, you just don't think twice,' said Erica. 'It's a four-star resort, you don't question it, which seems ridiculous now. We were only downstairs, like my husband said. It's kind of like being at home, isn't it? You leave your kids upstairs when you're at home, don't you? It's all the one building, a hotel at least has security, or should have had security. Now, of course, I'm thinking "how many people work at the hotel?", sure I guess most of them are good people, but who *are* all these people? Are they pedophiles, druggies, wife beaters? Are they psychopaths? Are their jobs just nothing to them, just what they do to make money to pay for child porn? Is the owner of this place a do-gooder, savior of mankind who employs ex-cons, or—? What if there's a guy who never touched a child, but suddenly decides, well, hell, I'll take these girls, I get caught, I get caught, I'll go out on a high, I'll give in to my sick fantasies . . .'

She didn't draw breath. She didn't pause. It was as if someone had popped the latch on the part of her brain that held her worst fears, and out jumped the demons . . .

12

Ren's heart-rate shot up as she listened to Erica Whaley. She hadn't taken a breath herself.

Do not take on these emotions. Step away from the panic.

'Mrs Whaley, if we talk through the evening,' said Ren, 'we'll be able to see things more clearly.'

'The first we saw of the sitter was when she showed up at our room,' said Erica.

'OK,' said Ren. 'And—'

'I can't believe it,' said Erica. 'It's like, "Hello, stranger, we know nothing about you. Here, why don't you look after the most precious things in the world to us, please take them, we'll see you in a few hours, while we're living it up down in the restaurant."'

'How did—'

'I mean, these days stranger babysitters are just part of the hotel's menu, right? Facials, massages, sitters . . .'

'Mrs Whaley—'

'I think she took her,' said Erica. 'I think she took her to order for some skanky druggie boyfriend she has, or for

some . . . desperate woman who can't have kids . . . or . . .'
She started shaking.

'Mrs Whaley,' said Ren. 'All over the world, parents leave their children with hotel babysitters.'

'Would *you*?' said Erica. 'Do you have kids?'

'I don't have kids,' said Ren, 'but I would have no problem leaving them with a hotel babysitter.' *And if you were listening very carefully, the word 'hotel' cracked with the broken cadence of doubt.*

Erica Whaley *had* been listening carefully.

Shit.

Erica Whaley started to cry.

'Mrs Whaley,' said Ren. 'Now is not the time to beat yourself up. Please don't turn this in on yourself—'

'I drank a whole bottle of champagne tonight,' she said. 'I started on a second. I know what that probably looks like to you . . .'

Erica Whaley gave her version of events and it matched her husband's until it came to their time in the restaurant, when it turned hazy.

'Mrs Whaley, a witness has said that you and your husband argued over dinner.' *The server saw. And he saw your tears when he delivered your champagne.*

Her eyes went wide. 'Yes,' she said. 'It was nothing. Just about his working hours. What woman doesn't complain about her husband's working hours?'

'So, your husband spends a lot of time at the office?' said Ren.

Erica nodded. 'Yes – then locked away in the den at home.'

'Can I confirm that you ordered the second bottle of champagne just before your husband left the table to check on the kids?'

'Yes,' said Erica.

'Did you argue about the second bottle?' said Ren. *Been there.*

'I'm mortified,' said Erica. 'I rarely drink. And the one night that I do . . . No, Mark didn't mind,' said Erica. 'He just reminded me about the championships tomorrow. He was just trying to spare me from a hangover.'

'OK,' said Ren.

'I feel like we're sounding like a different couple to who we are,' said Erica. 'That we've been caught at our worst or something. Fighting in a restaurant, drinking too much in my case . . .'

'You were out for dinner. No-one's judging you,' said Ren. 'How long do you think your husband was gone from the table?'

Erica paused. 'Twenty minutes? Hold on, I've got a text here. I texted my sister when he got back to the restaurant.' She picked up her cell phone. 'That was at twelve fifteen.'

Ren glanced down at her notes. 'The receipt for your second bottle of champagne says eleven thirty-five,' said Ren. 'Your husband was gone forty minutes, Mrs Whaley.'

Erica frowned. 'Why did I drink all that champagne, I'm so fuzzy – my timing always gets a little skewed . . .'

Yet your sober husband said twenty minutes too.

'May I look at your phone, please?' said Ren.

Erica handed it over. Ren scrolled back through Erica's texts. The previous one to her sister read:

Asked him, finally. Denied it. Hmm.

Erica blushed.

'The text to your sister,' said Ren. 'What had you asked your husband?'

'I didn't really think he was, but I . . . I just asked him if he was having an affair.'

'What made you think that?' said Ren.

'I jumped to conclusions,' said Erica. 'Because of the whole working late thing – it's a cliché, I know . . . but . . .' She shrugged. 'To be honest, it's probably just me being paranoid.'

'And from your text, you say he denied it.'

'Yes,' said Erica.

'But, you write "Hmm" . . .'

'I was tipsy,' said Erica. She shrugged. 'If you're asking me right now? I do believe him. Of course I do. I get a little dramatic. He's right. He's got a lot of work on. Making him sound like he's sneaking around behind my back sounds terrible right now.'

You bet.

'What was your husband's demeanor when he returned from checking on the kids?' said Ren.

Erica frowned. 'Fine – why?'

'Was there anything in his behavior that caused you concern?' said Ren.

'No – not at all.'

'What did he say?' said Ren.

'He said that the kids were sleeping, and that the sitter was watching television. Are you putting out an Amber Alert?'

'We're not in a position to do that,' said Ren, 'we don't have enough information to release. We don't know what happened to Laurie. We don't have a description of an abductor, we don't have a vehicle description—'

'But you have a photo of Laurie!' said Erica. 'Taken tonight! And I'm sure you have a photo of the sitter. She could be the . . . perpetrator here . . .'

'We have already released their photos,' said Ren. 'Their

images will be displayed around Breckenridge, they'll be on local news, in the newspapers first thing.'

'But . . . Amber Alerts, they're on the highway signs, right?'

'Yes, but without a vehicle description, drivers won't know what to look out for,' said Ren.

'What about at a rest stop? Someone might see them. Didn't a guy in California rescue a little girl when he saw her in a pickup? That was an Amber Alert.'

'There were witnesses to that kidnapping,' said Ren. 'The police had a description of the vehicle, and there was surveillance footage of the vehicle shown on television, along with the girl's photo.'

'Don't you have surveillance footage here?' said Erica.

'Most of the cameras were not operational at the hotel,' said Ren.

'I don't believe it,' said Erica. 'So, you're telling me you have nothing.'

'For an Amber Alert, we have to know that an abduction has occurred—'

'What do you think this is, *Adventures in Babysitting*?' said Erica. 'That they're out on the town somewhere having fun?'

'No,' said Ren. 'But we are limited by the amount of information we have to release.'

'I can't believe this, I can't believe any of this—'

'I know this is difficult,' said Ren. 'Just a few more questions.'

Erica nodded.

'Have there been any changes in Laurie's behavior over the last little while?' said Ren.

'No,' said Erica.

'Have a think about that,' said Ren.

'I'm telling you straight off, because I know. We have

Laurie Saturday during the day, every second weekend. I don't know what happens the rest of the time, but she's been the same as she always is. Oh . . . tonight, she had a pain in her stomach, that was all, but she was fine shortly afterward. We got out of the SUV, and she kind of got a sharp pain, she was bent double with it, but by the time we were checking in, she said it was gone. And she didn't look ill: no fever, rosy cheeks, and she was running around after Leo.'

'So, this weekend . . . you were picking her up from the Merritts' house?'

'Yes – on Saturday afternoon, it was about four o'clock. We told Laurie about Breck when we got there – it was a surprise. Obviously, we had run it by Cathy and Dale. So we headed for Breck, but then Laurie asked us could we go back so she could pick up her new ski jacket. We hadn't the heart to say no. Leo had spilled his drink all over himself, so it suited us to have the chance to get him cleaned up.'

'What time was that at?' said Ren.

'It was five by the time we left again,' said Erica.

'Who was there when you went to the house?' said Ren.

'The second time? Just Joshua – that's Dale Merritt's son.'

'Did you spend long there?' said Ren.

'Not long,' said Erica. 'I don't know. Laurie ran up to her room to grab her jacket. I went in after her to find somewhere to change Leo's clothes and then we left.'

'Did Mark go inside with you?' said Ren.

'Yes, he came to help with Leo.'

'How does Laurie get along with her stepbrother?' said Ren.

'He's a teenage boy, she's an eleven-year-old girl . . . you can imagine.'

Ren nodded. 'With three big brothers, I sure can. Could you elaborate a little?'

'Laurie bugs Joshua, he bugs her, but they get along just fine. You'll hear about them bickering one minute, then Laurie'll say that they were having fun playing *Shaun White Snowboarding* on Xbox or whatever. So it's up and down. Nothing unusual, as far as I can make out.'

'What kind of kid is Joshua?' said Ren.

'I don't know him very well,' said Erica, 'but . . . he seems like a nice kid. His mom died when he was five years old. He had his father to himself for quite a few years, and then Cathy and Laurie came along. It took him a while to adjust. He's sixteen years old, it's not an easy age . . .'

'And how would you describe your husband's relationship with Dale Merritt?' said Ren.

'Good, actually. There's no tension there. He's a very nice man, and he's very good to Laurie.'

'We'll be going through Laurie's cell phone records,' said Ren. 'Does she use it a lot?'

'Not really, she's still a little young, I think . . .'

'Is she ever secretive about who she's calling or texting?' said Ren.

'She isn't allowed to be,' said Erica. 'Cathy and Dale got her the phone and they explained to her very clearly that the only reason she has it is so that her parents can be in contact with her at all times, and that we all know she's safe. I know that Cathy told her about the rapist that's out there, so Laurie was aware that she had to stay safe, and that we would be worried if we didn't hear from her.'

'Mrs Whaley – what happened back there with Cathy Merritt?' said Ren.

'I know that didn't look good,' said Erica, 'and you're probably thinking all kinds of things about Mark . . . but it's just not how it seemed. I think that was a rant from somewhere in Cathy's past. I met Mark when he was in recovery. I guess I see him how Cathy did when she first met him. He's a wonderful guy. So I understand, to a point, how she could be so bitter that he left. I think she's still hurt. She sees it that he cleaned up his act for me, even though he was doing it for himself. Mark's been through a lot. Yes, he was an alcoholic, but he's in recovery – he's been sober for six years. And even still, Cathy didn't want him having access to Laurie.'

Ren nodded.

'Mark is a good person,' said Erica. 'I've never seen anything other than that. He told me all about his past, he's always been honest about it. He was a different person back then.'

'OK,' said Ren. She stood up and thanked her.

Bob was with a detective in the hallway when she walked out. The detective nodded at Ren and took her place in the room.

'Well, Mrs Whaley's still drunk,' said Ren.

'I thought she might be,' said Bob.

'Do you know what's sad?' said Ren. 'Millions of women will hear about this on the news, about the mother who was down in the restaurant getting drunk while her children were upstairs. And, really, there are lots of people everywhere who could just as easily be in the same position. Guilty, Your Honor. Of socializing.'

13

The Safe Streets team had made a command center out of the same office they had used for the Jean Transom investigation.

'It's like we never left,' said Ren. She glanced at Colin. 'Except you're not at cat lady's desk.'

'Cat lady appears to be gone,' said Cliff. 'There's no sign of any kitty pictures anywhere.'

'She's probably lying dead on her apartment floor and they're chewing on her remains,' said Ren.

'So . . .' said Gary. 'Erica Whaley?'

'Well, I'm not convinced of the whole notion of being scared sober,' said Ren.

One look at myself at 3 a.m. in a bar-room mirror would solve all my problems if that were the case.

'I think she's telling the truth in as much as she can,' said Ren, 'but attention to detail won't be her strong suit, and that's really agitating her. Not to mention the showdown with her husband's ex.'

'Which lady is telling the truth about Mark Whaley?' said Gary.

'I'm guessing they both are,' said Ren. 'But despite her big defense of him, Erica Whaley still suspected him of having an affair.'

'What's your reading?' said Gary.

'I'm not sure about the affair,' said Ren, 'but I am sure that he is lying.'

'What makes you say that?' said Colin.

'My gut,' said Ren. 'And a few other things.' She read from the statement she had taken. 'Exhibit A, when I asked him what time he left the table, and what happened, he said "I guess . . . eleven thirty? And then I came back down to Erica."'

'And?' said Colin.

'Think about it,' said Ren. 'The sitter has possibly taken your child. Wouldn't you analyze every single second of your last encounter with her, then recount the entire thing? Mark Whaley fast-forwarded to getting back to his wife. He skipped the entire time he was in the room i.e. the last time he saw the sitter, *and* his daughter. That usually means that someone has edited out their bad behavior in some way.'

'You don't think it was just that he's a nervous wreck?' said Bob.

'No,' said Ren. 'I also asked him was there anything out of place in the kids' room. He answered: "Absolutely not. Nothing." Who is absolutely sure of what is or isn't out of place in a hotel room they've just been in a couple of hours?' said Ren.

Bob nodded. 'Hmm.'

'It was like he wanted me to get out of that room, figuratively,' said Ren. 'Also, twice he answered my question with questions, as if he was stalling for time. Literally. Stalling for the time it took to come up with a time. Another weird thing was that twice he mentioned the sitter was wearing sweats. It's kind of random. Oh, and then there was his pause after suggesting fifteen minutes, then quickly giving twenty as an option, which, I would venture is because he figured his wife would be in the other room telling a version that wouldn't have added up. My conclusion is . . . there are two gaps in his story. At least.'

'What do you think is at the root of them?' said Gary.

'That I don't know,' said Ren. 'Maybe his wife is right – maybe he is having an affair. I don't know . . .'

'Maybe he stashed the mistress in another room,' said Bob.

'Is there a Mrs Smith on the guest list?' said Ren.

'Did you ask him to take a polygraph?' said Gary.

'I thought I'd wait a little while,' said Ren. 'I didn't want to freak him out right away, but if anything else shows up . . .'

'Let's go to the hotel,' said Gary.

He nodded toward Colin, Robbie and Cliff.

Robbie picked up his camera.

'You do the room,' said Ren. 'I'll follow you. I want to go talk to the desk clerk first. The statement he made earlier is . . . a little odd.'

Jared Labati was slouched in a chair in the office behind reception at The Merlin. He was staring at the floor, stretching a rubber band between his thumb and forefinger.

'I already gave a statement,' he said.

'Not to me you didn't,' said Ren. 'So, Jared, did you see anyone come in or out of the hotel after the Whaleys checked in?'

'Just guests,' said Jared, 'and whoever they were meeting up with, I guess.'

'Did you see Mr Whaley leave the hotel at any point?' said Ren.

'The Sheriff took the tape,' said Jared.

'I'm not talking about a tape right now,' said Ren. 'I'm asking you what you saw.'

You petulant prick.

'Then, no,' said Jared. 'I didn't see him leave the hotel. But I saw him leave the restaurant. Out of the corner of my eye. He headed for the elevator.'

'Where were you?' said Ren.

'At the desk,' said Jared.

'Did you notice anything about him?' said Ren.

'It was only out of the corner of my eye,' said Jared. 'He was walking fast. It's not like I was staring at him. He looked fine to me . . .'

'And did you see him come back to the restaurant?' said Ren.

'No,' said Jared.

'Were you anywhere other than in the lobby area last night?' said Ren.

'No,' said Jared.

'What did Mr Whaley say when he phoned you from the room?' said Ren.

Jared shrugged. 'I think, like, "help, my daughter's gone", something like that. And he asked me to shut down the hotel. He kind of hung up, he was in a panic. So, I just went over and locked the front door. Then I called 911.'

'How does it work if I'm a guest here and I want to book a sitter?' said Ren.

'Well, you call down or request a sitter at check-in and we put in a call to the agency.'

'What agency do you use?' said Ren, glancing at the notes.

'It's right there,' he said, 'Breck Sitters.'

'I just want to hear you say it,' said Ren. Her voice was flat. 'So Shelby Royce was sent by Breck Sitters . . .'

'Uh . . . yes.'

'You seem a little hesitant,' said Ren.

'I just . . . I have to answer all these questions . . .' said Jared.

'Has she been to The Merlin before to babysit?' said Ren.

'No,' said Jared.

'Can you tell me anything else about Shelby?' said Ren. 'Do you know her well?'

'Yeah,' said Jared. 'She lives on the same street, we went to the same high school. She was a couple years behind. But . . . we're friends.'

'And what kind of girl is she?' said Ren.

'Cr—, fun,' said Jared.

'What were you going to say?' said Ren. '"Cr—"?'

'Crazy?' said Jared. 'But, like, you would probably just take that the wrong way.'

'Do you think?' said Ren. 'I had a few crazy friends back in the day . . .' She glanced at her notebook. 'Does Shelby have a best friend?'

'Yes,' said Jared. 'Jane Allen, I guess.'

'Do you have a number for her?' said Ren.

'No.'

'Don't worry, we'll get a hold of her,' said Ren. 'Do you have any thoughts on where Shelby and Mr Whaley's daughter might be?'

'I only just saw the Whaley girl last night . . .' He shrugged. 'I don't have a clue.'

'Did any of your friends stop by the hotel last night to say hi to you?' said Ren.

'On a Saturday night?' He snorted.

'What about the staff?' said Ren. 'Did you notice anything different?'

'No.'

'Were any of the contractors here?' said Ren.

'Uh . . . four of them were here for dinner,' said Jared, 'but they left, like, at ten.'

'They weren't working . . .' said Ren.

'No.'

'Do you know their names?' said Ren.

'No, but I can find out.' He looked away. 'I can't think of anything else I can help you with.'

'That's not really your call,' said Ren.

'Look, it's Sunday morning,' said Jared, pointing to the reception desk, 'people are trying to check out. I need to be there.'

'It's nine a.m.,' said Ren. She looked at her notes. 'Didn't your shift end hours ago?'

'Oh, yeah,' said Jared. 'I guess with all the commotion . . .'

'Well, thank you for your time,' said Ren, standing up, shaking his sweaty palm.

Ew.

14

The door to Room 304 was open, and Sheriff's Office detectives were in the hallway outside, talking loud enough for Ren to follow the sound when she got off the elevator. She nodded to the men, flashed her badge to the officer at the door, and went in. She pulled on her gloves.

The room was more European capital city than Breckenridge ski resort, except that it was spacious. It had modern lines, but was decorated in warm shades of cream and beige.

A crime scene tech was sliding a cotton swab across the edge of the low walnut headboard. Ren recognized it from the photo of Laurie Whaley. The tech looked up at Ren. The tip of the swab he was holding was reddish brown.

Oh, no.

'We found a blood-stained pillow and a wet blood-stained towel in a plastic hotel laundry bag at the back of the wardrobe,' he said. 'Looks like someone used the towel to wipe blood away.'

Ren looked at the lamp shade on the nightstand beside him.

'There's an indentation there,' said Ren. 'Looks like it fell, and was put back up.' She turned it around. 'Yup – there are bloody prints here.'

The technician nodded.

Ren walked through the door into the adjoining room. The bathroom door was to her left. She could see another technician in there, swabbing the tiles.

'Looks like someone's head was bashed against the headboard,' said Gary.

'Yes,' said Ren. 'And someone tried to clean it up.'

Gary handed her an evidence bag.

'What's this?' said Ren. There was a small, torn string of blue and brown beads in it, with more loose beads at the bottom.

'They were found right here by the door,' said Gary. 'It's some kind of bracelet, could belong to either of the females, or a cleaner, or an unsub, or anyone else who could have been in the room.'

'They're ghost beads,' said Ren.

'So the girls were taken by spirits . . .' said Colin. 'Case closed.'

'Actually, ghost beads are meant to ward off evil spirits,' said Ren. 'They're Native American.'

'Your people,' said Colin.

Somewhere in Ren's past, there was Iroquois blood.

'Is there a dance you could do that would make an unsub rain down?' said Colin.

'Keep 'em coming . . .' said Ren.

She studied the bag. 'Laurie Whaley was wearing the bracelet in the photo. It's hers.'

'So she could have been pulled out of the room by the wrist,' said Gary.

'Or chased into it from the parents' room,' said Ren. 'I'm wondering how, assuming there was an unsub, he could have subdued Shelby out in the other room if she was close to the main door? Wouldn't she have just run?'

'Two unsubs?' said Gary.

'A planned operation, then,' said Ren.

'Two unsubs could have been planning a robbery . . .' said Gary. 'Got the wrong room, or got the right room, but thought it was going to be empty . . .'

'They could have been taking advantage of the fact that the hotel wasn't quite on its feet yet,' said Ren. 'They knew security was lax.'

'The contractors would know that,' said Colin.

Ren looked around the room. 'Anything else in here?'

'Nothing that jumps out,' said Gary.

'Which bed is whose?' said Ren.

'Leo Whaley's is the one by the window,' said Gary.

There was a portable DVD player on top of the rumpled bed clothes. Ren put on gloves and went over to open it. '"*Dora*",' said Ren. 'Not something Laurie would watch. Could Leo have been watching this in bed? Headphones on, which is why he didn't hear anything? Or he could have fallen asleep with the headphones on . . .'

Gary nodded. 'The child forensic gal – Sylvie Ross is her name – should be hitting Breck round about now. She's part of the CARD team.'

Gal . . .

'And then we can benefit from the wisdom of Leo Whaley's three years,' said Colin.

'Three-year-olds can surprise you,' said Gary.

'Even traumatized, pajama-wetting ones?' said Ren.

'Well, I'm not holding my breath,' said Gary.

'Ren will do a little rain dance,' said Colin.

'Yes,' said Ren. 'Then I could shove my peace pipe up your—'

'Ren – did you speak with the desk clerk?' said Gary.

'Yes,' said Ren. 'He's another candidate for my peace pipe.'

'Why?'

'Just – he's a dick. Probable stoner. Isn't remotely alarmed by the situation. Thinks he should hate the Feds because he saw it in a movie once . . .'

'Has anyone spoken to the owner of the hotel?' said Gary.

'He's not here yet,' said Ren. 'I'll go down and see if we've got an ETA.'

'I'll meet with the Royces,' said Gary.

Bob Gage was walking away from a couple who were sitting on a sofa in the foyer, the husband with a protective arm around his crying wife.

'The Royces,' said Bob when Ren came over to him.

'How are they holding up?' said Ren.

'Not good,' said Bob. 'Do you want to know what they just told me? They have a Child ID kit for Shelby at home. They got it a few years back; the mom figured that somehow, it would lessen the chances of her daughter going missing . . .'

'They thought "well, surely, if we have her fingerprints and a DNA sample, we couldn't possibly end up needing them" . . .' said Ren. *Ugh.*

'Do you want to talk to them?' said Bob.

'Gary's on his way down,' said Ren. 'Who's that guy?'

A man in his late thirties was standing at the corner of the reception desk, his face pushed into Jared Labati's, who was leaning back, but still with an expression that didn't reach concerned.

'That's the owner,' said Bob. 'Tom Olson—'

'Attempting the tricky feat of shouting under his breath,' said Ren. 'Let's go say hi.'

*   *   *

Jared Labati had been sent away by Olson and was gone by the time they reached the desk.

'My apologies,' said Olson. 'I'm a little frustrated, here. It's the weekend, Jared knows that the security system absolutely had to be re-connected on Friday afternoon. He was to tell the electrical contractor, and he was to stand over everyone until it was re-connected and fully functioning.'

'He's quite young to have such responsibility,' said Ren.

'I can see that now,' said Olson. 'I know his father well – Jared has done work experience with him for a few years. I figured he could handle telling a contractor a few things . . .' He shook his head. 'I cannot believe someone was able to walk into my hotel, and abduct a child . . .' He paused. 'And I'm sorry about Shelby Royce. I did *not* authorize that.'

'Authorize what?' said Ren.

'Hiring a sitter that wasn't from an agency – someone that hasn't been background-checked.'

'What?' said Ren. 'But Breck Sitters guarantee their sitters are background-checked.'

'But Shelby Royce wasn't with Breck Sitters,' said Olson. He looked at Bob and Ren. 'Didn't you know that?'

Ren could feel her blood pressure rise. 'No, we did not.'

'Shelby is just one of Jared's friends,' said Olson.

Jesus Christ. 'Where is Jared Labati right now?' said Ren.

'Gone to the staff room,' said Olson. 'He's about to go home.'

Not yet he isn't, the son-of-a-bitch.

15

Ren ran down the hallway, and caught up with Jared Labati. She took him by the arm.

'We need to talk,' she said. 'Back where we came from.'

Jared did as she asked, bumping off the door frame as he stumbled through the office door.

'Why did you lie about Shelby Royce?' said Ren.

'I didn't,' said Jared.

Ren stared at him.

'I mean, obviously, I did, but—' He shrugged. 'I didn't think Tom was going to be back so soon . . .'

Where do I start? 'I don't even understand what that means,' said Ren.

'I need this job,' said Jared. 'I really do. I couldn't risk—'

'Are you for fucking real?' said Ren. Jared flinched. Ren exploded. 'Risk *what*? Two children have been abducted—'

'Shelby's sixteen years old,' said Jared.

'A minor!' said Ren. 'A *child* in my book. And that hardly exonerates you.'

Oh my God, you don't know what exonerate means.

'You don't get off the hook is what I'm saying,' said Ren.

'There is an eleven-year-old girl out there, *and your friend*, and you tell me that Shelby works for Breck Sitters, and is therefore background-checked, when she is not.'

'There's no need to background-check her,' said Jared. 'Shelby's cool. I could vouch for her. If this hadn't happened, Tom would have been fine with it when he got back.'

Ren paused. 'Now I get it – you were hoping you could have a quiet word in Mr Olson's ear before we got to him, get him to back you up?'

Jared looked away.

'What difference does it make?' he said, his head snapping back to her.

'Every bit of difference,' said Ren. 'You lied at the beginning of an investigation, first off. That is the most crucial time for us. Do you have any idea the damage you could have caused?'

'They'll probably come back,' said Jared. 'They probably just went out . . . it's Saturday night.'

Sweet Jesus. '*How* did you get a job here?' said Ren. 'How?'

'Aw, my dad's buddies with Tom . . .'

You absolute idiot. 'Jared, you need to listen to me, OK?' said Ren. 'If there is anything else I should know about Shelby Royce, this is your time to speak up.'

'No – nothing,' said Jared. 'She's a regular girl. I don't know what all this is about, same as anyone else. I don't know why anyone would, like, burst into a hotel room and take them away. Seems crazy to me.'

'Is that what you think happened now? They were taken away by someone? Not that they just went out on a Saturday night for some fun?'

'No! I don't *know*, I told you. I haven't a clue what happened. If I did, I'd say.' He held some random fingers up. 'I promise.'

'You are looking at me like I'm supposed to believe everything that comes out of your mouth,' said Ren. 'The same mouth that did not open a crack to tell me that Shelby was just one of your buddies, and not even authorized to be here . . .'

'Look, I'm sorry, OK?' said Jared.

'Do you get the gravity of the situation?' said Ren.

'Yes, OK? Jesus. You're probably doing a background check on her now, anyway. What's the difference?'

'Just go,' said Ren. 'We're done here.'

Bob Gage was standing in the center of the foyer, talking to Mike Delaney. Ren walked over to them. 'That desk guy is such an asshole,' said Ren. 'How he could just bareface lie . . .'

'Lot of kids just don't give a shit these days,' said Mike.

Ren's attention was drawn to three men and a woman in dark suits and pristine white shirts walking through the lobby doors and moving her way. Three of them stopped just inside but one of them, the handsome one, kept walking, smiling, toward her. Late forties, fading tan, and hair that had gone very sexily gray.

Oh. Dear. God.

'Excuse me, gentlemen,' said Ren. She walked toward the man walking toward her. She could barely feel her legs, but they managed to move, and they managed to stop. And for the first time in eighteen months, she found herself standing face to face with the man who messed with her head like no other.

Damn you, Paul Louderback.

Paul hugged her lightly, and kissed her cheek. 'Hello, there.'

To what do I owe the discomfort? 'How are you?' said Ren.

'I'm good. It's great to see you.' He paused. 'Really great.' He pulled away. And stared a little too long.

Shit. Shit. Shit.

'You too,' said Ren. 'What are you doing here?'

'She said accusingly . . .' He laughed.

'More miserably than accusingly . . .' said Ren.

'I am here, Agent, because I'm the CARD guy,' said Paul.

'What?' said Ren. 'Since when?'

'You don't call, you don't write . . .'

'I'm . . . sorry,' said Ren. *Cold turkey was my only meal option.*

'Seeing that my emails clearly didn't interest you enough to warrant a reply, there was no point in writing to tell you that I've been out in the field as an SSA with the Violent Crime Squad . . . and, well, now I'm with CARD. At your service.'

'Wow, that's great,' said Ren.

'We were visiting with different agencies in Denver this week, so we were able to respond quickly. So, anything you need . . .' He smiled.

'Sure,' said Ren. *Two girls are missing and I'm thinking why didn't Paul Louderback tell me he was coming to Denver . . .*

'You do still *have* my number, don't you?' said Paul.

'Ha, ha,' said Ren.

He smiled. 'We should go for a drink.'

'We should,' said Ren. *In some other lifetime.*

'Maybe we could have dinner first?' said Paul.

Don't do it. Don't do it. 'If you insist. OK, I gotta go – there's a briefing at the Sheriff's Office.'

'Hey,' said Paul, 'fill me in before you go.'

Ren told him what she knew, and ran from him . . . as fast as her rattled heart could handle.

Dinner and drinks: way to get over Paul Louderback.

16

Ren stood up at the front of the conference room and addressed the team, giving them all the details she knew to date. She'd stood here before – when the walls were a little dirtier and the desk was a cheap version of the one she was now laying her notes on. She looked out at a sea of mostly men from the Summit County Sheriff's Office, Summit County PD, and the FBI. She counted just six women.

She could see a raised hand in the crowd.

'Ma'am? Detective Owens from the Sheriff's Office, ma'am.' He was no older than twenty-three and stood like a soldier. He was fair-haired and sweet-looking, the kind of guy who would never forget his mama. He was holding a small spiral notebook at waist height, and had his pen hovering over the page. There was a look of intense expectancy on his face. 'Could this have been a pre-meditated abduction?'

'Well, we'll keep an open mind on that,' said Ren.

'Could Mark Whaley himself have planned it?' said Owens.

'The abduction of his own daughter?' said Ren. 'I think that's unlikely – this is his first overnight visit with his daughter after what was, by all accounts, an acrimonious custody battle.'

'Maybe his daughter could have been like collateral damage in something, like he was planning something, and she walked in on it? Like, he was going to abduct the sitter?'

'We have yet to establish a prior connection between Mark Whaley and Shelby Royce,' said Ren. 'If Mark Whaley did know her before last night, and was genuinely planning to abduct her, it's unlikely he would have done so while on a weekend away with his wife and family.'

'But what if it was an opportunistic thing,' said the detective, 'he saw the sitter, he liked her . . .'

'By all accounts, Shelby Royce was an unexpected part of the Whaley family's weekend away,' said Ren. 'They could not have known that she would be their babysitter – she was not on any agency's books, despite what the desk clerk first told us.'

Owens sat down, but kept writing.

He stood back up again. 'Could the babysitter have taken the little girl?'

'That's a possibility,' said Ren.

'Maybe Laurie Whaley didn't want to stay overnight with her father,' said Owens. 'There could be an abuse issue. And things could have gotten violent . . .'

'That's a possibility,' said Ren.

'What if the little girl was injured and ran?' said Owens. 'The sitter would have followed her – she was in charge of her. If the little guy was asleep, she would have thought he was safe in the hotel.'

Ren nodded. 'In that case, with none of their warm clothes on, they wouldn't have made it too far from the hotel.'

'But wouldn't Shelby Royce have gotten in contact with someone if the little girl ran away?' said one of the female officers. 'Wouldn't she call her own parents? I know my daughter calls me if she's babysitting and something happens, or she's not sure what to do . . .'

'My boss has spoken with the Royces, so we'll see what they say,' said Ren. 'OK, moving on: with regard to vehicles in and out of Breck, there are almost ten thousand extra visitors here this weekend. Because of this, and because of a charity fundraiser on Saturday night, there were no road closures when the authorities were alerted, and without confirmation of a kidnapping, and without any license plates to go on, we don't know what we're looking for on the highway cameras, so until that changes, there's not a lot of point in pulling the tapes.

'On the Whaleys' finances, there's no indication that the family's going through any financial difficulties – they have $55,000 cash, $3 million in liquid assets, $2 million in a 401k, plus their paid-off $1.1 million-dollar home, and, at today's rate, $2.3 million in stock options with MeesterBrandt.'

Ren handed the briefing over to Paul Louderback.

'Thank you, SA Bryce. Good morning, everyone. I'm SSA Paul Louderback and I'm with CARD – the FBI's Child Abduction Rapid Deployment Team. For those of you who don't know, CARD works alongside agents from the BAU – Behavioral Analysis Unit – the National Center for the Analysis of Violent Crime, and the Crimes Against Children Unit. We're here as a resource to you all, so if there is anything you need, please, let us know.'

Ren had drifted from his explanation – she knew who Paul Louderback was, she knew why he was there. She knew more about him than anyone else in the room. So, she just watched. She had an opportunity she had not had since she was at the Academy – to stand in a room, and study Paul Louderback.

He was dictionary-definition handsome, the type who

comes from a long line of handsome men, men who wear chinos and button-down shirts, and smart shoes. He was too classically good-looking for other men to get Ren's attraction to him. They would think 'nah – he's too straight for her'.

Corruptible . . .

The thoughts that used to run through Ren's head were trying to run their course again.

Stop. Stop. Stop.

Part of Ren resented Paul Louderback. He should have known better. She was hardly the first student to have a crush on him.

But it wasn't a crush. It was more than that. It was just . . . complicated.

When they first met, she was with someone else, someone her own age, her hometown boyfriend, someone she really cared about. And what hundreds-of-miles-away twenty-four-year-old Catskill boyfriend could compete with a thirty-four-year-old FBI PT instructor? Especially when he didn't even know a starting pistol had been fired. The guilt had consumed Ren. She left her boyfriend, not because he had done anything wrong, but because she didn't know what to do with her feelings for Paul Louderback.

She took her eyes off Paul, physically shook her head as if that would get rid of the thoughts.

Jesus, stop thinking about men.

Gary Dettling caught Ren's eye, holding her gaze until she focused back on the top of the room. Gary had asked her once was she sleeping with Paul Louderback, and she was able to truthfully answer no, but . . . well. The important thing was that she had let the friendship slide, and she wanted to keep it that way.

But 'wanted to' and 'would' are two entirely different things.

* * *

Ren zoned back in when Gary Dettling took over and delivered what he knew about the Royces.

'Shelby Royce's parents are Cal Royce, sixty-five years old, and Connie Royce, forty-six years old. They're married twenty-eight years, and have lived for the past sixteen years in Blue River, four miles outside of Breckenridge. Shelby is their only child. Cal runs The Miner on Main Street. Connie works in Happy Days crèche, also on Main Street.

'Cal Royce is ex-Sons of Silence, a motorcycle gang – a one percenter. As it was famously said – ninety-nine percent of motorcycle gangs are good guys, any outlaw gangs are called one percenters. Sons of Silence are a hardcore gang – but Cal Royce straightened himself out, got married, moved to a nice house in a nice town, no trouble since. On Saturday night, he and his wife were eating together at the South Ridge Bar and Grill in town and stayed there until two a.m. Multiple witnesses confirm this.

'The Sheriff will be holding a press conference in an hour's time,' said Gary. 'But we're keeping details of this investigation at a minimum. It is crucial that the correct information is out there, so please, if you are approached by the media for a comment, refer them to our media team. I don't need to stress the importance of discretion here.'

Everyone moved into the hallway.

Gary came up to Ren. 'We'll meet in Bob's office, go through what we're going to say to the press.'

Bob walked over to them. 'There's already shit getting out there,' he said. 'It's not good, particularly for Erica Whaley – drunken step-mom. I just spoke with everyone's favorite dimwit-reporter, Casey Bonaventure: "is it true the Whaley step-mom was drunk?"; "did the Whaleys have a screaming match in the restaurant?"; "did the husband grab her by the arm?" "is Cal Royce a member of a violent gang?"; "was Shelby Royce drinking that night?"'

'And I've seen it's already on Twitter,' said Ren, '"OMG two girls kidnapped in Breck!" And "OMG such a cute town, v safe" and "OMG was going to stay in that hotel for the Dew tour". Shocked Smiley face.'

17

Taber Grace was wakened by a sharp slice of early morning sun beaming through his bedroom blinds. His dreams had been a mess he could barely untangle, shafts of faces and places, the vague sense of fear and pain. His hands were clenched, his palms sore from where his fingernails had been buried into them. The client file had fallen from the bed where he had left it, and was fanned out across the floor.

He checked his phone. There was a voicemail from his ex-wife, Melissa.

Taber, wherever you are, please call. TJ got in a fight in school Friday. It wasn't serious, but . . . just call.

TJ had gotten into a fight. TJ had no business getting into a fight. This was worth more than a phone call or a text. He checked his watch. He would pay TJ a visit. At nine a.m. on a Sunday morning, that would wake him up.

Melissa and TJ Grace still lived in the home that Taber once shared with them in Stapleton, North East Denver. Melissa's car was in the drive when he arrived. The drapes were closed. Taber walked up the path and rang the doorbell. There was no answer. He smelled burning. He ran to his car and grabbed the spare house key from the glove box. Things had never gotten that bad that Melissa had changed the locks.

He walked into the hallway, but stopped when he heard raised voices in the kitchen. They hadn't heard the doorbell. They hadn't heard him open the door and come in. The smell, he realized, was burnt pancakes. There were no flames, there was no smoke. He started to move toward the kitchen. He could hear Melissa's voice, but couldn't make out what she was saying. He walked closer.

'You screwed up my entire life!' TJ shouted.

Taber stopped dead. *Screwed up his life?*

Taber heard Melissa answer. 'I did what I thought was right,' she said.

TJ was sobbing. 'Do you have any idea what it's like to have to lie the whole time? Do you have any idea?'

Taber's heart pounded. This wasn't just teenage drama. TJ sounded traumatized.

'Yes, I have an idea!' said Melissa. She was crying too. 'Yes,' she said. 'I lied too, TJ. And it wasn't right, but . . . I thought it was. I swear to God, I thought it was.'

Taber was rooted to the spot. *Lied about what?*

'Are you telling me the truth now?' said TJ.

'What do you mean?' said Melissa.

'Are you?' said TJ.

'I don't know what you mean . . .' Her voice was shaking.

Taber could hear something hit the floor. He realized then that he could see his ex-wife and son in the reflection of the open glass door. Melissa bent down to pick up what TJ had thrown at her. It was a bottle of pills.

'Oh, God,' she said. 'Where did you get these?'

'You can't even remember where you hid them?' said TJ.

'Stop, TJ, please. I told you—'

'You did what you thought was right,' he said. 'I get it.'

'Please,' said Melissa, 'don't be mad.'

'Mad?' said TJ. 'Mad? You think I'm just mad? Are you for real?'

'You were depressed!' said Melissa.

'I was nine years old!' said TJ. 'My parents were divorcing! I was *upset*. My dad was gone.'

Taber thought about it: *Nine years old. When TJ was nine . . . when TJ was nine . . . Melissa tried to kill herself. TJ had found his mother covered in blood. He had called 911. Taber had heard the recording, TJ's desperate voice. 'I . . . my . . . mother is shot. My mother is shot. She—' They asked for his details, and he sobbed as he gave their name and address. They asked again what had happened. He had covered the phone, then spoken again ' . . . self-infected. She's self-infected.' The operator had said, 'Son, do you mean self-inflicted?' 'Yes,' Melissa had said in the background. 'Yes,' TJ had said.*

And the ambulance had been sent, and the wound was superficial, and lucky for Melissa Grace, and for all the family, her suicide attempt had been a failed one.

And here they all were, six years later. Taber tuned back into the conversation.

'Did dad know about these?' said TJ, grabbing back the bottle of pills.

Taber Grace could feel his stomach churn. He barely realized he had moved until he was standing in the kitchen in front of them.

TJ jumped. Melissa cried out.

'Please tell me what's going on,' said Taber.

They both stared at him.

'Someone, please tell me,' said Taber.

'Oh, God,' said Melissa.

'We're all going to sit down,' said Taber. 'And you're both

going to tell me what this is all about.' He reached out to TJ. 'Hand me those,' he said.

TJ handed him the bottle of pills. Taber read the label. It was a six-year-old prescription.

CERXUS. Melissa Grace. Take One Tablet By Mouth Twice Daily.

'How do I know the name Cerxus?' said Taber. He opened the pills and shook them into his hand. They were bright yellow and stamped with a C.

'These are . . . what the hell?' said Taber. 'These are . . . TJ's Vitamin C? When he used to stay with me, and you gave me that little plastic Monday Tuesday Wednesday pill box, you told me not to forget to give him his Vitamin C. It was this? What, exactly, is Cerxus?' He turned to Melissa. 'What is it? What was I giving to him?'

'It's . . . it's an antidepressant,' said Melissa. Tears streamed down her face.

'What?' said Taber. 'An antidepressant? I said no to that—'

'You wanted to change his *diet*,' said Melissa, 'get him into sports more, but I was the one who was going to have to do all that. I was going to have to be the one to make all these healthy meals, to fight with him every mealtime, say no when he wanted to watch television . . . I'd have to drive him to all his sports. I just didn't have the time.'

'You didn't have the time?' said Taber. 'So you gave him drugs? Were you out of your mind?'

'Yes!' said Melissa. 'I was! I had lost my husband! I was suddenly a single mom—'

'Single mom!' said Taber. 'I've been in TJ's life more than any other divorced father I know.'

'I'm sorry,' said Melissa. 'I know . . . It seems crazy to me now. But . . . I . . . I thought I was doing the right thing.'

'By giving him drugs meant for adults?' said Taber. 'I cannot believe—'

'They were being prescribed to children—'

'Were they even approved for that?' said Taber.

Melissa paused. 'No . . . not officially, but doctors were giving them to lots of kids. I talked to other moms . . .'

'Oh, Jesus,' said Taber. 'Now I know how I know the name Cerxus. It was taken off the market. There was something about the side effects in kids—'

'No, it wasn't,' said Melissa. 'It wasn't. It's still on the market. But—'

'There was a TV special too, wasn't there?' said Taber. 'Something about withdrawal symptoms—'

'But—'

'You better tell me the whole truth here,' said Taber. 'So help me God.'

'There were side effects . . . with Cerxus . . . with children,' said Melissa. 'It made them . . . it gave them suicidal thoughts. And could . . . it could cause psychotic episodes.'

'Psychotic episodes?' said Taber. 'Psychotic episodes.' He turned slowly to TJ. *Nine years old. Melissa's suicide attempt. The 911 call.*

'Oh, TJ . . .' said Taber. 'TJ . . .'

'Yeah, it was me,' said TJ, jumping to his feet. 'I shot her.' He stabbed a finger toward Melissa. 'It wasn't her, she wasn't trying to kill herself. It was me. I found your gun. I don't even know what happened. All I remember is being really angry. Mom told me what to say to the paramedics, she told me over and over . . .'

'And I got the same story,' said Taber. He turned to Melissa. 'You told him to tell his own father the same story. Jesus Christ, Melissa. What did I ever do to—' He broke down.

'You would have gone crazy—' said Melissa.

'I'm suddenly a monster, now?' said Taber. 'You think you could not have come to me with that?'

'Of course not,' said Melissa. 'I . . . I knew there would be no way back. I knew that—'

'All I do every day,' said Taber, 'is deal with liars. People who hide things. People who deny things, and screw people's lives up. And my job is to find out all their little secrets. That's my job. And for six years, my wife and son have been lying to me. Right under my nose. I cannot believe this.'

'I'm sorry,' said Melissa. 'I'm so sorry.'

'And whatever about you,' said Taber, 'you made TJ bury all that, have that rotting away inside him – what? For the rest of his life? How could you put him through that?'

'I didn't want TJ being branded as some psychopath,' said Melissa, 'or having some record because of it. I thought I was doing the right thing. I thought he was young, he was confused as it was, and I thought that his memory would fade.'

'Jesus Christ,' said Taber.

'I was not in a good place,' said Melissa. 'I can see that now, but at the time, I thought this was the only way out of a terrible situation. I was in shock. I was trying to think quickly, and . . . I guess once I started lying, there was no going back.'

'I can't . . .' said Taber. He stood up. 'I can't talk to you right now.'

'No, dad,' said TJ. 'Don't go, dad, don't – I'm so sorry, dad, I'm so sorry.'

Taber leaned down and grabbed TJ's shoulders. 'TJ – look at me, OK? Look at me.'

Tears were streaming down TJ's face.

'TJ,' said Taber. 'I love you very much. Nothing will ever

change that. Nothing. This is not your fault. I'm leaving right now, but it's because I have to process all this. I don't want to say anything I might regret.'

Melissa stood up and reached for Taber's arm. 'Taber, don't. Please don't—'

'I do not know what to say to you, Melissa. I . . . I'm at a loss. I don't know how to feel.'

'You hate me now, don't you?' she said. 'You hate me.'

'I don't,' said Taber. 'I don't hate you. I . . . I just have to go.'

Taber managed to make it down the hallway, out into the cold and sit into his car. He closed his eyes. Tears poured down his face. For six years, he had been haunted by a scene where his young son had found his desperate mother lying in a pool of blood after trying to take her own life. Now, he had a new scene, and it was more horrifying than he could ever have imagined. It flashed, strobe-like, in his head: TJ raising his gun, pointing it at Melissa, out of control, terrified . . .

Taber Grace slumped back in the seat, and started the engine. He couldn't bear the noise of his own pain. *Replace the sound, replace the images.* He turned on the radio and got the tail end of a commercial break. Then the lead news story was introduced, but instead of taking him away from his problems, it seemed to draw them all together and mangle them: his no-show client, his job, his wife, his son . . .

Most private investigators would do no more than the job they were paid to do. Taber Grace was no different. But, for the first time, the contents of the client file beside him meant a whole lot more to him than someone else's shit.

18

In the command center at the Sheriff's Office, extra desks had been brought in from other offices, making it almost impossible to move around the room.

'These desks are breeding,' said Ren, squeezing through them to reach Gary's at the back. He was sitting very still with his hands resting on the keys of his laptop. Ren leaned over the chest-height partition in front of him.

'If you ever wanted to bring the lab to a standstill, you could bag all your fears and send them in.' She went over to her desk and brought back anti-bacterial wipes. 'Here,' she said. 'Don't be a hero.'

Gary started wiping things down.

'Just wondering,' said Ren, 'how long will the CARD team be here?'

Gary shrugged. 'Just a couple days. Why?'

'Just wondering.' Ren pulled away, and glanced down at her white shirt. There was a line of dirt across it from the top of the partition.

'Ew,' she said. She could hear her cell phone ringing on her desk.

'Pardon me,' she said, running over to it. It was her brother, Matt.

'Hey, Ren, I wanted to say thank you for the gifts you sent Ethan.'

'My pleasure,' said Ren.

Silence.

Ren started walking toward the interview room.

'Are you sure you can afford them?' said Matt.

Ren stopped walking. 'Mm . . . what?'

'Just . . . I know that things have been a little tight . . . and I was wondering . . . don't get me wrong—'

'Oh, I'm not getting you wrong,' said Ren. 'I think I'm getting you right.'

'Don't be like that,' said Matt.

'What's your point?' said Ren. 'I shop, therefore, I'm manic?'

'Just . . . shopping when you can't afford it . . .' said Matt.

'Then there are a lot of bipolar people in the world,' said Ren. 'Many of them women with great shoes.'

'Just . . . there's no need to buy Ethan gifts, he's only a baby—'

'I can buy my only nephew whatever I like,' said Ren. 'Now you are calling me to complain about gifts? Who does that?'

'I'm not complaining about gifts,' said Matt. 'I'm thanking you for them, and hoping that buying them didn't put you under financial strain.'

Ren laughed. 'They're onesies from Target,' said Ren. 'I don't think I'll be on the streets . . .'

'Onesies from Target, a snowsuit from Saks, two sweaters from Baby Gap, booties from Macy's, two pillows from Pottery Barn Kids, a hat from somewhere . . .'

'Are you seriously reading labels?' said Ren.

'I'm just worried,' said Matt.

'Please don't worry, Matt. Please. Get on with your life.'

'I'm concerned your judgment is impaired . . . that's what happens.'

'Impaired judgment? How technical . . .' said Ren.

Matt took in a deep breath. 'OK, let's forget all that. Tell me, how is your new man?'

'Gorgeous, and sweet, and fun, and amazing. This could—'

'Be IT?' said Matt.

Ren paused. 'What's that supposed to mean?'

'Nothing,' said Matt.

'I can't just think someone is amazing without there being an issue?' said Ren.

'You know him two weeks,' said Matt.

'Unbelievable, isn't it?' said Ren, 'that someone can take less than ten years to propose . . .'

'Propose?' said Matt. 'What do you mean—'

'Not like that,' said Ren. 'I'm saying you took ten years to propose to Lauren, so you're hardly a swept-off-your-feet kind of person . . .'

'But being *repeatedly* swept off your feet is a true sign of love?' said Matt.

'Wow,' said Ren.

'I'm sorry,' said Matt. 'I am. That was—'

'No, no,' said Ren. 'Kick me when I'm up. I love that.'

'I didn't mean to—'

'I can't really talk,' said Ren. 'But thanks for your over-concern. It's *amazing*.'

Mark Whaley was sitting with a detective in the interview room. They were talking sport. He had a glass of water cupped between his hands. He stopped talking when Ren walked in, and looked up at her with hopeful eyes.

'How did the press conference go?' he said.

'We issued photos of the girls, the Sheriff made an appeal to the public, and corrected any misinformation they had,' said Ren. 'The media wants to help.'

And wants to demonize your wife.

She sat down opposite him. 'Can we talk about the forty minutes between when you left the restaurant to when you returned?' said Ren.

'What?' said Mark. 'Forty minutes? It was twenty. Where did you get forty minutes from?'

'There are forty minutes unaccounted for,' said Ren.

'There couldn't be . . . but even if there was . . .'

'Forty minutes,' said Ren. 'You left the table at eleven thirty-five p.m. You told us that yourself. And we have a text from your wife, sent to her sister at twelve fifteen a.m. saying "Gotta go . . . he's back".'

'But . . . forty minutes?' said Mark. 'I'm sorry – I had no idea. I . . .'

'It's quite a long time,' said Ren.

'Did that text send when it was supposed to send? This makes no sense to me.'

'It did send when it was supposed to send,' said Ren. 'So, it's a proven fact that you were gone for forty minutes. And thirty minutes later, you discovered that your daughter and her sitter were gone.'

'I . . . that might sound bad,' said Mark. 'But I had nothing to do with this. I don't know what's going on here.'

'Mr Whaley,' said Ren. 'The reason your wife was texting her sister was . . . because you were gone so long. We've talked to her, we've gone through some of her correspondence . . .' Ren paused. 'Did you know that your wife thinks you're having an affair?'

'I didn't know that – not until last night.'

'But you didn't think to mention that?' said Ren.

101

'Because I'm not having an affair!' said Mark. 'I didn't want you going down a route that would lead to a dead end. I would never have an affair. I've never cheated on anyone . . . if I didn't have affairs when I was a raving alcoholic, I'm not going to start now. I love my wife.'

'Are you saying, for the record, that you are not having an affair?'

'Yes,' said Mark. 'I am not having an affair. Never have, never will.'

'Your wife said that you spend a lot of time at the office.'

'Yes, I do,' said Mark, 'but I'm in the den at home more. Why is she saying all these things? I don't get it. Why now? This is just going to distract everyone.'

I'm ignoring that. 'As part of an investigation like this,' said Ren, 'we would ask close family members to submit to a polygraph.'

Mark Whaley stared at her. 'So you don't believe a word I'm saying.'

'It's standard practice to ask for a polygraph,' said Ren.

'Uh . . . I . . . well, go ahead, then. I've got nothing to hide.'

'You are willing to take a polygraph . . .' said Ren.

'Yes,' said Mark. 'Absolutely.'

She stood up. 'Thank you.'

He nodded.

'You've been stuck here for hours,' said Ren. 'Would you like to get a coffee in the break room?'

Mark nodded. 'That would be great. Thank you.'

19

Paul Louderback walked down the hallway toward Ren, his face red from the cold, his hair in tufts. His navy ski jacket was hanging open over a black fleece. Ren smiled at him.

She turned to Mark Whaley. 'Could you hold on there for just one moment?'

'No problem,' said Mark.

She walked over to Paul. 'So, how did the search go?'

'We had to abandon it for now,' said Paul. 'Snow is falling thick and fast. We had eighty volunteers show up – we searched a two-mile radius. We're still waiting to hear back from some of the owners of the vacant holiday homes nearby for permission to search their properties. We're hoping to get back out there at eight a.m. tomorrow, but the forecast is not promising – ten inches of snow are expected.'

'Shit.'

'Where are you two headed?' said Paul.

'To the break room, just so he can stretch his legs, and

grab a decent coffee. The walls of that interview room must be closing in on him. They're closing in on me . . .'

'OK – catch you later.'

Ren led Mark Whaley to the break room. She knocked on the door. There was no-one inside. Mark took a seat at the table. The television was playing silently in the corner. Ren turned around to the machine to make coffee. She reached out to hand a mug to Mark Whaley. He didn't move. The images on the television screen had changed, and a crimson strip across the bottom was detailing his pain:

BREAKING NEWS: MISSING GIRLS

Breckenridge, CO: Laurie Whaley, 11 years old, Shelby Royce, 16 years old, missing since midnight from The Merlin Lodge & Spa.

Mark Whaley reached for the remote control, his hand shaking. He struggled to find the volume button. Ren took the remote control gently from him, and turned up the volume. Mark looked around. 'Thank you,' he said. Then he watched, tears streaming down his face.

Detective Owens walked into the room. Ren handed him Mark Whaley's coffee. She nodded toward him. 'Can you keep an eye on him?' she said quietly.

Ren went down to Bob's office. The television screen was now showing the photo of a child who had disappeared from a motel in Park County two years earlier and had never been found.

'Any connection?' said Ren.

'Nah,' said Bob. 'My money's on the mother for that one. Everyone's money's on her. And that's without the public knowing some of the shit I know. Do you know something? In her second interview, an investigator asked her what she would like most in the world – bearing in mind her five-year-old kid is missing – and she says "a red Ferrari".'

'You are shitting me,' said Ren.

'That's what you're dealing with. How's Whaley?' said Bob.

'He's just been watching this, so not good, I'm guessing,' said Ren. 'I've left him with Owens.'

'What next?' said Bob.

'I wanted to let you know that he's agreed to a polygraph. We can have someone here from Denver right away.' Ren pointed to the television. 'Ooh – look,' she said, 'another Repuritan bites the dust. Or the tight ass of a hooker . . .'

'Mississippi Congressman, Shep Collier . . .' said Bob. 'This will be good.'

'And there we have it,' said Ren, reading the scrolling text at the bottom of the screen, 'the press conference that will address the prostitution claims . . .'

Congressman Shep Collier took the podium.

'Check out The Good Wife,' said Ren.

Shep Collier's wife was standing two steps to her husband's right, and one step back. She had brown hair, swept off her round face. She was full-figured, dressed in a lilac and mauve pants suit. She looked like a woman who never wore a skirt because she didn't like her legs. She looked like the woman in the grocery store who would pick up something you had dropped and hand it to you with a smile. She looked like the neighbor who would make you a casserole and leave it on your doorstep with a note. Right now, she was the woman who the women of America were rooting for.

'*Thank you all for coming,*' said Shep Collier. '*I am standing here today as a proud American, a proud Republican, and . . . a man—*'

'Thanks for clearing that up . . .' said Ren.

'*A man in whom, at this moment, I can take no pride,*' said Collier.

'What about at the moment of being caught?' said Ren. 'Or at the moment of . . . the money shot.'

Shep Collier turned to his wife.

'Now, that is one ashen-faced man,' said Ren. 'Yes, asshole, you have, indeed, been burned.'

On screen, Shep Collier had his eyes on his notes. *'On the evening of October 24th last . . .'* He glanced up, *'while on a business trip to Boston,'* he glanced down, *'I availed of the services of a prostitute.'* He glanced up. Flashes exploded.

Collier laid his hands flat on the podium.

'No other language can be used to make my actions sound any less deplorable. I am a carbon copy of those who have gone before me, public figures who have been branded liars and cheats.' He looked out at the crowd.

'Although we were certain of the promises we made to our supporters, we discovered at the nexus of political and private life, a misleading god and an abuse of power, the results of which you see here today.

'My wife, Marie, patiently bore the trials of being married to a politician for over a decade, and despite the devastating impact of my actions, remains by my side today, and is bravely dealing with the effects, both psychological and physical, on all our family, particularly on our children.'

He looked down.

'Strange-ass little speech,' said Ren. 'Most people would say "false god", not misleading. I mean, is he saying he was misled? Does that mean he's not really taking responsibility?'

On screen, Collier looked directly at the camera.

'Wow,' said Ren. 'He looks . . . genuinely anguished. That's a first.'

'I never believed . . .' said Collier, *'that my beautiful, and beloved wife, Marie, would become . . . The Good Wife.'*

'Holy shit,' said Ren, turning to Bob. 'No speech writer wrote that.'

'*And she is a good wife,*' Collier continued. '*To her core. She touches so many people—*'

'Just not her husband . . .' said Ren.

'*I never thought,*' said Collier, '*that I would be a man, like the others who have gone before me, men we have all watched, apologizing on national television for their transgressions.*'

A reporter shouted from the crowd. '*Tina Bowers was underage, Mr Collier. She was seventeen years old. Are you going to talk about that?*'

'*I was about to address that,*' said Collier. '*Under no circumstances was I aware of Miss Bowers' age.*'

'*It's your legal responsibility to confirm the age of a prostitute before you engage in sexual relations,*' said the reporter.

'*That's a matter for the Massachusetts Attorney General,*' said Collier.

'Shame it's not Eliot Spitzer . . .' said Ren.

'*I would like to take this opportunity,*' said Collier. '*To tender my resignation from the U.S. House of Representatives.*'

An explosion of flashes followed, and for a brief moment, Collier took the dazzling lights. But he didn't take the questions. Instead, he turned and took the hand of his good wife.

'Your commentary really added to my enjoyment of that, Ren,' said Bob.

'Why, thank you,' said Ren. 'OK – gotta get back.'

Ren walked into the break room. It smelled bad. She could see a dark patch of sweat down the center of Mark Whaley's back. There were rings of coffee on the white table in front of him, as if all he had done since she had left was move the mug around. It was almost full. He half-turned to her. His eyes were swollen.

'I've changed my mind,' he said. 'I don't want to take the polygraph.'

20

Bob was in the command center showing Cliff and Gary a map of the town when Ren came back from the break room.

'These are the six registered sex offenders in Breck,' said Bob, pointing to the red pins on the map that represented their location. 'We've got four solid alibis here, and these other two were home alone.'

'Sorry to interrupt,' said Ren, 'but did red-Ferrari-lady fail a polygraph?'

Bob nodded. 'She sure did.'

'And I'm guessing that while I was on my walk to your office earlier the news report mentioned that,' said Ren.

Bob paused. 'Did our guy change his mind?'

'He sure did,' said Ren.

'If he crosses his fingers for a black BMW, we're in trouble,' said Bob.

'Ren?' said Gary. 'A word, please.' He took her to one side. 'Go get some rest,' he said, his voice low.

'What?' said Ren. 'Did I do something wrong?'

Gary looked at his watch. 'By my calculations, you've had three hours' sleep in the last forty-eight hours.'

'Not quite,' said Ren. 'But . . . who else has had any sleep? Are you singling me out, here? That's not—'

'Ren, if I choose to single you out, you run with it,' said Gary.

Do not react.

'As it happens,' said Gary, 'Colin and Robbie went back to their hotels after the search. Robbie will be back to spend tonight at the hotel with the Whaleys in case a ransom demand comes in. Colin will be with the Royces. And look – Cliff is packing up too.'

'But—' said Ren.

'You won't be any use to the investigation unless you rest,' said Gary.

'I'm wide awake,' said Ren.

'Well, try not to be.' He moved past her. 'Goodbye, Ren.'

Ren put a call in to Karen Nyland, the owner of The Firelight Inn, a cozy Victorian Inn close to Main Street.

'Hi Ren,' said Karen, 'it's good to hear from you.'

'You too,' said Ren.

'I'm guessing you're here for all the wrong reasons,' said Karen.

'Sadly, yes,' said Ren. 'And I was wondering if there is room at the Inn. I'd need it right away. I'm on enforced rest.'

'Someone beat you to the suite by minutes,' said Karen. 'But I have a room on the second floor. It's yours for as long as you need it.'

'That's great, thank you,' said Ren.

'Those poor girls,' said Karen.

'Did you know Shelby Royce?' said Ren.

'No,' said Karen, 'but we know her parents to talk to in a small-talk kind of way. And we send people to The Miner and Cal Royce sends people here. We exchange bottles of wine at Christmas, that sort of thing.'

'Can I ask, off-the-record, about Tom Olson at The Merlin?'

'Sure,' said Karen. 'Well, Tony and I wouldn't share the same opinion of him, that's the first thing. Tony thinks Tom is the does-a-lot-for-the-community good guy,' said Karen. 'He organizes community events, that kind of thing. I think Tom's the Breck native who's spent his life getting by on his looks, and is ultimately out for his own gain . . . *ish*. If that can be an "ish". I don't think he's a bad guy – I just think that he wouldn't be beyond screwing someone over if he had to. Not in any terrible way, but . . .' She paused. 'Oh . . . I don't think that he would have anything to do with taking those two girls. Not at all. I can't imagine that.'

'OK,' said Ren. 'So . . . what did he do before he opened the hotel?'

'He owned an inn, not unlike ours,' said Karen. 'He was doing great.'

'Until . . .' said Ren.

'He overstretched himself with the hotel venture. It looked like he was going to run out of money by the end. He's broke, by all accounts,' said Karen. 'That's why he opened before he was ready. The Dew tour brings in a lot of visitors. Accommodation can be hard to find. Tom wanted to have a few weeks' practice before the real crowds showed up. Take this with a grain of salt – and I don't even know if it has any significance – but I heard that Tom's anywhere up to three million dollars in debt. But we're a small town, there are always rumors out there, and no-one really has a clue what goes on in people's houses or bank balances.'

'That's true,' said Ren. 'Is there anything else you can think of that might help?'

'No,' said Karen. 'Nothing that hasn't been in the news.'

'OK,' said Ren. 'Well, let me know if anything comes up. Anyway, I'll be seeing you in about ten minutes. I'm just packing up here.'

As Ren was about to close her laptop, an email popped up from Glenn Buddy in Denver. Subject: Kennington Witness Statement. It had two attachments – audio from the interview with the Kennington rape victim and a color scan of the drawing the rapist had left behind. Ren clicked on the drawing.

It was a simplistic black-and-white line drawing, but the artist was not without talent. A line down the center of the page bisected a primitive rendering of a monkey suspended by chains that were attached to his wrists. On the left-hand side of the page, the chain hooked on to a bed post with a bird perched on it. On the right, the chain – threaded with a life preserver – disappeared inside a megaphone.

Freaky.

There were bloody fingerprints at the edges of the pages, smears of blood, tiny droplets.

Blood that had been very real, but was now represented by red ink on a page.

Ren took her headphones from her desk drawer and put them in to listen to the audio file.

'This is Detective Glenn Buddy, with Denver PD. What follows is the witness statement of Ally Lynch, aged fourteen, from Skyland, Denver.'

Ally Lynch's voice was trembling. *'I was at a Hallowe'en party in Kennington Asylum with my friends. But I lost them. I met this guy I liked from school . . . I was talking to him . . . it was maybe midnight. Then . . . I saw this kid come in. He was around the same age as me, maybe a little older. It was like . . . he kind of appeared out of nowhere. He wasn't in the party all night. But . . . then, I'd been drinking . . .*

'I was talking to a guy-friend of mine, and this guy who walks in is totally staring at me. It was so creepy. My guy-friend was about to leave the party, but I told him to wait, that I needed to go to the ladies room. But as soon as I walked past the creepy guy, he started to follow me. There were people around, I thought I was safe, but suddenly there seemed to be no-one. I started to run, and I ended up in this room that was like some kind of office, and he backed me all the way to the wall, and I was trying to climb up on a table, but I only got as far as sitting on it, when he just dived for me, and started kissing me. I was so shocked, I froze. I . . . I . . . do karate. I always thought if something like this ever happened to me, I'd be one of those people who fights back, but I didn't. I was so terrified, and he was so strong. Like, angry strong. But he was kind of smiling at me too. He was biting on my lips, but then he would kiss them really gently. It was so messed up . . . ' She breathed in. *'Do you need all these details?'*

Ren could hear Glenn say 'yes', managing to put so much kindness into one short word.

'I don't know what happened with my hair,' said Ally, *'but he just pulled a bunch of it out . . . '*

She started to hyperventilate.

The tape clicked off, then back on again, with the same introduction from Glenn.

'He was . . . crazy,' said Ally, her voice composed again. She paused. *'I was terrified. But . . . I don't think I screamed.'* Ren could hear her voice crack. *'I . . . don't think I made a sound. It was like my throat closed up. Like in your nightmares you scream and nothing comes out. I thought that was just for nightmares. I didn't think it would happen in real life. I didn't think any of this would happen in real life. He smelled bad, like he hadn't showered and his clothes weren't fresh. His breath was disgusting. It didn't smell of alcohol. But maybe that was because I'd been drinking too. I don't know. His face was pale, kind of puffy.*

His eyes were . . . it was so strange . . . his eyes were almost, like, sleepy. I thought, like, with something like this, his eyes would look wild. But they weren't. They were sleepy.

'I wish I had been even more drunk than I was, then I'd have forgotten all this, I could have blocked it all out.'

She paused. *'He didn't speak. He seemed so angry, and so happy, but I don't know which it was. Because he didn't speak. He didn't say one word. At the very end, he muttered something, but I was so out of it. I think he thanked me. I think he actually thanked me.'*

21

Ren left the Sheriff's Office and dialed Ben Rader's number when she got into the Jeep.

'Talk to me about my girl,' she said.

'Well, Misty's a wonderful girl,' said Ben. 'And what about "how are you, Ben"?'

'Aw, you're a big boy,' said Ren.

'That's what you said last night.'

'Jesus.'

'I really like your friend, Janine, I wanted to say.'

'Thank you, I like her too.'

'She's kind of got that dry wit going on . . .'

'Is that code for she insulted you?' said Ren.

'No, not at all, she was really sweet,' said Ben.

'She is.'

'Your house is unbelievable,' said Ben.

'Do you really think that is my house? Isn't your pay check not too dissimilar to mine?' said Ren.

'I thought you might be, like, a secret heiress,' said Ben.

'Yes. And it turns out that Paris Hilton is actually an agent.'

'The place must be a hundred years old . . .' said Ben.

'Even more than that – it's a Gold Rush house,' said Ren. 'And the lucky lady who owns it is sadly not me. It's Annie Lowell, a dear family friend: an adorable, warm-hearted, white-haired angel who foolishly asked me to house-sit.'

'Yes,' said Ben. 'I saw the kitchen . . .'

'I was running late . . .' *Three mornings in a row.* 'We used to stay with Annie in the summer when we were kids.'

'I saw the family photo,' he said. 'I wasn't being nosy – I had to follow Misty into the living room. You were so cute.'

'Where did it all go wrong?' said Ren.

'Very right,' said Ben.

'You're not supposed to reply to those statements,' said Ren.

'And where is this Annie?'

'Traveling around Europe,' said Ren. 'Seriously. At eighty years old.'

'I want to do that when I'm eighty,' said Ben.

'You'll probably still be getting ID'd,' said Ren.

'And you'll be like, "no, I am not his mother".'

Hello? 'You are nuts.'

'It's very boring here without you.'

Ren smiled. 'Aw.'

'I miss you,' said Ben.

'Don't be a loser. OK – gotta go – I'm supposed to be in bed.'

'Yes – mine.'

Ren drove down Main Street, ignoring the turn for The Firelight Inn and going to The Crown café. She ordered a coffee with two espresso shots and took out the copies she had made of the victim/family questionnaires. She started reading through Mark Whaley's.

'Hello, there.'

The voice of Paul Louderback. Ren looked up. 'Well, hello there, yourself.'

He was standing with a coffee in his hand. 'I walked right by you.'

'So, did you send yourself off to rest?' said Ren.

'Yes. I didn't take it well, though. In fact, I'm quite resentful of myself.'

'My resentment, I can at least direct at Gary,' said Ren.

'Yup,' said Paul. 'Rest is for . . . other people.'

'Not pussies, then?' said Ren.

He smiled. 'Can I join you?'

'Of course you can,' said Ren. *Whose bed am I supposed to be in?*

'Can I get you a coffee?'

'The least you could do for beating me to the suite at The Firelight?' said Ren. 'I'm presuming it was you.'

'Guilty.'

'Damn you.'

'Did you get a room there at least?' said Paul.

'Yes,' said Ren.

'Well, that's something . . .'

Something . . . what? 'I'm still working on this,' she said, pointing to her coffee. 'Take a seat. Where are the other CARD shufflers?'

'Shuffling in a less cozy setting. Two of them will be with the Merritts at their hotel in case anyone calls.' He paused. 'I'm glad I'm here. I'm glad you're here.'

Stop. Stop. Stop. 'Me too.'

Four hours, six espressos, and twenty-five pages of notes later, Ren laid down her pen. Opposite her, Paul had his head buried in a file folder. She looked around and realized that The Crown had really filled up since they had arrived.

She watched parents watching their children. By the counter, a stack of newspapers showed the faces of two girls whose parents cared for them no less, but who, through an unknown series of events, for reasons Ren was trying to uncover, had vanished.

Families came to Breckenridge for fresh air, for powdery snow, for warm drinks and hot fires. They came for their breath to be taken by the stark outline of four Rocky Mountain Peaks against the night sky, not by the stark truth of the fragility of happiness, or security, or life.

'Out of curiosity,' said Ren, 'why didn't you let me know you were in Denver?'

Paul looked up at her. 'Abject fear.'

'Thought as much . . .' said Ren.

'OK, honestly?' said Paul. 'You're terrible company. And very hard on the eye.'

'True,' said Ren.

After a long silence, Paul spoke. 'The fear part is true . . .' he said. 'I was afraid that you'd drawn a line under us the last time.'

Yes – a lasting line, like a line drawn on a steamed-up mirror. She had a flash of Ben Rader in her shower.

'Whatever "us" means,' said Paul.

Us means you and your wife and me and . . . deep breath . . . Ben Rader . . . maybe . . . I don't know. Or you and me. And never to be.

22

Ren left Paul Louderback and walked down the steps of The Crown. Under the twinkle of fairy lights, she could see posters of Shelby and Laurie taped onto lamp-posts and in store windows. She got into the Jeep and called Matt on the short drive to The Firelight Inn.

'I think I would have to be electrocuted or strangled by a string of fairy lights to ever fall out of love with them,' said Ren.

'Good to know,' said Matt. 'Should I add this information to your existing instructions for your funeral?'

'Ooh – yes,' said Ren. 'Good idea.'

'Maybe the priest could wear them.'

'Speaking of dying,' said Ren. 'Or nearly dying . . . I'm in Breck and guess who shows up?'

'Too tired. Tell me.'

'Paul. Paul Louderback.'

Matt paused. 'The PT instructor guy? The married guy?'

'Yup,' said Ren.

'Oh, no,' said Matt. 'Where did he come from?'

'D.C. And what do you mean "oh no"?'

'Just . . . you could do without the complication.'

'What do you mean?' said Ren.

'Why is he there?' said Matt.

'To mess with my head,' said Ren. 'This is all about me . . . obviously.'

'And . . . how was it?' said Matt.

'You'd think I'd be over him by now . . .'

'You *are* over him,' said Matt. 'This is just a little dramz. And you like the dramz.'

'I do. But, it was a little . . . bam!'

'Didn't you sort this all out the last time?' said Matt. 'Didn't you decide—'

'Yes, yes, I know.'

'Well, then. You've had the conversation. Don't go back. And what about the new guy?'

'I know. I know,' said Ren. 'But I can't help how I feel. How I felt when I saw Paul.'

'You can't help how you feel, but you *can* help what you do about how you feel.'

'I know, but . . . I'm not great at helping myself,' said Ren.

'Paul Louderback is – let's not forget – married,' said Matt.

'I know,' said Ren.

'You said yourself you wouldn't go near a married man.'

'But I still have feelings for him . . .'

'And so the cycle goes,' said Matt.

'What—'

'Ren? Just get off the bike.'

Ren took the next turn onto French Street. A Missing poster for Shelby Royce was pinned to a tree and looked almost fluorescent in the glaring white light of a street lamp.

'Oh my God, Matt,' said Ren. 'I gotta go.'

The poster was just like the other ones lined along the street. Except this one had something extra. Across her pretty face, someone had scrawled: WHORE.

Ren pulled in to the curb. She grabbed an envelope from her bag, put on her gloves, and got out of the Jeep. She took a photo of the poster with her phone, unpinned it, and put the paper and pins into the envelope.

What kind of sick bastard . . .

Ren checked the clock. She was due back to work in less than an hour. She turned the Jeep around and drove back to the office.

No point sleeping now.

Gary looked up as Ren walked in, then glanced at the clock.

What are you, the fucking slumber police?

'Hi,' said Ren. She sat at her desk, then realized that Paul Louderback was sitting two desks away.

'Am I in some time–space continuum?' she said.

'I didn't have a bed-time,' he said. 'Did you go back to the Inn?'

'Shh,' said Ren. 'Of *course* I did.'

He smiled.

'No – I found this.' She called Gary over too.

She held up the poster. 'It was pinned to a tree. I saw it on my way back . . . here . . . just now.'

Gary took it and studied it. He let out a breath.

'I know,' said Ren. 'It's terrible. It was just on French Street. Anyone could have seen it. Look.' She showed him the photo on her phone.

Uh-oh. Shit.

'So, you managed to see the front of this poster, while driving in this direction?' said Gary. His face was set.

I'm dead.

He focused back on the poster. 'Well . . . what's this all about?'

'It's the only defaced poster in town,' said Ren. 'It

120

could be nothing, it could be some Mean Girl who hates the attention going someone else's way. It could be a girl whose boyfriend cheated on her with Shelby, I don't know . . .'

'Could just be an idiot,' said Paul. 'Or some young kids goofing around.'

'Or Shelby Royce could be an out-and-out ho,' said Ren.

'And there's that,' said Paul.

'Imagine if her parents saw this,' said Ren.

'We really need to get these high school kids to talk,' said Gary. 'They've told us nothing. I thought maybe that's because there's nothing to say . . . now I'm thinking maybe there's too much.'

Ren nodded.

'You haven't talked to any of them . . .' said Gary. 'You get on well with young people . . .'

'Jared Labati is my case-full of youth,' said Ren. 'Robbie *is* the youth, Cliff has sired the youth. I am nothing. They would do better.'

'I think kids would relate to you better,' said Gary.

Is this some kind of punishment? Resist. Resist.

'I've been de-stabilized by my dealings with Mr Labati . . .' said Ren.

'Leave it with me,' said Gary. 'I have several things to consider.' He left.

I'm dead.

Paul's expression told her the same thing.

Robbie and Colin arrived into the office at nine.

'Have all y'all got lists of who's been in touch with the Whaleys and the Royces since Saturday night?' said Ren.

'Yes,' said Robbie, handing her a print-out, 'they got a bunch of texts from their friends and family after the press conference – more texts than calls – I think people are conscious of tying up their phone.'

Ren read through the list and the text messages.

'So,' she said, 'who's getting through the net . . . in terms of who they're calling?'

'Close family,' said Robbie. 'Both sets of grandparents have passed, so it's siblings, really. And close friends.'

'OK,' said Ren. 'Detective Owens?'

'The Royces got a few texts,' said Owens, 'but they had a lot of people calling to the house. By about one a.m., everyone was gone.'

'Thanks for these,' said Ren. She looked down and scanned them.

Don't laugh. Don't laugh.

'Thank you so much, Detective Owens,' said Ren. She nodded as a way to dismiss him.

'He itemized what foods each visitor brought,' said Ren. 'Mrs X, beef casserole. Mrs Y, homemade bread.'

Colin laughed. 'What – in case someone was going to poison them? Are you serious?'

'As serious as young Detective Owens clearly was,' said Ren.

'That kid is an idiot,' said Colin. 'The kid in school who sat at the back, scribbling really hard like a freak.'

'Damn those Straight A students,' said Ren. 'Damn those people who lean heavily on their pens.'

Gary arrived back into the office. 'Conference room everyone, please.'

23

By nine thirty the extended team of investigators was crowded into the conference room.

'Welcome, everyone,' said Gary. 'Updates: the tip line has been swamped, we're going through the promising ones: they're in the minority. We've got nothing so far on calls to the Whaleys, the Merritts or the Royces overnight. I spoke with Mark Whaley's boss at MeesterBrandt Pharmaceuticals, he's the CEO, Nolan Carr. He confirmed what Erica Whaley said – that Mark Whaley's behavior has been a little strange for "*at least*" six months. He said "off-the-record" that he suspected Whaley of having an affair—'

'So another affair theory . . .' said Ren. 'Well, they both agreed he was working late, but he said it was mostly at home.'

'There's always lunch break,' said Colin.

Ren nodded.

'This could all be a high drama way for Erica Whaley to force the husband to admit it,' said Bob. 'She'd know that if his child went missing, he'd have to tell the truth . . .'

'That's very drastic,' said Ren. 'I can't see her doing that.

If I was going to go to extremes, I'd start by hiring a private investigator.'

'Maybe she did . . .' said Bob.

'If Whaley was having an affair,' said Ren, 'does that mean he's an all-round dirtbag, the type to hit on a sixteen-year-old babysitter?'

'He could have made some kind of move on her,' said Paul, 'and when she rejected him, he made her believe that it was her fault, that she was giving off the wrong signals . . .'

'He's an older man – he could easily manipulate a sixteen-year-old that way,' said Ren. 'Maybe afterwards Shelby could have thought of his wife and kids and decided, "I don't want to rock the boat here, he didn't *really* do anything, I won't say anything, I don't want to mess up the family that way—"'

'And then she ran?' said Gary.

Ren nodded. 'Yes. Just to get away from the situation.'

'And took Laurie with her?' said Gary.

'Maybe, maybe not,' said Ren. 'Maybe Laurie, if she walked in on something, could have been the one who was about to blow his cover, and he flipped. Or,' said Ren, 'he's not unattractive. Maybe Shelby Royce came on to him.'

'I'm glad you said that,' said Colin.

'Nothing is beyond the bounds,' said Ren.

'Well, Whaley's boss certainly suspected him of having some personal issues,' said Gary. 'He said that he has never had a problem with him up until this year, and several times he said that Whaley's alcohol problem was something that he had hopefully overcome. He labored that point, I didn't bring that up. He gave me details of Whaley's salary and expenses, and emailed me a PDF of his business calendar for the past twelve months.'

'Where does Jonathan Meester fit into the company now?' said Ren.

'He set it up – he's the chairman,' said Gary. 'He bought Lang Pharmaceuticals six years ago, hired Nolan Carr as VP Sales & Marketing, and basically lined him up to take over from him when he took early retirement, which he did last year.

'OK – on to Shelby Royce,' said Gary. 'A lot of Shelby Royce's friends have been interviewed and they're not saying anything other than the fact that she's a lovely girl, doesn't have a bad word to say about anyone . . . Her parents check out, so do the neighbors so far. The one interesting thing is that, according to Jane Allen, her closest girlfriend, Shelby Royce was *not* friends with Jared Labati. In fact, she refused his friend request on Facebook . . . the ultimate teen trauma according to my fifteen-year-old daughter. Jared Labati has already lied to us, so . . . we're not considering him a reliable witness. Jane Allen says that Shelby had been on Facebook talking about not having enough money for Lady Gaga tickets, and maybe to suck up to her, Labati offered her a way of earning money at the hotel. Yes, you can still read someone's Facebook profile without being "friends" with them . . .'

Gary Dettling, you dorky dad.

'So,' said Gary, 'Jared Labati could have been doing anything to get close to Shelby Royce. He certainly tipped the power balance in his favor on Saturday night. He may have seen her as "owing him one" after that.'

'Maybe he went up to the room to collect,' said one of the detectives. 'And the little girl got in the way . . .'

'That's a possibility,' said Gary.

'It's not really a break-in when the guy's got a key . . .' said Bob.

'What about the stepfather?' said Paul. He glanced at his notes. 'Dale Merritt?'

'Seems like a big friendly giant,' said Ren. 'I'm not getting evil stepfather vibes.'

'There is one other person who was in the room . . .' said Gary.

'A very little person,' said Ren.

Mark and Erica Whaley sat, holding hands, in Bob's office. Leo was in a fold-away stroller beside them. His little arm was wrapped around a Spiderman action figure, his fist curled into a ball.

Adorable.

'I am really uncomfortable with Leo being interviewed again,' said Mark Whaley, glancing down at his son. 'He's been through too much. First off, he wakes up alone in a strange room, God knows what he's witnessed, his parents come in and start shouting and screaming . . . then he's taken away from us at the Sheriff's Office, and he's put in a room with a stranger and asked a bunch of questions . . .'

'We'd like God not to be the only one who knows what he witnessed . . .' said Bob.

Risky.

Mark looked at him. 'He's been through enough.'

'He's three, Mark,' said Erica. 'He'll be able to get through this a lot quicker than he'd get over the loss of his big sister . . .' She slid her hand from Mark's.

No-one said a word.

Eventually, Mark spoke. 'He probably saw nothing. And if he did, it's unlikely he'd be able to vocalize it.'

Erica stared at him. 'Last week, you were calling him *"easily* one of the smartest kids" in pre-school, and saying how wide his vocabulary is.'

'Erica, this is completely different. What they're asking

for, ultimately, is for our three-year-old son to relive the most traumatic experience of his short life . . .'

'Mr Whaley, Leo won't be asked leading questions, so he won't be exposed to any scenario that's outside of his experience on that night,' said Ren. 'He won't have scary images planted in his mind. Child forensic interviewing is a real skill, and we have one of the country's leading interviewers here.'

'Well, she didn't find anything out the last time . . .' said Mark.

'This kind of interview usually takes place when the child is well rested, and has eaten. We couldn't afford the time to wait for that the first time. The circumstances early Sunday morning were not very conducive to a successful outcome, but we wanted to try.'

Erica was nodding. 'Mark – she's right. Leo isn't able to concentrate when he's tired. He's not himself when he hasn't slept. You say so yourself. His Spidey senses are weak.' She tried to smile.

'When do you want to do this?' said Mark.

'This afternoon,' said Gary. 'Some time around four p.m.'

Erica turned to Mark.

He was staring at the ground. 'Fine, then . . .' he said. 'Go ahead. But . . .'

'Thank you,' said Erica. She nodded toward Ren.
God bless you.

Gary followed everyone back into the command center.

'Ren and Colin,' said Gary. 'About our old Tinytoes Bandit case – there's a discovery conference at the U.S. Attorney's Office with the AUSA and the defense attorney at twelve today – I need you to go to that.'

'What?' said Ren. 'But—'

'Colin – you drive,' said Gary.

'Good,' he said. 'I get to hold on to my breakfast.'

Ren grabbed her purse. 'OK. I think I can channel Miss Daisy.'

Colin and Ren spent the first ten minutes of the drive in silence.

I want to slam your foot onto the accelerator.

'Why the hell do we have to go to Denver in the middle of all this?' said Ren.

'I think they can survive without us for a couple hours,' said Colin.

No, they can't.

'Do you mind if we go to Safe Streets first?' said Colin.

'No,' said Ren.

'I just need to pick something up.'

Much like your girlfriend needs to pick things up. Here goes: 'Naomi sure knows how to have a good time,' said Ren.

Colin smiled. 'She is a live wire,' he said.

'We had a blast that night we were out,' said Ren.

Colin nodded. 'Yes . . . I guess she doesn't have a lot of female friends . . .'

Probably because she's stolen their men. 'Really?' said Ren.

'Well, she's moved around a lot,' said Colin.

Probably because she was being hunted down by her female friends for stealing their men. 'That's hard,' said Ren.

'So, did she out-drink you?' said Colin, glancing at her.

'Not a chance,' said Ren. *Just go for it.* 'She definitely out-chatted me, though . . .'

'You two fighting for air time . . .' said Colin.

'More she was chatting with the people we met,' said Ren. 'This group of snowboarders . . .' *Male snowboarders. Men. Other men.*

Colin nodded. 'Tis the season . . .'
To be whoring. Fa-la-la-la-la . . .
Ren turned on the radio.

There was a package on Ren's desk when she arrived at Safe Streets. It had a Spyder logo. She ripped it open.

It was a new ski jacket. Her heart soared. She had bought it on a second screen while she was buying Ethan's gifts.

I had forgotten about you.

She was shaking off her jacket to try the new one on, when the phone rang. It was Glenn Buddy.

'Did you listen to the Kennington tape?' he said.

'Yes,' said Ren.

'She's still swearing she doesn't know who organized the party,' said Glenn. 'Neither does the guy-friend or the boy from school she said she liked.'

'We need to find out who was behind that party,' said Ren. 'And whether there's any significance in the choice of venue.'

'The significance is kids' fascination with asylums,' said Glenn. 'There are websites devoted to this, there are asylum "fans" . . .'

'I'm fascinated myself,' said Ren. 'But I wouldn't go to a party in one . . . especially the condition it was in.'

'Even when you were sixteen . . .' said Glenn.

Colin stuck his head around the door. 'Ren – that meeting with the AUSA's canceled.'

Ren covered the phone. 'Wait. I'm nearly done.'

Colin shrugged. 'Gary just called.'

'But, we've come all this way—'

'Don't look at me,' said Colin.

WTF?

'Sorry, Glenn, I'm back,' said Ren. 'Are you looking at

the people running these asylum "fan" sites, or posting on them?'

'Yup,' said Glenn.

'If you need any extra eyes on that, let me know,' said Ren.

'What do you make of the drawing?' said Glenn.

'That's one freaky little monkey,' said Ren.

'Is it a see-no-evil hear-no-evil thing?' said Glenn.

'I don't know,' said Ren. 'I'd like to think about it some more. My phone's ringing, Glenn, I have to take this. It's Gary.'

'Sure, go ahead,' said Glenn. 'Thanks for all this, Ren.'

'I'll keep you posted.' Ren switched calls.

'How are you doing?' said Gary.

'I'm good, but . . .'

'But?' said Gary.

'Colin just told me the meeting's canceled—'

'Yes,' said Gary. 'Nothing we can do about that. What time is it?'

'Now?' said Ren. 'Twelve thirty.'

'OK – you should be able to make that appointment,' said Gary.

'What appointment?' *Shit. Shit. Shit. The psychiatrist.* 'What appointment . . . time have you got there?' *Like that's convincing.*

'Same as it always has been, Ren. One p.m. No change . . .'

'Just checking,' said Ren. She paused. 'I've no car.'

'Grab a cab.'

'OK.'

Shit. Shit. Shit.

How did I fall for this?

24

Dr Leonard Lone was in his early fifties, sitting in an office that appeared to have been designed in the decade leading up to his birth.

Next client: brittle housewife with closeted husband.

Dr Lone sat cross-legged in a chair beside his desk. He was dressed in a mauve shirt, a pale green round-necked sweater, ghostly blue slim-fit jeans, and beige sandals with thick gray woolen socks. He pointed Ren toward a seat two feet in front of his.

Men should not cross their legs.

Ren pictured a website of psychiatrists, like a shopping website, where the images sped across the screen, and you could stop briefly and click on an image to get a closer look. She would have scrolled past the priestly Dr Leonard Lone. He smacked of downplaying your sexual exploits.

Ren wondered whether psychiatrists could tell how quickly she summed them up. Or if they cared. It averaged two minutes, but she always stayed for the full session to have her mind changed. She wondered if psychiatrists also noticed when they didn't click, and did they hope she wouldn't come back.

'Hello, Agent Bryce . . .' he said, reaching out to shake her hand.

'Ren is fine,' she said.

'And *is* Ren fine?' said Dr Lone.

Oh. Dear.

'I'm . . . OK,' said Ren. *And not into you enough to feel like telling you otherwise.* She slid her chair back a fraction.

'So,' said Dr Lone. 'I've gone through your file, and . . . well, you're obviously an FBI Agent. That must be quite a challenge.'

'It can be,' said Ren. *But you'll never understand exactly how.*

Dr Lone waited. 'So, tell me how is everything at work right now?'

Why are people always interested in my work? Ask me about relationships. I'll get a gold star: one man. No pressure. No drama. No crime or drug history.

'You're smiling,' said Dr Lone. 'That must be a good sign.'

Of me entertaining myself. 'Work is fine, actually,' said Ren. *And I need to get back to it. And I've already sent you out of the first round of Shrink Idol. So this pricey hour is a total waste. And I am sick of psychiatrists. And I already found the perfect psychiatrist. And now she's dead. And it was my fault. And . . .*

Dr Lone tilted his head. 'How are you coping with the loss of your last psychiatrist?'

La. La. La. La. La. 'As well as can be expected,' said Ren. *I can not believe I said that.*

'Have you had any grief counseling?' said Dr Lone.

'No,' said Ren. *That would be sensible and terrifying.*

'Maybe that's something you could look at,' said Dr Lone. 'Along with your visits to me.'

Internal eyebrow raise.

'So . . . what do you hope to gain from coming to see me?' said Dr Lone.

Zero? A pain in my ass? Weight? 'Em . . .'

'Do you feel that you're here under duress?' said Dr Lone.

Ren paused. *Be nice.* 'I understand why I've been sent to you,' said Ren. 'To a degree . . . actually, I don't really. Because I've been fine.'

Dr Lone nodded. 'It's a condition of your employment that you are under a psychiatrist's care, isn't that right?'

'Yes,' said Ren. *Sadly.*

'Well, maybe that's all this is . . .' said Dr Lone. 'A formality. To keep your boss happy.'

Oh, you don't believe that.

'What are your concerns about coming here?' said Dr Lone.

Let me think: I'm not sure I like you. Or you're right for me. Or there's any need for me to be here. 'I don't want to be put on medication.' *You said that last part out loud.*

'We've only just met,' said Dr Lone. 'I won't be handing you a prescription today.'

'And . . . any other day?' said Ren.

'I don't necessarily believe in medication,' said Dr Lone.

What? But I want you to. Even though I don't want to take any. I just want to know it's there. And that you believe there's a quick fix. If, at some point, I need one. Which I don't right now.

'Why do you think I would medicate you?' said Dr Lone. 'If everything is fine.'

Damn you.

'Everything's great,' said Ren. 'Really good. I'm getting a lot done.'

Dr Lone nodded. 'And are you getting much sleep?'

No. I don't need it, but that's the wrong answer. 'Yes.'

'How many hours are you getting each night?' said Dr Lone.

None to one. 'Seven.'

'And what about eating?' said Dr Lone.

And the correct answer is: 'I'm eating well . . . regularly.'

'And your caffeine intake?' said Dr Lone.

Beautifully, wonderfully excessive. 'Maybe a little more than usual, but we're on an intense case.'

'So everything is fine,' said Dr Lone.

It actually is, people! 'Absolutely.'

'Yet, you think I might have put you on medication . . .'

'Just . . . psychiatrists like to medicate.'

'Not all of them,' said Dr Lone.

'So, how else would you correct a chemical imbalance . . . if you felt there was one?' said Ren.

'Assuming a chemical imbalance is what lies behind mental illness . . .' said Dr Lone.

'But—'

'No study has ever proven that depression, for example, is caused by a chemical imbalance . . .' said Dr Lone.

'But, serotonin,' said Ren. 'Dopamine . . .'

Dr Lone nodded. 'No study has shown that depression is caused by a lack of dopamine or serotonin.'

'But . . . I've spent my whole life thinking I had a chemical imbalance,' said Ren.

'I would venture,' said Dr Lone, 'that you spent a great part of your life not thinking there was anything wrong with you and being oblivious to the field of psychopharmacology . . . until a psychiatrist diagnosed you in your mid-twenties. And then when you read up on bipolar disorder, you were assaulted with very clever advertising campaigns that reinforced the chemical imbalance theory.'

'But I've read studies . . . in medical journals . . .' said Ren.

'You may have read that antidepressants raise dopamine and serotonin levels, and yes, that's true – they do,' said Lone. 'But perhaps what you may not have read is that low levels of dopamine and serotonin have never been shown to cause depression.'

What?!

He nodded. 'One could argue that fevers are caused by too little aspirin . . .'

'That's insane,' said Ren.

'It's easy for someone to feel that they haven't been treated if they don't leave a doctor's office without a prescription. Desperate people want help,' said Dr Lone. 'Or at least hope. They like to think there's a quick fix. And I think differently.'

'What do you think?'

'I think medication can work for some people, absolutely. But I think it's over-prescribed. I think antidepressants can work in the short term to get people back on their feet, but that diet, exercise and talking are the key. The right diet and exercise can work as well, and, in some cases, better than antidepressants. It's just very difficult to persuade people. Either way, I certainly wouldn't be prescribing medication after the first consult. All my sessions are typically one-hour long, by the way, not just the first session. They are that length so that we have time to talk.'

Oh. Dear. God. No. How is work even paying for that? Because I'm not worth it. Gary is the one who should be here. He's lost his mind.

'For today, Ren, I'd like you to go through some of your history . . .'

Noo. 'Normal childhood, happy home, trained with the FBI, went undercover, came out from under the cover, psychiatrist died, here I am.' She glanced up at the clock behind him.

He noticed. He slid his chair back a little from the desk. 'I'm afraid that our time has run out.'

Oh. 'OK,' said Ren. *But . . . no, it hasn't. And aren't you even going to mention the skimming over of the background?*

'Shall I see you again next week, Ren?' said Dr Lone. 'What would you think about that?'

No. Way.

'Two weeks?' said Dr Lone. He smiled.

'Yes, that would be great.' *Who said that?*

'Two weeks it is,' said Dr Lone. 'Can you please call Betty to confirm? She's my right-hand woman.'

'Yes,' said Ren. 'And . . . will it be for a whole hour?'

Dr Lone nodded. 'Your boss has sanctioned that.'

Ren jogged down the stairs and out to her Jeep. She pulled out her phone when she got there. She texted Ben Rader.

Am in twn. Hav 2 go 2 my place 2 pck up clothes . . . . 5 mins of ur time?

Ben texted right back:

U bet.

Who needs therapy?

25

Ren pulled out her cell phone and texted Matt.

> Saw shrink: priestly (not Jason). Next contestant to the stage to perform! Or not . . .

> Matt: There has to be a next! Hang in there!
> Ren: Not teetering on cliff edge just yet . . .
> Matt: It's not the teetering. It's the jumping off drunk and nekkid for fun ☺

Ren didn't reply. She leaned her head against the window and stared out at the snow.

Matt, you're like a dark cloud of doom.

Ren got back to the office at six. Gary had forwarded her the email with Mark Whaley's calendar. She opened it and started to go through it.

She called Gary. 'Did Nolan Carr mention someone called Hillier?'

'Yes,' said Gary. 'It's not a person. It's MeesterBrandt's

Contract Research Organization – the company that takes care of their clinical trials.'

'MeesterBrandt don't do that themselves?' said Ren.

'No,' said Gary.

'So, it's pharma-ed out . . .' said Ren.

Silence.

I deserve silence.

'So, Hillier's in Boston?' said Ren.

'Yes,' said Gary.

'So it would be standard practice for the CFO of a pharma company to visit with their Contract Research Organization . . .'

'Yes,' said Gary.

'It's here in his calendar that Mark Whaley had two appointments: Thursday afternoon/Friday morning. He stayed at The Lowry Hotel . . .'

'And in terms of recent hotel stays – is that it?' said Gary.

'Yes,' said Ren. 'I'll get in touch with The Lowry, see if there's anything there . . .'

'What are you thinking?' said Gary.

'Hotel room precedent,' said Ren. 'And I'm thinking affair. Was he meeting a lady friend? A man friend? A paid-for friend? A Fisherman's Friend? I could go on all day.'

'Hold up,' said Gary. 'Where are you right now?'

'In the office. Why?'

'Can you hear that?' said Gary.

'What?' said Ren.

'Crying,' said Gary.

'No,' said Ren. 'Oh, I do . . . it's coming from reception.'

'Meet you there.'

Erica Whaley was standing in reception with Leo in her arms, her hand pressing his head to her shoulder. They were both crying. Bob Gage was standing beside her, a bewildered look on his face.

'What's wrong?' said Ren, rushing to Erica. 'What happened?'

'Mark's gone,' said Erica. 'He's . . . he went for a walk after lunch, he didn't come back, I figured he just lost track of time. So I came here for Leo's interview with Agent Ross, and I just . . . I really thought Mark would be here by the time it was over, but he's not. He's not, and I don't know where he is. His car keys and his cell phone were at the hotel. I . . . I . . . I don't know where he is.'

'OK, there's no need to panic,' said Ren. 'Why don't we take you somewhere quiet, you can sit down, we can put on some cartoons for Leo, get you a glass of water . . .'

Paul Louderback appeared as Erica was heaving for breath, struggling to calm herself down.

Now, what the hell is going on?

Ren turned around to the grim faces of Bob Gage, Gary Dettling and Paul Louderback.

Ren followed Erica down the hallway. Leo was staring at her from over his mother's shoulder.

I have a bad feeling about your daddy.

Ren turned on the television in the break room for Leo. She tried to talk to Erica, but she had descended into a disturbing silence. Ren asked her if Leo had seemed OK after his interview with Sylvie Ross, but Erica didn't seem to hear. After ten minutes, a Sheriff's Office detective came in to relieve Ren.

Ren walked into Bob Gage's full-to-capacity office.

'We got a match on the blood on the headboard,' said Gary. 'Blood is Laurie Whaley's, prints are Shelby Royce's . . .'

'What the . . .?' said Ren.

Sylvie Ross appeared in the doorway.

'I think I know why Mark Whaley disappeared,' she said.

Everyone turned to her. 'Leo said he saw Shelby Royce's privates.'

'What – he walked in on her in the bathroom?' said Ren.

'No,' said Sylvie, 'he saw her in his parents' room.'

'Was she alone?' said Ren.

'No,' said Sylvie. 'He said that his daddy was there.'

26

Mark Whaley's three-year-old son had walked in on him with a naked sixteen-year-old girl. Mark Whaley, poignant victim of a family tragedy, had just lost his victim status.

'No wonder he ran,' said Bob.

'What – the hell – exactly happened in that room?' said Ren.

Colin spoke in a flat tone: 'Mark Whaley made a move on the sitter, the sitter went nuts, his kids woke up in the commotion, they walked in, Whaley warned everyone to shut their mouths. The little girl – the daughter – ran for the phone by the bed, Whaley pushed her away, she cracked her head on the headboard, maybe she was knocked out. Sitter went to help her, or whatever. Whaley hooked the little guy up with the DVD player and put him to bed. He took both girls away, threatened that he'd kill them if they didn't keep quiet. Maybe now he's gone to wherever they are to finish them off.'

'A tidy theory,' said Cliff.

And one in which – not once – did he mention the girls' names.

'I don't think that's a forty-minute-window theory,' said Ren. 'But . . .'

Cliff nodded. 'All that would take a lot of time. And where would he have taken them? He didn't use his car. Maybe when Laurie Whaley struck her head, he was able to carry her out easily, then he threatened Shelby Royce and forced her to go with them? But, where?'

'Well,' said Ren, 'there was enough time for him to make a move on Shelby Royce, assault her, I don't know, and go back down to his wife, giving Shelby Royce enough time to take Laurie. Like, her message to Mark Whaley is, "How would you feel if someone did something to your little girl?"'

'If he *had* assaulted her,' said Gary, 'wouldn't she have screamed the walls down? There was obviously a struggle. Would he have risked leaving her there in the room with his kids if he had just done something to her? And would you even do something to a sitter right there in the room?'

'Look, none of it really makes sense.' Ren let out a breath.

'OK everyone,' said Gary, 'we'll keep a lid on this for now. We'll get officers all over town looking for him. He can't have made it too far without his car. If anyone asks, we're obviously still looking for the girls. The high school kids are holding a vigil tonight. It would make sense that we're out there to ask questions. Ren, could you go speak with Whaley's wife now? Then take her back to their hotel – that's where he'll show if he shows at all.'

Erica Whaley was sitting in the break room with Leo on her knee.

'Hey, there,' said Ren. 'How are you holding up?'

Erica shook her head. 'I'm . . . I'm not.'

'A team of officers are setting out now to look for your husband,' said Ren.

'He could have just gone to get some air, he probably needed some time to think,' said Erica. 'He's worried sick.'

Ren spoke gently. 'Erica, I know Mark didn't want Leo to be interviewed again. Did he talk any more to you about that since you left here?'

'Just what he had said to you already,' said Erica. 'That he was worried it would upset Leo.'

Ren nodded. 'Did he mention any other concerns?' said Ren.

'No – it was all about Laurie, and getting her home safe, and, just everything you would expect under the circumstances. Nothing else. Nothing any different to how we've been feeling since all this happened.'

'Do you know did he speak with anyone before he left?' said Ren.

'Yes,' said Erica. 'Jonathan.'

'Do you know what they spoke about?' said Ren.

'Jonathan called him just to check in . . . I called Jonathan just before the interview to see did he know anything or had Mark said anything. But he said no.'

'You're very close to Jonathan,' said Ren.

Erica nodded. 'He's like family. He supported Mark through all his problems, through rehab, everything. Jonathan founded MeesterBrandt, but basically, he and Mark were partners, he consulted with him on pretty much everything.'

'Where is the Brandt?' said Ren.

'That was Jonathan's wife. She passed five years ago. But she never took an active part in the company.'

'Is there any tension between Mark and Jonathan?' said Ren.

'My goodness, no,' said Erica. 'They're best friends.'

'Did you get the sense there is any work-related stress for Mark?' said Ren.

'He loves his job,' said Erica. 'He's been very busy. Maybe that was stressing him out. He was talking about taking early retirement next year, but he said that was so he could spend more time with me and the kids.'

'Was Jonathan or anyone in the company aware that he was planning to do that?' said Ren.

'No,' said Erica. 'I don't think so. He told me not to say anything to anyone.'

'Do you think work would have had a problem with it?' said Ren.

'No,' said Erica. 'Of course, it would create the problem of having to find his replacement, but they've always been supportive of Mark and any personal decisions he makes.'

'OK,' said Ren. 'Why don't we think about where Mark could have gone? Is there anywhere you can think of? Do you think he might drink again under this kind of pressure?'

'No,' said Erica. 'I really don't think he would.'

'Is he a spiritual man?' said Ren. 'Would he maybe look for a church, for example?'

'I didn't think of that,' said Erica. 'I don't know is the answer. He doesn't go to church, but he believes in something up there. He believes that something or someone is working for us all up there.' She paused. 'But he probably doesn't believe that any more.'

27

Erica's cell phone rang and she grabbed for it. 'Oh,' she said when she saw the name. 'It's not him.' She held the phone to her ear. 'Jonathan, hi,' said Erica. 'Really? OK. OK. Thanks for coming. I'm here, yes.' She held her hand over the phone. 'Ren – Jonathan is outside. Can he come through?'

'Yes,' said Ren. 'I can meet him in reception.'

'Thank you.'

Jonathan Meester was dressed in casual clothes, and even though they had tiny logos, Ren still recognized four different designer brands.

He held out his hand and shook hers. 'You must be Agent Bryce, thank you for this.'

Ren nodded.

'Erica called me earlier wondering if I had heard anything from Mark, and I told her, yes, we had spoken around one o'clock, but she said he'd gone missing not long after that.'

'Was there anything he said that caused you concern?' said Ren.

'I know that he was afraid that you were targeting him as a suspect—' said Jonathan.

'We weren't targeting him,' said Ren. 'We were simply trying to clear up the inconsistencies in his statements.'

Jonathan ran his hands through his hair. 'He was in a panic that you'd focus on him to the detriment of finding the real person – or people – responsible.'

Ren let this go. 'Were you aware of any changes in his behavior over the past few months?' said Ren.

'He was a little quiet,' said Jonathan. 'At one point I thought maybe it was some kind of mild depression, but then I just thought it was work. I've been there. We all put in a lot of hours.'

'And there's nothing else you can think of?' said Ren.

'No,' said Jonathan. 'Nothing.'

Ren nodded. 'I'll bring you through to Erica and Leo, and then we can all go back to the hotel.'

'And pray that Mark will be there,' said Jonathan.

It might just be too late for that.

Ren left the Whaleys' hotel room after midnight and went to The Firelight Inn. It was always especially quiet, even when it was full.

It's good to be as home as I can be.

She walked into the shared kitchen. 'Stop! Thief!' she said.

Paul Louderback stood up from the refrigerator. 'Foiled again,' he said.

'I know that there's nothing in that student/snowboarder refrigerator that could possibly belong to you,' said Ren.

'Force of habit.'

'It's one a.m. Do you know where your missing guilty-looking father is?' said Ren.

'Gone never to return,' said Paul, closing the refrigerator door.

'Swinging from a tree somewhere . . .' said Ren.

'What did he do?' said Paul. 'What did that man do?'

'Fooled everyone, by the looks of it,' said Ren. 'I've just come from their hotel. Grim.'

'Anything?' said Paul.

'No,' said Ren.

A text came in on Ren's phone. She glanced down. It was from Ben: I feel used. :-D

'Was that Gary?' said Paul.

'No,' said Ren.

Something hovered in the silence between them, an understanding – or a lack thereof.

And you've probably just gotten off the phone to your wife.

'Come into the living room,' said Paul.

'I think it may be time to admit defeat,' said Ren.

'Sleep?' said Paul. 'No.'

Ren smiled. 'I know. But I don't think I'm getting the same buzz off my sleep deprivation . . .'

'Well, I'm sure I won't be far behind you.'

The wrong image flashed into Ren's head.

A newspaper was open on the kitchen table. Ren twisted it toward her. 'Were you reading this?'

'Yes.'

Ren read out the headline, '"*Bad Shepard: The Fall of a Congressman*".' The article opened with '*Shepard Collier was not watching over his flock at night. Nor was he under a haystack fast asleep. Looks like he was wide awake – just not to the Big Bad Wolf that was about to come knocking at his door.*'

'I was surprised by him, to be honest,' said Paul. 'I see him about the place in D.C. Seems like one of the good guys. I wouldn't have put him in the fall-from-grace category. You struggle up the mountain, but the way back down is like an elevator with a slashed cable.'

'A hooker in a hotel room,' said Ren. 'Not the most original of bow-outs.'

'No,' said Paul.

Ren scanned through the article. There was a photo of Shep Collier at a charity auction with his wife. Beside it was a full-length photo of the underage hooker in question. The caption read: *'Tina Bowers in a photo taken outside her parents' home when the news broke of her relationship with Congressman Shep Collier'*.

'Ah, yes,' said Ren, 'the off-duty hooker/stripper/exotic dancer look: makeup free, dressed in track pants, a sweatshirt, a baseball cap and Uggs. Stylist's brief: vulnerable, girl-next-door.'

The second photo undid all the good work of the stylist: it was Tina Bowers' professional shot. The girl had worked hard with what God had given her: a light-handed measure of prettiness. Everything that drew the eye was fake: tits, lips, eyelashes, and nails.

You go, girl. Make things bigger and longer. That's your job.

'I've done with it,' said Paul. 'Take it.'

'No, I need sleep,' said Ren, still scanning the article.

'Go,' said Paul, folding up the newspaper and handing it to her. 'Sleep.'

'OK, goodnight,' said Ren.

They hugged.

That was too good. Run, run for the hills.

Ren sat on her bed and started to read the article. It seemed that Shep Collier's first brush with negative press was when he caused a racism scandal after being caught on video backstage at a fundraiser: his daughter had tried to hand him her adopted African-American son before he was to go on stage to have his photograph taken, and he had shaken his head and refused to take him.

Holy shit.

Yet, in a side bar to the article was the heading:

Constituent Breaks Silence on Collier Racism Claim

Ren skipped to the quote from a woman called Diana Moore. *'I am an African-American woman, representing one of the most under-privileged African-American communities in the state of Mississippi, and I am coming forward today because I believe in Congressman Shepard Collier. I should not be speaking up about this, because of a confidentiality agreement that has been in place for over thirty years. But that doesn't bother me. I want everyone to know that Congressman Collier funds the nursing home of which I am director, with proceeds from his own private business interests. His generosity has changed lives. I had a hard time believing that Congressman Collier would be involved in a scandal such as the one that has cost him his position. But what I can address are the rumors that he is a racist. They are false, and they are malicious. Congressman Collier has only ever been kind and generous to everyone in our community. And every member of his family is the same. I know for a fact that the reason he did not take his grandson in his arms at his fundraiser that time was that he was suffering from a virus. Unbeknownst to his family, he had been briefly hospitalized that morning. The fact that he never chose to dignify these rumors with a response goes to show what an honorable man Congressman Collier is.'*

Ren put the newspaper on the floor by the bed.

Wow. An anti-Obamacare Republican sponsoring a nursing home for underprivileged African-Americans? That would horrify a lot of his Conservative supporters more than him paying for a hooker.

*   *   *

Ren lit the small white candle by the bed and turned off the light. She sat down, then lay back, staring at the ceiling.

Shit. I've no clothes.

She sat up and turned on the bedside lamp. She opened her bag. There was clean underwear in the small zipped compartment.

Phew.

She picked up her phone and called Ben. 'Hello, I'm looking for a discarded, previously perfectly-happy-to-be-used sex addict . . .'

'Speaking.'

'Did I not even kiss you goodbye?' said Ren.

'No,' said Ben. 'It cheapened the whole thing.'

'Just when you thought it couldn't get any cheaper?'

'How are you doing out there?' said Ben.

'The father has disappeared,' said Ren.

'No way.'

'There was a way, apparently.'

'Shit. What does that mean?'

'It means I won't stay on for long, I've a lot to get through, including maybe even an hour of sleep. But I promise I'll think of you right beforehand.'

'Me too. Stay in touch.'

'I will.'

Ren grabbed her bag and took out the photo of Laurie Whaley sitting cross-legged on the center of the hotel bed, fresh from the shower. She was eleven, and she was smiling, and she was in pink pajamas, and she was missing.

She looked at the photo of Shelby Royce. She was in sweats, no makeup, her hair up in a high ponytail. The word *whore* flashed in her head, but she let it go. Ren laid the photos of the two girls on the nightstand and rested her head back on the pillow. That night, hundreds of people had gathered in town to light candles and pray for their safe return.

Night, night, girls. I will not rest. I will not rest.

And up Ren got, and downstairs to the living room she went.

At five a.m., Ren jerked awake on the sofa. She was lying down, tucked inside a red fleece blanket. The fire had died and her face was cold. Paul Louderback was asleep in the armchair beside her, his head slumped down on his chest. Their cell phones started to ring at the same time.

'You take yours, I'll go,' said Ren, grabbing her phone from the floor and running to take the call upstairs.

She got off the call and walked back down.

'Well . . .' said Paul.

'All will be revealed . . .' said Ren.

28

Ren was dressed in her new ski jacket: black, technologically advanced, biker style, $400. The model in the photo online had been wearing it on a shining white ski slope, under a brilliant blue sky, with a look that said *Add to Basket*. Its first outing for Ren was part of a very different picture, one that would sell nothing other than the message that life was cruel, and bleak, and without hope.

At Ren's feet lay the naked body of Shelby Royce. She was face up, covered in a light dusting of snow. Her limbs were splayed in a terrible way. Her right arm was bent at the elbow, the small hand almost closed, the fingertips bright with blue nail polish. The other arm was by her side, palm up. Her blonde hair was streaked across her face. Underneath the frosty strands, her eyes were open, their irises frozen and cloudy. A gaping hole had been blown through her torso, the burnt black edges dotted with tiny snowflakes.

Beside her, what looked like a black G-string was curled into a tiny ball, and beside that, a black ribbon lay twisted like a telephone cord.

Ren spoke to Paul Louderback, who was by her side; neither of them took their eyes off the body. 'You know, I wasn't much into dolls,' said Ren. 'But my friend had a Barbie doll, and every now and then we'd play with her. She was mainly naked, and we took her limbs and we stretched them into the most extreme poses we could, and it would be fun, and then we'd throw her away . . . until the next time.' She turned to Paul. 'It was ultimately joyless.'

Paul looked like he was in a trance. All he could do was shake his head.

Robbie Truax walked up with his camera. 'This is terrible.'

He moved solemnly around the scene, capturing every element with forensic detail, every photo a stone tablet for a future judge and jury. He always took extra photos – the stunning landscapes, the snow gathered on the fork of a branch.

There was a series of five framed photos on a wall in Robbie's living room. Not one of them gave any indication that the photographer was between one foot and five feet away from a dead body.

When he told Ren, she called him The Morbid Mormon.

But then he explained: for every one photo of the horror of death, he took one of the beauty of life, or art, or humanity: anything to restore the balance. Photos to make people think of life.

And that is the Robbie Truax I know and love.

Bob Gage came up beside Ren.

'The kids who found the body had been to the vigil,' he said. 'They say they were just going for a drive, got out to stretch their legs. Bullshit,' said Bob. 'None of them live out this direction. There are six vacation homes here, that's it. None of these kids' families own any of them . . .'

Ren looked around. They were impressive timber-frame

houses on half-acre lots, set back off the road, accessed by a curved driveway. The body was not outside any one house, but at the edge of a wooded area at the end of the street.

'Do you know any of the kids?' said Ren.

'A couple of the parents,' said Bob. 'I'll talk to them. We're trying to get a hold of the owners of the houses too. They're all out-of-towners.'

'Are there property management companies taking care of the places while they're gone?' said Ren.

'Mike's on it,' said Bob.

Summit County Coroner Denis Lasco made his heavy-footed way across the snow, puffed up by a giant orange parka that added more bulk to his bulk.

'Agent Bryce,' he said. He was heaving for breath.

'Hi Denis,' said Ren. 'Good to see you. If only we were meeting for another reason.'

'No-one meets me for another reason,' said Lasco.

'Aw that's not true,' said Ren.

'It's the way I like it,' said Lasco.

'That's not true either,' said Ren.

Lasco trudged a little closer to the body.

'Trust me it's a dead body,' said Bob Gage.

Lasco was known for his reluctance to commit to anything at a scene.

Bob kept talking. 'Female, sixteen years old, photo's been all over the newspapers recently, gunshot wound to the chest. Resulting in? The girl's dead.'

'I have yet to confirm her demise,' said Lasco.

'This is what you're dealing with,' said Bob to Ren.

'What we're dealing with is all of you dancing jigs on crime scenes,' said Lasco. 'Can we all please stand back? Right the way back. All of you.'

'Yeah, yeah, yeah,' said Bob. 'We've done this before.'

'With varying degrees of success,' said Lasco. 'And when I say success, I mean "effective evidence preservation on the part of the Sheriff's Office".'

Bob's eyes flashed. He didn't reply, but turned and retraced his steps to the trees. Ren did the same. Bob's cell phone rang.

'Let the shitstorm commence,' he said, as he hit Answer.

Ren noticed a green and navy parka lying against the tree trunk beside her.

'I've seen that before,' said Ren, turning to Bob reflexively.

Bob had walked away.

Ren heard Mike Delaney's voice behind her. 'Yes, you have,' he said. 'And the owner is in his shirt a hundred yards away, minus his face.'

29

Mark Whaley was slumped against a tree trunk, with most of his skull missing. The shotgun had fallen away from his body and lay half-covered in snow. His pale blue shirt was filthy and sweat-stained. His beige pants had turned a yellow-gray and were soiled. Like Shelby Royce, he was lightly dusted with snow.

'Please tell me Laurie Whaley isn't around here somewhere . . .' said Ren.

'Search and Rescue is on its way,' said Mike. 'We'll find her if she is.'

Bob came back to them. He stood over the body, shaking his head.

'Murder-suicide?' he said.

'Looks like it,' said Mike.

'These big business guys,' said Bob. 'They just can't help themselves. Whipping their dicks and their wallets out.'

'Power and money, power and money,' said Mike.

'Beautifully put, everyone,' said Ren.

It looks like Erica Whaley didn't know her husband. She didn't know him at all.

Denis Lasco appeared behind them.

Bob spoke loud: 'Male, forty-nine years old, name of Mark Whaley, photo's all over the newspapers. Gunshot wound to the head. Resulting in? The guy's dead. Very cold. Ice cold, brewed in the Rocky Mountains.'

'I will be ignoring you from now on,' said Lasco.

Gary came up beside Ren.

'I'm going to go with Detective Owens to notify the Royces. But I want you to go back there later today with Bob and go through Shelby Royce's room again. It's been searched, but it hasn't been searched by a female.'

There was no sexism. Sometimes it did make a difference.

Ren nodded. 'OK. Am I looking for anything in particular?'

'Every particular,' said Gary.

'At least you're taking care of the notification,' said Ren.

'I've built up a rapport with the Royces.'

Oh no. Please don't make me.

'You know what I'm going to ask you to do,' said Gary.

Ren and Bob arrived at the Whaleys' hotel room and knocked on the door. From inside, they could hear someone rush toward them. They glanced at each other. Erica Whaley unlocked the door and pulled it open. She crumpled to the floor in front of them before they had even spoken.

'What happened?' said Erica, already crying. 'What happened? What happened?'

Ren crouched down beside her, and laid her hand gently on Erica's arm. 'Let's take you inside, let's get you to the sofa.'

'Who is it?' said Erica as Ren helped her to her feet. She clung to her. 'Who is it? Who did you find? Is it Mark? Is it Laurie? Who is it?'

Ren's eyes started to well.

Shit. Shit. Shit.

Then the tears were gone.

'Let's get you sitting down, Mrs Whaley,' said Bob. 'Let me help you.'

When she was sitting down, Ren sat beside her. Erica gripped Ren's hands.

'We've found your husband,' said Ren. 'And I'm afraid the news is not good.'

Erica blinked several times. 'Is he . . . is he . . . are you saying he's . . . dead?'

'Yes,' said Ren. 'I'm afraid your husband is dead.'

'But . . . but . . . what happened?' said Erica.

'We can't say for definite until we get the coroner's report,' said Ren. 'But we suspect that your husband took his own life.'

'No,' said Erica. 'No, he would never do that. Mark would absolutely never do that. I know him. I know him.' She glanced to Bob, then back at Ren. 'Laurie! Where's Laurie? Did you find Laurie?'

'No, ma'am,' said Bob. 'But we have officers out there looking for her.'

'I love him so much,' said Erica. 'Oh my God, I love him so much.'

'I know you do,' said Ren. 'I know you do.' Ren looked at Bob over Erica's head.

Erica raised her head suddenly. 'Shelby Royce,' she said. 'Did you find Shelby Royce?'

Bob Gage stepped in and told her the worst news she was ever likely to hear. Ren watched as Erica retreated somewhere so far away from this new reality that it was shocking to watch.

'Jonathan!' Erica cried. 'Jonathan!'

Jonathan Meester rushed out from the bedroom. He ran to Erica. 'I'm sorry,' he said to Ren and Bob. 'I had to take a call. I . . . what's going on?'

Erica could barely speak, but managed to get out what happened.

'No,' said Jonathan. 'No. This has to be a mistake. This can't be . . . this is a mistake. Mark would never do this. He would never harm another living being. I've known him my whole life. He'd never do anything like this. And he'd never leave Erica and the kids. Never.'

Ren could hear Bob's cell phone ring. He picked up.

'What the—?' he said. Pause. 'Are you sure?'

He walked into the hallway. Ren followed.

'You better be one hundred percent—' Bob was saying.

Ren could hear a man raising his voice at the other end of the line: '*Jesus, Bob. Of course I am! For Christ's—*'

Bob was already hanging up. He turned to Ren. 'That was Mike. Gary's on his way for you. You're going to Denver Children's Hospital.'

'What's going on?' said Ren.

'It's Laurie Whaley. She's alive.'

'What?' said Ren. 'Denver? But . . . where did they find her?'

'Kennington Asylum.'

Oh, no. No. No. No.

159

30

Gary Dettling cut thirty minutes off the ninety-minute drive to Denver. He ran with Ren through the hospital doors. The doctor came to meet them.

'Wonderful news, isn't it?' she said. 'We checked Laurie over – she suffered quite a blow to the back of her head. We patched her up. She must have blacked out – she has no recollection of what happened.'

Shit.

'Were there any signs of a sexual assault?' said Gary.

'No,' said the doctor.

'How's her mental state?' said Gary.

'Well, she's suffered a trauma,' said the doctor. 'We ordered a psych consult, but . . . her mother is here, and she's reluctant to put her through anything more.'

There was a commotion by the hospital doors. Ren and Gary turned around. Reporters and camera crews, now familiar faces, struggled through with their equipment.

'I'll take care of it,' said Gary.

'I'm outta here,' said Ren.

Ren turned to the doctor. 'Thank you, doctor. Where's the family now?'

She directed Ren down the hallway to a private room. Ren knocked on the door. 'Mrs Merritt? It's Agent Bryce.'

'Come in,' said Cathy. She was sitting on the bed with her arm around Laurie, who was buried under the covers. Cathy looked up at Ren with a look of relief, and fear, sadness and happiness.

'Thank you, Agent Bryce. Thank God.'

Ren smiled. 'I'm so happy you have your daughter back.'

'Laurie, sweetheart,' said Cathy, 'this is Agent Bryce, one of the people who was trying to find you. She's with the FBI.'

'Hey there, Laurie.' Ren walked a little closer to the bed. 'I'm Ren. It's so good to meet you.'

Laurie said nothing. Her stare was desolate, two huge eyes in a face too young to be so lost.

'You are a very brave young lady,' said Ren.

Laurie managed a smile. 'Thank you.'

Cathy locked eyes with Ren over Laurie's head. There was a strange hysteria in them, as if Cathy wanted Ren to tell her that this haunting image of her eleven-year-old daughter was all in her mind, that this clearly terrified, bereft little girl, was going to be fine.

If I could wave a magic wand . . .

'I won't stay long,' said Ren. 'I'll leave you guys to it. I just wanted to check in . . .' She paused. 'Laurie, do you mind if I talk to your mom for two minutes? We'll be right outside.'

Laurie nodded.

Ren waited in the hallway.

'Has Laurie said anything to you?' said Ren when Cathy came out.

'Nothing,' said Cathy. 'I'm trying to stay calm here, but . . .

I'm . . . what happened to her? She's like a zombie. I . . . what am I supposed to do? I have no idea what . . . Am I supposed to allow a psychiatrist to talk to her? I don't want to do that. Is that the right decision, though? I mean . . .'

'She hasn't told you what happened that night, or where she's been or . . .'

'No,' said Cathy. 'Nothing. I'm just so glad to have her back, I . . . I . . . don't want to push her.'

'That's understandable,' said Ren. *Here goes.* 'Cathy, I'd like you to sit down. There's something I need to tell you.'

'No, no, I don't need to sit,' said Cathy. 'Just tell me.'

Cathy Merritt stood, motionless, as Ren told her that around the same time Denver PD found her daughter alive, someone else was finding her ex-husband dead.

Cathy started shaking violently. She ran for the nearest garbage can, but she didn't make it, and she threw up all over the floor.

Laurie had come to the doorway. She started to cry.

'Go back in the room, Laurie,' said Cathy. 'Go back in the room.'

'What's wrong, mommy?' said Laurie. 'What's wrong?'

'Nothing, sweetheart, go back in the room. I'll be with you in a little while. Mommy's not feeling well . . .'

'Why don't we sit down,' said Ren. 'There's a seat right here.'

A nurse came into the hallway. Cathy was sobbing, apologizing to her for the mess she had made. The nurse was reassuring her that it happens all the time, she had nothing to worry about.

If only she did have nothing to worry about.

Cathy went to the ladies room. Ren waited for her outside, but could hear the most terrible, wracking sobs, then the faucet running.

Cathy emerged moments later, as if all the emotion she

had toward her dead ex-husband had been laid to rest in the previous five minutes.

'What the hell has he done?' she said to Ren. 'What the hell will this do to our daughter? Is this what he wanted all along? Was this the overnight visit he wanted all along? Was this why?'

Ren arrived back in Breckenridge and talked through the grim hospital encounter with Bob on the drive to Blue River. They pulled up outside Cal and Connie Royce's pristine little ranch house.

'If it's any consolation,' said Bob, 'apparently young Owens had a very good cry along with them.'

'Gary fed him to the lions,' said Ren. 'Was this his first notification? Telling the parents of a missing sixteen-year-old that their only daughter was found naked and shot?'

'Toughen him up,' said Bob. 'In fact, no it wasn't his first. I think he told a little old lady that her cat had made it down out of a tree in the worst way possible.'

'Sniper?'

Bob laughed.

'I guess there had to be some tempering,' said Ren. 'Gary slash Owens.'

They got out of the car.

Cal Royce stood up from shoveling snow.

'You've got to keep going . . .' he said as they walked toward him.

'You sure do,' said Bob. He shook Cal's hand. 'How are you holding up?'

'Not good,' said Cal. 'Not good at all. Not even as well as can be expected.'

'It's a very tough time,' said Bob. 'You remember Agent Bryce.' He turned to Ren.

'I do,' said Cal, shaking her hand.

'I am so sorry for your loss,' said Ren.

'Thank you,' he said. 'Thank you for everything you did. Is there something in particular I can help you with?'

'We'd like to take a look around the house, and at Shelby's room if that's OK,' said Ren. 'We'd like to piece together a few things.'

'Go ahead,' said Cal, 'you can do whatever you like, anything that helps.' He walked up the path, and let them into the house.

'I'm right out here, if you need me,' he said. 'Connie's inside, she's just laying on the sofa, won't talk to no-one, won't accept visitors. You can go up ahead.'

An hour into the search, Ren found an oversized bag stuffed into a laundry bag and wedged in the bottom of another laundry bag that was filled with Cal Royce's dirty clothes. Ren took it out, and laid it on the bed. She unzipped it. A red-and-white cheerleading uniform was folded neatly on top. She pulled it out. It wasn't a regular cheerleader uniform: the top was a tiny racer-back bra-top, the skirt was extra short, and the matching panties were not quite complete. Ren laid them out on the bed. She pulled out the next outfit. It was a tiny sailor suit, with cutaways at the sides, and other places, places that meant that neither of these costumes were for a regular costume party.

Ren looked into the bag to see the rest. It was filled with lingerie: red, black, stockings, suspenders, lace, satin, rubber.

Sixteen years old . . .

31

Ren called Bob in to the bedroom. 'How did nobody find this?' said Ren. 'It was tucked away like Russian dolls in the laundry room. Size 2, so they're not Connie's. They've got to be Shelby's. And, unless Shelby was planning on getting arrested for indecent exposure, these little numbers were for private viewing only. And there are more.'

As she opened the bag wider, a sweet smell wafted out. She stared into the bag. 'You know something,' she said, 'I stumbled on a TV show for teens recently – regular day-time scheduling, and the nanny in it caught the fifteen-year-old daughter watching porn, because the guy she liked had a previous girlfriend who was "really experienced" and she didn't want to let him down when they had sex for the first time. So . . . yup, things are different these days. But . . . this . . . this is like a stripper's bag.'

'Surely, our pretty little cheerleader wasn't a stripper . . .' said Bob.

'I hope not,' said Ren. 'Bob – maybe it's just us. I mean, is this just a teenage girl's bag for a night at her boyfriend's house? I know I always hid my . . . things . . . from my mother when I was younger.'

Bob raised an eyebrow.

'Not *these* kind of things,' said Ren. 'When I say things, I mean any underwear that was not white and one hundred percent cotton.'

Bob smiled.

'One of the Royces obviously found this bag,' said Ren. 'And I'm guessing it was Connie.'

'We need to go talk to her,' said Bob. 'Do you think Shelby ever even brought this bag out of the house?'

'It's a very cool bag,' said Ren. 'I wouldn't just use this as storage if I were her.'

Ren turned the bag sideways. 'I didn't see this bit,' she said. She unzipped a section at the bottom of the bag that was meant for laundry. She reached in and pulled out the contents. Bob looked down, then they both locked eyes.

Children's picture books. The dual roles of Shelby Royce.

'There's our answer,' said Bob.

'In this kind of bag,' said Ren, 'well that's just a whole pile of wrong.'

Connie Royce sat on the edge of the sofa, shattered, not looking at the bag beside her.

'I found it at the back of her wardrobe on Saturday night,' she said. 'I was going to ask her about it when she got back, but . . .' Tears welled in her eyes. 'And after everything that happened, I just . . . they were very private things, I didn't want you to think badly of her. She's a good girl. I didn't want to think that her underwear . . . or whatever you would call these . . . was relevant.'

Ren laid a hand on Connie's arm. 'I understand why you kept this from us,' said Ren. 'But you really need to be honest. You need to tell us everything – no matter how bad it might sound to you. Nobody here is going to think ill of Shelby. We don't judge anyone, we couldn't do our jobs if we were in the business of judging people. Everyone we've spoken to says such lovely things about Shelby, she seems to have been a very special young lady. That's all that matters.'

'Thank you,' said Connie. She held a tissue up to her nose. 'Thank you. I . . . I was Shelby's age when I met Cal . . . I was young. But we fell in love. That man out there is the love of my life. I've had a wonderful life, I don't regret a thing . . . I didn't regret a thing. But I still wanted Shelby to do more, to go out and see the world . . .'

'Can I ask, did you have a reason for looking in Shelby's wardrobe on Saturday night?' said Ren.

'For cigarettes,' said Connie. 'I know she smokes. Cal was at work, and I wanted to sneak a cigarette. I haven't smoked in years . . .'

'Was there anything else going on with Shelby that you can think of?' said Ren.

'No,' said Connie.

'You said in your interview that Shelby didn't have a boyfriend,' Ren said. 'Are you sure about that?'

'As sure as any mother can be with a girl that age,' said Connie.

'Did you have any suspicions that she might?' said Ren.

'No,' said Connie.

'What did you think when you saw the bag?' said Ren.

'I thought, well, me and Shelby are going to have to sit down and have a talk.'

'OK, we're going to take this bag away for now,' said Ren. 'We'll return it when we're done.'

'Saturday night,' said Connie, 'I was looking at my

daughter, thinking how cute she is, with the ponytail elastic thing wrapped around her wrist, and I knew she's going to twist her hair into a high knot later, and wrap it in that thing, and there'll be little wispy bits spiking out the top, and she'll be reading stories to whoever's kids she's looking after. And a couple of hours later, I find this bag. I'm just . . . so confused. And then she's gone. She's gone. And here I am with a bag of . . . this. And she's gone.'

'These are just clothes,' said Ren. 'Remember that. They don't change a thing about your relationship with Shelby.'

'Secrets change relationships,' said Connie. 'Secrets do.'

Bob and Ren walked into the command center and laid Shelby Royce's bag on the table at the top of the room.

'This is Shelby Royce's,' said Ren.

Everyone went over to it.

'Yikes,' said Cliff.

'Gloves please, people,' said Bob, eyeing his men.

'There are kids' picture books in the compartment underneath it,' said Ren.

'What was going on with her?' said Gary.

'We don't know,' said Ren. 'Her mom had found it in the back of Shelby's wardrobe on Saturday night and hid it in a bag in a laundry bag in a laundry bag. She didn't want us to be affected by it, to think badly of Shelby, which is understandable. I wish I wasn't thinking about the "whore" poster right now.'

'We all are,' said Gary.

'But what was she doing with all this?' said Robbie.

'Thanks for directing that my way,' said Ren.

Robbie blushed. 'Sorry . . . I . . . just . . .'

'I'm kidding,' said Ren. 'She could have been wearing it for someone in particular, she could have been photographing herself, videoing herself, doing stuff on line, or . . . selling herself . . .'

'A lot of visitors come to Breck,' said Gary. 'If she had links in a hotel . . . she could make herself available.'

'That creepy Labati kid could be lining men up for her,' said Ren. 'When he's not too busy trying to line himself up for her.'

'She didn't have the bag with her on Saturday night,' said Robbie. 'Does that mean she had no plans in that sense? Could Mark Whaley have expected she would, and got mad at that? Maybe he had been here before and we just didn't know.'

'We have to get these high school kids to talk,' said Gary. 'I think I'll go with an unorthodox maneuver . . .'

Gary and unorthodox?

'Mark Whaley raped her, or she was a ho and seduced him, he shot her, killed himself, Laurie Whaley's been returned safe,' said Colin. 'The end.'

Gary stared at him. 'Colin, I'd like you to go to the autopsies with Ren, Robbie and Bob.'

'But—' said Colin.

'It matters what happened in that room,' said Gary.

Colin's jaw twitched.

You can't hide behind your computer screen now, you dickhead.

32

Taber Grace still had the client file. It was fatter than it used to be. For days it had been like a lump lodged in his throat. Now it was sitting on top of his shredder, where he stockpiled papers until he could bear the sound of the motor grinding through secrets. Or when he needed a little more time to think about whether he really wanted to make something disappear.

He checked his phone. There were seven missed calls from Melissa. And five messages.

'It's me. We need to talk.'

'Tabe, where are you?'

'Taber, wherever you are, please call.'

'Call me, please. I'm starting to get worried.'

'Taber, it's Melissa again, I don't care if you can't talk right now, but just let me know you're OK. Just send me a text . . .'

He called her. 'Hey,' he said. 'It's me.'

'Thank God,' said Melissa. 'I was worried. So was TJ.'

'I texted TJ. He's fine.'

'Well, TJ and I haven't exactly been on speaking terms . . .'

'I'm sorry to hear that, Missy. He'll come around.'

'I just wanted to know that you're alive. You've kinda disappeared since . . . everything. I was afraid you'd never want to talk to me again.'

'No,' said Taber. 'No.'

'I was worried about you.'

'There's no need, but thanks for your concern.'

'OK . . . thanks for letting me know,' said Melissa. 'Thanks for calling.'

'Take care.'

'You too.'

Taber Grace closed his eyes and the scene in the kitchen kicked off again, like a movie, the images even tinted and sharpened, the voices like surround-sound.

Taber Grace had locked himself away since he walked out on Melissa and TJ that morning, sitting at his laptop, reading about what Cerxus had done to the children it had been prescribed to: some had attempted suicide, others had violent outbursts, some had complete personality changes. Melissa was right – Cerxus was still on sale. The makers, Lang Pharmaceuticals, had just put a black-box warning on the insert saying that it could cause suicidal thoughts and psychotic episodes in children.

Taber Grace didn't stop with Cerxus – he was sucked into one article after another about drugs that had been rushed to market, marketed illegally, over-prescribed, reacted badly with other medications, increased the risk of strokes or heart attacks, caused fatalities. Every pharmaceutical company he had ever heard of had been sued because of one drug or another, and between them they had paid out billions of dollars to settle claims. And he knew a settled claim meant sealed documents that the public was unlikely to see.

Taber Grace got up from his desk, his head filled with images of TJ's terrified nine-year-old face, and Melissa bleeding and clutching him, and telling him what to do, and how to lie.

Replace the sound, replace the images.

He walked into his bare living room. He sat on the sofa, and turned on the television. He watched microphones being pushed into the face of a man called Bob Gage, Summit County Sheriff. Behind Sheriff Gage and back a little, was definitely an FBI Agent. A BuBabe. A Bureau Babe. He knew that case agents weren't authorized to speak to the press, but she would have been a better face for the camera.

The sheriff was speaking: *'At four a.m. on the morning of Tuesday, November 17, the bodies of Mark Whaley, 49, and Shelby Royce, 16, were found on Wildcard Drive here in Breckenridge. Following yesterday's autopsy results, we can confirm that Shelby Royce died of a gunshot wound to the chest. Mark Whaley died from a gunshot wound to the head which evidence confirms was self-inflicted. At nine a.m. on the morning of November 17, Mark Whaley's daughter, Laurie Whaley, was reunited with her family and is recovering at a private location.'*

A reporter asked: *'Sheriff Gage, can you tell us the extent of her injuries?'*

'Laurie Whaley is recovering well. That is the last comment I will make on her condition.'

'Sheriff, is it true that Shelby Royce was sexually assaulted before her death?'

'Our investigation is ongoing.'

'Was this a murder-suicide?'

'All evidence points to a murder-suicide. Thank you for your time.'

'Sheriff Gage—'
'Sheriff Gage—'
'I have no further comment at this time.'

Taber Grace stood up from the sofa.

'Hate to break it to you, people – that was no murder-suicide.'

He hit the red button and the screen went black.

'But you're going to have a hell of a time proving otherwise.'

He walked over to the shredder, took the file from on top of it, and laid it on his desk.

33

Ren Bryce sat at her desk with her handbag open, throwing in everything she could see that belonged to her.

Gary called her over to his desk. She leaned over the partition, then quickly checked her shirt.

'I cleaned it,' said Gary.

'Good for you, not suffering in silence.'

He smiled. 'I wanted to ask – how was your appointment with Dr Lone?'

'Did you know that his sessions are all an hour long?' said Ren. 'Not fifteen minutes, not even half an hour. How does that work? Financially? And missing-work-wise?' *And boredom-threshold-wise.*

'You just concentrate on making the most of that hour,' said Gary.

'But—'

'If it makes you feel better,' said Gary, 'he only charges a fifteen-minute fee for a one-hour session.'

'What?' said Ren. 'Who does that?'

'People who like to help people, I guess.'

'No wonder he can't afford full shoes . . .'

'What are you talking about?' said Gary.

'Just . . . he wears sandals,' said Ren.

'Jesus, Ren. Maybe if your approach was not to stare at the floor, you wouldn't notice his footwear.'

Helen Wheeler had beautiful shoes.

Gary looked up. 'Are you OK?' he said. 'Did I say something?'

'No,' said Ren. 'I'm fine.'

But Helen had beautiful shoes.

Paul Louderback stuck his head in the door.

'Ren, could I have a word, please?' he said. 'If you don't mind, Gary. I just have to clear something up.'

'Sure, go ahead,' said Gary. 'We're done here.'

'Hey,' said Paul, when she walked out, 'as we will shortly be parting company, would you like to go for dinner tonight?'

'Ooh,' said Ren. 'I would. Here? Would that be wise?'

'Wise now that I know your boss is traveling to Denver tonight.'

Ren smiled. 'Dinner it is, then.'

Her cell phone rang on her desk.

'I'll leave you to it,' said Paul.

Ren ran over and grabbed it.

'Agent Bryce, it's Kevin Crowley from The Lowry Hotel in Boston – I just sent you an email – the details you wanted, if you'd like to take a look at it.'

'Thank you,' said Ren. She hung up, and opened the email and clicked on the attached files. There was one PDF, and six JPEGS. She started with the PDF. It was Mark Whaley's bill from his stay.

For three nights. Even though his last meeting was on Friday, he stayed on in Boston Saturday night.

She looked at the photos. In the first, a short, smiling blonde was leaning over The Lowry's reception desk.

Ren clicked on the next photo. It was the lobby bar on the same night. A man was sitting on a sofa in the corner with the same smiling blonde. Her coat was off, and she was dressed in a short, dark-colored, low-cut dress.

'Gary,' said Ren. 'You need to see these.'

Gary came over to her desk.

'It's Mark Whaley,' said Ren, pointing. 'In The Lowry Hotel in Boston.'

Gary leaned in closer to the screen.

'So there is a hotel-room precedent with Mark Whaley,' said Gary. 'Underage blondes.'

Nail. Coffin.

Paul Louderback was waiting for Ren at a table upstairs in the furthest corner of Modis on Main Street. He stood up as soon as she walked in. He kissed her on both cheeks, and pulled out her chair for her.

Manners. I love it. 'Thank you,' said Ren.

'I've taken the liberty of ordering a bottle of Bordeaux,' said Paul.

Ren raised her glass. 'Here's to the first time I've ever heard that sentence anywhere other than in a British mini-series.'

Paul made a sad face.

She smiled. 'Aw, your crest has fallen.'

'I didn't want to sound lame *right* away,' said Paul. 'I was aiming for somewhere in the middle of dinner.'

'Don't worry,' said Ren, 'feel free to take wine-related liberties at all times and go on to tell me about them in quaint ways.'

He relaxed back into his chair. 'So . . .' he said.

'Mark Whaley . . . can you believe it?'

'I can,' said Paul. 'Especially after those Lowry photos.'

And they were off, talking about work, and movies, and books, and music, and shoes.

Eventually, after a lull, Ren looked across the table at Paul.

'So,' said Ren. *The question I hate asking, but feel bound to.* 'How's Marianne?'

Your wife of twenty-four years, the mother of your two daughters.

Paul drained his glass.

'Oh, some comedy glass-draining,' said Ren.

'She left me,' said Paul at the same time.

Ren waited for him to smile or laugh or say, 'just kidding' – anything that would stop him from sensing the visceral reaction that had just rocked through her. 'Oh my God,' she managed.

'She walked out, and took the girls with her,' said Paul.

'When?' said Ren.

'Three months ago,' said Paul.

'Why didn't you say?' said Ren.

'Because I wanted to hear you talk about shoes.'

'I'm . . . mortified.'

'Don't be ridiculous, I've had the most fun I've had in . . . I can't tell you when.'

'But you should have told me at the time,' said Ren. 'I would have—'

'Confused me,' said Paul.

Uh-oh.

34

Ren's heart was pounding.

I could do without the complication.

'But . . . why did she leave?' said Ren. 'What did she say? Do you mind if I ask?'

'Are you surprised that she left?' said Paul. 'Really?'

Yes. Kind of. No. 'Yes,' said Ren.

Paul laughed.

'I can't believe you laughed at that,' said Ren. 'I *am* surprised. But . . . I suppose . . . maybe . . . I will now stop speaking.'

'Don't worry,' said Paul. 'I'm not in total denial. I know the kind of husband I was. I love Marianne because she is the mother of my children. I don't know in the end if I loved her as, you know, my lover. And . . . well, I guess she found someone who did.'

No-one should use the word lover. 'Oh . . .' said Ren.

'Yes,' said Paul. 'She met a man who is my polar opposite. Hurtfully so, if I'm honest.'

'I'm curious as to what you consider your polar opposite,' said Ren.

'Someone attentive,' said Paul. 'Someone relaxed, fun, loving, optimistic.'

'There's a barman in Gaffney's who calls that kind of talk "hindshite",' said Ren. 'Hindshite: looking back on things and distorting them, seeing everything in a negative way. I understand how everything looks like crap right now, because you're going through something terrible. But there is no way Marianne got married and had two beautiful daughters with a man she thought was inattentive, uptight, or boring.'

Paul shrugged.

'I don't buy that,' said Ren. 'If this new man's all that—'

'He is,' said Paul. 'I swear to God. I have no problem with the guy. Can you believe that?'

'He had an affair with your wife,' said Ren.

'Nope, that's the kind of stand-up guy he is,' said Paul. 'He fell in love with my wife. And respected her too much to destroy her marriage, and our girls' lives, and all the rest of it. So he walked away. He told her if she ever changed her mind, she knew where to find him. This was two years ago. He waited for her all that time.'

'Wow,' said Ren.

'And Lord knows, she tried to make it work with us,' said Paul. 'I can see that now . . .'

'Do you think she still wants to make it work?' said Ren.

Silence. 'I don't know,' he said, eventually.

'Hmm,' said Ren. 'Maybe leaving you was a cry for help. Terrible expression, but you get the idea.'

'I'm in no position to help anyone,' said Paul.

'Are they living together?' said Ren.

'No.'

'Has he met the girls?' said Ren.

'No. She's not ready for that.'

179

'Well, that could be a good sign,' said Ren. 'I'm so sorry to hear all this. None of it sounds easy. How are you feeling?'

'I don't think I want her to keep trying . . .' said Paul. 'I think . . . I think it's been over a long time.'

Ren poured more wine. 'I'll be the wine guy,' she said.

'Stick to what you know best,' said Paul.

Ren laughed.

'You are a master side-stepper . . .' said Paul.

'What am I side-stepping?' said Ren. *Apart from the I-don't-think-I-want-her-to-keep-trying-so-I'm-finally-available thing that we both know I'm side-stepping.*

'Not a thing,' said Paul.

Good.

Paul smiled. 'Remember that night at the sexual assault convention . . .'

'OK, if anyone overheard just that part of the conversation . . .'

Paul laughed, then stopped. 'I don't know what's happened to me,' he said. 'It's like my own laughter is an alien sound.'

'Your laughter *is* an alien sound,' said Ren.

'Why didn't you reply to my emails after the last time in Breck?' said Paul. He had locked eyes with her.

Please refrain from staring at the animals. 'I . . . I don't know,' said Ren. 'I've . . . been busy.'

Paul nodded. 'So I believe, you cartel queen.'

'Domenica Val Pando was the cartel queen, I was just the—'

'Agent of her downfall.'

'I like it,' said Ren.

He glanced at the second bottle of wine Ren had ordered. 'I suspect you'll be the agent of *my* downfall too.'

*　　*　　*

At one a.m., Paul Louderback and Ren Bryce stood in the small foyer of the restaurant, sandwiched between two glass doors, looking out at the snow. He helped her into her coat. She buttoned the huge collar under her chin.

'Look,' said Ren, pressing a finger against the glass door. 'Here's our cab.'

She turned around to him. 'Thank you so much for dinner.'

'Thank *you*,' said Paul. He kissed her cheek. They hugged.

Ren went to pull away, but Paul's hand was still pressed against her lower back. She leaned away from him, and looked up.

'It was just what I needed,' said Paul.

Stop looking into my eyes. 'Sure,' said Ren. 'My invaluable insight into relationships.'

'You're not as bad as you think,' said Paul. 'Although, you were wrong about one thing.'

'Highly unlikely,' said Ren. 'What?'

'Well . . . not everything looks crap right now.'

No. No. No. In a strange cross-purposes move, he released his hold, and started kissing her. It was the most extraordinarily intimate kiss Ren had ever experienced. She could not have pulled away quick enough. She reached behind her for the door, and staggered back against it.

'OK,' she said. 'Let's go. Thanks.'

'Sure,' said Paul. He held the door open for her. She banged her elbow off of it on the way out.

Ren slumped into the back of the cab. Paul sat in front with the driver.

I'll laugh or joke with yo' man, but I don't want him. He's all yours. I think I make that clear. I've never taken anyone's man. She let out a breath.

Her cell phone vibrated. Two messages.

The first was from Paul: R u OK?

She looked up. He was smiling at her in the rear-view mirror.

The second was from Ben: R u alive?

No/Barely.

She sent Yes to Paul. And nothing to Ben.

Shit. Shit. Shit.

And then she texted Paul Louderback one more time.

Paul Louderback sat on the edge of his bed. Ren stood in front of him.

'Take off your clothes,' he said. A slow, polite, Southern command.

Ren started with her black top, pulling it slowly over her head.

'I was watching that pink strap all through dinner,' he said.

And I was watching you watching it. 'Really?' said Ren.

'Keep going,' said Paul. His voice was firm.

Ren turned her back to him, and pulled the zip of her tight black skirt down, so he could see the cutaway of her pink low-ride lace shorts with the keyhole and the satin ribbon trim. She moved her hips twice until the skirt fell to the floor. She stepped out of it, and turned to face him.

'Keep the shoes on,' he said.

When Ren was naked, but for black patent high heels, Paul stood up in front of her, and started to pull off his tie.

Ren smiled. 'Imagine if I said to you "keep the shoes on".'

Paul laughed. 'I've thought about this moment for a very long time, Ren. There's pretty much nothing you could say that could possibly ruin it.'

Not even *'what the fuck am I doing here?'* or *'I have to go'* or *'this will destroy our friendship'*, or *'I hate plaid boxers'*?

Paul held his hands against Ren's lower back, moved them lower, and pulled her gently toward him. He kissed her again, like before, but more.

Ren kissed him back.

I am going nowhere.

She kissed him harder.

I need to follow through.

35

Ren sat in her Jeep outside the Sheriff's Office. A giant coffee was steaming up the windows. She held her cell phone pressed to her ear.

'I swear to God, Janine, my fingerprints on the door of that restaurant must have looked like a horror movie poster,' said Ren. 'Someone clawing out of something for their dear life.'

'What is wrong with you?' said Janine.

'I have no idea,' said Ren. 'I feel like I'm a fourteen-year-old girl, and Taylor Lautner has just shown up at my door, saying "Hey! Here I am! I'm free."'

'But you've been crazy about this guy for years,' said Janine. 'He's available. What's the problem?'

'Or did I just *think* I was crazy about him?' said Ren. 'Because I couldn't have him – he was a safe person to love.'

'Unlike all those unsafe people . . .'

'Yeah, but love really is shit,' said Ren. 'You've got to admit. So, someone who wasn't going to love me back . . . that was quite appealing.'

'That's the spirit,' said Janine.

'It is, though. I'm sick of it.'

'Dare I ask – what about Ben?' said Janine.

'I love Ben!' said Ren. 'They're both so different . . .'

'And . . .' said Janine.

'There's a lot to be said for an untroubled man.'

'That would be Ben,' said Janine.

'Yes – Ben just fails to see a problem with anything. You could tell him your deepest darkest fear, and he would listen, say sweet things, but not psychoanalyze you, like an older man would. It's very refreshing.'

'OK,' said Janine. 'My opinion? Don't kid yourself on the following: psychoanalyzing is not a younger man/older man thing. It's on a man-by-man basis. And Ben is not *that* young. I think that because he looks so young—'

'He does,' said Ren. 'Sometimes I feel like those high-school teachers who get arrested for sleeping with their students . . .'

Janine laughed. 'As I was saying, you associate him with youth, light-heartedness, and a time when you didn't have a worry in the world. That really appeals to you. You see him as someone who has not really been damaged by the world like you have. Which is a really attractive trait in anyone. Paul Louderback, however, is a grown-up. Which scares the crap out of you. You run from the grown-ups. You run from the ones who try to get inside your head. And—' said Janine, Ren could see her raising her finger, 'don't say it. Don't. Do not make some joke about Ben only wanting to get inside your pants—'

Ren paused. 'I can hear you rolling your eyes.'

'Must get eyeballs tightened in socket,' said Janine. 'Ren, let's try this – who do you want to be with – Ben or Paul?'

'Baul.'

'OK, let's try maturity first,' said Janine. 'Then, answer the question: old, married dude. Or young, hot dude.'

'Paul's hot too. And he's not . . . really . . . married.'

'OK,' said Janine, 'old, hot, not-really-married dude. Young, hot, single dude. You're the only one who can make that decision.'

'Sentence least likely to inspire . . .' said Ren.

'That's your problem,' said Janine.

'That and your unhelpfulness,' said Ren.

'Neither is your answer, then. You want to be with neither man.'

'Because *that's* an option,' said Ren.

'It is an option,' said Janine.

'I don't like people who suggest being alone as an option.'

'And therein lies the problem,' said Janine.

'Leave me alone,' said Ren.

'That's a start.'

Janine had kindly not asked what happened after the horror-movie scene in the restaurant foyer.

God bless you, Janine, for not making me have to say I'm a whore out loud. For not having to say I've been up all night again. And for not knowing I'm bipolar, so I don't have to deal with another concerned tone.

Ren walked into the Sheriff's Office reception area. Gary Dettling was standing by the front desk. When he turned toward her, she could see, behind him, the familiar figure of Ben Rader.

Oh. Dear. God.

Stop appearing from behind my boss.

'Hello,' said Ren.

'Ren, you remember Ben Rader,' said Gary.

In all kinds of ways. 'Yes, nice to see you again.' *Your timing will keep me in guilt-ridden thoughts for months.*

'Hi, Ren,' said Ben. Then his big smile.

Mental picture: double-date: me, Ben, Gary and his wife. And Jesus Christ.

'I thought you'd gone back to Denver, Gary,' said Ren.

'Change of plan,' said Gary. 'Shelby Royce's funeral was yesterday – it's still going to be quite raw for the kids. They'll be out tonight – it's Saturday night – partying, drinking . . .'

'And I'll swoop in and prey on their vulnerability,' said Ben.

'Sounds like a plan,' said Ren. *Gary's unorthodox plan. There's a reason he shouldn't do unorthodox.*

She couldn't take her eyes off Ben, standing there with his black hair gelled messy, his flawless skin, his hands in the pockets of his jeans.

Effortlessly cool. Even for an eighteen-year-old . . .

'But, hey,' said Ren, 'what if no-one invites you to party?'

Ben gave her a big smile. 'I'm sure someone will . . .'

You bet your cute ass.

'OK,' said Gary. 'Come in to the office, Ben, take a look at whatever you need.'

Ben raised his eyebrow at Ren. 'Sure,' he said.

They went in to the office, and Gary started to talk Ben through the case.

Ren watched Ben nodding intently. She realized he almost pouted when he was concentrating. And still managed to look good.

Stop risking eye contact with me.

She glanced around the room.

Everyone knows I am sleeping with Ben Rader. Everyone.

36

Ren grabbed a coffee and pulled out a magazine she had stolen from reception. It was promoting Summit County, and each town had its own section. It was made up mostly of advertorials, with columns or pages of relevant ads beside them. She saw one ad for The Merlin, then a general article for luxury holiday home lets, and beside that an ad for a company called York Property Management. One of the employees was a fit-looking cheery man with a strong, chiseled face, who by virtue of his age, and unusual surname, appeared to have spawned a most unlikely child.

'Bob,' said Ren. 'Could I pick your tiny mind?'

Bob came over. 'Sure. Go ahead.'

'I was flicking through these ads masquerading as a magazine, and came across a gentleman by the name of Gabriel Labati.' She pointed to the picture. 'Is the ungainly Jared Labati the offspring of this rugged specimen?'

'Yes, he is,' said Bob.

'So, Gabriel Labati works for York Property Management. Do they manage any of the homes on Wildcard Drive?'

'Yes. I got Mike's report here. Two.'

'Has anyone taken a look around them?' said Ren. 'We still don't know where the girls were kept.'

'Mike and a few of the other detectives had a look around the outside and there were no signs of a break-in anywhere,' said Bob. 'We don't have probable cause to go inside. The owners won't give us permission because they're deferring to York and obviously York is maintaining that no-one could have gotten into the houses because they had the keys, and they're such an outstanding management company that there was no way anyone could have gotten their hands on them.'

'OK,' said Ren. 'Do you know is York where Jared Labati did the work experience Tom Olson mentioned?'

'I presume so,' said Bob. 'Gabriel Labati only has one job.'

'So Jared would have had access to keys for a lot of houses . . .'

'What are you saying?' said Bob.

'Just that sometimes people have things that we don't expect them to have.'

'Deep,' said Bob. He glanced down at her mug. 'You need to slow down on the coffee, missy.'

Ren grabbed the empty mug and stood up. 'Coffee anyone?'

Bob shook his head. 'You'll have a stroke.'

'I'll have a coffee, thanks,' said Cliff.

'Yeah, me too,' said Colin.

No thanks.

Ben shouted yes from Gary's desk at the back of the room. Gary had left him with a stack of statements and was walking toward the door.

Ren stood up.

Whoa. I do not feel right.

She took a few more steps.

Whoa. Something is . . . I'm going to . . .

She reached out for the desk.

My head. I need to . . . zzzzzzzzzzzz . . .

Ren slumped to the floor, landing hard on her side, striking her head off the ground.

'Jesus Christ,' said Bob. He bent down beside her and rolled her onto her back. He started to loosen her shirt collar. Gary rushed over and knelt at Ren's feet, lifting them onto his lap. 'Cliff, grab me a cushion or something to prop her feet up.'

'Do you think maybe her belt is too tight?' said Bob.

They stared at each other.

Ren's eyes opened. *What the . . .?* She struggled to get up.

'Jesus Christ, Ren,' said Bob. 'You scared the crap out of us.'

She looked at Bob beside her, and Gary at her feet. She started laughing. *Ow.*

She started to sit up. Bob and Gary took an elbow each. She realized Ben was right there in the middle of them.

'Sit down over here,' said Gary. 'Take it easy, take it easy . . .'

'The color just drained from your face,' said Robbie. 'It was freaky.' He handed her a cushion.

'What am I supposed to do with this?' said Ren, holding it on her lap.

'It's all that caffeine,' said Bob.

Don't take my sunshine away.

'You need to get checked out by a doctor,' said Gary.

'I fainted,' said Ren. 'That's all.'

'Yes, that's all . . .' said Gary. His voice was flat. 'You've had a head injury.'

'"Head injury" sounds very dramatic,' said Ren.

'You didn't see it from here,' said Bob. 'That was a dramatic tumble.'

'I'm not taking any risks,' said Gary. 'You go to the doctor, then you go back to the Inn to rest. Come back in the morning.'

No, no, no, no. 'Gary, please don't.' She started to get up. 'I'm fine. Seriously.'

I need to get back to Denver. I need to flee people. Paul. And Ben. And myself.

'Ben here has got some great reflexes,' said Bob. 'He came to your rescue almost as quick as me . . . and he was at the back of the room.'

Ren smiled inside.

'Damsel in distress,' said Ben.

'Seriously, Gary,' said Ren, 'I am fine—'

'Bob, could you recommend a doctor to Ren?' said Gary. He left the office.

'I am going to lose my mind if I have to relax for the day,' said Ren.

'It's only until tomorrow morning,' said Bob. 'I hate to say this, and I never thought I would, but you look like crap.'

Ugh. 'I've bolted,' said Ren, 'you can't lock the barn door now.'

'It's not that bad,' said Bob. 'You get to sit back and have a rest. I'd love a day off.'

'It was funny coming to, though,' said Ren. 'You and Gary were right there, and your hand is hovering over my belt and Robbie's standing to one side. And Ben. It was like those "special" movies you get in hotel rooms . . .'

Bob laughed. 'Ren, you brighten up my life.'

'"Please Officer" could be the title,' said Ren. '"Or Officer (Going Down)" or "The Long 'Charm' of the Law." That would be you.'

'If I said something like that, it would be sexual harassment,' said Bob.

'And I'd love every minute of it,' said Ren. She stood up. 'I can't believe I have been rendered invalid. This "head injury" business. I haven't eaten – that's all. I forgot to eat.'

'Really?' said Bob. 'Is that really something people do? I don't buy it.'

'I swear to God,' said Ren. 'I haven't eaten since . . . I had dinner last night.'

'That is not good,' said Bob. 'I'm on Gary's side.'

'Bob, you know me, you know I eat like a horse . . .'

'I see you drink coffee and eat my Jolly Ranchers.'

37

Ren sat in her bed at The Firelight Inn, propped up by four pillows. She was dressed in lemon-colored flannel pajamas with a pink ribbon trim. Her hair was in a messy bun. She scrolled through her contacts and decided on Matt.

'Hey,' she said. 'I am so pissed off. Gary made me go back to the Inn for rest – for the entire night.'

'Why? Did you fall asleep at your desk?' said Matt.

'No, I just fainted, big deal,' said Ren. 'I hadn't eaten and, big deal, I fainted. But because I hit my head he was, like—'

'You hit your head?'

'Just, I had a minor encounter with the floor.'

'Don't tell me – no big deal?'

'Yes!' said Ren.

'He was right to send you home,' said Matt.

Silence.

'OK. Why hadn't you eaten?' said Matt.

'Jesus, who gives a shit? I forgot to. Everyone forgets to eat . . .'

'Not so much,' said Matt.

'That is bullshit,' said Ren.

'Even if it was bullshit,' said Matt, 'not everyone who doesn't eat is as . . . affected by that as you are.'

'Seriously, Matt . . .'

Silence.

'You buy an entire wardrobe for Ethan,' said Matt. 'You don't eat, you stay up half the night, you're sleeping with two men, or about to, I don't know and I don't want to know. Yet, you can not see the pattern, here—'

'Screw you.' Ren hung up.

Breathe. Breathe.

There was a knock on the door.

'Two-two-three? It's your fellow inn-mate.'

Ren laughed loud. Years earlier, Paul Louderback had nicknamed her two-two-three after the bullets: 'slim, elegant and golden' as he described them. Then he quickly added that they were 'stable until they hit the human body, then . . . they would rapidly become unstable'.

'Are you alive?' said Paul.

'No,' said Ren.

'Can I come in?' said Paul.

'Do you have revivifying elixirs?' said Ren. 'Have you taken liberties? Come in.'

Paul pushed open the door and held up a bottle of wine. He had two glasses upside down between his fingers.

'You actually have taken liberties,' said Ren. 'You clearly agree that there is nothing wrong with me.'

'Apart from the drink problem, yes.' He looked at her nightstand. 'Have you taken painkillers?'

'No, Your Honor.'

'But I shouldn't go counting puncture wounds in blister packs . . .' said Paul.

'Exackily.'

He leaned down and kissed her on the cheek, then sat down on the bed and poured them each a glass of wine.

'Thank you,' said Ren. 'I am so pissed off with Gary. Feel free to join me in that.'

'Gary's one of the good guys,' said Paul. 'Unfortunately for you. He is your great defender and protector . . .'

'Anyhoo,' said Ren.

Paul tilted his head. 'Have you been crying?'

'No . . .'

'About this?' said Paul. 'About being sent home?'

'No,' said Ren. 'My brother is giving me a hard time. It's no big deal.'

'Your wet eyelashes . . .'

'Yes – looking good,' said Ren.

Paul reached out and took her hand. 'You always look good. But, particularly tonight. You had me at pajamas.'

Ren smiled. She leaned back against the pillow and closed her eyes.

This is too hard. You shouldn't be here with me. I shouldn't be here with you. Ben Rader is out working on the case, and here we are drinking wine. And popping painkillers . . .

'Let's watch a movie,' said Ren.

'Sounds great,' said Paul.

That's the pressure off.

Just after midnight, Ren's phone beeped.

'Sorry,' said Ren, 'let me just check this.'

u knw ur spendng 2 mch time wth 16 y/os, whn ur wondrng if sme1 wnts 2 b ur girlfrnd . . . XBen

Ren's heart did a little flip.

She sent him back a Smiley face.

'I should be too old for Smileys. I should hate them,' said Ren, putting the phone down. 'But I just don't. They say so much.'

'Who are you sending Smileys to?' said Paul.

'Everyone,' said Ren. She held out her glass. It swayed. Paul poured more wine.

'Thank you,' said Ren. She drank more, and her eyes started to close. Paul took her glass and put it on the night-stand.

'Sorry,' she said. 'I'm . . . exhausted.' *And guilty. And so, so suddenly drunk.* She closed her eyes as the room started to spin.

'Shall I stay with you?' said Paul. 'Do you want me to?'

No. I want to do the right thing. I want to be kind to Ben Rader. Ben Rader is kind to me.

'Yes,' said Ren, opening her eyes. 'But, just so you know, I'm probably going to . . .' Her eyes closed.

'Fall asleep?' said Paul, smiling. He watched her for a minute until he was finished with his wine. He undressed to his plaid boxers and t-shirt and pulled back the covers. He lay behind her and wrapped his arm gently around her waist. He kissed her neck and pulled her closer.

'Sweet dreams,' he said, as quiet as he could.

Ren's breathing was steady.

Paul's eyes started to close. He spoke one last time, even quieter. 'I think I might just be falling for you, Sleeping Beauty.'

Shit.

38

Ben Rader was standing alone outside an empty conference room when Ren arrived in the morning.

'Hey,' he said, 'are you feeling better?'

'Not quite on top of the world,' said Ren. 'Maybe a third of the way up. How did last night go?'

'I hope you didn't think my text was too dumb,' said Ben. 'I was just trying to be funny.'

'I know that,' said Ren. 'It made me laugh.'

'So, what is our story?' said Ben.

Put me down, you don't know where I've been.

'I mean, are we . . . you know . . .?' said Ben.

I'd be the last to know. 'I don't think I'm ready for a relationship right now,' said Ren. *Because whores don't go in for relationships much.*

'Oh,' said Ben.

'I'm sorry,' said Ren. 'It's just . . . well . . . I've never been alone for very long. And I probably should be.' *Either that or with two people . . .*

'Why?' said Ben.

197

Because that's what people tell me. And that's what healthy people do.

'Good point,' said Ren.

Ben looked at her with a tilted head. 'So, do you want to hook up tonight?'

'In Breck? No way,' said Ren. 'With Gary hovering around?'

'But you had dinner with that CARD guy the other night. That was just the two of you.'

'Yeah, but that's different,' said Ren.

'Unless you're sleeping with him too.' Ben laughed.

Ren laughed too. 'Jesus, keep your voice down.'

'Relax,' said Ben. He looked like he was about to hug her.

'Hey, we're back in Denver tonight,' said Ren. 'It's Sunday. I forgot. I feel like I lost a day. I could call over to your place tonight?'

'That would be great,' said Ben.

'So, last night?' said Ren. 'What happened?'

'It was something else,' said Ben. 'I ended up hooking up with a group of kids at Big Mountain Brewery, and they invited me along to a house party five minutes from town on the road to Fairplay.'

'What did you get?'

'A few six packs, a couple bags of chips—' He smiled. *Gorgeous, gets-under-your-skin smile. That I don't deserve.*

'This was a party full of high-schoolers, and some a little older. We were in the basement of a house. There were two girls, I'm not making this up, they were in the games room on the pool table . . .' He glanced at Ren. 'They had . . . sex toys . . .' He paused. 'That they were using . . .'

'As opposed to holding them up like on the adult tele-shopping channel?' said Ren.

'It was unbelievable,' said Ben. 'It was the kind of thing guys should have to pay for.'

Hello?

'You know what I mean,' said Ben. 'That kind of stuff shouldn't happen at a teen party. It was basically a sex show.'

'And the crowd went wild,' said Ren.

Ben nodded. 'But, the party was kind of split,' said Ben. 'This was the basement action. Upstairs, were the more regular kids. Less skeevy. So, anyway, when I went back down to the basement, two guys passed me in the doorway, they were leaving the room, and I heard one of them say, "She's no Shelby."'

'It was obvious that one of the girls was less experienced than the other, she was trying too hard, and I think he was referring to her. So I figure Shelby was the regular, and this girl was her replacement. I tried to get up to talk to the other girl when they were finished, but there was a line of guys waiting to move in . . .'

Grim. 'And how was she reacting?'

'Her boyfriend was there,' said Ben. 'Standing in the wings. She didn't acknowledge the other guys.'

'But . . . what was the deal? Was she getting paid?' said Ren.

'So cynical,' said Ben. 'I didn't see any money being handed over, but who knows what could have happened before or after?'

'If she wasn't getting paid, what's the point?' said Ren. 'She has a boyfriend, he was right there . . .'

'Getting off on it probably.'

Ren nodded.

'Anyway, I got talking to the guy who left the room, told him I thought one of the girls was a total fail, and he was like, yeah, there was another girl here before, she was way better, and I said "Who?", and he said, "Doesn't matter, she's not around any more." Looked like he got an attack of speaking-ill-of-the-dead guilt. I said, "Oh, she just left?", hoping to hear more about her, and he said, "No, she stopped, like, a year ago."'

'And her legacy lives on . . .' said Ren. 'If she stopped a year ago – when she was fifteen – how old was she when she started? Jesus.'

'I know,' said Ben. 'But if she stopped a year ago, what's with the bag at her house? Was there a layer of dust on it?'

'There could have been before the mom moved it,' said Ren. 'Who knows? Maybe she just reduced the size of her market to one man at a time and a guaranteed payment at the end.'

Ben Rader stood up at the top of the conference room, and started to go through the details of the party when the room filled up. Ren stood at the side wall, watching him. There he was, looking like a college kid, but speaking better than Gary, better than Paul. He was passionate about what he did. He really cared about people.

And look at the piece of shit he wants to have a relationship with.

Ren turned her head as Paul Louderback arrived into the room looking deathly. His face was gray, and for the first time since she had known him, he hadn't shaved. She turned back to Ben.

Beautiful Ben.

Ren bumped into Gary in the hallway afterward.

'I wish we weren't leaving,' she said.

'I think we both know that this isn't about Breckenridge,'

said Gary. 'I don't believe there's anything more to be found here or anything to be gained by being here. I don't know what exactly this is, but our official line is out there, sadly, we've got the bodies . . . we can do more in Denver. At less expense.'

'I know . . . but still.'

'See you in the morning,' said Gary, walking away.

Bob came out of his office. 'I hate to see you go,' he said.

'Yes,' said Ren. 'This whole "tidy" ending . . . I feel like I'm going home from the party early . . . with the wrong guy.'

'Now why would you ever go home from the party with the wrong guy?' said Bob.

'Because my friends told me he was perfect or I thought he was a better option than the unknown. Or . . . you get where I'm coming from,' said Ren. 'I'm leaving this party with the wrong guy. What do you do when all the evidence is there and it aligns and the only hole is the one in your gut, because something is eating away at you? If the autopsy results said that he didn't pull the trigger, that would be helpful. But we know that he did. He killed Shelby Royce. There was semen in her mouth, he more than likely raped her, and he killed her.'

'There are two words that come to mind at a time like that,' said Bob. He put his arm around Ren and squeezed her shoulder. '"Case" and "closed".'

'You don't believe that,' said Ren.

'Nope,' said Bob. 'So, go out there, little lady. Spread your wings and fly.'

'I think I might have a problem with my landing gear.'

'I can't help you with that.'

Ren laughed. 'Will you help me when I come back with the real story?'

'I'd help you, Ren, no matter what the hell you showed up with,' said Bob.

'Thank you, Bob. You are a wonderful man.'

'So my beloved wife tells me.'

Ren went back to see if Ben was finished. He was tidying his notes with his talented hands, talking to some of the detectives. Paul Louderback came up and stood beside her in the doorway.

'He's a good speaker, that guy, Rader,' said Paul.

'He is,' said Ren. 'Thanks for looking after me last night. I know I was such good company.'

'You were lovely,' said Paul.

'You look . . . like . . . not great.'

'Fight with Marianne this morning.'

Like hearing her name even less now.

'Ah,' said Ren. 'I hope it wasn't anything too serious.'

'No . . . just about the girls, and her having a weekend away with her . . . boyfriend . . .'

OK, thanks for sharing.

'Well,' said Ren, 'we better say goodbye. I guess you're going back to D.C. now that we're all done.'

Paul nodded. 'I'll be back in Denver soon, though. Us CARD shufflers still have to give that talk we were meant to give when we got called away for this.'

'Well, keep in touch,' said Ren.

Paul frowned. 'Of course I'll keep in touch . . . what's that supposed to mean?'

'Nothing,' said Ren. 'Just keep in touch.'

'I really want to kiss you now . . .'

Ugh.

Ren smiled. 'OK, I gotta go. Safe trip back.'

Why do I do this? Why? Why? Why?

39

Ren made it to work for eight thirty on Monday morning. She had canceled Ben. Instead, she had read one of Annie's obscure novels and pushed men out of her mind for the two minutes it took her to fall asleep. She wanted escape. She wanted a world where nothing bad happened.

Her office phone rang. It was Glenn Buddy. She listened quietly as he delivered more bad news.

There was a third rape: a woman, alone on the street, surprised by a man who had violently assaulted her, beating her relentlessly as he raped her. She had just left a beauty salon and the first person to see her was a man who didn't care about all the things she had done to make herself as beautiful as she wanted to be. He had pushed her down onto the ground, and dragged her by the feet into a laneway. He had slammed her up against a dumpster, and her head had banged off it, over and over, and the stench of garbage, and of wet animals, had filled her nostrils. A rat had fallen from the dumpster right by her face, and had run, disappearing under an empty bag of fun-sized chocolate bars. Three of the gold stars that had been glued to her nails had broken off. She noticed that the polish had smudged on one of them, she guessed, when she put her coat on at the salon, even though the girl had helped her with it . . .

The victim remembered all these details clearly because she would rather watch a rat, and smell a stench, and read the five fun flavors in an empty bag of tiny chocolate bars than focus on what this man on top of her was doing. He was gone, she had figured, he was somewhere else, and she didn't want to go wherever that was. She wanted to be right there in a filthy alleyway, focusing on everything but an unreality. She knew women could disassociate at a time like this, and she didn't want to, she was too afraid. There would be too much, already, in the aftermath, too much physically to overcome. She didn't want to add to that a search for her mind.

He left her a drawing too.

Ren sat at her desk, staring at the new drawing – a cityscape, towering buildings, and lightbulbs scattered across the sky. That a rapist could draw this, with the same hands he had used to restrain these girls, this woman, the same hands that he had pressed over their mouths, the same hands he had used to tear at their clothes, and punch, and choke them, was incredible. That the same mind that had composed the image she was now looking at could create, and make real, his unspeakable fantasies, could violate a human being so thoroughly, was too much to make sense of.

The FBI profiler categorized the rapist as anger-retaliatory: short, impulsive, blitz attack, displaced anger, victim likely to represent someone else/women in general, extreme violence until the anger goes, possibly comes from a broken home, possibly spent time in foster care, socially competent, athletic, not seeking to kill, drug/alcohol abuser, mid to late twenties.

Each rape appeared to be unplanned, which meant that the rapist had not gone to the Kennington party with a victim or even a rape in mind. He had only been there for a short period of time, he had seen Ally Lynch and he had pounced. Ren removed elements of the profile based on Ally Lynch's account: her rapist was younger than his twenties, which Matt had backed up, the rapist was strong, but he was not athletic, and, at least on the night he had attacked Ally, she said that he had no alcohol on his breath.

Who the hell are you?

Ren picked up the phone and called Matt.

'Matt, I need some art theory help. I've got a drawing here from a crime scene . . .'

Silence.

Yes, let's not mention the whole 'screw you'/hanging-up-the-phone thing.

Matt decided to go along with Ren in forgetting their last encounter.

'A drawing?' said Matt.

'Yes,' said Ren. 'A drawing. It was found at a crime scene.'

'You really are Nancy Drew,' he said. *Nancy Dwew. Dwawing.*

I could listen to your endearing voice all day long. That's the Matt I love.

'It's weird,' said Ren. 'It's like a monkey on a skewer with chains coming out of his hands. On the left, the chain is attached to a bed with a bird on it. On the right-hand side, the chain disappears into some kind of megaphone. And there's a life-preserver hanging off it.'

'See-no-evil hear-no-evil?' said Matt.

'That's what one of the detectives said, but I don't think so.'

'Can you send me a JPEG?' said Matt.

'Sure . . . burn on reading, OK?' said Ren.

'Of course. I'll call you back.'

Ten minutes later, Matt called back. 'You have to look with better eyes,' he said.

She stared at the drawing.

'First off, it's not a monkey,' said Matt. 'It's a man's face or boy's face split in two – one side looking left, the other looking right. The downturned mouths are joined up – that's what's making it look like a monkey. The left side is chained by the wrist to a bed, with a cuckoo on it. That would be the proverbial cuckoo's nest, I'm guessing—'

'Really?' said Ren. 'Minus the actual nest?'

'Looks like a hospital kind of bed to me,' said Matt. 'And look at the right-hand side of the picture: the shape of the links on the chain is different. The chain looks like it's made of pills.'

'Pills are my thing these days,' said Ren.

'Crushing them up and snorting them?' said Matt.

'Only when I sense a random drug test on the horizon.'

'See in the picture,' said Matt, 'the pills are forming a megaphone . . .'

'And look at the bed,' said Ren. 'The thing that looks like a medical chart at the end of the bed also looks like a sliding volume control. It's up to the max.'

'You're getting the hang of this,' said Matt.

'So . . . ' said Ren. 'In terms of the artwork itself . . .'

'It's very simplistic, but it's detailed,' said Matt. 'And the message isn't terribly sophisticated—'

'Thanks for that . . .' said Ren.

Matt laughed.

'So,' said Ren, 'this picture was drawn by . . .'

'I would say a teenager . . . a teenage boy.'

Ally Lynch said the rapist was not much older than her.

'Well, that makes sense,' said Ren. 'So what's he saying? That he's being restrained by pills and chains and nobody's listening to him . . .? Is he a psych patient?'

'Possibly. But he's not actually in the bed. If he was, I would venture he would have drawn the monkey-boy in there. Instead, he's been left hanging. It looks to me like he's being pulled in two different directions: one toward physical restraint, one toward pharmacological restraint. I'm not sure that's a word, but you get the gist.'

'As if a hospital isn't going to medicate him anyway . . .' said Ren.

'True. But some people really do need meds, Ren.'

Silence.

Matt sighed. 'I do *not* mean you at this moment in time.'

'Well, when the moment arrives when you do mean me, do let me know.'

'Not-fighting-dot-com,' said Matt.

'Not-wanting-to-fight-dot-e-d-u,' said Ren.

'E.D.U. – I love it. A higher purpose.'

'Hey,' said Ren. 'Look again on the right . . . that chain, the one made of pills . . . it's going into his head, not onto his wrist like on the other side. Could the pills be making the voices louder?'

'Maybe,' said Matt. 'And . . . look. The life preserver . . .'

'Has a hole,' said Ren.

'It's a sad piece of art,' said Matt.

'It is,' said Ren.

'I'm taking it the red dots on the picture are not to indicate a sale.' There was no humor in his tone. 'What did he do?'

'He raped a fourteen-year-old girl, and possibly more.'

'And you're on the hunt . . .' said Matt.

'Not my case,' said Ren. 'But, I'm assisting . . . hopefully. OK, gotta go.'

Ren took out the second drawing from the rapist. There was something in these drawings . . . or the sense of something . . . she just wasn't quite sure what. She sat forward.

The curve. It's the curve of the bird's wing, the bird perched on the bed. It's like the curve of a scythe. She had seen it before. She had seen that shape . . . on the lightning strike that marked the path to Kennington Asylum.

40

Ren put a call in to Glenn Buddy. 'Glenn, those drawings – the curves in the bird's wings and on some of the buildings in the second drawing . . . they're the same curves on the lightning strikes on the ground at Kennington. I think they were drawn by the same person.'

'Really?' said Glenn.

'It looks that way,' said Ren. 'I'm looking through my notes here, and I was thinking – we should go talk to the boy that Ally Lynch said she liked that night. If the feeling was mutual, if he had any connection with her, he could be the one to break his silence and tell us who organized the party or who did the artwork that led to it.'

'OK – I'll pick you up,' said Glenn.

Ren followed Glenn into the Principal's Office of St John's Academy in Park Hill. There sat the object of Ally Lynch's affections: Rigg Raskin. A name straight from *Gossip Girls*.

Rigg was handsome, athletic and devastatingly unattainable to most girls. And, in the way he moved to settle himself in the chair . . .

Possibly devastatingly unattainable to all girls.

'So, Rigg . . .' said Ren. *Where the hell did you get your name?*

'I know you gave your statement about the party,' said Ren, 'and you said you didn't know who was running it—'

'That's correct, ma'am,' said Rigg.

Nice and polite. I'll cope with the ma'am.

'I just showed up,' said Rigg.

'But who told you it was on, and where to go?' said Ren.

'The same bunch of people you guys interviewed already. We were all, like, afterwards saying that it seemed to go in a circle – we all thought we heard from each other, but no-one had an outside source.'

'OK,' said Ren. 'I have a different question for you.' She placed the image of the lightning strike on the table. He sat forward.

'This, as you know, was used to guide you to the door of the party, and everyone's hands were stamped in invisible ink with the same logo.'

'Yes.'

'Who did the stamping at the door?' said Ren.

'I don't know, they were older, bouncer types, there for the start of the party, and apparently they were gone by the time any late people arrived.'

'Do you know who drew this?' said Ren.

'Who drew it?' said Rigg.

Ren nodded. 'It's important.'

He frowned. 'I don't know.'

'Do you think you can find out for me?' said Ren.

Glenn Buddy leaned forward. Very far forward. 'I don't think giving us that information will expose whatever dealer was behind the party that everyone is afraid of.'

A trace of fear flashed in Rigg's eyes.

'We're not interested in the dealer,' said Glenn.

For now . . .

'Or,' said Glenn, 'their suppliers, despite what movies you've seen. Special Agent Bryce and I want to know where this symbol originated, and we figure that it wasn't with whoever threw the party.'

If he was the rapist, he wouldn't have been arriving after midnight to his own event.

'I guess I could try,' said Rigg.

'No trying,' said Glenn. 'That's not what we want here. We want a name.'

Rigg turned to Ren with an imploring look in his eye.

'It's an important part of our investigation,' said Ren.

Rigg nodded. 'Agent . . . ma'am . . . there's a rumor . . . about Ally Lynch . . .' He stared at the ground. 'I haven't seen her. I know you can't say, but . . . if it's true, please . . . I'll do . . . I'd like to do what I can. Ally's . . . Ally's a cool person. She's a really good person.'

'Here's my card, Rigg,' said Glenn. 'If you find out who drew this, call me right away. And don't speak about this to anyone.'

'Sure,' said Rigg. He turned to Ren. 'If . . . if you see Ally, tell her I said hi . . .'

Rigg Raskin, you sweet boy. Poor Ally Lynch is not ready to hear that you care, because the idea of you even having a clue what happened to her would crush her spirit even more.

Ren arrived back at the office to an email from Matt.

OK, Ren, I do not want you to hate me for this, but I'm sending you an email that I'd really like you to read. Call me afterwards, if you like but . . . look, I'm not saying it will be easy reading, but please just think about it, OK? I love you very much. Just remember that.

She opened the email:

> Ren, I've gone back over some of our emails from earlier this year, and I've taken out some of the things you wrote me, so you can, hopefully, see a pattern. I know it won't seem a fair or a kind thing to do but . . . I just hope you can understand why I'm worried about you. Love, always, Matt.

Ren frowned. *What?*

> Jan. 02 to Jan.11: No emails (same thing for last three years).
> Jan. 12: OMG – Livestock Show Party! Amazing night! Roped v cute extreme rider (LOL!!!). THE worst hangover. EVER.
> Jan. 15: On trail of Tiny Toes Bandit – guy with tiny feet who robs banks while wearing shoes that are too big. Left a teeny tiny footprint at one scene, lost a shoe at another!!! Idiot!!!
> Jan. 17: Asleep at desk . . . ☺
> Jan. 18: Caught bandit. Here's link. Totally nailed it.
> Jan. 19: Hangover from hell . . .
> Jan. 21: Started dance class. What a blast! Teacher said I was a natural.
> Jan. 24: Extreme rider rides off into sunset . . . ☹ ☺
> Jan. 25: Phone company total IDIOTS!!! Hate them!!!
> Jan. 27: Took delivery of some very nice dance gear.
> Feb. 12: Gave up dance.
> Feb. 18 to Feb. 24 (no mails).
> Feb. 25: Note to self: don't open credit card statement when miserable.
> Feb. 27: Off work for a while. Gary great. Feel like shit.

Feb. 28: Not going to make it to NY. Sorry. ☹
Mar. 06: Back at work. Ugh.
Mar. 05: Yes, saw Helen. Helped, as always.

At the end, Matt had written: Ren, try that psychiatrist again.
For me.

Ren deleted the email.

41

Ren opened an email to Matt and typed: Nice.

She deleted the email. She called Matt.

'Nice,' she said.

Matt took a breath. 'I was just trying to get you to—'

'That was unbelievably mean,' said Ren. 'They were emails I sent to you that you've managed to turn into something shitty. Who the hell goes back over emails and—'

'That's not what I—'

'Just because you have zero social life,' said Ren.

'Yes, I have zero social life,' said Matt, 'but it's from looking after my baby son, Ren. And looking after my wife. I don't want any other kind of life. And all I want for you is to be happy.'

'Yet,' said Ren, 'you make out the emails where I am clearly happy and having fun prove some kind of negative.'

'No,' said Matt, 'that's not it, it's . . . think back to the emails that came after the happy ones—'

'Just answer me this,' said Ren, 'am I ever just allowed to be happy? Have you created this threshold where . . . if I cross it, some alarm rings somewhere? You're turning into

Jay: *your* judgment is the only one.' Jay was their eldest brother.

'That is not true,' said Matt.

'It's starting to be,' said Ren. 'How you see the world is how it is. Don't look at yourself, just look at me, right? Then you don't have to face any of your own shit—'

'Ren, I've got to go,' said Matt.

'Of course you do,' said Ren.

'I'll talk to you soon,' said Matt.

'Wait,' said Ren. 'Wait. What if you called me and "I had the most amazing day, Ren. Ethan, Lauren and I went for breakfast, then we went to the playground, and he just *loved* the little baby swing, and then we took a walk around the park, and there were these cute new ducks, and then we went for ice-cream, and then we went home and got a sitter, and Lauren and I went for dinner in this great new Italian place, and then" . . . then I said to *you*, "whoa, Matt, be really careful, that sounds really good, you've got a lot of happiness going on there, you need to be careful—"'

'Ren, I really have to go,' said Matt.

'Yes,' said Ren, 'as soon as I've got something to say, you—'

'Look after yourself, OK?' said Matt. 'I love you.'

'Sure you do.' Ren cut the call before Matt could.

She grabbed her keyboard and went to Apple movie trailers.

Her email pinged. She opened it.

Matt had forwarded her another email that she had sent him late the previous year:

Hi Matt,
I'm so sorry. I was way out of line. I know you understand me – in as much as anyone can . . . and sorry for the threshold thing again.

You're always there for me. And I'm so grateful.
And I love you too. Please ignore all evidence to the
contrary . . . ☺ x

Ren stared at the screen. She could feel her face burning.

Delete. Delete. Delete.

Ren's office phone rang.

If it's Matt, I'm hanging up.

'Hi Ren, it's Cathy Merritt . . .'

'Oh . . . hi, Cathy.'

'Sorry to bother you, but I was wondering . . . do you
have someone watching our house? Or keeping an eye on
Laurie?'

What? 'No,' said Ren. 'Why do you ask?'

'A neighbor came by and asked me were the police still
looking out for us,' said Cathy. 'They'd seen a black sedan
at the end of our block, but within view of our house – once
when Laurie was getting dropped off from a friend's house.
And once at the weekend. Apparently it drove by when
she was out in the garden, making a snowman. That was on
Saturday.'

'Really?' said Ren. 'OK, let me look into that for you.'

'Thank you,' said Cathy. 'The neighborhood is on high
alert – the girl who was raped at the Kennington place lives
only two blocks away, and with Laurie and everything . . .
it could just be paranoia, but, if it isn't . . .'

'I understand,' said Ren.

Gary walked into the office while she was on the call. Ren
told him about the black sedan.

'Could it be Denver PD watching the Merritts?' said Ren.

'No,' said Gary. 'At least not to my knowledge. Why would
they?'

'It's just weird,' said Ren.

'Did the neighbor get a license plate?' said Gary.

'No,' said Ren. 'She just said black sedan.'

'And when was the last time she saw it?' said Gary.

'Saturday,' said Ren. 'What do you think it could be?'

'I think there are some real sick people in the world and one of them might have liked the pretty little girl on the news . . .' said Gary.

'Ugh,' said Ren.

'Could have been just a reporter,' said Gary.

'Yup,' said Ren, 'a grown-up who thought it would be nice to freak the shit out of a kid who has already been abducted and lost her father,' said Ren. 'There are no boundaries in the world any more. Zero.' She paused. 'Want me to go check it out? Let me re-phrase, I'll go check it out.'

'Don't go anywhere, yet,' said Cliff, calling from his desk. 'JeffCo pathologist's on line one for you.'

Ren picked up. 'Dr Tolman . . .'

'Hello Ren, I wanted to let you know that the results on Shelby Royce have come back from the lab – the oral sex didn't happen the night she disappeared, but somewhere within the twenty-four hours leading up to her death,' said Tolman. 'And the traces of semen are not a match for Mark Whaley.'

'What?' said Ren.

'There was another man with Shelby Royce the day before she died,' said Dr Tolman. 'Someone else appears to have been involved.'

42

Ren couldn't believe what Dr Tolman was saying. Someone else was involved. Someone who was stupid enough not to know that the semen could have been tested, or reckless enough not to care. Someone who knew they weren't on a database anywhere.

'Wow,' said Ren.

'It's not a match for Mark Whaley or any dirtbag in CODIS,' said Dr Tolman.

'Well, thanks for letting me know,' said Ren. She put down the phone.

'So,' she said, 'Mark Whaley was not alone. The semen found in Shelby Royce's mouth was not a match. Neither was it a match with anyone in CODIS.'

'Whether he was alone or not, he pulled the trigger,' said Colin, 'that's a proven scientific fact.'

'Yes, and now we have another proven scientific fact,' said Ren. 'Some other man had a sexual encounter with Shelby Royce in the twenty-four hours leading up to her death. Maybe this isn't all about Mark Whaley. Where had she been for those two days? Was she with Laurie Whaley?'

Clermont Street was in Park Hill in North East Denver. All the houses on the street were decorated similarly for Christmas as if the residents had gotten together and made a plan. A modest plan, but a cheery one.

The Merritts lived in a bungalow with a small garden. There were five stone steps up to the door. A Christmas wreath was hanging from it.

Cathy Merritt opened the door.

'Hi Cathy,' said Ren.

'Hello, Agent Bryce,' said Cathy. 'And, it's Agent Truax, isn't it?'

'Yes,' said Robbie.

They shook hands.

'Come on in,' said Cathy.

She led them into the living room. It was decorated almost entirely in oranges and reds – the walls, the throws, the cushions, the lamp shades. A fire glowed in the hearth, amplifying the strange effect. Even the small Christmas tree had red lights.

'Would you like some hot chocolate?' said Cathy. 'I was just about to make some.'

'Thank you,' said Ren. 'That would be great.'

'Yes,' said Robbie.

Cathy went through a small door into the kitchen.

Ren looked at Robbie. His blond hair and the right side of his face were glowing.

'Brothel chic . . .' Ren mouthed.

'What sheet?' said Robbie, sitting forward.

Ren shook her head. *Never mind.*

'Brought what sheet?' said Robbie.

Shut up!

Cathy Merritt came back in with a tray of hot chocolate and a plate of muffins. 'They're cinnamon,' she said.

And what about the hash ones you were eating when you were styling the room?

Ren took a muffin and a mug of hot chocolate. 'Thank you. How's Laurie doing?'

'She's OK,' said Cathy. 'It's been tough. She actually wanted to go back to school today, but I said no. I'll have to let her go tomorrow, though. She just wants to be back to normal. She's going to get a lot of attention, and I don't think that's going to ease up any time soon. The school principal called, the teachers are all going to do their best, but . . . the kids, well . . . she's like a superstar and a freak at the same time. And then, there's what happened to Mark . . . parents are obviously talking, and the kids are picking up on it.'

'The poor thing,' said Ren.

'There's no chapter in the parenting manual for this,' said Cathy. 'I'm sure you're thinking I should be forcing her to talk about this – to someone, even if it's not us. But she's already been taken somewhere against her will. Her father has . . . died. She's had no control over anything, so I'm reluctant to take any more control away from her. She was a sensitive little girl before this ever happened . . .'

'We understand that Laurie has been through a lot,' said Ren. *But where was she? Who was with her? What did she see? Who brought her to Kennington? Could someone have threatened her into silence?*

'But, she will have to talk to Sylvie Ross very soon,' said Ren. 'Agent Ross is the child forensic interviewer who spoke with Leo after the abduction. She's wonderful with children, and she understands how to talk to a child who has been through a trauma.'

'I'll talk to Laurie,' said Cathy. 'I'll try.'

'And the black sedan . . .' said Ren.

'All I know is that it was parked about five houses down from here, but across the street.'

'And apart from the neighbor who came to you,' said Ren, 'did you talk to any of the owners of the houses near where it was parked?'

'Not all of them,' said Cathy. 'Should we be worried about this?'

'It could be a coincidence,' said Ren. 'We have people out there now canvassing the neighborhood. Maybe someone was visiting with someone. Maybe it was nothing to do with you. Obviously, everyone is on high alert with what you've been through, so it's easy to jump to conclusions.'

'Yes,' said Cathy. 'I'm sure it's nothing. It's just . . . it's making me feel . . . that maybe there's something more to all this . . .'

'Like what?' said Ren.

'I don't know,' said Cathy. 'It's this whole thing . . . I'm just not sure about any of it. Mark had his problems. But what happened with the sitter, him taking Laurie too? When things were bad, I'm sure there were so many times he dreamed of taking Laurie from me and he didn't,' she said. 'I know you saw me losing it with him, but I don't . . . I didn't feel those things for him, not really. It was just years of built-up pain, I guess. Now he's gone, and it's . . . it's devastating.'

'Did you ever think he was capable of something like this?' said Ren.

'Sometimes . . . sometimes I think that all along, alcohol was . . . maybe more a kind of tool to block out his demons. Maybe when the alcohol was gone from his life, the demons could roam free. Or a new addiction replaced it? Maybe sex addiction . . .?'

Sex addiction, the manufactured get-out-of-jail free card.

'So, what should we do about the car if it comes back?' said Cathy.

'If you see it, try to take down the license plate number. We're going to go talk to the neighbors. And if there's anything else, call me.' She handed Cathy her card. 'Any time. The same goes for Laurie.'

Ren and Robbie walked back to the car.

'Sex addiction: give me a break,' said Ren.

'It's a psychiatric condition,' said Robbie.

'And the winner of the world's most convenient psychiatric disorder ever goes to . . .'

'But—' said Robbie.

'And the winner of the award for the only psychiatric disorder a man would gladly suffer from, is . . .' said Ren.

'It ruins people's lives,' said Robbie.

'I'm not disputing that *infidelity* ruins lives,' said Ren.

'Well, how do you explain men throwing away their careers by their philandering or porn addiction or whatever?' said Robbie.

'Because it's amazing!' said Ren. 'Not because they have some mental illness. If they *didn't* want to have sex, *that* would be a mental illness. I think non-addiction to sex should be classified as a mental illness.'

Oh shit. Robbie is a virgin.

'The addict has to *want* to get help,' said Robbie.

'But who *wants* to be stopped from having sex with someone?' said Ren.

'We'll agree to disagree,' said Robbie.

'You sound like you're taking this personally,' said Ren.

'I'm obviously not,' said Robbie.

'Well, who knows what might happen when you get a taste for it.'

Robbie stopped. 'I actually found that really insensitive, Ren.'

'Oh my God, Robbie, I'm so sorry. I didn't at all mean it that way. I just . . . I'm sorry.'

'It's OK, but . . . maybe . . . not everything has to be so light-hearted.'

Ren's phone beeped with a text. Ben Rader.

Agent down(town). Agent down(town).

Ren replied: Your place: 6? Can't stay, though . . .

Ben replied: Cheap.

Ren replied: Nasty.

Ben replied: Perfect.

Who wants to be stopped from having sex with someone? And why can't everything be light-hearted?

43

Ben opened the front door, grabbed Ren's hand, and pulled her upstairs into the bedroom. He sat on the bed.

'Take off your clothes,' he said.

How am I supposed to stop comparing these men?

'You do it,' said Ren. She took his hands and put them where she wanted them. He slid them up, and started with her top button.

He paused. 'Was this expensive?'

Yes. Shockingly. 'No,' said Ren.

Ben grabbed the fabric, and yanked it hard, popping all the buttons. Then he grabbed the back, and ripped it off. He unhooked her bra with one hand, and threw it on the floor with the top, and everything else that was getting in his way.

Ren turned around, and looked into his eyes for the longest she had since they met.

I like you Ben Rader. I like you a lot.

Ren lay on the floor afterwards and stared at the remains of her top, and some buttons. Something was clawing at her, somewhere in the back of her mind, mixed with thoughts of people throwing their careers away, and photos, and this.

Whores.

She jumped up, grabbed her phone and called Bob Gage.

'I need to speak to your most promising newcomer,' said Ren.

'Owens?' said Bob.

'See?' said Ren. 'I knew you thought he was good.'

'Shit,' said Bob. 'OK, I'll give you his cell.'

Ren wrote down the number.

'What's this all about?' said Bob. 'Looking for help with a thousand-piece jigsaw puzzle?'

'Leave him alone,' said Ren. 'He may be about to give me some case-altering information.'

'About—'

'B'bye.'

Ren punched in Owens' number.

'OK – Owens, it's Ren. Can you talk? This is important.'

'Sure I can,' said Owens. 'Shoot.'

She could hear him shuffling pages.

'Remember the break room,' said Ren. 'When I left you there with Mark Whaley?'

'Yes.'

'What was he like, do you remember?' said Ren. 'What did he do?'

'He just kind of sat there in a daze,' said Owens. 'He was watching the television.'

'Did he say anything?' said Ren.

'Just . . . he said thank you for the coffee. But . . . he didn't touch it. He looked ill. I had to go get him some antacid.'

'Did you leave him alone?' said Ren.

'Uh, yes,' said Owens. 'He was sick . . . I didn't want him to throw up. I was only gone five minutes, max. Just to reception – the ladies have a supply.'

'And when you got back . . .' said Ren.

'Nothing,' said Owens. 'He was there, same place.'

'How did he look?' said Ren.

'No better. More sweaty. I gave him the Tums, he said thank you. And shortly after was when you came in.'

Ren remembered the sweat, the strong smell. *The smell of fear.*

'Is there a phone in the break room?' said Ren.

'Yes . . .' said Owens. He paused. 'Oh, God. Do you think he made a call? But he really didn't look well. He was telling the truth, definitely.'

'I have no doubt that Mark Whaley was looking very sick,' said Ren. 'But there are many reasons why a man can look sick, and sickness isn't always top of that list. Especially when he's sitting in the Sheriff's Office . . .'

'I am so sorry,' said Owens.

'I know you are,' said Ren. 'And I know it won't happen again.'

'No, ma'am.'

'Nor will you call me ma'am again,' said Ren. 'Just so we're clear. So, what do you think could have made Mark Whaley change his mind about his polygraph . . . from when he left the interrogation room with me to when I returned to the break room?'

'You're asking me . . .' said Owens.

'I'm asking you,' said Ren.

'Uh, OK. He comes in to the break room. He sits down. He's waiting for coffee. He's watching the news. Was the girls' disappearance on it when you got there?'

'Yes,' said Ren.

'Maybe it was all too real,' said Owens. 'When he saw it all there on the news, his daughter, it made him sick, and the whole idea of a polygraph was too . . . polygraphs scare people.'

Ren nodded. 'And one of the stories on the news afterward was about a woman who failed a polygraph, and has been considered guilty ever since.'

'Oh, he didn't watch that story,' said Owens. 'We were talking over that . . .'

Oh. My. God. And again, the answer was pulling at Ren.

'You're sure of that,' said Ren.

'Absolutely,' said Owens.

It wasn't the red Ferrari lady that stopped Mark Whaley taking the polygraph. It was the next story. It was Shep Collier's press conference.

Ren ran back into the bedroom. 'That was amazing, gotta go.'

Ben was asleep. She ran into his office, grabbed a stapler and stapled her top together. She put her jacket over it and buttoned it up as far as it could go.

Ren got back to Safe Streets and opened her laptop on the photos of Mark Whaley that had come in from The Lowry. And there was the young lady, getting close to Mark Whaley.

Tilting her head in a way that I should have recognized. Shit. Shit. Shit.

It was Mark Whaley and Tina Bowers. Ex-Congressman Shep Collier's lady of the night.

Ren searched on line for the article she had read on Shep Collier. He had slept with Tina Bowers on October 24th. He had stayed at The Crawford Hotel. Ren Googled The Lowry, where Mark Whaley had stayed. It was two blocks away.

And Saturday the 24th was the third night he had been staying in Boston.

Republican Congressman Shep Collier, secret supporter of healthcare for the poor, was the antithesis of big-business pharmaceutical companies.

What was his connection with Mark Whaley?

44

Ren didn't run her plans by Gary. Instead, the following morning, she sat in the conference room with her phone to her ear as she tolerated a series of questions, bad hold music and transfers until she got as far as leaving Shep Collier a voicemail. Half an hour later, her phone rang.

'Hello – is that Special Agent Ren Bryce?'

It was an older man's voice, a warm, voiceover voice.

'Ren Bryce speaking.'

'This is Shep Collier. I'm returning your call . . .'

'Yes, thank you,' said Ren. 'I'm currently working on an investigation and I wanted to ask you what you know about a man called Mark Whaley.'

'Mark Whaley? Should that name be familiar to me?'

'Well, I'm calling to find that out, sir.'

'I can't say I've heard of the man,' said Collier.

'Are you familiar with MeesterBrandt Pharmaceuticals?'

'I'm aware of MeesterBrandt, of course,' said Collier.

'Mark Whaley is their CFO,' said Ren.

'Ah,' said Collier. 'I'm sorry I can't be of any help to you, but I've had no personal or business dealings with MeesterBrandt or Mark Whaley.'

Here goes. 'Mark Whaley was found dead last week,' said Ren. 'An apparent suicide.'

'I'm very sorry to hear that,' said Collier. 'I'm sorry for the man's family.'

'Did you hear about the two young girls who went missing from a hotel in Breckenridge, Colorado just before that?' said Ren.

'For my family's sake, the Collier household has been in media blackout since my announcement,' he said. 'As you might expect . . .'

'I wouldn't expect that, actually,' said Ren. 'I'd like to know what people are saying about me . . .'

When Collier spoke, there was a smile in his voice. 'Well, it's clear I don't necessarily behave as expected . . .'

What can I say to that?

'I suspect there will be many awkward pauses for me to look forward to in life from now on,' he said.

'My apologies,' said Ren. 'It's . . . hard to know what to say.'

'At least you're honest.'

'As were you . . . I watched your press conference,' said Ren. 'I admit, I was impressed by parts of your resignation speech. They didn't sound scripted.'

'Most of it was,' said Collier. 'But that's the world we live in. It's about the party, not about me.'

'True,' said Ren.

Why am I getting into all this?

'Agent Bryce,' said Collier. 'The missing girls you mentioned . . . they were obviously connected in some way to this Mark Whaley?'

'One is his eleven-year-old daughter – she was found safe.

The other is the sixteen-year-old babysitter who was looking after her. Sadly, she was found dead.'

Silence.

'Manner of death was murder-suicide,' said Ren. She waited for him to react.

'Mark Whaley murdered a sixteen-year-old girl, then took his own life?' said Collier.

'Yes,' said Ren.

'That's a very tragic situation,' said Collier.

'Mr Collier . . . there is something else I'd like to ask you. It's a delicate question . . . and I'd appreciate your discretion on this matter, as I would on our entire conversation.'

'Go ahead, please,' said Collier.

'I have a photo of Mark Whaley,' said Ren, 'and he's in the company of Tina Bowers. Would you know anything about that?'

'You're asking me if I would know the details of a prostitute's clients?'

No – just the prostitute you slept with . . . 'Can I ask how you found Tina Bowers?' said Ren. *Enthusiastic? Perfunctory?*

'On a website,' said Collier.

'What website?' said Ren.

'I can't remember,' said Collier.

'Did you type in a website address?' said Ren. 'Had the agency been recommended to you? Or did you search for something in particular?'

'I . . . don't remember,' said Collier.

Really? Haven't you replayed that moment over and over again? Haven't you paused at the first step you made on this disastrous journey? Even I'm picturing a website with a screen full of hookers and their vital stats.

'Well, thank you for your time,' said Ren.

'Good luck with your investigation, Agent Bryce. My thoughts are with the families.'

'Thank you,' said Ren. 'Good luck with your . . . with everything.'

She put the phone down and sat back.

You do, indeed, behave unexpectedly, ex-Congressman Collier. How else could I not have taken an immediate dislike to a cheating frequenter of underage prostitutes?

Ren went on line and Googled Tina Bowers. According to every gossip website, she had gone underground, and would only reappear for an interview that would pay six figures. According to her celebrity lawyer, when Ren called her, she was hiding out in her grandmother's house in Maplewood, New Jersey.

An email popped up in Ren's Inbox from Bob Gage.

I never get emails from Bob Gage.

She opened it:

Read this before you kill me.

It was a link to *The Summit Daily News*:

Mack Yarnwood, 42, from Silverthorne, CO, might want to cancel his Facebook account quick fast. Yarnwood was arrested at his home early today on charges of Class 1 misdemeanor theft. Yarnwood, who had been working for Holder Electrical Contractors in Breckenridge, CO, posted Facebook images of himself with his loot, stolen from various jobs he had been working on in the previous twelve months.

When Yarnwood's boss, Danny Holder, saw his employee's Facebook photos, through his own son's Facebook page, he looked into Yarnwood's past and uncovered prior convictions for robbery and possession of a controlled substance.

Holder set up CCTV cameras, which captured Yarnwood taking a range of items, including clothing, bottles of liquor, appliances, even bed linen, and yes – you've guessed it – hotel towels.

Ren called Bob.

'I'm guessing Mack Yarnwood wasn't showing up for work at the Sheriff's Office,' said Ren. 'Can't seem to find his name here on any list . . .'

'I didn't even know the guy existed,' said Bob. 'I had to buy that journalist a slap-up meal not to put in that Holder was working at the Sheriff's Office. It doesn't look good.'

'What I would like to know,' said Ren. 'Is when and where your buddy Holder set up his cameras . . .'

'Meaning The Merlin . . .' said Bob. 'And yes, he did. I spoke with him. We have tape from the parking garage the night the Whaleys checked in . . .'

Ren slammed a hand on the desk. 'What the fuck was Danny Holder thinking?'

'He went through the tape,' said Bob. 'He saw nothing, so he figured he wasn't doing anything wrong.'

'Like he'd have a clue,' said Ren. 'I cannot believe he didn't come forward with this.'

'He wanted to handle the whole thieving thing privately,' said Bob. 'He was just trying to protect his business.'

'You mean his ass,' said Ren.

'His livelihood.'

'Jesus, Bob. Two little girls were missing out there. And, so you know, we just found out that the buccal swab from Shelby Royce's mouth wasn't a match with Mark Whaley. There was somebody else involved.'

'I'm not trying to defend Danny Holder,' said Bob. 'I'm pissed at him myself. It's just he thought he had a crew he could trust, and next thing, he's thinking not only could he have a thief, he might have even hired a pedophile.'

'I don't care about Danny Holder right now,' said Ren.

'Don't get mad at me,' said Bob.

Even though the small-town bullshit has everyone covering everyone's asses.

'I'm just telling you he's a good guy,' said Bob. 'His kids are in school with mine.'

'Oh, well then,' said Ren.

Silence.

'I'm sorry,' said Ren. 'But I just, I can't stand—'

'We have the tape, OK?' said Bob.

'Yes,' said Ren. 'Yes.' *Retract your claws.*

'According to Danny,' said Bob, 'the only thing in the tape is the Whaleys getting out of their SUV.'

'You have got to be shitting me,' said Ren.

'No,' said Bob. 'He said they're just getting out of it, unpacking it, and disappearing out of shot. He didn't think there was anything crucial going on . . .'

'Yes, to his trained eye. But . . . when did he set the camera up? His crew weren't working that weekend.'

'Friday lunch-time, before he left,' said Bob. 'He takes Friday afternoons off . . .'

'And how long was the camera set to run? All weekend?'

'Not the whole weekend,' said Bob, 'but he chose whatever setting compromised the quality of the footage so that the camera could run for longer. And it makes sense – he can see them on Friday night if they're leaving with any shit, or, if the team's on the beer for the weekend and they run out of it by Saturday night, or in the early hours of Sunday morning, one of them could be dumb enough to try to sneak in again. They didn't tell him they were going away for the weekend because they figured he would hang around to make sure they didn't knock off early Friday. Some of them were going for dinner in The Merlin, now that I think about it – maybe he thought it was those ones who were going to steal . . . while they were there.'

'Where's the tape now?' said Ren.

'It should be with you shortly. And you get the fun job of going through it. But, I wouldn't hold out much hope.'

Ren put down the phone and her office phone rang.

Go away everyone.

'Ren, it's Cliff, I just happened to be talking to Glenn. Apparently some guy got the crap kicked out of him this afternoon in Park Hill. He was by the basketball courts, got dragged out of his car by a man, he used a baseball bat, really went to town on him.'

'Is he in the hospital?' said Ren.

'No. He managed to get back in his car and drive away.'

'Don't tell me,' said Ren, 'was it a black sedan?'

'Yup. That's why I called. The basketball court's only a few blocks from the Merritts' house.'

'What is going on here?' said Ren.

'Beats me,' said Cliff.

'Beats him,' said Ren.

'Denver PD's canvassing the neighborhood . . . we'll see what comes up.'

'Hopefully they'll find some paranoid neighbor with a telephoto lens pointed at the street.'

'Oh, and Ren,' said Cliff, 'one eye witness said that the guy doing the beating was a big guy with a beard . . .'

Like Dale Merritt, for example.

The tape from Danny Holder showed up in the afternoon with a note from Bob.

'Saturday 6 pm 'til 4 a.m. Enjoy!'

Ten hours. Yay. Thank you, Danny Holder.

Ren hit Play. It was low res and didn't capture every frame, so objects flashed on and off the screen.

Shit.

The camera had been placed lower than it should have, and Holder hadn't allowed for the dim lighting so the footage was in shades of mid-gray to black.

Ren fast-forwarded through much of it, stopping when she saw some action. She rewound, and lined it up. It was 19.05 – the Whaleys' SUV pulled into the parking garage. The camera faced the driver's side. Mark Whaley got out and went around to open the back door. Erica Whaley appeared beside him having come around from the passenger side. Then Laurie Whaley appeared from the driver's side with Leo on her hip. She handed Leo to Erica. Then she staggered forward. She was at the front of the frame, bent over, clutching her stomach. Erica and Mark followed her around. Mark crouched down to see if she was OK. Erica was bending down as much as she could with Leo in her arms. Laurie moved her hands to her knees, and looked like she was taking deep breaths. Her father was rubbing her back. She slowly came to her feet a minute later. She was nodding. She was OK. Mark handed her a bottle of water. Erica walked with her and Leo out of shot. Mark continued to unpack the car.

Despite the stomach-ache drama, it was the standard family preparing to go into a hotel. Except within seventy-two hours, the father was involved in a murder-suicide with the sitter they were about to call for.

Ren rewound and hit Play. She watched it again. And again. And again.

Oh. My. God.

She pressed Pause.

What the fuck?

She squinted at the screen, paused at when Laurie was bent over. Laurie's feet. Mark Whaley's feet. Ren hit Play again. Then Pause. Laurie's feet. Mark Whaley's feet. And there, in the middle, another pair of feet. At the passenger side.

Ren watched five more times. And flashing on and off, was an extra pair of feet, visible under the SUV.

She rewound the tape again, and looked out for more movement, for anything coming from the direction of the entrance, but there was nothing. No cars drove by to the left of the SUV, none to the right.

What? I'm going blind . . .

Ren ran into Gary's office. 'Come down to the AV room,' she said. 'You've got to see this.'

He followed her. She sat him down and stood by his shoulder, talking him through what she saw.

'Someone was in that parking garage,' said Ren. 'And they were right by the Whaleys. They could have been waiting. They could have heard exactly what their plans were. They could have heard that Laurie wasn't feeling well, meaning she could have been vulnerable. They would have known her name, Leo's name.'

'*Are* they feet?' said Gary, leaning into the screen.

Ren enlarged the image. 'It's still very blurry.' She looked at Gary. 'But I think they're feet.'

'But one looks higher than the other.'

'It's probably the angle,' said Ren.

'Is there any other footage – another camera, another angle?' said Gary.

'No,' said Ren. 'It's the missing frame thing – the feet are gone in the next shot, and they don't reappear.'

Gary slid the chair back from the desk and stood up. 'Leave it for the techs to have another look at, see if there's anything they can do . . . because this . . . doesn't really give us anything.'

'It does. Gary, you know that there's more to this. This *is* something.'

'I'm still not sure they're feet,' said Gary. 'It could just be a shadow.'

Ren slumped back.

Don't rain on my feet.

'Did you hear about the guy that got the crap kicked out of him in Park Hill?' said Ren. 'It was right by the Merritts' house? Gary, this might have been someone coming back to finish the job. If, for example, Laurie was let go and she wasn't meant to be . . .'

'We can't know what happened to Laurie Whaley, other than she whacked her head in the hotel, until she's been seen by the child forensic interviewer.' He started to walk out of the room. 'OK,' he said. 'Go talk to Cathy Merritt and Laurie Whaley – see if they saw anything. But don't press her about the abduction . . .'

Mixed signals alert.

46

Cathy Merritt opened her door and hovered in the doorway.

'I'm sorry,' she said. 'Should I have been expecting you?'

'Denver PD got in touch,' said Ren. 'About an assault that happened in the neighborhood yesterday.'

Cathy's eyes went wide. 'Really? Oh my goodness. Come in.'

Ren followed her into the living room.

Ugh.

'We're trying to locate the victim,' said Ren. 'He managed to drive away from the scene.'

'And . . . what can I do to help?' said Cathy.

'Did you notice anything unusual yesterday afternoon?' said Ren.

'No,' said Cathy.

'The vehicle that this man was driving,' said Ren, 'was black, like the one that was reported on your street.'

'And where did the assault happen?'

'By the basketball courts – two blocks from here.'

'Oh my God,' said Cathy. 'Laurie plays basketball there.'

'Was she there yesterday?' said Ren.

'She was over at a friend's house – they may have gone

there, but she certainly didn't see anything happen, she would have said.'

'OK,' said Ren. 'We'd like to talk to Laurie about it, if you don't mind. We also need to ask her about the night she went missing.'

Cathy sat back. 'I can't allow that. She's not ready.'

'Mrs Merritt, I don't want to ask her about what happened in the room, or anything to do with what happened afterward. I've been reviewing tape of the parking garage, and there may have been someone there when the Whaleys arrived.'

'But . . . it's a parking garage. Of course there were people there . . .'

'Well, neither your ex-husband nor Erica saw anything, but I took a look at some footage, and . . . I'd like to ask Laurie a few questions . . .'

Cathy took in a deep breath. 'OK,' she said. 'Let me go get her.'

Laurie Whaley had lost weight – her clothes swamped her. She stood against the door frame with a bent knee, and one foot on top of the other. Her legs were like twigs. She had pulled her hands up into the sleeves of her sweatshirt.

'Hi, Laurie,' said Ren. 'I'm Ren. We met in the hospital.'

Laurie nodded. 'I know. Hi.'

'Would you like to sit down?' said Ren.

Laurie sat beside her on the sofa, but shifted back into the corner.

'How've you been doing?' said Ren.

'Good,' said Laurie. She shrugged.

'I'm wondering if I could ask you a few questions,' said Ren.

'I guess,' said Laurie.

'It's just about arriving at the hotel that Saturday night,' said Ren. 'I know that night was a very difficult time for you, and it was very frightening, but I just want to know, do you remember seeing anyone . . . or anything in the parking garage?'

Laurie was very still. 'No,' she said. Her eyes were wide. 'No.'

'Did you hear anything, maybe?' said Ren. 'Any sound?'

Laurie paused. 'No.'

'You felt unwell,' said Ren. 'What was the matter?'

'I just got a stomachache,' said Laurie. 'I ate too much candy earlier, and being in the car, and everything . . .'

'So, there was nothing that upset you?' said Ren.

'No,' said Laurie.

'You didn't see anything?' said Ren.

'I'm sorry. I . . . there was nothing there,' said Laurie. 'No-one.'

'OK, Laurie, thank you for that,' said Ren.

She could hear footsteps coming up the path.

She glanced out the window, then turned to Cathy. 'That's Robbie who you met already. I'm going to have to go talk to him.'

'Sure,' said Cathy.

'Thank you again,' said Ren. She stopped in front of Laurie. 'If you think of anything at all, you let me know. You can get your mom to give me a call.'

Laurie nodded. 'OK.'

Ren opened the door to Robbie. 'Well?' she said.

'The neighbor in number four saw the car yesterday afternoon, about 3.30 p.m.,' said Robbie.

'Where?' said Ren. 'On the street?'

'No. At the basketball court on the next block. Laurie Whaley was there with a group of kids.'

'They were there on their own?' said Ren.

'No,' said Robbie. 'Dale Merritt was there too, talking to one of the other fathers.'

'Did the other father get a license plate number by any chance?' said Ren.

'No.'

'And he didn't call the cops?' said Ren.

'He said he didn't see any assault.' He raised his eyebrows. 'In the words of your people, "oh, Lawsy".'

'In *your* words,' said Robbie, 'well . . .'

'It's all asterisks, hash and dollar signs,' said Ren.

Robbie dropped Ren off outside Safe Streets, and went to buy lunch. Ren walked into the foyer to catch the elevator. Colin was standing waiting.

'Hi,' he said.

'Hi,' said Ren.

They stepped into the elevator, known for having a personality of its own, suspected of being operated by a ghost. It moved to the first floor, and between that and the second, it stopped, and started to rattle.

'Colin,' said Ren, 'it isn't my business, and I've thought about whether to say this to you, but . . . it's about Naomi . . .'

'What about her?' said Colin, turning to her.

'It's . . . well, you know I really like Naomi. And hanging out with her is such a blast. But when you're not around . . . she's kind of . . . she just seems interested in other men.'

'Really?' said Colin. 'So, she drinks and gets flirty? Imagine that.'

Why, Ren, why? 'This is not about me,' said Ren. 'And it's more than flirting, OK? Why would I bring up drunken flirting, for Christ's sake?'

'You tell me,' said Colin. He stared at her. 'What's really going on here, Ren?'

Oh, sweet Jesus. 'Nothing is going on. I am trying to tell you, I just thought her behavior was . . . a little off for someone in a relationship.'

The elevator struggled back to life. Ren banged her head off the wall.

'Ow,' she said. 'I'm not dating her but if I was . . . maybe I'd be a little wary if I were you.'

'Look, whatever,' said Colin. 'You've said what you've said. You can relax now. Your hours of agonizing can come to an end. Your message has been delivered.'

He stepped off the elevator, and walked quickly down the hallway.

I thought that went well.

Ren's office phone was ringing when she walked in.

'It's Robbie – are you at your desk?' He paused. 'Obviously you are . . .'

'Yeees,' said Ren.

'I'm getting lunch,' said Robbie, 'but I got a call from one of the parents at Laurie's school who heard we had called. We've got a license plate if you want to run it.'

Ren took down the details. She put down the phone, and ran the plate through CCIC, the Colorado Criminal Information Center, and NCIC, the national one.

The car was registered to a man named Taber Grace. Ren read more.

Holy. Shit.

Taber Grace:

Private Investigator.

Ex-FBI.

Ex-Rocky Mountain Safe Streets Task Force.

What. The. Effin. Crap?

47

Ren's heart was pounding. An ex-member of Safe Streets – whom she had never even heard of – had the crap kicked out of him for loitering outside the house of an eleven-year-old girl who was the victim in a Safe Streets abduction investigation.

Ren took a deep breath.

Who the hell do I ask about this?

She looked around the office at everyone. None of them had ever mentioned a man called Taber Grace. There must be a reason for that. And asking about him, without being armed with a little more information, was not a wise move.

Ren walked down the hallway into one of the conference rooms. She called Paul Louderback.

'I believe you are back in Denver,' said Ren.

'I am,' he said.

'A couple of things have come up in the Mark Whaley case,' said Ren. 'Are you free to meet up?'

'I'm intrigued.'

'How about Gaffney's? Just to be original.'

'Isn't there anywhere else you go?'

She could hear him smiling.

'The champagne bar on Larimer Street,' said Ren, 'but I'm trying to watch your wallet. Gaffney's is all about the wings, and the jalapeno poppers. I've been obsessing about them all morning.'

'What time is it now?' said Paul.

'Two o'clock,' said Ren.

'Can we say seven?' said Paul.

'Perfect,' said Ren. She paused. 'This is between us, OK?'

'Of course,' said Paul.

Why break a seventeen-year tradition?

Colin let out a whistle from his desk.

'That Sylvie Ross is hot,' he said. He turned his screen toward Cliff, and a little toward Ren. It was on a charity website. Sylvie Ross was in shorts and a tank, smiling at the finish line of a race, holding up a medal.

'The forensic child lady?' said Cliff.

'Paul Louderback's little protégée,' said Colin.

The what now?

'She was *not* hot,' said Robbie.

'Her shoes were terrible,' said Ren.

'I noticed the shoes too,' said Cliff. 'That's what you've done to me, Ren. That was not a well-designed shoe.'

Could I love you any more?

Don't ask. Be cool. 'What do you mean Paul Louderback's protégée?' said Ren.

'One of his ladies. He gets off on it. They follow him around like little puppies,' said Colin. 'I don't get it. Do you, Ren?' He gave her a shit-eating grin. 'Do you like Paul Louderback's shoes?'

Does that even the score, you piece of shit? And while I'm at it – Paul Louderback, you're a piece of shit too.

Gaffney's was uncharacteristically quiet. Paul Louderback was at a table facing her, wearing a blue flannel shirt.

Very old-school . . . for a multi-protégée-timer.

Beside him were two gorgeous young girls.

Uh-oh. Not ready for this.

'Hey, there,' said Paul, standing up. 'Girls, this is Special Agent Ren Bryce, we're working together in Denver. And Ren, these are my girls, Emma, and Lucy.'

'Hello, there,' said Ren. 'How are you doing?'

They smiled politely. 'Nice to meet you.' They both shook her hand. *Adorable.*

Emma was twelve years old, tall and thin, dressed in skinny jeans and a sweater, with long auburn hair in a ponytail. She had a perfect white smile, and the same sharp cheekbones as her father. Lucy was eight years old, and had blonde curly hair, a cute little face, and bright blue eyes.

'Would you care to join us?' said Paul.

Ren smiled. 'If it's OK . . .' *A warning might have been nice.*

'The girls' nanny was held up,' said Paul. 'We're just finishing up. And the girls like the idea of getting rid of their father and having a table to themselves . . .'

'No, we don't,' said Lucy, but she was smiling at Emma.

'They have things to discuss, apparently,' said Paul.

'And we don't have a nanny,' said Lucy. 'We're not babies.'

'What is she, then?' said Paul, smiling.

'Our entourage,' said Lucy, laughing.

'She got you there,' said Ren.

Lucy turned to Ren. 'You can stay if you like.'

'Sure,' said Ren. 'Thank you, Lucy.'

Emma moved closer to her father to make room for Ren. Her eyes were slightly narrower than Lucy's . . .

'Would you like some fries?' said Lucy.

'Thank you,' said Ren, grabbing one.

They talked about all the things the girls had done in Denver, and what they liked to do at home, and who their friends were. Lucy was the more outgoing, performing every story she told.

The girls went to a table of their own for dessert – two tables away. They started taking pictures of each other on their cell phones.

'I think they like their independence,' said Paul.

'I think they like their dad,' said Ren. 'They might even adore him.'

'Oh, I don't know . . .'

'I wanted to ask would Sylvie Ross talk to Laurie Whaley for us?' She waited for a reaction.

He frowned. 'Yes . . . why?'

Ren filled him in.

'Sure,' said Paul, 'I can't see that being a problem.'

The door of Gaffney's opened and a cold breeze shot through.

'Ah,' said Paul. He smiled. 'Gary.'

Ren turned around. Gary walked over to the table. Ben Rader appeared behind him.

And for the second time that night, Ren heard Paul Louderback say, 'Would you care to join us?'

You have got to be kidding me.

Ren had no time to talk to Paul Louderback and find out if he had ever worked with or trained an agent called Taber Grace. She had time, however, to sit through one of the most excruciating gatherings of her lifetime, second only to attending a charity dinner with the parents of her high-school boyfriend . . . an hour after they had walked in on their beloved son and his girlfriend in their newly installed en-suite shower.

Ren zoned back in on the conversation. There was great news – Paul Louderback was leaving to take the girls back to the hotel. Next to go was Ben, who had tried desperately to hold eye contact with Ren.

Ben to the left of me. Paul to the right. Here I am . . .

Ren spent half an hour more with Gary, talking about all the developments, and what they could mean. He slid his chair back, about to announce his departure.

'Wait,' said Ren. 'Sorry, but . . . I have to ask you something.'

'Sure,' said Gary. 'Go ahead.'

'Who is Taber Grace?'

Gary's poker face performed as expected. 'Why do you ask?'

'Because he was the man in the black sedan watching Laurie Whaley . . . until he got the crap kicked out of him.'

The poker face was struggling.

'What is it?' said Ren. 'Who is this guy?'

'Taber Grace originally had Colin Grabien's job,' said Gary. 'For the first three months of Safe Streets. And then he fucked up.'

End of story.

WTF? 'In what way?' said Ren.

'He had lied on his application,' said Gary.

'What do you mean "lied"?' said Ren.

'He wasn't entirely honest about his past.'

'Was it something serious?' said Ren.

'That he lied?' said Gary. 'Yes, Ren. That happens to be serious.'

Dig. Dig.

'But you hired him,' said Ren. 'He was here for three months . . .'

'It only came to light after three months,' said Gary.

'How?' said Ren.

'This is old ground,' said Gary.

But I am dying to know what this guy did.

All eyes had been on Gary when he was setting up Safe Streets. Multi-agency task forces were new, and it took him a long time to convince everyone it would work.

And in the first three months of the task force, something had failed. Taber Grace had failed. Therefore, Gary Dettling had failed. And Gary Dettling had zero tolerance for failure. Even his own.

'Just – you're very thorough . . .' said Ren. 'I'm surprised anything slipped through the net.'

Silence.

'Why do you think he was watching Laurie Whaley?' said Ren. 'This isn't some elaborate revenge thing is it? I mean, could he be trying to get back at Safe Streets or something?'

'This is not a movie, Ren,' said Gary.

'But . . . it's all so weird,' said Ren. 'Why would—'

'I have no idea,' said Gary. 'And it's Denver PD's responsibility.'

'But – the Merritts . . . that's our—'

'Taber Grace is not my concern,' said Gary. 'And he's certainly not yours.'

48

Ren walked up the path to the Graces' house, contemplating the ghosts of Dettling's past freak-outs. It was a fleeting contemplation, not because the ghosts were few but because Ren had successfully filed them in the la-la-la-la-la file. Whatever Gary Dettling told her not to do, she would do if her gut told her otherwise. Her gut beat everything.

'Hello, Mrs Grace,' said Ren, holding up her badge. 'I'm SA Ren Bryce from Safe Streets. Can I come in?'

Melissa Grace frowned. 'Safe Streets?'

'Yes.' *I'm afraid so.*

'But . . . is this about Taber?'

'Could I please come in, Mrs Grace?' said Ren.

Melissa swung the door back. 'Yes, yes. Is Taber OK?'

'It appears that your ex-husband has been the victim of an assault, but—'

'Oh my God,' said Melissa. 'What happened? Is he OK?'

'He was badly beaten,' said Ren. 'We don't have all the details. But what we do know is that he was well enough to be able to drive away from the scene.'

'He drove away?' said Melissa. 'But . . . did anyone see where he went? Did he make it to the hospital?'

'No hospital has admitted anyone matching his description,' said Ren.

'But . . . if he was beaten . . .' said Melissa. 'If . . . maybe he didn't look like himself. Or . . . did he get a head injury? Maybe he's lost his memory or is passed out somewhere.'

'According to witnesses, he did receive a head injury,' said Ren. 'We were hoping that maybe he had come to see you. Detectives from Denver PD have been to his apartment, and he's not there.'

'No,' said Melissa. 'No. Oh my God – I can't believe this.'

'Is there anywhere you can think of that he might go?' said Ren. 'Any family he might have gotten in contact with, any friends?'

'I . . . I don't know,' said Melissa. 'We're divorced, and Taber . . . well, he does his own thing. I don't know what he's doing most of the time. I have to keep on at him to know where he is or what he's doing . . . for our son's sake, more than anything.'

Hmm. Not just for his son's sake if your face is anything to go by.

'Did your ex-husband mention a case that he was working on—'

'No,' said Melissa, shaking her head. 'No – he worked confidentially, and he was very protective of us. So he would never have told us anything. Who did this to him?'

'We don't know that,' said Ren. 'That's why we need to talk to him. He could be in danger.'

'Is that a line you throw out there to get me to cooperate?' said Melissa.

'I'm presuming you're already cooperating,' said Ren.

'I am,' said Melissa. 'Of course I am.'

'Your ex-husband was seen watching the house of an eleven-year-old girl,' said Ren.

'If he was doing that, he was hired to do it, to protect her,' said Melissa. There was no pause before her answer.

'Do you know that for sure?' said Ren.

'No,' she said. 'I don't . . . But I know for sure that Taber watching the house of an eleven-year-old girl could only be because of an assignment.'

'We've looked into that,' said Ren. 'We have no evidence that he was hired to protect this girl.'

'That doesn't mean that that evidence doesn't exist,' said Melissa.

'Is your son here?' said Ren.

'Yes,' said Melissa. 'TJ. Why do you ask?'

'I'd like to speak with him,' said Ren.

'Do you have to?' said Melissa.

'Yes,' said Ren.

Ren knocked on TJ Grace's door. He didn't respond. She told him that she was an FBI Agent and he told her she could come in. He was lying on his bed, his long hair covering his face. He pulled himself up as she walked in.

'Mind if I sit down?' said Ren. She pointed to the chair in front of the computer.

He shrugged. 'Sure, go ahead.'

'TJ – have you seen your father?' said Ren.

Eye dart. 'No.'

'It's very important that you let us know if you have, OK? Your father's been injured, and he might need medical help.'

Or someone might want to go back and finish what they started.

253

TJ nodded.

'Are you telling me that your father has not come to visit?' said Ren.

He looked down, and nodded. 'Yes,' he said. 'He hasn't been here.'

Ren glanced down at the shelf under TJ's desk.

'Ah, you have Wii Sports,' she said. 'I am a Hula Hoop champion.'

He smiled.

'Mind if I take a look?' she said.

'You want to play Hula Hoop here?' he said.

Ren smiled. 'No – I just want to have a look at your game.'

'But if you've got it already—'

Her expression was enough to get him to hand her the controls.

'Could you switch the TV screen to the right channel?' she said.

'Sure,' he said.

'D'oh – you've hit the wrong button,' said Ren. She took the control from him, and brought up the Wii Sports screen. It was paused on a wakeboarding game. There were two players' names on the bottom: TJ and P.I.

'TJ, can I check out your Miis?' Miis were characters designed by players: you chose their features, hair, body shape, even their birthday. You could clone yourself and use that, or you could choose a different player every time you played.

'Did you make this Mii?' said Ren. 'The one called P.I.?'

'Yeah . . . I make all the Miis.'

'I'm guessing it's your dad. It looks really like him,' said Ren.

TJ nodded. His face was grim.

'Based on experience,' said Ren, 'your friends are not going to choose your father as their Mii when they're going wakeboarding . . .' said Ren. 'Unless your father is a world-champion wakeboarder.'

He half-smiled.

Ren looked back at the screen. 'Looks like you were whuppin' him.'

'I always whup him,' said TJ.

'What time was he here?' said Ren.

TJ's shoulders slumped. 'About eleven thirty. Mom doesn't know. She was at the gym. Don't tell her he was here. She'd kill me.'

'Was he badly injured?' said Ren.

'He had patched himself up,' said TJ, 'but he didn't look too good. I asked him was he OK, and what happened, but he just told me not to worry.'

'Did he mention that it was anything to do with a case he was working on?' said Ren.

'No,' said TJ, 'he never tells us anything about his cases.'

'OK,' said Ren. 'I can't stress how important it is for you to tell me the truth, TJ. I'm going to have to tell your mom about this, you know that.'

TJ nodded.

Ren glanced to another desk, where a small blue laptop was half-closed.

She popped it open. She looked to her right. It was attached to a printer. She called up the last document it had printed. An airline ticket. For Newark, New Jersey. Leaving that night.

'He never said anything to me,' said TJ.

'If your father gets in touch with you again, can you please ask him to call me?' She handed him her card.

'You're from Safe Streets?' said TJ, reading the card. His face changed. 'He hates you guys. There's no way he's ever going to call you.'

'Please,' said Ren. 'This is not about Safe Streets, it's about your dad. I wasn't with Safe Streets when your dad was. He'll know that.'

'Is your boss that Gary guy?' said TJ.

Ren nodded. 'Yes.'

'Dad hates his guts,' said TJ. 'I know that much.'

Ren went back down to Melissa Grace. TJ followed her.

'Safety in numbers,' he said.

Ren smiled.

'Mrs Grace, TJ thought he was doing the right thing by not saying anything, but he just told me that his father came by here when you were at the gym today, and spent some time with TJ. Physically, TJ thinks he patched himself up OK, but there are no guarantees. Here's my card, I've given one to TJ too. Please call me if you know anything more.'

'You'll understand if I'm wary about anything to do with Safe Streets,' said Melissa.

'I don't know the facts about your ex-husband's time there,' said Ren. 'It was before I started. What I do know is that he may be in danger right now.'

'Could this not have been a random assault?' said Melissa.

'I don't believe that it was,' said Ren. 'And that's all I can say right now.'

Ren walked down the path and got into the Jeep. She saw TJ coming out the front door and walking toward her.

'Hey,' he said.

Ren rolled down the window. 'Hey, there.'

'Is that your dog?' He put his face up to the back window.

'Yes,' said Ren. 'That's Misty.'

'I saw her head popping up,' he said. 'Can I pet her?'

'Sure you can. Go ahead.' Ren lowered the back window.

TJ reached into the back seat. Misty pushed her face toward him and he petted her gently.

'She's a beautiful dog,' said TJ.

'She is,' said Ren.

'Mom won't allow dogs in the house,' said TJ.

'Well, I had to wait until I moved out of home to get Misty,' said Ren.

He smiled. 'Then I don't feel so bad.'

Ren started the engine. 'Well, OK, I better go—'

'Um, I heard mom and dad talking,' said TJ. 'It was, like, years ago. And . . . all I know is that they don't really know why dad was fired. I mean, they know why, but they just don't know how.'

'How?' said Ren.

TJ shrugged. 'I think that Gary guy found something out, but mom and dad didn't know how he could have done that.'

'OK . . .' said Ren.

'Well, OK,' said TJ, 'I gotta go.' He nodded. 'Thank you.' His hand briefly rested on Ren's arm, as he pulled it past her.

Ren drove away from the house. Taber Grace Jr. was a sweet kid. She thought of him trotting down the path after her, and his hand on her arm, not in a weird way, just a small, kind gesture.

Ren glanced back at Misty.

'Misty, he seems like a good kid to me . . . what do you think?'

And he has brought me the closest I have come to finding out what the hell happened with Taber Grace.

49

Ren got back to Safe Streets and went straight to Gary's office. He told her to take a seat.

'OK,' said Ren, 'I know you told me—'

Gary stared her into silence. 'That's a familiar opener, Ren. And finishes every goddamn time with you telling me you've done something I have specifically asked you not to do.'

'This is—'

'Different!' said Gary. 'I know. I am not screwing around here, Ren, but I am not going to be able to tolerate this for much longer. I like you on a personal level, you know that, but professionally, it is getting to the point that when I see you walk in my door—'

'But I haven't even—'

Gary shook his head. 'I can separate personal feelings and professionalism, Ren, so I'm telling you that this has got to stop. Or I will have to transfer you. I'll have no choice. Some day it's going to blow up in my face.'

Ren's heart was pounding. 'I . . . I'm sorry, Gary. I always only try to do the best for the case. And I haven't screwed up if you think about it . . .' She held her breath.

'Officially? No. But that's because I have covered your ass. How many times have I covered your ass?'

'Many times.'

'Now, what were you coming in to tell me?' said Gary. 'Finish the sentence "I know you told me" . . .'

'I know you told me you didn't want coffee, but I was wondering—'

'Jesus Christ, Ren. How do you have the fucking balls?'

Ren smiled. 'OK. It's about Taber Grace, but please give me a chance. Here's what we've found out: someone else was in the parking garage around the time the Whaleys were checking in. Someone was watching the Merritts' house i.e. Taber Grace. I went to see his ex-wife and son, because Taber Grace obviously knows something we don't, he's been assaulted because of it, and he's gone underground. So, I'm there, and I decide to go up to the kid's room to speak with him and I realize that Taber Grace has been there. I missed him by an hour. But I went to his son's computer, and the last thing he had printed out was a ticket to Newark. New Jersey. Which is where Tina Bowers, Shep Collier's hooker, lives – Maplewood, New Jersey.'

'OK . . .' said Gary.

'So, what we have now is an undeniable link between a private investigator, a congressman, a hooker, and the Merritts/Whaleys. There's also mystery semen . . .'

'Mystery semen . . .' said Gary.

Ren nodded.

Gary nodded. 'What do you want to do?'

'Go to Maplewood in the morning. Taber Grace is a smart man. His son has probably got a message to him that I was at the house and saw the airline tickets. I doubt he'll catch that flight.'

'He probably booked another one,' said Gary. 'He's probably there right now.'

'I'd like to go talk to Tina Bowers,' said Ren.

'OK,' said Gary. 'Go ahead. But don't take that as a sign that it's going to be worth going against my orders again.'

'I'd like to talk to Mark Whaley's boss too. It's clear that whatever went on between Mark Whaley and Shelby Royce, there is a business-related issue here.'

'Do your homework, Ren,' said Gary. 'Don't go in there without knowing as much as you possibly can about him. This is politics, it's big business, and it's two cases that have already had huge media attention in the last month.'

Hmm. 'In that case, I'll wait until I speak with Tina Bowers, before I talk to Nolan Carr,' said Ren.

Gary nodded. 'OK.'

'And thank you for your understanding,' said Ren.

'I don't understand,' said Gary. 'I don't understand you at all.'

That evening, Ren sat with Janine Hooks in Woody's in Golden, not far from Janine's office. Ren had made it three-quarters of the way through a ham and arugula pizza. She paused, watching the movement of tiny bones in Janine's hand as she picked a carrot stick from a glass of crudités.

She wondered how Janine could get through the day, how she could walk, and run, and exercise, and think, without food in her belly.

You are so pretty, and endearing, and kind. Yet you torture yourself.

Ren watched as Janine put the carrot stick on her plate. It had one bite taken out of it.

Will you ever talk to me about it?

Ren glanced at her phone, making sure that it was not dialing a number by accident, thereby allowing someone to listen in to their conversation.

And will I ever talk to you about being nuts?

Ren and Janine looked at each other at exactly the same time.

Do either of us really need to?

'So,' said Janine, 'Paul Louderback, a man who promised you nothing, has, indeed, delivered on that promise?'

'So it seems,' said Ren.

'How surprising and disappointing that must be,' said Janine.

Ren smiled. 'But I do feel like an idiot.'

'Did you think he was not allowed to have other friends?' said Janine. 'Did you let him know?'

'Friends, yes,' said Ren. '"Little protégées?" Noo. There's only one little protégée. I'm the little protégée.' *Me me me me me.*

'That's sad,' said Janine.

'I know, I know,' said Ren. 'I just want to hear someone say it out loud.'

'So . . . Paul Louderback has fallen behind in the polls this week,' said Janine.

'That sounds terrible,' said Ren.

'I'm kidding.'

'Would it also sound terrible if I said that I think you're using the protégée thing to back off? I seem to remember he made his intentions very clear to you when you were leaving Breck . . .'

Hmm.

'Colin Grabien likes to stir things up, he obviously guessed you had some fondness for Mr Louderback, and he got his dig in. I think you really know that Paul is interested in you. But, hey, you've got an excuse to not get involved.'

'You're evil,' said Ren.

'Ben is adorable,' said Janine. 'He is smiley and sweet and yes, very cute. He has a strange innocence about him.'

'Don't say innocence,' said Ren. 'I'm the innocence quencher.'

'You could be a rapper, that could be your name,' said Janine. She paused. 'Can I stand up for the little guy? I want to say – do not underestimate Ben Rader. You'll end up hurting him.'

'He doesn't care that much,' said Ren.

'Be careful,' said Janine. 'For someone who loves men, you are very quick to assume they're cold and heartless . . . when it suits you.'

'I'm not saying he's cold and heartless,' said Ren. 'Just that, he's not that into me.'

'Hasn't he broached the whole girlfriend thing? Why would he bother? It's not like he lives here full time. Have you been looking for reasons to go off him too?'

'You're a white witch.'

'How can you live with that brain of yours?' said Janine. 'I would go crazy.'

'Oh, I do,' said Ren. 'You have no idea.'

That night, Ren sat in front of her laptop and searched for Tina Bowers to make sure that Hugh Hefner hadn't flown her to his mansion for a party. She had posted a new photo on Facebook from that afternoon – with her black Labrador and two clear Maplewood, New Jersey markers in the background.

The girl trying to hide from the media . . .

Ren was about to shut her laptop. But words came back to her – words from Matt, words from Janine; cycle, pattern, threshold, crazy. She went to Apple movie trailers, and watched five. She sat back and stared at the screen. And Matt's words came back again; "jumping off drunk and nekkid for fun".

Ren leaned forward and opened Google. She typed in the name Dr Leonard Lone.

Show me what you're made of. Show me why you should be the winner of this year's Shrink Idol. Who have you worked with? Who are your influences?

At first, Ren found very little information except his business address and contact details. There were no images, no videos, no academic papers.

Ren worked some more magic. And there it was – everything she could want to know. Her hands froze on the keys.

Dr Leonard Lone. Trust-fund billionaire. Philanthropist. Resident in multi-million-dollar mansion.

Holy psychotropics! My shrink is Batman.

50

Maplewood, New Jersey was a beautiful, quiet, old-school town, a great place to bring up a family. There was no sign in the town center that read Birthplace of Teen Hooker Tina Bowers.

Ren sat in her car down the street and waited until she saw Tina, running down the path of her aunt's house with a black Labrador on a leash. Tina was dressed in a white down parka and skinny blue jeans tucked into black suede knee-high boots. The fur-trimmed hood of her parka was down, its pointed edges reaching out past her narrow shoulders. Her white-blonde hair was loose and piled inside it.

Ren got out of the car and walked toward her.

'Tina Bowers,' said Ren. She was better-looking up close than Ren had expected. Her skin was flawless, several shades paler than in her promotional shots. Without makeup, her eyes looked smaller, her blonde lashes almost translucent. The effect was angelic.

'Ohmygod, how did you find me?' said Tina. 'I'm not doing any more interviews.' She tried to go back into the house. Then she saw Ren's badge.

'Oh,' she said.

'I'm Special Agent Ren Bryce, I'm working on the murder of a young girl, not much younger than you . . .'

'Oh my God,' said Bowers. 'Really? That's terrible.'

Ren nodded. 'Can we go grab a coffee somewhere?'

'But . . . what have I got to do with a . . . murder?' said Bowers.

'Let's go get coffee,' said Ren. 'Let's start with that. Where's good?'

'Um . . . right down the street,' said Bowers

The coffee shop smelled of disinfectant. A skinny, wrinkled waitress with a spray bottle was the person responsible. Ren sat opposite Tina Bowers in a booth at the back.

'Tell me about Shep Collier,' said Ren. 'The truth . . .'

'I . . . told the truth,' said Bowers. 'Do you seriously think—'

'Tina, tell me the truth,' said Ren. 'This is a murder investigation. And it's a crime to lie to a federal agent. That would be me.'

'Who was murdered?' said Bowers. 'You said a girl.'

'A sixteen-year-old girl,' said Ren. 'So, I need you to tell me about what happened with Shep Collier.'

'You think he murdered someone?' said Bowers.

'No,' said Ren. 'I do not. Talk to me. What happened?'

'How do you know anything happened?' said Tina.

Ren's expression stopped Tina asking another question. Instead, she looked around her, behind her, over Ren's shoulder.

'Tina, what happened the night you were at the hotel with Shep Collier?' said Ren.

'I got a call from the agency to go to The Crawford Hotel to room whatever,' said Bowers. 'So, I did. Shep Collier opened the door. I had been told by my boss that the role play would start as soon as he did, so I played along – tried to force my way in, told him I knew what he wanted.' She shrugged. 'He was like, what the hell is going on here, but I kept pushing it. For a while. It was obvious real soon that this was all bullshit. It was real awkward. I kind of apologized, I think . . . I can't really remember . . . but I left.'

'You did not have sex with Shep Collier,' said Ren.

'No. I was mortified. I left the hotel, and I called the agency. They said that he probably got cold feet, but that they had been paid, I would be paid, so it was all cool, I could go home if I wanted.' She took a breath. 'So, I did. And when I get home, there's a man waiting at the steps to my building, and he stops me, and says "Tina Bowers, here's the thing . . . " And he tells me that he will give me $20,000 to tell that story I told about Shep Collier, and the guy says he can email me photos of me at the room as backup . . . so that the story would be realistic. So, I did.'

'Did he say why he wanted that story told?' said Ren.

'No.' She shrugged.

'But you agreed to do this . . .'

'For the money,' said Tina.

Hello? 'Did you know who Shep Collier was?' said Ren.

'Not really,' said Tina. 'I mean, I realized when the story went huge.'

'Who did this man say you were to tell that story to?' said Ren.

'I had to email blownpolitics.com. It was supposed to be anonymous. But, I think they tricked me. Next thing, my name was everywhere . . . my actual name. It was the worst day of my life.' She looked at Ren. 'You're probably thinking getting $20,000 couldn't be the worst day of anyone's life . . .'

'That's not at all what I'm thinking,' said Ren. 'You were used very badly in all this.'

'Well, that's m'job,' said Tina. She tilted her head.

'And I don't think that either,' said Ren.

'It's pretty shitty,' said Bowers. 'And all those wives bitching about me on line. And meanwhile, their husbands are, like, Googling me like crazy. I'm right up there.' She took out her phone. 'But check this out.' She opened up her photo folder, and turned the screen to Ren. She started scrolling through photos she had taken of herself with different wigs, and sunglasses.

'I guess I could go anonymous for a while. I'll put them up on Facebook, see which look my fans like the best.'

Anonymous. Let me know how that works out.

'Can you give me a description of the man who came to your house, and gave you that $20,000?'

'Yes, but even I know that it won't help you. He was like any other guy. Tall, thin, skinny face, short light brown hair, combed to the side. Black leather jacket, black jeans, black boots.'

Ren wrote it all down. 'Thank you.'

'Will I have to testify?' said Tina.

'I don't have enough information to answer that,' said Ren. 'Now, I want to show you two photos.' She handed her a photo of Mark Whaley. 'Have you ever met this man?'

Tina stared at the photo. 'Yes,' she said. 'This one was different. It wasn't an agency thing. I was just to go up to him, chat to him in the hotel foyer, in the bar, places where the hotel had cameras.'

'Did he show any interest in you?' said Ren.

'No,' said Tina. 'Not at all. He showed me a picture of his kids. I pretended I was just a tourist, waiting to meet my mom and dad, that they were up in the room getting ready for dinner. He was a nice man.'

'And was it the same man who gave you the $20,000 that asked you to do this too?' said Ren.

Knowing that both men's photos hitting the media would cause a shitstorm.

'Yes,' said Tina. 'He didn't pay me extra for that.'

'One more photo,' said Ren. 'Have you spoken to this man?' She put down a photo of Taber Grace.

Tina looked away, slumping in the chair.

'Remember, Tina, you are legally bound to tell me the truth,' said Ren. 'This man is not a law enforcement officer . . .'

Tina groaned. 'Yes. He was here. He wanted to know about the congressman too.'

'Is there anything else you can tell me about him?' said Ren.

Tina shrugged. 'No. He wanted to know the same things you did. The only difference was that he had a photo of the man who paid me.'

Shit.

'Well, he had four photos,' said Tina, 'and I had to pick the one who paid me. Which I did. But he didn't tell me who he was or anything.'

'Were they mugshots?' said Ren.

'No – they were just regular photos. But they're ones that look like the person doesn't know they were being taken.'

Funnily enough.

'When did you meet this man?' said Ren.

'This morning. He's not going to come back for me, is he? I mean, he told me not to tell anyone . . .'

'No,' said Ren. 'He's not going to come back for you.' She stood up. 'Tina, thank you for your time.'

'No problem,' said Tina.

'So, what are you going to do now . . . with your life?' said Ren.

'I'm staying safe,' said Tina. 'Webcam probably. When I get back to my apartment.' She pointed to herself. 'No-one gets to touch this anymore.'

She rubbed the frayed cuff of her jacket. She looked at Ren. 'Probably until I need new stuff, anyway.'

Sweet Jesus.

51

Ren went to Gary's office when she got back. She told him what happened with Tina Bowers.

'Gary, you have got to let me go talk to Shep Collier,' said Ren. 'Tina Bowers was paid off – Shep Collier *was* set up, Tina confirmed that. She was paid $20,000 to tell a tall tale. And the same guy who paid her to trash the congressman sent Tina to The Lowry to entrap Mark Whaley . . .'

'Where does Shep Collier live?' said Gary.

'Florida,' said Ren. 'Sarasota.'

Gary raised an eyebrow.

'I wish he lived next door,' said Ren. 'I have zero interest in getting on another flight, even if I do end up in warmer, more glamorous climes . . .' She paused. 'I just have a feeling Collier will talk to me,' said Ren.

Gary waited for more.

'It was just . . . it was how he was on the phone with me,' said Ren.

'That's it?' said Gary.

'My bag is still packed,' said Ren. 'This will be an easy transition.'

'OK, go,' said Gary. 'But, Ren – Shep Collier stood up in front of America and admitted this. Can you trust what this girl is saying?'

Ren stopped at her desk, and sat down to type up her conversation with Tina Bowers. Paul Louderback called as she was finishing.

'Well, you were a big hit with my girls,' said Paul.

'Aw.'

'They thought you were "so cool" . . .' said Paul.

'Well, you can tell them I thought *they* were so cool,' said Ren. 'They are really great kids.'

'I know . . .' said Paul.

'You are allowed to take some credit for how your kids turned out,' said Ren. 'There was a little hesitation in your voice, there.'

'Marianne has done the heavy lifting,' said Paul. 'I . . . well, I don't know what exactly I contributed.'

'That's ridiculous.'

'So, what happened with Whore du Jour?' said Paul.

'Shep Collier was framed,' said Ren. 'Tina Bowers didn't sleep with him. She was paid $20,000 to say she did.'

'Any idea who's behind this?' said Paul.

'I'm flying to Florida in the morning to talk to Shep Collier,' said Ren.

'Can I come?' said Paul.

Ren smiled.

'I hope you didn't mind Wednesday – that I didn't tell you the girls were with me,' said Paul. 'I'd been sitting there, thinking, "How am I going to talk to the girls for two more hours?" I love them so much, and I'd be just fine sitting there quietly with them, but that's not what they want. They would have gotten bored, and I would hate the idea that spending time with me was a duty. You came along and you were able to talk to them about movie stars, and clothes, and computer games, and pop singers.'

Movie stars and pop singers. Quaint.

'Were we at the same table?' said Ren. 'They were just excited to be there with you. They adore you.'

'Thanks,' said Paul. 'And you weren't the only big hit. They seemed to take quite a shine to Ben Rader.'

Pause. Reflect. 'Probably because he looks roundabout their age,' said Ren.

'In fact, they thought you and Ben would make a great couple,' said Paul.

Yeah . . . until their father showed up in town and messed it all up.

'Kids adore Ben,' said Ren.

'He's quite the charmer,' said Paul.

Stop where you're going.

Ren kept working until late. Until she got a call from Naomi.

'Ren, get your butt into Gaffney's. I'm here with your office, and they're talking work and sport. Like that's any kind of revelation to you, but please. Save me.'

Ren looked at her watch. 'Ooh,' she said. 'I'd love to, but I've got a five-thirty flight in the morning.'

'That's hours away,' said Naomi. 'No excuse. Get to your locker, do a Superman. Text me when you're two minutes away and I'll even have your beer lined up.'

'OK . . .' said Ren. 'A few beers won't kill me.'

'Yay!' said Naomi.

'See you there,' said Ren.

Gary was standing in the doorway. 'Are you going to Gaffney's?'

'Yes,' said Ren.

'You're flying out early in the morning, right?'

'Yes . . .'

'So, can you drive?' said Gary. 'So I can have a beer?'

You evil genius. 'Sure,' said Ren. 'You don't need a ride home, do you?'

'No,' said Gary.

They got into the Jeep. Ren started the engine. She reversed out of the spot in a sweeping arc that finished with a deafening crunch of metal, and a forward motion that slammed her head hard against the steering wheel, and split the skin at her eye.

'Jesus Christ,' said Gary. He had grabbed the dashboard and his arm had taken all the impact.

'Fuck,' said Ren. 'Fuck. I'm sorry, Gary.'

Gary let out a breath. 'Are you OK?' He turned to her.

She still had her head down, and was holding the steering wheel. She touched her cheek. She looked at her fingers. *Blood. Lots of blood.*

She lifted her head up slowly, and looked at Gary.

You are very, very handsome.

'I'm OK,' said Ren. 'I think.' She pressed her fingers along her eye socket. 'Ow.'

'That's a black eye,' said Gary. 'And stitches.'

'And it didn't even happen in the line of duty . . .' said Ren.

'It's your duty to drive well,' said Gary. 'What the hell happened?'

'I . . . have no idea, I was just pulling out, I didn't see anything . . . I didn't think there was a car there. I don't know. I'm so sorry, Gary. I can't believe this. I've never crashed in my entire life . . .'

They both unhooked their seatbelts and got out to check the damage.

'It's not a Safe Streets car, that much I know,' said Gary. 'I'll call it in.'

'Thank you. I'm so sorry.'

'Let's get you to a hospital, get checked out,' said Gary.

'No,' said Ren. *I want to curl into a ball and cry.*

'Come on,' said Gary, 'let's get you fixed up.'

Tall order, Mr Dettling. Tall order.

52

Ren sat on the sofa in Annie Lowell's house with a glass of water in her hand and a packet of painkillers minus four beside her. The doorbell rang. She went into the hall and opened the door to Ben Rader.

'Wow,' he said.

'I know,' said Ren. 'Not the prettiest of pictures.' Six dissolvable stitches had zipped her cheek wound closed. She had a black left eye.

'Does it hurt?' said Ben.

'Not when numbed by narcotics, no.'

He gave her a long hug. 'You're my height again,' he said. He glanced down at her bare feet.

'Don't get used to it,' said Ren. She kissed him. 'Thank you so much for coming, so late.'

'Of course I was going to come,' he said. 'I was worried about you. How was Gary?'

Ren made a face. 'Not my pal.'

'It was an accident,' said Ben. 'Accidents happen.'

'I wasn't really paying attention,' said Ren.

'I didn't come over here to listen to you beat yourself up.

I actually came here to be your knight in shining armor. Even though I know I won't even get sex in return.'

'What makes you think that?' said Ren.

Ben walked down the small hallway. 'It's such a cool place,' he said. He turned back to her. 'But I came to the conclusion last time I was here that we would never have sex under this roof.'

Ren laughed.

'It would be too weird, right?' said Ben.

'How do you even know that I'd think that?' said Ren.

Ben shrugged. 'Same as I know I bet your bedroom here is pink and frilly.'

'Frilly – I love it.' *Did he go up into my room?*

'And before you ask, no, I did not snoop up there.'

Freaky.

They went into the living room and Ben sat on the sofa. Ren stood in front of the floor-to-ceiling bookshelves.

'I was looking for a book to read on the flight,' she said. She checked her watch. 'Which is about four hours away.' She crouched down. 'This is an amazing collection.'

She slid a small, blue-covered hardback from one of the shelves.

'I was expecting a cloud of dust,' said Ben. 'That was kind of an anti-climax.'

'Em, you have noticed that the place is clearly cleaned maniacally every week?'

'I'm not saying the place is dirty,' said Ben. 'Just – it's an old bookshelf, like something out of a movie. Or maybe a book . . .'

Ren smiled. She stood up, and opened the cover. She read the inscription, holding her hand to her heart.

'Oh my God,' she said.

'What?' said Ben. 'Is it worth millions of dollars?'

'Annie's been a widow most of her life,' said Ren. 'She adored her husband, never looked at another man since he died.' She held up the book. 'He obviously sent her this as a gift,' said Ren. 'In 1952. He must have been away somewhere.' She looked up at Ben. 'If I read this out loud, I may not make it to the end, I'm warning you.'

> *To my beloved Annie,*
>
> *Since we met, I don't know the measure of anything. Folks talk of the beauty of a golden sunset, or the joy of sweet birdsong on a summer morning, or the wonder of a roaring waterfall.*
>
> *But you are beautiful, Annie, and you are wonderful, and you are joyful. Is there any more beauty or joy or wonder to spare?*
>
> *If there is, the answer is two months and four days away. For the golden sunsets, the sweet birdsong, and the roaring water will come to life for me only when you are by my side, only when they can draw from your endless reserves.*
>
> *My dearest Annie, just as you are beautiful, wonderful and joyful, I am thankful and I am grateful.*
>
> *Your ever-love,*
> *Edward*

Ren sat down on the sofa beside Ben. He put his arm around her. He didn't say a word. He leaned forward, and pulled a Kleenex from the box on the table in front of them.

Ren took it from him. 'Thanks,' she said.

'That was for me,' said Ben.

Ren laughed through the tears.

'I'm serious,' he said. 'You're a heartless one.'

She looked up at him. 'I thought you were joking,' she said. 'You sensitive soul.'

'But, love is amazing,' said Ben.

There's a lot to be said for an untroubled man.

'I slept with someone else,' said Ren.

Ben looked at her. 'Really?'

'Yes,' said Ren. 'And I feel terrible about it.'

'Why?' said Ben.

'Why did I do it or why do I feel terrible?' said Ren.

'Why do you feel terrible?'

Uh-oh. 'Because . . . of you.'

'Well, don't,' said Ben.

'OK, but I can't help it,' said Ren.

'Who was it?' said Ben.

'Someone from before,' said Ren. 'Someone . . . I had unfinished business with.'

'Did sleeping with him finish the business?' said Ben.

'Yes,' said Ren, 'the business is wound up, the shutters are down, the auditors have been and gone, there were rumors of fraud, but it turns out it was ultimately unfounded, and really, the business never stood a chance, and was probably only two silent partners who had more important businesses elsewhere, but were loyal to their little start-up that never really started-up.'

'Is there potential for a new start-up, do you think?' said Ben.

'I do think,' said Ren.

Ben smiled. 'Good.' He paused.

'How come you're cool with this?' said Ren.

'Because I know why you did it.'

'Well, I don't . . .'

'Because you like me, and you don't really want to, so sleeping with someone else was your way of seeing how you really felt about me, or him, or both of us . . . I don't know . . .'

Ooh.

He smiled. 'Rader: 1. Louderback: 0.'

'Oh, God,' said Ren. 'Take that to your grave.'

'It's in a grave, trust me.'

'I do,' said Ren.

'Paul Louderback, though . . . I don't really get it.'

Ren laughed.

'I'm sorry,' said Ben. He took her hands and looked her in the eye. 'It's OK to care about someone. No-one's going to die.'

Shut. Up. 'I know. Thanks. And I really am sorry. It's just . . . that letter was beautiful, and I . . .' *. . . am not. And I love that kind of love. And I need everything to be perfect and if it isn't . . . I can't bear it. I can't believe in it. It scares the crap out of me. I need you to know what you're letting yourself in for. I can't have you thinking I'm better than I am. Because I'm a piece of shit. And really, you should know better. And weren't you trained to have better instincts? And . . .*

Ben kissed her, and took her in his arms. 'There's no need to sabotage this.'

Ren slept on the flight to Atlanta, and slept on the flight to Sarasota. It was an exercise in anthropology watching people's reaction to her facial injury as she walked through the airports.

She rented a car and drove to Armand Circle where she was meeting Shep Collier in a restaurant called Venezia. She found him sitting in the corner with a coffee. He was dressed suitably expensively in tones of beige and cream. When he reached out to shake Ren's hand, she could smell lemon cologne.

'Thank you for meeting me,' she said.

He nodded. 'That's not a problem.' He called the waiter over and ordered them coffee.

'Excuse my appearance,' said Ren. 'I had a minor car issue last night.'

'It looks sore,' said Collier.

'It is.'

'So, what can I help you with?' said Collier.

'I don't have a lot of time,' said Ren. 'I know that whatever is going on, you must be under incredible pressure, or in danger. I can't see another reason why you would lie to your family, to the entire nation, and to the FBI.'

His face stayed impassive. 'I don't know what you're talking about.'

Ren leaned in to him. 'I spoke with Tina Bowers. That girl is frightened . . .' *Or naively buoyant, one or the other.*

Collier blinked. 'She is seventeen years old, and she's been embroiled in a national scandal. Of course she's frightened.'

'It's more than that,' said Ren.

'I'd rather not talk about Tina Bowers,' said Collier. 'There is nothing more that I can say to you about her.'

'Think of Mark Whaley's wife and children,' said Ren. 'I presume you looked up the story after we last spoke.'

Collier nodded.

'I don't believe that Mark Whaley murdered Shelby Royce,' said Ren. 'I believe he was set up. There was no evidence at first, but now it appears that there may be . . .'

'I just don't know how I can help you,' said Collier.

'You didn't sleep with Tina Bowers, Mr Collier.'

Something in his face changed. 'Why would I admit to sleeping with an underage prostitute if I hadn't?'

'Well, you tell me,' said Ren. 'She said that she didn't sleep with you.'

'She hasn't gone on the record with this . . .' said Collier.

'You seem very sure of that,' said Ren.

'My lawyer would have informed me.'

That or you know the ruthlessness of the people behind this.

'I am *not* giving up on this,' said Ren.

Collier stared at her, for what seemed like minutes. 'I said everything I have to say one month ago . . .' He paused. 'I was standing in front of the whole country, and I thought that was it, that was the end. I just can't have this coming into my home any more. My family is too important to me. I love my wife too much.'

His eyes were boring into Ren's, she could feel the intensity.

Something is going on here. What the hell is it?

'I'm sorry I can't help you,' said Collier.

'I can't say that this will end here,' said Ren. 'I'm sorry.'

'Well, I can only hope,' said Collier. 'It's difficult for a man like me to lose control over events in his life.' He paused. 'If just *one person* could take another look at what it was that first impressed them about me . . . well, it would be a positive step. Who knows what that could lead to?'

'Thank you for your time, Mr Collier,' said Ren.

Ren ran to the rental car and jumped inside. She grabbed her notebook from her purse. Paul Louderback's advice came back to her: 'write everything down verbatim: skim over what an interviewee is telling you and you miss vital verbal clues.'

It was simple advice that had been implanted early on, and reinforced constantly by Gary Dettling in UC training.

You can't pull a notebook out during a drug deal.

Ren wrote down as much as she could remember of what Shep Collier said to her. She shoved the notebook in her bag, put the car in gear, and made it to the airport in half the time it had taken her to get to the restaurant.

She checked in, went to the airport shop, and bought two

boxes of candy. She sat in the lounge and began to read what she had written. She underlined, she separated phrases, she closed her eyes, she remembered the nuances in his delivery: where he paused, when he stared.

She finished by writing out again the words she believed that Shep Collier wanted her to hear.

"I said everything I have to say one month ago. I was standing in front of the whole country."

He's talking about his press conference. When he resigned, a month ago . . .

'I just can't have this coming into my home any more.'

Whatever 'this' is, he is protecting his family.

'It's difficult for a man like me to lose control over events in his life.'

What he's gone through is out of his hands.

'If just *one person* could take another look at what it was that first impressed them about me . . . '

Me! He didn't mean his voters. His eyes had riveted hers. And the first thing that had impressed Ren about him was his resignation speech. She had told him that on the phone.

'I was impressed by parts of your resignation speech. They didn't sound scripted.'

He had ended today with: ' . . . *it would be a positive step. Who knows what that could lead to?'*

Holy shit. Whatever 'this' is, if I can work that out, it would be a step forward, it would lead to something.

Ren pulled out her laptop, and fired it up. Her flight was being called.

No. No. No. Not now.

She went on line, she opened YouTube. She searched for Shep Collier's press conference. Then she heard her name being called out over the tannoy.

No. I have something I have to watch right now.

Ren heard her name again. She looked up at the desk, and the three uniformed staff members with their bored faces, filing things away, shutting things down, and stretching a piece of fabric from one pole to another to stop anyone . . .

Ren slammed the laptop shut and ran for the desk.

Shit. Shit. Shit.

'Have you got Wi-Fi on board?' said Ren as she held out her ticket.

The attendant looked at her as if to say, 'You barely have a seat.'

'No, ma'am,' she said.

'Shit,' said Ren. 'I'm sorry, but shit.'

'Ma'am, you really will have to make your way to the aircraft.' A fake smile stretched across her face.

I want to punch you all. You assholes.

53

The plane landed at Denver airport and Ren ran. She found a bank of seats and sat down. She pulled out her laptop. Beside her, a mother leaned forward suddenly and picked up her son who had been whining on the floor in front of her. For a moment, Ren wondered if the woman thought she looked dangerous, with her black eye and air of panic, but she was focused only on her son. She stood the little boy in front of her, and held his shoulders.

She said very seriously, 'You mustn't pretend to be sick, just because you don't want to be here. It is dangerous. What if you really were sick, and mama just thought you were pretending?'

The little boy stared at his feet.

'Now, sit up here beside your mama, read your book.'

She smiled at Ren.

'Beautifully done,' said Ren.

The mother laughed. 'He is a trying child.'

Ren went to YouTube. She put on her headphones and watched Shep Collier's speech. She watched it again.

Nothing. What am I supposed to be hearing here, what am I supposed to be seeing?

She watched it again. She took off the headphones.

Nothing.

Ren drove down I-70 toward the office. She was thinking about Shep Collier. He was framed. He had clearly been stepping on toes.

And what about Mark Whaley? What had he done?

She dialed Gary's cell.

'Gary, it's Ren. There's something going on with Shep Collier, but I don't know what. He stuck to his story, but it seems to me that he has no choice. He was dancing around something. I think he was implying that I should watch his press conference, but I did, several times, and I got nothing. He must be under surveillance. If I was listening in, everything he said was solid, it sounded like he was giving me nothing. But I think he was giving me something. I just . . . don't know yet what that is.'

'So, it was a wasted trip . . .'

'No,' said Ren. 'I don't think so. I've built up a trust with him . . . to some degree.'

'That's great, Ren.' His voice was flat.

Shit. Shit. Shit.

Ren dialed Colin's cell phone. 'Colin? It's Ren. Will you come with me to MeesterBrandt headquarters on Monday?'

'Why?' said Colin.

'I need your charm to talk to the boss.'

'Well, it's in no short supply,' said Colin.

'R-O-T-F-L,' said Ren.

'Why are you calling me now?' said Colin.

'Why not?' said Ren.

'Hey, hold on,' said Colin. 'Naomi wants to talk to you.'

'Hey, girl,' said Naomi. 'We missed you the other night! Heard about your fender bender. Get your ass out here. You owe me. We're in . . . where are we, Col?'

'I can't,' said Ren. 'I've got to—'

'I'm not taking no for an answer,' said Naomi.

'I'm afraid you're going to have to,' said Ren. 'I gotta go!'

She's more nuts than me.

Ren's phone beeped with a text: It's Saturday night. Do you know where your tutu3 is?

Ren laughed and texted back. Tutu3 – love it. Am back.

Paul Louderback replied: Drinks it is!

Paul was sitting in a Larimer Street bar, with a lite beer in front of him.

'Girl's drink,' said Ren.

Paul smiled. 'Ouch. Your face is worse than I thought.'

'I look like a thug.'

'Let me get you a glass of champagne to counter that.'

'Then I'll look like a moll.'

'Why I oughta . . .' He called the waiter and ordered the drink.

Ren sat down. She filled him in on Shep Collier.

'The thick plottens,' said Paul.

Ren nodded. 'It sure does.' She could hear her cell phone vibrate. *I bet that's Ben.*

She stared into her drink.

'Where have you gone?' said Paul.

She turned to him.

'You look serious,' he said.

'Paul, I think you need to go back and work things out with Marianne.'

'What?' said Paul.

'I hope I'm not being too blunt . . . ' *But I feel sorry for Marianne, I feel bad for being in on a secret that she isn't.*

'But . . . I thought . . .'

Me and your protégées could share?

'What did you think?' said Ren.

'I . . . don't know,' said Paul. 'Maybe that you and me could try and . . . maybe we could work.'

The romance.

'You and Marianne still love each other,' said Ren. 'It's obvious.' *Her cry for help is echoing all the way to Denver.*

Paul stared down at the table.

'It sounds to me like Marianne only left you as a last resort.'

He looked up. 'Maybe.'

Then how did you let it go so far? 'It's not too late, is it?' said Ren.

'Maybe not,' said Paul. 'I . . . I wasn't there for her. I can see that now. Or the girls. They are spending more time with me now than they were when I was living with them. They have hours of my time in a row . . .'

'And look how happy they are,' said Ren. 'At least with that part of it. Go call Marianne. You can work this out.'

'What about her . . . new man?' said Paul.

'I think her old man is the one she wants,' said Ren. 'That old man is her husband. For better or worse . . .'

Paul said nothing.

'Men need sex to feel loved,' said Ren. 'And a lot of women need to feel loved to have sex. I'm not one of them, but you get the picture. I think you thought I'd solve the sex end of things for you, and maybe Marianne thought her new man would solve the emotional end of things for her. We look elsewhere for the things we're not getting at home . . .'

'I think you're being harsh on everyone with all that,' said Paul. 'I wasn't just interested in you for sex.'

'I actually know that,' said Ren. 'I don't think you're that much of an asshole. But, I also know that you were never really looking at me as a serious contender . . .'

'And neither were you looking at me . . .'

'That's probably true,' said Ren. *Yet how foolish was I to let it muddy the waters for so long?*

'So,' said Paul.

'So,' said Ren. 'Without managing to do each other any great harm, we're not really good for each other, are we? We're in that strange gray area. But, despite being someone who I think is wonderful, well, I think you're going to have to be someone else's wonderful.'

She thought of the inscription on the little blue hardback.

'But you are beautiful, Annie, and you are wonderful, and you are joyful.'

She smiled at Paul Louderback.

You can be someone else's. I'd like to be someone's Annie.

54

Colin and Ren stood in the foyer of MeesterBrandt Pharmaceuticals, waiting for the elevator.

'Do you think that up there in those offices,' said Ren, 'they feel any connection with the rest of the world? Or do they just stare at accounts and see massive figures and think "high five" and keep on trucking?'

'Keep on trucking . . .' said Colin.

'I'd love to just grab one of them and say, "sorry to bother you while you're counting your profits, but come with me," and take them to some broken-down home, where a mother, doped up on antipsychotics, is laying on her sofa watching daytime television, while her three children, diagnosed with behavioral disorders to qualify for disability, are crying because they miss their big brother who's in prison because he's been doped up too and went crazy and killed someone and he's fifteen . . . and say to this pharma guy "You know those amazing drugs you make? Congratulations, you really are changing lives."'

People had started gathering around the elevator. Colin was frowning at Ren. She stopped talking. The doors opened and they rode to the thirty-fifth floor. Ren took a deep breath as she got off.

Bring it on, bitches.

Nolan Carr was as close to attractive as he could ever be, and it was money, not taste, that had brought him there. He was well-groomed, he wore the right clothes. His shoes, his watch, his cuff links were high end, but ultimately, he was a plain man with a water-retention problem.

'Nice to meet you,' said Ren.

'Likewise,' he said, shaking her hand.

Eye-dart to the tits.

Carr shook hands with Colin.

'Mr Carr,' said Ren. 'We're here because new evidence has emerged that casts doubt on our belief that the deaths of Mark Whaley and Shelby Royce were a murder-suicide.'

'Oh,' said Carr, nodding. 'OK. I had assumed that . . . what happened was . . . what happened.'

'We're now looking at the possibility of foul play,' said Colin.

'I'm not sure how I'm the best person to help you,' said Carr. 'I know very little about Mark Whaley's personal life.'

'We're here because we don't think this concerns Mr Whaley's personal life,' said Colin.

'You think it's about his professional life?' said Carr.

'Yes,' said Ren. 'You work in a multi-billion dollar industry, and it's not uncommon in an industry where there's that much money at stake . . .' She paused at his reaction. 'I'm sorry. Are you surprised by that?'

'I know you might find this hard to believe,' said Carr. 'But MeesterBrandt doesn't feel that way to me. It feels like a small company to me. I see a company whose staff works very hard to make it a success. I find it hard to see it as part of something sinister.'

Small company, my fat ass.

Colin leaned forward. 'Did MeesterBrandt have any significant business deals in progress? Anything that might have impacted on Mark Whaley or on the company?'

'Mark was our CFO,' said Carr. 'It's a behind-the-scenes job, effectively. He was in charge of the financials, but he wasn't out there making deals, or . . . he just wasn't visible.'

'What kind of relationship did you have with Mark Whaley?' said Ren.

'I spoke to another agent about that during the investigation,' said Carr.

'That was more about what you suspected about Mark Whaley's private life,' said Ren. 'I'm interested in whether or not you and Mark Whaley got along.'

'I was his boss,' said Carr. 'That was our relationship. We wouldn't have socialized outside of work, if that's what you mean.'

'Did you know that Mark was planning to take early retirement next year to spend more time with his kids?'

'No, I did not know that,' said Carr.

'But you can understand,' said Ren, 'how a man one year from retirement mightn't be the number one candidate for suicide.'

'A married father caught sleeping with underage girls would always be a candidate for suicide,' said Carr.

'Why did you say underage girls, plural?' said Ren.

'Well, I hardly suspect this was his first time,' said Carr.

'Is there something you know about Mark Whaley and underage girls, Mr Carr?' said Ren.

'No. I . . . it just came out, there's nothing to it.'

'Are you familiar with Title 18, United States Code, Section 1001?' said Ren.

'No,' said Carr.

'It's a crime to lie to a federal agent,' said Ren.

'I don't know anything about Mark Whaley and underage girls,' said Carr. 'I swear to God.'

'We'd like to get your permission to search Mr Whaley's office and to take his computer away for forensic examination, please.'

'That won't be a problem,' said Carr. 'Can I ask what new evidence came to light?'

'No,' said Ren.

He paused.

Well, that's someone who's not used to hearing no.

'Could you please take us to Mark Whaley's office?' said Colin.

Carr stood up. 'Yes, absolutely. Follow me.'

'I find it fascinating,' said Ren, as they walked along the hallway, 'I read a quote recently about Henry Gadsden. Who was he again? Merck's Chief Executive. Thirty years ago, he said he'd like the company to be like Wrigley's. He'd like to sell drugs to healthy people, because then he could sell to everyone.'

She could see a smirk at the corner of Carr's mouth. 'Gadsden was a very successful man.'

'Was he, though?' said Ren. 'Define success in that instance. Couldn't we all sit down and come up with a diabolical plan? I have no doubt, for example, that I could commit the perfect murder. If I went ahead and did that, would that make me successful?'

Nolan Carr slowed and turned to her.

'Or,' said Ren, 'would it only be successful if I made a huge amount of money from it? Or if I didn't get caught?'

'Agent . . . I'm sorry, I've forgotten your name?'
Asshole.
'How do you make sense of things?' said Ren.
'I'm sorry?' said Carr. 'Of what?'
'Just how people talk about the amazing advances in the pharmaceutical industry, yet the number of people on disability because of mental illness more than doubled in the twenty years since Prozac was launched. And it gets worse when it comes to kids: in the same time period, the increase was thirty-five fold.'

Ren and Colin walked to his SUV. Colin was carrying Mark Whaley's computer.

'What the fuck was that about?' said Colin.

'What?' said Ren. 'Nolan Carr's a lying son-of-a-bitch. I did my research on him. It's like a six degrees of Kevin Bacon thing. The first pharmaceutical company he worked for had a painkiller that was taken off the market for causing heart attacks and strokes – not before it made hundreds of millions of dollars, of course. The most recent company he worked for – Lang Pharmaceuticals – the one MeesterBrandt bought over – their drug, Cerxus, was meant to have all kinds of side effects, but it's still on the market, just with a black-box warning. Unlike almost all the antidepressants out there, Cerxus managed to escape without paying fines or settlements because of the side effects. Each time, Nolan Carr walked away with a clean sheet. They couldn't prove he did anything—'

'Anything what?' said Colin.

'Off-label promotion of drugs, for example,' said Ren. 'Getting doctors to prescribe drugs for uses that they haven't been approved for,' said Ren. 'So, say the FDA approves Cerxus to treat depression. That's great, but Lang's sales reps fly off like evil flying monkeys and whisper in the docs' ears, "actually, this really works for insomnia or migraines or whatever" . . . while stuffing cupcakes in their mouths, tickets for ball games in their pockets . . . it's not illegal for the doctor to prescribe a drug for something it hasn't been approved for. It's just illegal for him to take money for doing it. And the companies get around this anyway by paying doctors and psychiatrists speaker's fees and shit like that to say how wonderful the drug is or to enroll patients in trials. The FDA only needs two successful trials to approve a drug. You can run fifty that prove nothing, but if you get two that show your drug works better than a placebo, you're in luck. It doesn't even have to be compared to an older drug.'

'And Nolan Carr was the boss of these companies?' said Colin.

'No,' said Ren. *You awkward prick.* 'That's not the point. He clearly has no problem being involved in all kinds of shit. Do you want some gum?'

'No,' said Colin.

Ren took a packet of gum out of her purse, slid out a stick and started chewing it.

'You were still out of line in there,' said Colin.

Go fuck yourself.

She was about to get into the SUV. She dropped her gum. She bent down and saw Colin's feet.

She thought of Laurie Whaley, and the boy at the airport with the fake stomach ache, and Laurie Whaley and her stomach ache, and the feet at the other side of the SUV, and how Laurie had cried out, she was bent double, her parents rushed to her side, as any parent would. And from the passenger side of the SUV – feet. And as Gary said – one looked higher than the other.

Oh my God. Someone was getting out of the SUV. Someone had been inside The Whaleys' all along.

Cathy Merritt was taken aback when she opened the door to Ren.

'I need to speak to Laurie,' said Ren. 'Can I come in?'

'You can come in, of course,' said Cathy, 'but I'd rather you didn't speak to Laurie. We've already agreed to speak with Agent Ross . . .'

Fuck Sylvie fucking Ross!

'I can get Agent Ross here too, if you like,' said Ren, 'but I need to talk to Laurie right away.'

I'm not fucking around, bitch. Can you see that in my fucking face? Can you respond to that, you weak fucking bitch? Do you fucking get any of this? I swear to God, I want to punch that fucking face of yours.

Ren's heart was pounding. She became acutely aware of her firearms, and aware of her fists. She briefly imagined punching Cathy Merritt, pushing her gun against her forehead.

What is wrong with me?

Cathy Merritt looked scared.

Good. I could care fucking less. Fuck you. And let me the fuck in to your house.

Laurie Whaley sat on the sofa beside Ren.

'Laurie, I'd like to ask you about what happened before you went into the hotel on that Saturday night. We don't need to talk about what happened in the room, I just want to ask you about the parking garage.'

'OK,' she said. 'But . . . nothing happened.'

'I know you told me you had a stomach ache – what kind of stomach ache?' said Ren.

'Um . . . like . . . what do you mean?' said Laurie, glancing at her.

Frightened eyes.

'Was it a sharp pain?' said Ren. 'Or did you feel like you wanted to throw up, or . . .?'

'A sharp pain, I guess,' said Laurie. She was staring at the floor again.

'Can I ask you another question?' said Ren.

Laurie nodded. Her little fists were clenched, squeezed together, resting on her lap. Her legs were shaking.

Ren reached out and laid a gentle hand on hers.

'Sweetheart,' said Ren. 'Who was in the SUV with you the night you went to the hotel?'

Laurie kept her eyes on the floor. Then she looked up at Ren, her shoulders rigid. 'In the SUV?' she said. 'Dad and Erica and Leo.'

Ren nodded. 'OK.' She allowed Laurie some time. 'Was there someone else?' said Ren.

'No,' said Laurie, shaking her head. 'No . . . who do you mean, someone else? Like, who?'

'I don't know,' said Ren. 'I'm wondering did you notice anything unusual during your trip.'

'No,' said Laurie. 'But . . . why are you asking me all this?'

'Because we have a video and it really looks like someone might have been getting out of your dad's SUV while you had your stomach ache. But – not your dad or Erica, because they were busy looking after you. And Leo was in Erica's arms. I watched it all. So, I'd like you to tell me who was it that could have been getting out of the SUV.'

Laurie said nothing.

'I think you know,' said Ren. 'You're not going to get into any trouble for telling me, Laurie. I can promise you that. Was there someone in the SUV that night?'

Tears welled in Laurie's eyes. 'Do you have to tell my mom?'

Ren nodded. 'I do,' said Ren, 'but we really need to know, because we have to make sure that we have all the right information so that we can do our job properly.'

Laurie took in a big breath. 'It was Joshua. My stepbrother, Joshua.'

55

Ren allowed the weight of what Laurie said to sink in.

'And how come Joshua had gone to Breckenridge?' said Ren.

'He is going to get in so much trouble,' said Laurie. 'He's going to kill me.'

'He won't,' said Ren. 'Why don't you talk through what happened and we can go from there.'

She began tentatively. 'That day, dad and Erica brought me to my house to pick up my new jacket,' said Laurie. 'Joshua was there. He was grounded, because . . . a couple of months ago, Mrs Ronson, down the street, she's, like, really old . . . she was on vacation, and someone broke into her house. And it was terrible; they smashed up all her stuff, and emptied out her liquor cabinet, and all kinds of things. They broke an urn, and threw her husband's ashes all over the floor. Mr Ronson had always been so kind to everybody. And they did other terrible things.

'There's a group home a few miles away, and everyone was saying that some kid there did it and . . . It was so sad. Poor Mrs Ronson, she's all alone.'

Laurie took a few breaths. 'Mom and Dale . . . I heard them asking Joshua about it. I couldn't believe it. He said he didn't know anything about it, but it was like they knew that he was lying or something. They said that they wouldn't tell Mrs Ronson, or anyone, but he still said he didn't know anything about it. But they must have known something, because they still grounded him – for four whole weekends. Mom said that she was sick to her stomach, that she didn't want to even look at him. They told him he could only come out of his room for meals. They took his Xbox. But I got to have it in my room. That drove him nuts. They let him have his television, but that's because that was the only other way to keep him in his room. They were so mad. I even saw Dale crying about it one day. I heard him tell Mom that he thought things were going to get better, but they'd gotten worse. And Mom told him to give it time.

'That Saturday was the last day Josh was grounded. And when I called to the house, I told him I was going to Breck and that Shaun White was going to be there. He's a famous snowboarder, we play his game. And I was going to get to see him up close, and I was going to get his autograph. I wanted Josh to be jealous. I liked the Ronsons a lot. They were really old, and really kind to all the kids, and even though Joshua said he didn't do it, I know he did.

'He totally flipped out when he heard about Breck. He was super jealous. Anyway, Dad and Erica had fixed Leo's clothes and we got in our car, and next thing, we've been in the car, like, twenty minutes, and I see Joshua there . . . just by my feet, under this blanket thing. I jumped, but he had his finger up to his mouth. Leo was sleeping, he always sleeps in the car. And I was just totally freaked out. I was thinking "What the heck is Joshua doing, where does he think he's going?" But I knew . . . I knew he was that jealous. He's obsessed with Shaun White. But . . . I just didn't get what he was thinking. He knew we were going to be gone until Sunday evening, and Mom and Dale could easily have checked on him. And, like, he might not have even gotten a ride home. But he obviously didn't care. It was crazy dangerous.

'When we got to the parking garage in the hotel, everyone got out of the SUV, and Joshua whispered to me, like, "distract them", so I pretended I had a stomach ache, and when I went back into the car to get my bag, he was gone.'

'Do you know where Joshua went?' said Ren.

'A bunch of his friends were going to Breck – he was probably going to hook up with them, go see Shaun White.'

'He didn't have a lot of time before he left the house,' said Ren. 'Do you know was he planning to call them when he got to Breck?'

Laurie stared at the floor. 'Um . . . Dale took his cell phone when he was grounded. Same thing they say to me – "It's our cell phone, we pay the bills, it's so we can keep in touch. If you're grounded, we know you're in your room, why would we need to phone you" . . .'

'So . . . what happened after Joshua left?' said Ren.

'Me and dad and Erica and Leo were in the room, we watched a movie, dad and Erica went down for dinner. Shelby and I hung out for a little while . . .'

Please tell me what happened next. Please.

Laurie broke down. Her crying was heart-wrenching.

'It's OK,' said Ren. 'It's OK, sweetheart.'

Laurie cried harder. 'It's not,' she said. 'It's not.'

'Is there something else, Laurie?' said Ren.

Laurie started to cry, but her head was bowed, and her tears dropped onto the carpet in a continuous stream. 'No,' said Laurie. 'No. Are you going to talk to him? Are you going to ask him about all this?'

'Yes,' said Ren.

'Don't tell him I told you,' said Laurie.

Ren stood up. 'Let me call your mom and Dale in here, OK?'

Laurie looked terrified.

'They won't be mad at you,' said Ren. 'I can tell them what happened, you don't have to worry about that.'

Cathy and Dale came in and took the chairs opposite the sofa.

'I didn't say anything,' said Laurie. 'She had a video. She saw Joshua in the parking garage.'

Cathy and Dale looked bewildered. They turned to Ren.

'We got hold of some surveillance footage of the parking garage at The Merlin,' said Ren. 'It was clear that someone was getting out of the SUV, and that they couldn't have done that without Laurie seeing them or without Laurie's help.'

'But . . . Joshua?' said Cathy. She looked at Laurie. 'What was he doing in Breckenridge?'

'He went to see Shaun White,' said Laurie. 'He just didn't want to be grounded any more. He was jealous of me.'

'Where is Joshua right now?' said Ren.

'He's staying at a friend's,' said Cathy.

'Is he close by?' said Ren.

'No, gosh, he's an hour away at least.'

'Could I ask you to do me a favor?' said Ren. 'Now that we know he was there, well, he could have been a witness to something. And also, I need to know how he got home that night. That could also reveal something.'

'What is happening here exactly?' said Cathy. 'I thought the investigation was closed.'

'No,' said Ren. 'No it is not.'

*   *   *

Ren went back to the office and took out all the statements from everyone who was in the hotel that night. She had read through them before – who was there around seven, who was there between eleven and twelve-thirty. There were enough people to look at the inbetween times. But she was rattled by Joshua Merritt, the fact that there was someone there that nobody knew about. He may not have been the only one.

She stopped at a couple, the Obermanns, Bill and Stella. They checked in at 9.30 and their statement said that they were alone checking in. There was no-one else in reception.

What about behind the desk?

Ren dialed Bill Obermann and asked him to confirm his statement.

'Yes, that's correct,' said Bill. 'We didn't see anyone else in reception.'

'And was the desk clerk there when you arrived?' said Ren.

He paused. 'Yes,' said Bill. 'He was. He was on a call, but he took care of us right away afterward.'

'OK,' said Ren. 'Well, thank you for your time.'

'My pleasure,' said Bill.

'Could I speak with your wife, please?' said Ren.

'Sure,' said Bill. 'Let me go get her.'

'Hello, this is Stella Obermann.'

'Hello,' said Ren. 'I'm following up on your earlier interview about the night you checked into The Merlin.'

'Yes,' said Mrs Obermann.

'Were you at the check-in desk with your husband?' said Ren. 'Or did you sit it out?'

'I was with him,' said Mrs Obermann. 'Although I had a mind to sit down. The desk clerk took his time to attend to us.'

'But he was there when you arrived?' said Ren.

'Yes, he was,' said Mrs Obermann. 'But he was on a call. A *personal* call.'

Why am I not surprised?

'Bill was not very happy about that,' said Mrs Obermann, 'but the poor boy was consoling a friend – I could allow for that.'

'Consoling a friend . . .?' said Ren. *Indulge me.* 'Can you remember any of the details?'

'I think he was talking to a friend who had broken up with someone. He said something like "chill, she'll be back" or "I'm sure she'll be back".'

Okaay.

'And could you hear the other side of the conversation?' said Ren.

'No, I couldn't,' said Mrs Obermann. 'But I got the impression it was a male, because it sounded like another boy was trying to move in on the girlfriend, because the desk clerk said, "you have got to watch him. He's like Superman."'

Oh. My. God. 'Mrs Obermann, could he by any chance have said "Spiderman"?'

Mrs Obermann paused. 'Oh, yes, yes,' she said. 'Yes. You're right. I knew it was a superhero. And, sorry, yes – it was Spiderman, because I remember thinking about this other boy catching this girl, whoever she was, in his web.'

Jared Labati was not talking to a friend about a break up. He was talking to Shelby Royce. And he was telling her that Laurie Whaley would be back. Laurie Whaley was not in the room. Laurie Whaley was gone. By 9.30 p.m.

56

Ren called Gary from her Jeep. 'Gary, I'm on my way to Breck. Laurie Whaley was gone from the room by 9.30 p.m. Jared Labati was overheard speaking at reception, telling someone to "chill, she'll be back", which had to have been a reference to Laurie. He also made a reference to Spiderman, which we know has to be Leo.'

The sign for Golden flashed by. She was half an hour from Breck.

'Jared Labati definitely knows what happened in that room,' said Ren. 'He was telling Shelby Royce to chill, but still, he was telling her that Laurie would be back. You wouldn't say that if a child had been abducted. Why would he say that?'

'Go talk to this kid with Bob,' said Gary. 'Do not talk to him alone.'

Jared Labati was on a day off. He was dressed in his regular clothes – oversized jeans, navy hoodie. He listened to Bob Gage tell him what they knew.

'Why were you so relaxed about it?' said Ren. 'Why were

you telling Shelby Royce to chill when an eleven-year-old girl went missing?'

He stared at the ground. 'Because I didn't think it was a big deal.'

'HOW?' said Ren. 'How could you not have thought that it was a big deal?'

'Because . . .' He shrugged. 'Because she was with family.'

You are insane. 'She was gone, Jared! Her family were in the restaurant! She was not with her family!'

'I meant her brother,' said Jared. 'Her brother, stepbrother, whatever . . .'

'Her brother?' said Ren. *WTF?*

She glanced at Bob.

Jared nodded. 'All I know is what Shelby told me. He showed up at the room, he went nuts at the little girl, he pushed her and she hurt her head. He freaked out, and told Shelby to stay where she was and shut her mouth. He took his stepsister away. He said they'd be back before eleven. When they didn't show by eleven thirty, Shelby was flipping out. The only thing she could think of to do was be naked – she knew that the dad wouldn't come in to the room any further. It happened to her once when she was babysitting, by accident – the dad walked in when she was getting changed, and she said he ran from the room like he was on fire. So she knew that this guy would do the same. Except, he waited outside the room, then knocked and came back in when she said she was dressed. Shelby said he was looking for something in his suitcase. The miracle was he didn't check on the kids.'

'And when Laurie didn't come back, Shelby just left?' said Ren. 'She left a three-year-old boy alone—'

'No,' said Jared. 'That's not fair. I called her when I saw the Whaleys leave the restaurant, and she waited a minute or two, so she was only out of the room, like, one minute, and she knew they'd be back.'

'So Shelby Royce was not abducted. She ran.'

Jared nodded.

'And you gave her somewhere to stay . . .' said Ren.

His eyes went wide. 'Uh . . .'

'You gave her the keys to one of the houses on Wildcard Drive, didn't you?' said Ren.

He nodded again. 'I screwed up. I know I did. I screwed up really bad. I liked Shelby. I cared about her . . .'

'Did you?' said Ren.

Jared paused. 'I . . . I did. Why?'

'Did you look for anything in return for helping Shelby out?' said Ren.

He stared at the ground. 'I don't know what you mean . . .'

'I think you do.'

'I don't.'

'Jared. I can get a warrant for a DNA sample.'

'She wanted to do it,' said Jared. 'She was the one who wanted it.'

Take a look at yourself. Inside and out. And say that again.

Ren sat in Bob's office with Gary on speaker.

'So, the mystery semen is a mystery no more,' said Ren. 'Jared Labati blackmailed Shelby Royce into oral sex.'

'That kid gives me the creeps,' said Bob.

'And even worse, it's his word against ours,' said Ren. 'He can keep saying it was consensual, we can keep saying it was rape, but we've nothing to back it up. That skeevy piece of shit will still be out there spiking drinks or whatever other fucked-up shit he wants to do.'

'We can still get him on lying to a federal officer,' said Gary. 'Where was he hiding her?'

'In number three, Wildcard Drive,' said Bob.

'We'll send an ERT,' said Gary.

'He went back and forth to her over the weekend,' said Ren. 'The last time he says he saw her was Monday night while everyone was at the vigil . . . when he claims they had this consensual experience. He says he doesn't know what happened after that.'

'So,' said Gary. 'We know where Shelby Royce went, but where did Joshua and Laurie go? Did Joshua bring her with him and his friends? Did she want to see Shaun White too?'

'And how did they make it back to Denver?' said Ren.

'We need to get Laurie and Joshua in separate rooms and find out what the hell is going on,' said Gary.

'I'll call Cathy Merritt,' said Ren.

'Cathy, it's Ren, did you speak with Joshua?'

'Yes, yes, I did,' said Cathy. 'And I approached it calmly so he wouldn't flip out and go silent on me. I told him he wasn't in trouble, but he needed to let me know how he got back from Breckenridge that night. And he refused to tell me.'

Hello? And you're OK with that? 'Did he acknowledge he got a ride back with one of his friends?'

'No,' said Cathy. 'He's saying nothing.'

'Did your husband speak with him?' said Ren.

'Yes,' said Cathy. 'But it's the same thing – he won't say anything.'

'But, Cathy, this is a criminal investigation, he can't just say nothing.'

'I don't know what else to do,' said Cathy.

Be a parent.

*   *   *

Ren called Gary.

'His parents are being obstructive. If we can't get the truth out of Josh, I'd like to call the school, get the names of his friends, take a trip to the wonderful world of Facebook, find out which of them went to Breck that night, then stock up on some traffic cam or tunnel footage. Or both.'

'Where was Laurie Whaley during all this?' said Gary.

'Not with her father, that's for sure.'

By eight o'clock that night, Ren and Colin were sitting in the Merritts' living room facing Dale and Cathy.

'Is Joshua still saying nothing about who drove him back from Breckenridge that night?' said Ren.

'Yes,' said Dale.

'We have tried so hard to get a name from him,' said Cathy. 'But you know teenagers. They're loyal to their friends, they won't "rat them out", as they see it. No matter what you threaten them with.'

'Well,' said Ren. 'I tried hard too . . .'

Cathy frowned. 'Pardon me?'

'I tried hard to get the name,' said Ren. 'And here's what I've got: ten thirty-two p.m., a car drives through the round-about in Breckenridge – from the direction of Denver. Eleven twenty p.m., the same car drives back through the round-about, in the direction of Denver. Then, three a.m., the same car drives through the roundabout and exits toward the Sheriff's Office.'

Dale and Cathy said nothing.

'So,' said Ren. 'My question is: what were you doing in Breckenridge between the hours of ten thirty-two and eleven twenty p.m. on Saturday, November 14? Because I know that after three a.m., you were in the Sheriff's Office with me.'

57

Dale Merritt sat forward in his seat and Ren realized for the first time the intensity of a man she had thought was a gentle giant. He was clearly someone who would do anything to protect his young.

'What would you do?' said Dale. 'Your son calls you to say that he accidentally hurt his stepsister. *Accidentally*. He's in a state of panic. What was I meant to do apart from going to him, and helping him?'

What about Laurie, helping her?

'Was it accidental?' said Ren. 'It doesn't look accidental to me. You'd have to push someone pretty hard to split their head open on a headboard. This wasn't just him bumping into her and knocking her down. Colin is going to go talk to Joshua after this, and I'll be talking to Laurie.'

'But—' said Cathy.

Try to argue with me.

'I'm sorry,' said Ren. 'We need to find out what happened for once and for all. I understand your need to help your son, Mr Merritt. What I don't understand is all the rest of it. All the lying, the covering up . . .'

'We know absolutely nothing about what happened between Mark and the babysitter,' said Cathy. 'We were as shocked as anyone else. I have no idea what happened there. I didn't think Mark was capable of anything like that. We just . . . we just . . . we did the wrong thing, but we thought . . . I don't know what we thought.

We just needed a few days until we worked something out. I don't know. We didn't have a plan. We wanted to make sure she wouldn't tell on Joshua. Dale couldn't bear to have him taken away.'

'He was grounded for breaking into a neighbor's home, is that correct?' said Ren.

Silence.

'Laurie had a head injury that night,' said Ren. 'What did you do about that?'

'We monitored her,' said Cathy.

'You didn't bring her to a doctor to get it checked out?' said Ren.

Cathy paused. 'We . . . didn't think she needed that. If she blacked out, maybe, but she didn't.'

'How could you watch your ex-husband go through so much anguish over his missing daughter?'

'Because he never noticed mine,' said Cathy. 'He never noticed my anguish for all those years.'

You scary, scary bitch.

Laurie Whaley was sitting cross-legged against a pile of pillows on her bed. There was an iPod on the bed beside her, a bottle of purple nail polish on the nightstand. She smiled at Ren when she came in.

'Can I grab this seat?' said Ren, pointing to the one at Laurie's desk.

'Sure,' said Laurie.

Ren sat down. 'How are you doing?'

'I'm good,' said Laurie. Her gaze was unsteady.

'I've got a few more questions for you,' said Ren.

'OK,' said Laurie.

'We know now that Joshua came to your hotel room, Laurie.'

Laurie's eyes went wide. She opened her mouth to speak, but she couldn't.

'Do you know why Joshua came to the hotel room?' said Ren.

Tears welled in Laurie's eyes. 'Did you ask him about it?'

'My colleague Colin is speaking with Joshua right now.'

Laurie looked everywhere she could, apart from at Ren. She pulled her iPod by the headphones toward her, and started rotating it between her little fingers.

Ren waited. 'You have to tell me the truth, Laurie. You're free to talk to me about anything.'

Laurie nodded. She started to wind and unwind the headphones around the iPod.

'Joshua wanted the code to my cell phone,' she said eventually. 'I have two cell phones – one my parents gave me, the other one's a secret. Joshua got it for me. We both think mom and Dale's rule is dumb, that they get to see everything in our phones. None of my friends' parents look at their phones.'

D'ja think?

'I never take my other cell phone with me when I'm with my parents,' said Laurie. 'I'd left it in my room back home.'

'Is there a particular reason why you need two cell phones?' said Ren.

Laurie nodded. 'To have fun. To send jokes to my friends, and to talk to boys and stuff. I know I'm too young to have a relationship . . . but . . .'

Relationship. Sweet Jesus.

'So . . . the phone . . . and Joshua . . .' said Ren.

'Joshua knows where I keep it, so he took it, so he could phone his friends in Breck when he got there. But when he went to turn it on, duh, he didn't have the code. So he came back to the hotel to get the code. He called the desk from a payphone, and asked what room we were in . . .'

And idiot Jared Labati told him, and said nothing. 'And what time did he call to the room?' said Ren.

'Just after Erica and Dad went to dinner. Like, just after nine.'

'And what happened?' said Ren.

'He totally pushed in the door, and was, like, "what's your code, Laurie, what's your code?" I was, like, "Calm down, what's your problem, what are you even doing with my phone?" And he was, like, "Just give me the effing code, you effing b." He was crazy,' said Laurie, out of breath, finally releasing everything she had been holding back. 'It was freaky. I hadn't done anything to him. I had actually covered for him, and now he's, like, going insane.'

'Where was Shelby Royce at this point?' said Ren.

'She was freaking out, too,' said Laurie. 'I told her it's OK, he's my stepbrother, but she was, like, "It's not OK. It really is not OK. Something is wrong with him." She looked terrified. I said "There's nothing wrong with him, he's just crazy." That really bugged him.'

'What did he do next?' said Ren.

'I told him no way was he getting the code,' said Laurie. 'No way. I told him that he scared the crap out of me earlier, hiding in the car, and that he was in so much trouble, and that I didn't want to get the blame, and that he was spoiling everything.'

'And what did he do?' said Ren.

'I told him he was a fat freak . . .' Her lips started to tremble.

'It's OK,' said Ren. 'Take your time.'

Laurie burst into tears. 'Joshua has never ever hurt me,' said Laurie. 'We'd have these little fights, he'd tease me, whatever, but . . . this was so scary. He kind of jumped at me, and he grabbed my arm, and threw me down on the bed. He pinned my arms above my head, and he, like, stuck his face in mine, and shouted, "Put in your code, you stupid b."'

'Where was Shelby at this time?' said Ren.

'She tried to reach for the hotel phone, and he threw it across the room. Leo started crying next door, and Joshua said to Shelby, "If you touch that effing phone, if you call one person, I will effing kill you. Go in there, and shut that little shit up."

'I've never seen Joshua so mad,' said Laurie. 'So I grabbed my phone from him, and I punched in the wrong code. Then I did it again. And then I did it one more time.'

'So he was locked out of the phone,' said Ren.

'I told him I knew what he did to the Ronsons and that he was a psycho, but that made him even madder . . .'

'And where was Shelby at this point?' said Ren.

'She was in the bedroom calming Leo down.' She took a deep breath. 'Then she came out and Joshua asked her for her car keys, and she said she didn't have a car. He pulled out this big pen-knife and started waving it about. I couldn't believe it.

'I told him he had to stop, that this was going to get him in so much trouble. Even more trouble. I said that if he just

313

left we wouldn't say anything, we promised, but he kept saying "You will, I know you will."

'Then Joshua grabbed me up by the pajamas and he shook me real hard, and hit my head off the headboard. And then . . . I passed out. I woke up after that, and he took me out of the room. And then mom and Dale met us and took us home.'

58

Ren sat at her desk with her morning coffee and no food. She had typed up her interview with Laurie.

Gary came in and put a Danish on the desk beside her.

'I had one left over,' he said.

Ren smiled. 'Thank you.'

Colin sat back from his desk. 'OK – I'm done with my interview with Joshua. He is one nervous, jumpy kid. He could barely sit still. You want to keep snapping your fingers in front of his face to get him to focus. He was all over the place. Did you see his room? Shelves of shoot-em-up games. The kid just sits on his ass playing that shit all day. I'd say there were, like, two sports games.'

'There is something weird about all this,' said Ren. 'Something I can't put my finger on.' She paused. 'Hold on – does this latest version of events mean that Jonathan Meester stayed in the Merritts' house while they went to Breckenridge the first time to get Joshua and Laurie? Or did he leave and come back to make sure someone was there with Joshua and Laurie while the Merritts went back to Breckenridge to address the problem of their "missing" daughter?'

315

'The neighbor didn't say anything about Jonathan Meester's car leaving,' said Gary.

'Whatever the case,' said Ren. 'This means Jonathan Meester lied to us too. But why would he cover for them?'

'Because they're friends . . .' said Gary.

'Even if his own goddaughter had been hurt?' said Ren. 'Wouldn't his feelings for Laurie Whaley trump any desire to protect Joshua Merritt? I mean, what does he care about Joshua Merritt . . .'

Gary nodded.

'At the very least,' said Ren. 'Wouldn't he have called a doctor? MeesterBrandt would have to have a list of doctors they deal with . . .'

'Not at chairman-of-the-board level he wouldn't . . .' said Gary. 'Cell phone records.'

'I'm on it,' said Colin.

An hour later, the details came through.

'We got a call here from Jonathan Meester's cell phone to a Bradley Temple, MD, at two thirty a.m. Sunday, November 15,' said Colin.

'When the Merritts were heading back to Breckenridge,' said Gary.

Ren Googled Bradley Temple. 'He's a doctor here in Denver,' she said. She searched his name with Jonathan Meester's. 'I got another hit here – they were at a pharmaceutical conference in Vegas together two years ago. Nolan Carr was there too. Bradley Temple was one of the "spokespeople" at the event, which was sponsored by MeesterBrandt, and he spoke very highly of their drug Cerxus, and produced some remarkable results of a clinical trial he ran . . .

'Weirdness,' said Ren, scrolling down the list of hits. 'On the Saturday night of the conference, there's a small piece in the *Las Vegas Sun* about a fourteen-year-old boy going missing from the conference hotel. His father was one of the delegates. But it doesn't name names.'

Ren looked it up in VICAP.

'A-ha' she said. 'Bradley Temple's *wife* filed a missing persons report for the Temples' fourteen-year-old son, Cameron . . . but he was found alive and well a few hours later. He had gotten into a fight outside a strip club . . .' She shook her head. 'Jesus. Outside a strip club.'

'I'd say he knocked and he knocked . . .' said Colin.

'So the whole family was in Vegas,' said Gary.

'No doubt at the expense of MeesterBrandt,' said Ren. 'The kid's probably in high school at the expense of MeesterBrandt. Note to self: find owner of pharmaceutical company and jump in pocket.'

'Male goes missing in Vegas . . .' said Colin.

'He was fourteen,' said Ren. 'Seriously? Does Vegas strike you as the type of place you'd feel safe wandering out into at that age?'

Colin held out his hands and squeezed two handfuls of air. 'As long as I could find comfort in a big pair of—'

'Yeah,' said Ren. 'Let me guess: you lost your virginity when you were twelve . . . or your dad brought you to a hooker to make you a man . . . or the Swedish babysitter jumped you on the sofa one night . . .'

'I remember, I had a red Mustang, The Colonel,' said Colin, 'and a girl called—'

'No, no, no,' said Ren. 'No. Information. And aren't cars supposed to have girl names?'

'Back to our case,' said Cliff. 'What are you saying, Ms Ren?'

'What happens in Vegas doesn't always stay in Vegas?'

'If it did,' said Cliff. 'Vegas would have fallen into a sink-hole years ago . . .'

'All that silicone wouldn't help,' said Ren.

'Saline is the way to go,' said Colin.

'Thanks for that,' said Ren. 'Let me call my surgeon.' She pretended to pick up the phone. 'Hello? I'm calling on behalf of colleague. Mmm-hmm, yes, yes . . . gender reassignment. He'd like to find comfort in his very own big pair of . . .'

Ren went back to her computer and ran Bradley Temple through CopLink.

'Meanwhile,' she said, 'it appears that Bradley Temple has been thrown out of two casinos – one in Vegas, one in Baton Rouge. Apparently, both times, he was having drunken money-loss-related meltdowns.'

Ren went back to the Google search results and scrolled down further. She began to get hits on the Cerxus lawsuit.

'Talk among yourselves, people,' she said.

A name had jumped out at her: Diana Moore, head of the nursing home in Jackson, Mississippi that Shep Collier funded. A children's clinic she had run was mentioned in a piece about a consultant psychiatrist, Patrick Kilgallon, who had been questioned in 2008 in connection with accepting kickbacks from Lang Pharmaceuticals to prescribe Cerxus to children between 2002 and 2006.

59

Ren found the nursing home website and called Diana Moore.

'Hello, Diana, my name is SA Ren Bryce, I'm with the FBI in Denver, Colorado. A clinic you ran came up in connection with a case I'm working on. And I was wondering if you could give me some more information on the consultant psychiatrist, Patrick Kilgallon.'

'How do I know you are who you say you are?' said Diana.

Ren gave her her number and waited for her to call back.

'I'm sorry to have to do that,' said Diana, 'you just can't take any risks these days.'

'I understand,' said Ren.

'What is this in connection with?' said Diana.

'I'm working on a homicide investigation and I'd like to ask you about the pediatric clinic, Dr Kilgallon and Cerxus.'

'OK,' said Diana. 'You're talking about when he was questioned about the Cerxus class action suit?'

'Yes,' said Ren.

'Dr Kilgallon had prescribed Cerxus to kids at the clinic and to a lot of other kids in the hospitals he worked in. He had close ties to the pharmaceutical company that made it, he carried out paid speaking engagements for them, etc., but when it came to prescribing Cerxus, there was no proof that he had been acting with anything other than integrity and the best interests of the children he was treating.'

'So nothing happened,' said Ren.

'No,' said Diana, 'and we believed in him. That's why I was happy to hire him when I took over the nursing home after my mom passed; it was our family business.'

'And how did that work out?' said Ren.

'Well, he didn't prescribe any more Cerxus, but for a year, up until earlier this year, he was prescribing an atypical antipsychotic to dementia patients . . .'

'To subdue them . . .' said Ren.

'Well, yes, but that was the least of it,' said Diana. 'Atypicals haven't been approved for treating dementia, but worse – it's not just that they haven't been proven effective, they're actually dangerous for dementia patients. That's been proven with other atypicals. It's even been proven with the older antipsychotics. They all have black-box warnings. This one was newer, so it wasn't linked to any deaths or lawsuits.'

Ellerol.

'Six patients being given the drug died during that year,' said Diana. 'Strokes and heart attacks mainly. We can't prove that it was because of the drug. Except, one day, I got a call from Congressman Collier – I can't call him anything else – and he asked me what Dr Kilgallon had been prescribing. I told him and he was furious – not at me, at the situation. He told me to fire Dr Kilgallon, which I did.'

'Did he tell you why?' said Ren.

'He said "our patients did not come to this stage of their lives to be strung-out victims of someone else's greed". I have never heard him so angry.'

'When did this happen?' said Ren.

320

'Back in August,' said Diana.

'Did Mr Collier say anything else?' said Ren.

'No,' said Diana. 'He said he hadn't got time to get into the details, but that he'd explain everything another time.'

'And did he do that?'

'No,' said Diana. 'We spoke, but not about that. And the next time I saw him was at his press conference.'

'Yes,' said Ren. 'I saw that.'

'The whole thing stank,' said Diana. 'It was like watching a stranger. He didn't even sound like himself.'

He didn't sound right when he was talking to me either.

'I will defend that man to the last,' said Diana. 'Congressman Collier's housekeeper spent the last eight years of her life in our nursing home. She suffered a stroke when she was in her late sixties and the Collier family, the Congressman's parents, paid for her to stay here. That family has kept our little nursing home going, ever since – and that was thirty years ago. The Colliers were devastated when she passed, she was like one of their own. The day her family came to take her personal effects, Congressman Collier and his siblings were there, and they made the announcement to all of us that they would fund this nursing home in her honor. And they've done that ever since.'

'That's such a wonderful thing to do,' said Ren.

'It is,' said Diana. 'I just hope I haven't ruined everything by going public.'

'I doubt that very much,' said Ren. *You've probably done him a huge favor.*

'That's kind of you to say,' said Diana.

'Best of luck with everything you do,' said Ren.

'Thank you,' said Diana. 'I don't care what anyone says, the world needs more Shep Colliers.'

* * *

Ren went to her laptop and opened up Shep Collier's press conference again. She put on her headphones and pressed Play. She watched the speech. She played it again. She realized there were stresses on certain words. She played it again, typing the entire speech. She listened to the audio only, and she highlighted where Collier laid emphasis.

'Thank you all for coming. I stand here today as a proud American, a proud Republican, and a man in whom, at this moment, I can have no pride.

'On the evening of October 24th last, while on a business trip to Boston, I availed of the services of a prostitute.

'No other language can be used to make what I did sound any less deplorable. I am a carbon copy of those who have gone before me, men branded liars and cheats. Although certain of the promises they made to their supporters, they discovered at the nexus of political and private life, a false, misleading god, and an abuse of power, the results of which you see here today.

'My beloved wife, Marie, patiently bore the trials of being married to a politician for over a decade, and despite the devastating impact of my actions, remains by my side today, and is bravely dealing with the effects, both psychological and physical on all our family, particularly on our children.'

Ren read what she had highlighted: the words where the stresses fell:

No lan car(r) brand(t) liars and cheats Cerxus misleading results of patient trials for over a decade devastating side effects both psychological and physical on children.

Holy. Shit. Shep Collier – I knew there was a reason I liked you. You daring bitch.

Ren played the press conference for everyone in the office, and talked them through her notes.

'We need proof if we're to touch Nolan Carr,' said Gary. 'Shep Collier's press conference could be a man with a grudge giving a "screw you" on his way out the door.'

'But Collier clearly knows about Nolan Carr—'

'"Knows", Ren?' said Gary. 'Unless you've got proof, Shep Collier "suspects".'

'Or allegedly alleges . . .' said Ren. 'If Collier is talking about Cerxus trials,' said Ren, 'that pre-dates Nolan Carr's move to MeesterBrandt. Either way, he's mentioning Cerxus, so that's Lang Pharmaceuticals too. Nolan Carr is the common denominator. Who knows what was going on . . . allegedly . . . in my opinion . . .'

She filled everyone in on Diana Moore and Shep Collier asking her to fire Patrick Kilgallon. 'The firing happened in August,' said Ren. 'Maybe it kicked something off with Shep Collier, and, whoever first set it up, Mark Whaley was able to tell Collier more. It sounds to me that whatever dirty practices were going on while Nolan Carr was at Lang, he brought them with him to MeesterBrandt.'

Ren called up another screen. 'And for my pièce de résistance,' she said. 'Check this out – I've got a picture here of Nolan Carr in 1999 with his ex-wife at a Lang Pharmaceutical charity event. Get this, people – Valerie Carr is now Valerie Trent, a lawyer specializing in class action lawsuits against – guess who? – the pharmaceutical industry.'

Ren raised her eyebrows.

'Now, that's what I'd call a big "screw you" on the way out the door.'

60

Valerie Trent's office was in a historic building in downtown Denver. She was an unlikely match for her ex-husband. She was classically good-looking, naturally stylish. She had shoulder-length sandy blonde hair, and wore a beige Armani skirt-suit with a cream pussy-bow blouse. Like her ex-husband, she was perfectly groomed, but she had the striking looks to make it incidental.

Judges must love you, Valerie Trent.

'What's this all about?' said Valerie.

'I'm working on an investigation,' said Ren, 'and I'd like to ask you about your ex-husband, Nolan Carr.'

'Who did you say you were with?' said Valerie.

'The Rocky Mountain Safe Streets Task Force.'

'Aren't you a violent crime squad?' said Valerie. 'Has something happened to Nolan?'

'No,' said Ren. 'But it is a homicide investigation.' Ren watched as the lawyer processed the information.

'Is this about the MeesterBrandt CFO? The murder-suicide?' said Valerie.

'Yes.'

'You think he didn't do it?' said Valerie.

'The investigation is ongoing,' said Ren.

Valerie smiled. 'Ah, yes, the investigation is ongoing . . .'

Ren smiled back. 'Can I ask you some questions?'

'Sure,' said Valerie. 'Go ahead.'

'I watched your ex-husband's interview with CNN in 2000,' said Ren. 'The show about the dangers of antidepressants.'

'Yes,' said Valerie.

'He used you as an example to illustrate the safety of Cerxus,' said Ren. 'You divorced by the end of that year. Was that a coincidence?'

Valerie nodded. 'No.'

'Can you talk to me about what happened?' said Ren. 'I'd like to hear your side of things. I'd like to know your experience of your ex-husband's time with Lang Pharmaceuticals.'

'Well, I had thought that time was great,' said Valerie. 'We were young, recently married, happy. He had a good job, I was studying law. We were lucky. Lang had a blockbuster drug in Cerxus and it was making hundreds of millions of dollars for them. It was the newest one on the market, while some of the others' patents were running out. Some antidepressants were getting bad press because of side effects, but in the show you saw, they were talking about sexual dysfunction, and about the drug's withdrawal symptoms. A lot of people had come forward to say that the withdrawal symptoms were so bad, they had to go back on the drugs. It was a big scandal at the time and Nolan was on damage-control. He was a clean-cut, attractive, young man who was presenting a good case. And Lang had spent thousands on media training for him. Nevertheless, he was dealing with an aggressive interviewer.

'So I'm watching it at home,' said Valerie, 'and I hear him

say, "I wouldn't allow my wife to take it if it wasn't safe." And as you saw, he didn't stop there. He said that our baby had been stillborn and that I had taken Cerxus to deal with the aftermath. What he said about our baby was true. But absolutely not something I wanted to share with America. So, in a few sentences, he managed to plant several ideas in the viewers' heads: that Cerxus was safe, that it could be used to treat grief or post-partum depression . . . and what man is going to approve of his wife taking a drug that could cause sexual dysfunction? It was clever.'

And so screwed up. 'So you weren't taking Cerxus,' said Ren.

'No,' said Valerie. 'There's no shame in taking meds if you need them. But Cerxus had huge issues. People were being misled. And I knew that what Nolan had said about me would reassure the public, and it made me sick to my stomach. It made me sick to think that people could die because of what he said. Can you imagine watching that, and it's your husband on the screen, and he's telling the whole of America about you? I was speechless. I just sat there. I couldn't move. Nolan rushed home afterward, "I'm so sorry, sweetheart. It just came out. You saw the guy, he was on my case, it just came out. He was asking me was this drug safe, you saw him, he was pummeling me, and it just came out."

'He apologized over and over, and I believed him,' said Valerie. 'A few weeks later, I was looking for something in his study and I found some papers. There were memos back and forth from the head of Lang's research lab to the sales and marketing department, drawing attention to the side effects of Cerxus, patients suffering from severe withdrawal symptoms, suicidal thoughts, terrible anxiety. Then there was a page with bullet points and on the top was written

Cerxus/CNN. It was basically how to tackle the task of reassuring the public, how to minimize the fallout. Halfway down the page, I see, hand-written in the margin "personalize/empathy/Val". The print-out was dated one week *before* the interview. And the note was in Nolan's handwriting. So this wasn't even an order from the top – mentioning me was something Nolan came up with himself.'

'What did you do?' said Ren.

'I went crazy. I confronted him when he got home, and then I walked out.'

'What did he say when you confronted him?' said Ren.

'Well, he couldn't deny it,' said Valerie. 'He pleaded with me, he told me again that he had been under huge pressure from his bosses to deliver. But I know Nolan. His ambition is quite something. It's like a force all of its own. When he's in a room with people who are senior to him or more powerful than he is, his ambition is palpable. I used to find it attractive at the start. And I was foolish enough to think that I was separate from that, that our marriage was ultimately the most important thing to him, and that his career success was something I could watch unfold, something I could be proud of. And then this happened. I couldn't forgive him for his lack of concern for all the patients taking these drugs, I couldn't forgive him for using me, no matter what pressure he was under. It was too late. I'm a very private person, and that was so public. I knew I would never trust him again.'

'So,' said Ren, 'do you believe your ex-husband would go to great lengths to protect his career?'

'Absolutely,' said Valerie.

'Knowing what you know, would you ever do anything about Nolan or Lang/MeesterBrandt?' said Ren.

'No,' said Valerie. 'I wouldn't do that.'

Ren nodded. 'I understand.'

'Oh, not because Nolan is my ex-husband,' said Valerie. 'But because he has covered his tracks so well.'

'So, you didn't keep any of the documents you saw?' said Ren.

'I wish I had, but, no. I threw them in his face.' After a moment, she went on, 'Do you want to know what's even more screwed up? When Cerxus' patent was set to expire, Lang applied for pediatric exclusivity with the FDA. That meant, if they could prove that it was an effective treatment for depression in children, then they could get an extension of six months or so on their patent, which was still worth a lot of money to them – over half a billion, at least. It was trialed on kids and the results were positive, so the patent was extended. Doctors began prescribing it to kids . . . but gradually, it became clear that the side effects were devastating – kids were committing suicide, harming themselves, lashing out. The drug was banned in Europe.

'There's a law firm in Denver currently working on putting together a class action suit, but I know for a fact that they are having a hard time gathering enough evidence that Lang Pharmaceuticals knew of the dangers of Cerxus. There are question marks right the way back to the original trial results. They skewed the negative side effects by slotting them under different categories or using "milder" words to describe them. Also, how the trials were carried out in the first place was likely flawed. For antidepressants and antipsychotics, doctors use a scoring system, and you need to reach a certain score to be eligible to take part in the trial. And if I'm a doctor, getting paid five to ten thousand dollars for every patient I enroll, I might just say you're a little more depressed than you really are. And then when your symptoms improve, I can attribute that to the medication. Lang are not the only company to do this—'

'But that's ultimately unprovable, right?' said Ren.

'Unless you find an email or a memo from a pharmaceutical company or CRO to a doctor spelling that out, yes – it's unprovable. And that kind of document just does not exist. No-one would be that dumb. It's understood. There are also concerns that Lang illegally marketed Cerxus for treating childhood depression well before they even went for patent extension.'

'So what happens if lawyers do find evidence on Lang?' said Ren.

'Well, MeesterBrandt Pharmaceuticals, because they bought Lang, will have to shell out a lot of money in fines and settlements. Other companies have paid billions of dollars to make these things go away. Lang was one of the few firms to have so far escaped a lawsuit. Worse than that for MeesterBrandt, though, Cerxus could actually be withdrawn—'

'Even after all these years?' said Ren.

'Absolutely,' said Valerie.

'If the evidence is there . . .'

Valerie nodded. 'Basically, what these lawyers need is someone who knows where the bodies are buried.'

Maybe they already found that someone.

*   *   *

Misty Bryce looked up at Ren with an expression that Ren was trying hard not to read as "dejected". Ren leaned down and gave her a rub.

'I'm sorry if you've been feeling lonesome,' she said.

Misty pressed her body against Ren as they walked up the path to Melissa Grace's house. Ren rang the doorbell and crouched down for hugs from Misty as they waited.

'Hi,' said Melissa.

'Hi,' said Ren, standing up.

Melissa glanced down at Misty with the look of a non-dog-lover.

'I can tie her to the . . .' Ren glanced around.

TJ came down the stairs. 'Hey,' he said. His face lit up when he saw Misty.

Result.

'TJ, if your mom doesn't mind, maybe you could take Misty for a walk? She's been in the house quite a lot recently because of my work, and I'm afraid she's going to end up the dog equivalent of those people who have to be removed from their house by a crane through their second-floor window.'

TJ laughed. He looked at his mom. 'Can I?'

'Sure,' she said. 'OK. Don't go too far.'

TJ rolled his eyes.

'Thank you so much,' said Ren.

TJ went down the hallway to grab his coat.

'Melissa, why don't you wait in the living room in the heat? Close over the door. I'll stay here with Misty.'

TJ came out onto the step with a bright red jacket on.

'No-one's going to miss you in that,' said Ren. She walked down the path with him, and pretended to show him how to operate a leash that was an old-school leash with no fancy system.

'TJ, I need you to do me a very important favor,' said Ren. 'I know your father wouldn't go anywhere without keeping in touch with you.'

TJ said nothing.

'Can you pass on a message for me, please?' said Ren. 'If he responds, you call my number, the one on my card, OK? If he doesn't, he doesn't.'

TJ still didn't commit.

'Can you tell your father to check out the rapper Too Short?'

TJ frowned. 'My dad's into rap?'

'He might be into one of his tracks, yes,' said Ren.

The one called Blow the Whistle.

TJ Grace called Ren that night. His father told him to tell her that was a good track, and that he'd meet her the following morning at ten. TJ gave Ren the address. And he thanked her for Misty. He actually said 'Thank you for Misty.'

Bless his heart.

61

Taber Grace sat in his brother's living room, staring at the family photos lined up along the wall. It felt strange being in a warm, feelgood home, drowning in other people's shit. The doorbell rang. He went to the door and Special Agent Ren Bryce was standing there . . . the BuBabe he saw behind the Summit County Sheriff at the press conference.

'Hello,' she said. She reached out and shook his hand. 'Nice to meet you.'

'You too,' said Taber. 'Come in, take a seat.'

'Thanks. So . . .' said Ren, 'Mark Whaley . . .'

'Mark Whaley came to me because he wanted to blow the whistle on MeesterBrandt,' said Taber. 'He believed that they were involved in illegal practices. The problem was that I found no evidence of that. I found no evidence of anything illegal at MeesterBrandt. I used every method available to me, and that's what I found out.'

What? 'But why did he think there was?' said Ren. 'And he's not alone in that belief.'

'Mark Whaley stood to gain anywhere between $40 million and $80 million for whistleblowing,' said Taber. 'As you know – he was entitled to fifteen or twenty percent of what the government would recoup. He wanted to retire next year and he wanted to have a lot of money to do it in style. The second issue was that I was able to access Mark's computer too, and what I found there wasn't very pleasant. Photos of teens. Lots of them. The same ones your agents are about to find.'

'So, do you believe that Mark Whaley sexually assaulted Shelby Royce and took his own life?' said Ren.

Taber Grace nodded. 'I think Mark Whaley finally got caught doing what he loved to do. *I* would have put a bullet in my head if I were as screwed-up as he was.'

'Do you know anything about ex-Congressman Shep Collier?' said Ren.

'Just that he didn't have the guts to put a bullet in his head when he was caught.'

'But, what about his connection with Mark Whaley?' said Ren.

'I knew nothing about a connection until afterward. I know as much as you do.'

She nodded. 'So why were you watching the Merritts' house?'

Taber stared at her. 'Uh . . . I know it sounds dumb, but I wanted to find a way to give back the money Mark Whaley paid me: to get it back to his daughter . . . '

WTF? 'How did you think you were going to do that?' said Ren. 'Give money to a little girl and expect that to not be noticed?'

'No, not just give it to her like that. Just, maybe to leave an anonymous package in the mailbox.'

Ren frowned. 'OK,' she said. 'Thank you for your time.'

* * *

Taber Grace sat down at his desk. His heart was pounding. His shirt was soaked in sweat. His hand was shaking as he picked up the phone.

'Did you get all that?' he said.

'Yes,' said the voice at the other end.

'Then tell me where . . . tell me where my wife and son are.'

'Isn't she your ex-wife?' said the voice.

'Screw you,' said Taber. 'Screw you.'

62

Ren walked away from her meeting with Taber Grace in a trance.

I could not have had this all wrong. All this time? I'm trying to clear the name of a man with a thing for teenage girls?

She remembered Matt: 'I'm concerned your judgment is impaired . . . that's what happens.'

Oh my God. Maybe he's right. Maybe I can't trust myself. Maybe I can't trust anything.

Ren went through her conversation with Taber Grace over and over.

Or maybe I just can't trust Matt.

Then she remembered one thing Taber Grace had said: 'I was able to access Mark's computer . . . and what I found there wasn't very pleasant. Photos of teens. Lots of them. The same ones your agents are about to find.'

Oh. My. God. He could only have known that we were about to access Mark Whaley's computer if Nolan Carr had told him. Taber Grace was lying. But why would he lie?

* * *

335

Ren called Cliff.

'Cliff, it's Ren. Is there anything you can tell me about Taber Grace?'

Silence.

'He's a good guy,' said Cliff. 'And he's an excellent P.I. He's an IT expert, obviously.' He lowered his voice. 'Better than Grabien.'

I love it.

'I met with him,' said Ren. 'He says he was hired by Mark Whaley, because Whaley suspected MeesterBrandt of illegal practices and he wanted to blow the whistle, and to have as much evidence as possible to back that up. Instead, what Taber Grace discovered, apparently, was evidence that Mark Whaley was into teenage girls . . .'

'Really?' said Cliff. 'Did that ring true to you? We found nothing like that.'

'I don't know,' said Ren. 'No. Cliff, why was Taber Grace fired?'

'I don't know why he was fired, just that he was,' said Cliff. 'And I was sad to see him go. Afterwards, I know that his wife tried to kill herself, and that it was really hard on him. Taber Grace's life took a sad turn. It was like it just drifted away from him. One thing I do know, married or not, he would do absolutely anything for Melissa and Taber Jr.'

'Like lie in a big way?' said Ren.

'If they were in any danger, Ren, you bet your ass. I'd do the same myself, and I wouldn't lose one night's sleep over it.'

Ren's phone rang. It was Glenn Buddy.

'Meet me at Fuller Park by Humboldt Street and 29th,' he said. 'We've had a report of an attempted rape.'

'Shit,' said Ren. 'Bad news is I'm forty-five minutes away.'

'Could you swing by anyway – we'll probably still be there, we need to talk to as many people there as we can.'

'Sure,' said Ren.

Thirty minutes later, Ren pulled in behind Glenn Buddy's car. She could see him in the driver's seat. She knocked on the passenger window and he told her to hop in.

'Turns out,' said Glenn, 'that the park is practically empty, because of the last rape. There was barely anyone there to ask questions to.'

'And what about the victim?' said Ren.

'We took her down to the station to try to work with the forensic artist,' said Glenn.

'So, my work here is done,' said Ren.

'Yup, sorry I didn't text you, but I figured you were only a few minutes away at that stage.'

'That's OK,' said Ren. 'Depending on what the victim says, if he fits the bill, we'll at least have a fourth location – enough to get a decent geographical profile.'

Glenn nodded.

'You know who to call at the FBI for that,' said Ren.

'Yup, thanks,' said Glenn.

Ren got back in her car and pulled out. She took a right onto 29th Avenue. She started to drive back to the office. Then she thought of Bradley Temple, MD. Then she thought of Gary's words.

Back off. Until we have proof, back off.

Bradley Temple could have proof.

Casinos. Losing money.

What would I do if I wanted a man with a gambling problem in my pocket? Bring him to Vegas, shower him with money and strippers, then ask for one teeny-tiny favor. Then repeat. For two decades.

Ren drove toward the left-hand turn-off for Steele Street. Gary's words were there, solid, at the forefront of her mind: 'I don't understand. I don't understand you at all.'

Me neither.

She took the left.

63

Dr Bradley Temple had a medical practice attached to his home on Steele Street. Ren rang the doorbell – there was no answer. She looked at the sign with the opening hours. It was 5 p.m. She was half an hour too early for his evening clinic.

It's a sign. Go back to the office. Do not incur the wrath of Gary Dettling.

She was turning to leave when a teenage boy walked up the path toward her, shrugging off his backpack.

'Hi,' he said. 'Are you looking for the doctor?'

'Yes,' said Ren. 'I see I'm a little early.'

'You can wait if you like,' he said.

'And can I ask who you are?' said Ren.

'Cameron, I'm Dr Temple's son.'

Cameron, the Vegas tearaway, all growed up.

'I'm Ren.'

'Let me open the waiting room door,' he said. He started to unlock the front door. 'I have to open it from inside the house,' he said.

It started to snow. Ren pulled up her hood.

'You can come inside for a minute,' he said.

'I can wait here,' said Ren. 'It's fine. Or, I can go to my car. I'm not sure your father would want me in his waiting room if he's not here.'

'It's cool,' said Cameron. 'I've done it before. You need a security code to get into his office, so . . .' He shrugged.

'OK, thanks,' said Ren. She walked into the house.

'I'll be right back,' said Cameron.

Ren took out her BlackBerry and checked her email. One had come in from Glenn Buddy with an attachment. She was about to open it, but she was distracted by a door further down the hallway, banging softly. She walked toward it. Her phone started ringing. Glenn.

'Hey,' said Ren.

'Did you get a look at the geo-profile?' said Glenn.

'The email just came in,' said Ren.

'You're not going to believe this,' said Glenn. 'That Rigg Raskin kid just called me. He found out about the lightning strikes. What happened was this kid in school, in art class, signed all his paintings that way, like a graffiti artist has a tag. So the day of the party, the guy organizing it thought it would be cool to rip off this guy's tag for the route to the asylum. It really pissed this kid off, he went crazy. So, I don't know, maybe this artist guy showed up to—'

The door swung back on its hinges beside Ren.

'What was that noise?' said Glenn.

'A door banging. Let me go get it.' She went to close the door. It was a bedroom, with the curtains drawn and the scent of teenage boy.

'Anyway, the Raskin kid gave me the name of the artist,' said Glenn, 'and it's right there, smack bang in the jeopardy zone. We're on our way now.'

Ren was transfixed by the walls of the bedroom.

Glenn was still talking. 'The kid's name is—'
Cameron Temple.
'Cameron Temple,' said Glenn.
'Jesus, Glenn—'
'What the fuck are you doing in my bedroom?' roared Cameron.

Ren spun around. He pushed her hard on the chest. She landed on the floor, her back slamming off the side of the bed. Her phone bounced across the floor and disappeared under his desk. Her head was spinning, and as she looked up, all she could see were lightning strikes jumping out at her from his paintings.

'What the fuck is that?' he said. He pointed at her. 'Is that a gun?' Her pants leg had slid up over her ankle holster. Cameron jumped down on the floor beside her and grabbed her ankle, trying to get the gun free.

Do not fuck with me.

Ren reached down, gripped his head on the pressure point, and buried her thumb behind his ear, pushing up hard to get him to drop his hold.

'You fucking bitch,' he said. Ren punched the side of the neck and he collapsed onto the floor. He rolled behind the foot of the bed. Ren stood up and pulled the gun from her ankle holster.

'Don't move,' she said. 'Don't move a fucking inch.'

But Cameron had reached under the bed and before she realized it, he had pulled out a baseball bat. He slammed it against her knee, and she dropped. The pain was excruciating. The gun was gone. Cameron picked it up, and laid it on the desk behind him.

Ren's eyes were streaming. He started to walk toward her, his eyes dead. Ren's heart started to pound.

You are a psychopath.

Ren froze.

No, no, no.

He was on top of her, now, straddling her. He pulled open her jacket, and ripped the gun from her shoulder holster. His knees were digging into her ribs. She could barely breathe. He threw the gun behind him, and it slid under the desk by her phone. He pulled off his belt and pushed her onto her stomach. He smashed his hand against her knee again. Ren cried out. He wound his belt tight around her wrists, and pulled her onto her back again, with her hands underneath her and her pelvis tilted up.

No, no, no.

Cameron stared down at her, almost in a trance. She could smell what she had read about, see what all the victims had described, how gone he looked – to a place where no words of reason would reach. She could see his hands moving toward her.

'Don't,' she said. 'Don't do this. I'm an FBI—'

'I don't care,' shouted Cameron. 'I don't care who you are.' He slapped her hard across her face, and split open her lip. He grabbed her breasts, then slid his hands down and pushed them up under her top, pushing her bra up out of the way.

Ren gagged. 'Please,' she said. 'Please don't do this to me.' Tears started to flow down her face. 'Please.' It was like she wasn't speaking. He was hearing nothing, was now completely shut off from reality. He was smiling. He reached down and started opening the button of her pants.

No. No. No. This is not happening. No.

With all her strength, she reached up and slammed her head against the side of his nose. She heard a crack. He fell off her. Blood poured down his face. He rolled onto his back. Ren was about to run past him to grab her guns.

Channel the dark side. Use it. It will work. Use your anger. He will not be able to beat you.

Cameron Temple slammed Ren to the ground one last time. He grabbed her ankles and yanked her toward him. He knelt down and pressed his hands around her neck and started to squeeze.

Ren's body went limp underneath him. She closed her eyes.

No. No. No. No. No.

The sound of footsteps came toward her, and suddenly the weight of Cameron Temple was off her, and she was being pulled up, and taken in someone's arms and passed into someone else's and she was standing in the hallway with two Denver PD detectives as Glenn Buddy and two more were handcuffing Cameron Temple in front of her.

Ren ran for the bathroom and threw up. There was nothing in her stomach except a bright green energy drink with a sugary stench that made her throw up again. Her head exploded in stars.

And everything went black.

64

Ren woke up in her pink frilly bed in the arms of Ben Rader. It was five a.m. He had arrived at eight the evening before, as soon as she was back from her doctor. Janine was not far behind him.

Ren had talked to them about her memories of Annie's house, how she and her brothers used to play here, all the little hiding places in the house, and all of Annie's old dolls, and trinkets, and Janine and Ben had let her talk until her eyes closed and Ben had nodded across to Janine, and Janine had given him a sad smile, and he had led Ren into her bedroom, where he helped her into her pajamas.

She crumpled into a ball on the bed. Ben held her close until she cried herself to sleep. He didn't speak, but every now and then, he kissed her head or wiped teary strands of hair from her face. She knew by his eyes when he came out of the bathroom earlier that he had shed some tears too. She could hear him breathing beside her, and she wanted to cry she liked him so much. He was a good man to the core. She rolled over and buried her head into his chest, and he stirred awake and kissed her.

'Are you OK?' he said.

'Yes,' said Ren. *Because you're here.*

They got up for breakfast at ten. Ben took a package out of his bag.

'Here,' he said. 'This came for you this morning.'

He handed it to her.

'What do you mean it came for me?' said Ren. 'To where?'

'To my apartment.'

'But . . . it's a rental apartment. And . . . how would anyone know? I mean, no-one knows about us yet.'

Her heart started to pound. She opened the package and pulled out a letter with a note on the front that said: 'Early Christmas present. It was good to meet you. Keep fighting the good fight.'

There was a separate package addressed to Taber Grace and postmarked Breckenridge. It was mailed on Monday, November 16.

'Oh my God, Ben,' said Ren. 'I've just been sent a package that was mailed by Mark Whaley on the day he went missing.'

Ren opened her letter first:

Dear Ren,

Yes – you were correct. Mark Whaley was about to blow the whistle on MeesterBrandt, but he started to worry that they were on to him. He hired me to find that out. I did. The night he went to Breckenridge, he was supposed to be meeting me. He must have gotten cold feet or decided it could wait until after the weekend. That same night I heard that Shep Collier was about to offer his resignation because of a scandal – it hadn't been announced yet what that was. But I knew right away that this was not good. Especially after what I had discovered about MeesterBrandt. Mark had a second cell phone for us to communicate on, I tried to get a hold of him on that, but I couldn't. You know the rest.

The people hired by Nolan Carr to destroy Shep Collier and Mark Whaley (and probably more) are, effectively, private investigators whose specialty is smear campaigns. Tina Bowers identified one of them from a photograph. And it's not just rummaging around your garbage that these people do. It is the total destruction of everything – their target's family life, career, everything. And they will stop at nothing. They employ ex-law enforcement, ex-military, ex-disgruntled anyone, mercenaries to carry out their dirty work. And they will only take on jobs if they have the license to do whatever they want. If they can't find anything on their target, unlikely as that is, they will go after spouses, siblings, children. And that is the hornet's nest that Mark Whaley took a stick to. They did some of their finest work on Mark Whaley. And some poor little Breckenridge babysitter got caught up in it all.

Here's what I got – do your worst.

TG.

Ren opened the package that Mark Whaley had sent to Taber Grace.

Holy shit.

She spent the next hour reading through all the evidence that Mark Whaley had gathered that would bring down MeesterBrandt and Nolan Carr.

There were memos from the late 1990s on Lang Pharmaceuticals headed notepaper, signed by Nolan Carr, detailing Lang's marketing campaigns, with directives to pay physicians for prescribing Cerxus to children, and for a range of conditions it wasn't approved for. There were emails to the lab directing them to re-word or bury negative findings. There were reports about suicides in the children who took

Cerxus, and it was clear that Nolan Carr had known all along. There were emails between Nolan Carr and one of his lobbyists in Washington about the rumors that Shep Collier was talking to the action group trying to introduce tighter regulation of the pharmaceutical industry.

There was one final set of documents.

'Jesus,' said Ren, spreading out more papers. 'Taber Grace hacked Bradley Temple's patient files.'

He is better than Grabien.

There were print-outs of Temple's files. Ren scanned through the list. She came to details of an Ellerol trial from two years previously.

Her anger spiked again.

There were eight drop-outs during the trial – no reason was documented. There was a second note from Taber Grace saying that five of Dr Temple's patients died during the time frame of the trial, although there was no evidence linking the deaths to the trial. Yet, all of the patients were teens/young adults who had been treated at one point for schizophrenia.

Then there was the most recent trial: a combination drug trial for Cerxus/Ellerol.

Then there were the two patients whose names she knew.

Cameron Temple. And Joshua Merritt.

65

Cathy Merritt broke down when Ren confronted her about Joshua and the clinical trial.

'It's too late, Dale,' said Cathy. 'It's too late. I cannot lie any more.'

'I told Jonathan about Joshua's behavioral problems,' said Cathy. 'They were causing huge issues in my relationship with Dale, and with Laurie. The tension in the house . . .' She took a breath. 'Jonathan told me that they'd started trialing Ellerol and Cerxus together for use in teens to treat a first psychotic episode . . . and he suggested that Joshua try it.'

'And when did Joshua have this first psychotic episode?' said Ren.

'After the incident at Mrs Ronson's house . . .' said Cathy, 'what we grounded him for . . .'

'That he denied doing,' said Ren.

'Well, yes, he would,' said Cathy.

'But, accepting that he had done it, who diagnosed it as a psychotic episode?'

'Dr Temple,' said Cathy.

'Joshua didn't see a psychiatrist?' said Ren.

'No,' said Cathy.

'Had you tried anything else to help him with his anger before what happened at the Ronson place?' said Ren.

'Other antidepressants and antipsychotics . . .' said Cathy.

Holy shit. A junk-food-eating, video-game-obsessed kid and you don't think there's a better solution than drugs?

'I was furious at Jonathan when we got the call from Joshua in Breck,' said Cathy. 'Jonathan had assured me that the drug combination was safe . . .'

'And Joshua had never been violent toward anyone before . . .' said Ren.

'He would get angry, just over the last year or so,' said Cathy. 'But, he was a good kid . . . he'd get a little unruly, talk back . . . but, no . . . he was never violent.'

'Was he suffering from delusions?' said Ren.

'No.'

'Hallucinations?' said Ren.

'No.'

And the ambiguity in the name antipsychotic is . . .?

'Jonathan was trying to help us,' said Cathy.

You just don't get it. You just do not get that Joshua was slotted into a trial for money and for favorable statistics.

'Jonathan Meester was trying to save his own ass,' said Ren.

'That's not true,' said Cathy. 'Jonathan's like family to us.'

'Do you remember standing in the hospital hallway, wondering out loud why your ex-husband wanted the overnight visit with Laurie, asking me was that how twisted and sick he was?'

'That still stands,' said Cathy. 'Look what happened with the sitter!'

You have no clue. 'Cathy, do you really think Mark raped and murdered Shelby Royce? Really?'

'Yes!' said Cathy. 'Yes. Don't you? Aren't you the people who solved the case?'

'Didn't you know what was going on with Mark? With MeesterBrandt, with Nolan Carr?'

Cathy looked shocked. 'What do you mean?'

'Mark was about to blow the whistle on Nolan Carr, MeesterBrandt and Lang Pharmaceuticals,' said Ren. 'He had been working on it all year. That's what he was doing and they knew it. They had already taken Shep Collier down. Mark was next. Nolan Carr tried setting Mark up in Boston – they tried to do what they'd done to Shep Collier.'

Cathy looked confused. 'But . . . Jonathan would never have let that happen . . . Jonathan would never—'

'Jonathan knew,' said Ren. 'He knew damn well what was going on. He was part of the whole thing. And you and your husband gave Jonathan Meester and Nolan Carr the perfect opportunity to cover up the side effects of their drug, as well as taking Mark out of the picture.' She took out a piece of paper and handed it to Cathy. 'This is a print-out of your home phone bill that I just received. We had never checked it, because it had never needed to be. And Jonathan Meester knew that. Look at that number circled. The call was placed from the house at five after ten on Saturday night, November 14. The call was made to Nolan Carr. He was tipping him off about Joshua, and the opportunity that had opened up to frame Mark.'

Cathy stared at the page.

'And here,' said Ren, handing her photos. 'These are from traffic cams in Breckenridge. This is Jonathan Meester's car in Breckenridge on Monday, November 16. The day Mark went missing. Mark called Jonathan, asked for his help, and of course, Jonathan was happy to oblige . . .'

Cathy was crying quietly.

'Nolan Carr had already brought in the same firm who arranged the Shep Collier set-up. Their scumbag investigators followed Jared Labati and found Shelby Royce in the house where Jared had allowed her to hide.

'Jonathan arranged to meet Mark, but, while he waited, as insurance, Mark had mailed all the evidence he had on Nolan Carr to Taber Grace. His only mistake was thinking that Jonathan Meester was innocent. Instead of Jonathan, this dirtbag hired by Nolan Carr turned up to meet Mark, and told Mark that he had Laurie – and he had a photo to prove that she was alive. Of course, this photo had been taken by Meester before he left Denver. And Mark was allowed to speak with Laurie on the phone, a call easily set up, again, by Meester. This man forced Mark to shoot Shelby Royce. And to kill himself. Or Laurie wouldn't be released.'

'But . . . I thought . . .' Cathy broke down. 'Oh, dear God. Oh, dear God.'

'Do you know why Laurie was found at Kennington?' said Ren.

'No,' said Cathy. 'I . . . Jonathan said he would drop her somewhere nearby, I didn't think it would be there. I would never have done that. He watched her from the car until she flagged someone down, I know that much.'

Well, good for him. 'Erica told me that you had warned Laurie about the rapist that was out there,' said Ren. 'I'm guessing Jonathan was aware you had too.'

Cathy stared at the ground. She could barely nod.

'So,' said Ren, 'he wasn't just trying to give the cops something to think about, trying to make them waste time looking for a link between the abduction and the rapes that were happening in Denver. He knew that what he was doing would scare the crap out of Laurie. He was showing her how much control he had over her. I know it would have scared the hell out of me when I was eleven. I'd pretty much go along with anything anyone said to me after that.'

How could you let this happen to your child?

'What did you think happened?' said Ren.

'I thought . . . I thought . . . Jonathan was on our side. Oh my God. What have we done? I thought Jonathan was on our side.'

'No,' said Ren. 'Mark was set up by Nolan Carr and Jonathan Meester, Cathy. Not only that, but they knew that the side effects of Ellerol and Cerxus taken together had likely caused Joshua Merritt to attack his sister, and Cameron Temple to have violent, psychotic episodes, that led to three rapes. Jonathan Meester was involved every step of the way. That's what a wonderful godfather he was. That's the man you thought loved your daughter. And the man who really did love her, killed for her, and died for her.'

66

Ren arrived into the office – an email had come in from Taber Grace. The subject was 'Nolan Carr talking to Sales rep'.

It had an audio file attached. Ren played it. Nolan Carr was speaking.

'. . . *the missing link for us is not having an ADD drug. But obviously, we can at least step in after that. So, a kid's diagnosed with ADD/ADHD, given whatever stimulant, which brings on manic symptoms, which more than likely is going to lead to a bipolar diagnosis next time he visits the doctor – he's bouncing off the walls.'*

Laughter.

'Now,' said Carr, 'we're talking – with bipolar on the table – down the road, the kid's in line for an antidepressant, for an antipsychotic . . . so they're coming our way. Cerxus and Ellerol. If you could see Cerxus and Ellerol as, you know, a duo, a Laurel & Hardy, a Ben & Jerry . . .'

Laughter.

'Every child diagnosed with bipolar disorder,' said Carr, 'that's $5,000 per annum. Multiply that . . .'

The pre-cursor to the combined pill.

*　　*　　*

Ren's phone rang.

'Thank you for giving me the great pleasure of watching Nolan Carr in handcuffs. Congratulations, Agent Bryce.'

'Thank you very much,' said Ren. 'Thank you for everything you did.'

'It was a risk worth half-taking.'

Ren laughed. 'I saw your interview on CNN. I'm so happy that you had the chance to clear your name.'

'I can't tell you my relief.'

'I can imagine.' She paused. 'Can I ask what happened in Boston?'

'One of Nolan Carr's lobbyists in Washington had tipped him off that I was liaising with the action group that were trying to introduce tighter regulation of the pharmaceutical industry. As you know, that's not exactly my party's traditional stance. When I was in Boston, I got a phone call from a man, he didn't identify himself – he said that he wanted to arrange a meeting, so I agreed to see him that evening.'

'Why did you agree to meet with a man who didn't identify himself?' said Ren.

'Well, because he identified me: he had information about me, and about my family, that only I knew. This man told me to "quietly resign". Obviously, I refused.'

'He was threatening to reveal this information?' said Ren.

'No – he used it to prove the extent to which they could invade my life, and find things out, and that he'd do the same thing to my wife, my kids . . . he told me I could choose what way I bowed out. I had to pick my poison: child porn discovered on my computer, or I slept with a hooker. I told him he was insane and I left. He fired a warning shot that night: when I connected to the internet, a pornographic image of a child appeared on my computer screen . . .' He paused. 'I've never seen anything like it.'

Just like the teen girls on Mark Whaley's computer.

'Could you not have gone to the police with it?' said Ren.

'I was afraid to,' said Collier. 'It was as simple as that. I was afraid what would happen to me, to my family.'

'What exactly happened at The Crawford that night?' said Ren.

'The night Tina Bowers showed up at my door, I was sitting on my bed in the hotel room, polishing my shoes. My wife called and I put her on speaker. She heard the knock on the door, I told her to stay on the line, that I wasn't expecting anyone.'

'And what happened?' said Ren.

'I opened the door, and Tina Bowers started to walk in. I asked her who she was, she told me that I knew "damn well" who she was. She tried to push me back into the room. She was very forceful. She was saying that she knew that this was what I wanted, and that . . .' He paused. 'She was speaking . . . in graphic terms,' he said. 'I told her that she was mistaken, that she had to leave, but that appeared to encourage her more. I had to physically remove her from the doorway, which is why my hands were on her arms in the photo. I had to almost push her into the hallway . . . which was terrible, I know, but she was very determined.'

'Did she say anything after that?' said Ren.

'She just looked confused,' said Collier. 'I closed the door when I got the chance, but when I looked out of the spyhole, she was looking at the number on the opposite door like she was checking whether she had gotten the right room . . . and then I could see her sort of moving quickly back down the hallway.' He let out a breath. 'The whole thing was very unnerving.'

'What was your reaction?' said Ren.

'I . . . I assumed she did get the wrong room, and that

she thought my reluctance was part of a game, role-playing . . . I went back to my call with Marie. She didn't hear exactly what happened, but she was aware that there were raised voices. I told her that someone had come to the wrong room. I didn't tell her that it was a call-girl – that wouldn't look good, no matter what.

'So Marie knew when she saw the date-stamped photos that she had been on the phone with me before and after they were taken, for a total of forty-five minutes, so I couldn't have had sex with Tina Bowers at that time. If you look closely at the photograph, you can see a dark patch on my shirt – polish, which is why I put Marie on speaker – I wanted to polish and talk at the same time. Because of the black mark, I had started to take off the shirt when Tina Bowers called. I assumed it was a room service guy. That's why I looked a little rumpled, I opened the door just as I was, without thinking.'

'What reason did you give your wife for confessing to something that didn't happen?' said Ren.

'I did tell her that I was the victim of a smear campaign, but I told her it was to do with financial irregularities related to a hedge fund I was involved in. I told her that I could go to jail. She had seen what happened to the Madoffs . . .'

'And she would do anything to stop that,' said Ren.

Collier nodded. 'I admitted to a hooker because the other option was child porn.' He paused. 'MeesterBrandt knew it was in trouble. If Mark Whaley's evidence got out, Nolan Carr was about to saddle the company with a massive lawsuit over Cerxus and off-label marketing at the very least. There was a serious possibility that Cerxus could have been withdrawn from the market – it was clear that the benefits were negligible and the side effects were catastrophic. It got approved in the first place by all kinds of string-pulling. And Ellerol, it now seems, is not the wonder drug it claims to be . . .'

And the combination pill they were so banking on clearly isn't either.

'It seems to me that Jonathan Meester hired Nolan Carr because he had managed to avoid any lawsuits with Cerxus, and had helped make billions of dollars for Lang,' said Collier. 'By getting hold of Cerxus, MeesterBrandt made billions more. Meester also got Nolan Carr in time for him to work his magic on Ellerol, especially as Meester knew there were issues with the drug's claims.'

'Jesus,' said Ren.

'This action group I was listening to is pushing for new legislation: that all clinical trial data, positive and negative, is available to the FDA and to the public, that more research is carried out on polypharmacy, that placebos are used in blind drug trials, etc., etc. And, with Mark Whaley's evidence, MeesterBrandt would have been the poster child for all that was wrong in the industry. And there was no doubt it would have gone under.

'I liked Mark Whaley a lot,' said Collier. 'He was a very modest man. He described himself to me as a "forty percenter" – it was an expression he and his family used: there are people out there who earn their degree or their post-grad by coming top of their class. But, you can still get a degree by scraping forty percent. So, if you're in the hospital, for example, you want to hope that the doctor treating you isn't a "forty percenter".'

'That's a great expression,' said Ren.

'Mark Whaley told me he was a forty percenter. He told me that CFO was a great title, but ultimately, he wouldn't describe himself as top of the class. It made him miss a few tricks over the years, but it also meant that Nolan Carr and

Jonathan Meester underestimated him. He took a course in forensic accounting, on line. He used his wife's home computer. He tracked down people who had worked for Lang in the past. This was a methodical project. He told me he treated it like a dissertation, and put more effort into it than anything he ever had done before. The wheels fell off when he got suspicious that they were on to him . . . you know the rest.'

'Your party is not exactly known to shun big pharma dollars,' said Ren. 'Why the change of heart?'

'Life,' said Collier, 'old age, a doctor trying to medicate my beautiful five-year-old grandson who lashed out because he was bullied for not being white . . .' He paused. 'My businesses are successful. But I don't suffer from greed. That's a disease I don't have. From what I know, it appears to be an incurable one. I don't need anyone's money at this stage of my life. I need peace of mind.'

67

Ren walked back into the office. Colin, Robbie, and Cliff were huddled in a group in the middle of the floor. Cliff had a hand on Colin's shoulder, and was leaning into him. They were laughing.

'I'm telling Colin the rules of the game,' said Cliff.

'What game?' said Ren.

Gary walked into the room. 'Hey,' he said. 'What's going on here?'

'Laughter,' said Ren.

'Colin's got some news,' said Robbie.

Colin locked eyes with Ren as Cliff delivered the news: 'Colin and Naomi are getting married.'

Oh. Wow. Way to hang on to your errant girlfriend.

Gary strode toward him. 'Congratulations,' he said, shaking Colin's hand, patting him on the back.

'Yes,' said Ren. *That's all I've got.* 'When?' *And that's an extra effort.*

'We haven't set a date,' said Colin.

'How did you propose?' *That's better.*

'Over dinner last night,' said Colin.

'Down on one knee?' said Gary, smiling.

'The whole nine,' said Cliff.

'Well, I'm happy for you both,' said Gary. 'She's a good woman.'

'Yes,' said Ren. 'Congratulations.' She walked over to Colin, and gave him a brief hug. 'She *is* a good woman.'

But a bad, bad girl.

Ren sat at her desk, and pulled her keyboard toward her. She wrote an email to Matt.

Subject: PsychoSis(ter)

Dear Matt

I, Orenda Bryce, solemnly ask you to solemnly swear, that if I ever have a psychotic episode, that you will allow the administration of antipsychotics only as a last resort, and if necessary, in the lowest dose possible, for the shortest time possible. Please find me a non-drugs-company-sponsored psychiatrist (I'm tentatively saying Dr Leonard Lone) who will treat my potential psychosis as a short-term blip in an otherwise flawless psychiatric history, and who will treat me with the proven group-therapy-style approach (see attached article). I hereby authorize you, the rest of the family/Gary/Janine/ and Misty to take part.

Regards,
Orenda Bryce

Re: PsychoSis(ter)
Dear Ren
Who will I forward this to in case you murder me during
aforementioned psychotic episode?

Re: PsychoSis(ter)
Dear Matt
No one. TRUST NO ONE.

Re: PsychoSis(ter)
Dear Ren
Then, say hi to Nurse Ratched . . .
I'll be back to haunt you. She'll never believe the visions
are real.

Re: PsychoSis(ter)
Dear Matt
You are sick.

Re: PsychoSis(ter)
Your nephew is crying.

Re: PsychoSis(ter)
Because he misses me. Give him giant hugs. XXXX

Ren looked around. Cliff and Robbie had left for Gaffney's.
Colin had gone into the hallway to take a call. Gary had gone
to his office to grab his coat. He stuck his head back in.

'Are you joining us for the celebration, Ren?'

'I don't know . . .' said Ren.

Gary walked over. 'How are you doing?'

'I'm good . . .' said Ren. 'Just . . . this case . . .' She shook
her head.

Colin walked back into the office while she was talking.

'Cameron Temple may or may not have ended up being a rapist,' said Ren. 'We'll never know. But that first drawing definitely shows that he saw, or he was told, that his only options were hospital or drugs. You should read the questions on the trial. How can anyone expect a teenage boy to know the difference between regular teenage angst or anger, whatever, and actual psychosis?' said Ren. 'His face will be everywhere, and all people will see is a rapist. He could have been a famous artist or sculptor, or . . . anything. We'll never know.'

Gary nodded. He zipped up his jacket. 'OK, Ren – time to give yourself a break. I'll see you in Gaffney's.'

'Is that an order?' said Ren.

'I don't think anyone needs to order you to a bar,' said Gary.

Ren smiled.

Gary left.

Colin was shutting down his computer.

'You're obsessed with analyzing people, and relationships, and all kinds of other people's business,' said Colin.

Eh, hello? 'So you keep saying,' said Ren. 'Probably because it makes you deeply uncomfortable on a personal level.'

'I could care less,' said Colin.

'You *think* you could care less,' said Ren.

'What the hell is that supposed to mean?' said Colin.

Back away. Back away. Actually, no. Don't back away. Do it. Now.

'You've always been freaked out by me analyzing people's personality or motives, or whatever. And now I know why.'

'I'm not freaked out. I told you. I could care less.'

'Yeah, I get it,' said Ren. 'I get it. But it's not true.'

'Shut the fuck up,' said Colin.

Ren stared at him. *I have spent three years giving you the benefit of the doubt. I've wasted time feeling sorry for you . . .*

'Not any more,' said Ren.

'What do you mean "not any more"?' said Colin. 'What the hell are you talking about?'

'Nothing,' said Ren. She got up, and grabbed her bag. 'I'm going home.'

'Wait,' said Colin. 'What the hell is going on here?'

'Nothing,' said Ren. She walked down the hallway, and started to jog down the steps.

Colin followed her down. 'Wait up, for Christ's sake. What's your point?'

Ren spun around. 'I know what you did to get this job,' she said.

'What?' He started to walk past her. 'The shit you talk.'

Ren grabbed his arm. 'Don't fucking walk away from me—'

Colin froze. Ren didn't let go.

'You fucked that man's entire life up,' said Ren.

'What man?' said Colin.

'Taber Grace, you asshole! Taber Grace.'

'What?' said Colin. 'I replaced a loser who got fired.' He pulled away from Ren's grip. 'I was second in line for the job, so . . . obviously, I was the one who would take his place.' He started to walk away again.

'You *got* him fired,' said Ren. 'Quit the fucking bullshit, Colin. When I tell you I know what you did, that means I fucking know, OK? It doesn't mean I'm guessing, or I've got a sneaking fucking suspicion, it means I know.'

Colin was staring at her.

'You set him up,' said Ren.

'You're insane,' said Colin. 'You are nuts.'

'You sent an email to Gary that showed Taber Grace had

lied about some piddling little misdemeanor from his teens about a fire that one of his friends had set, but that he ended up getting sucked into and being in court about – nothing of consequence when you look at it. You knew that Gary Dettling particularly hates lies and you emailed him the information. *Anonymously*. I found it in Taber Grace's personnel file.'

Oh my God. Not a flicker.

'You used a BellSouth account with the user name "colonel". Like your car. Delusions of grandeur there too.' Ren's heart started to pound. 'Didn't you?' she said. 'You hacked into his home computer and you used personal emails to his old buddies to set him up.'

'Why would I have to do that?' said Colin. 'I graduated top of my class, I could have had a job anywhere in the entire country. Why would I be so desperate to—'

'You didn't get this job, though, did you?' said Ren. 'You failed your first big interview after the academy. You followed a Denver woman all the way here, proposed and everything, assuming, because you're an arrogant prick, that you'd get this job. But she dumped you, no doubt realizing that you were an arrogant prick, and then, to add insult to injury, you didn't get the job. Making you a double loser.'

Colin's eyes were lit with anger.

'And you don't like being a loser,' said Ren. 'Everything is about winning with you, isn't it? And being seen to win. Here's Colin Grabien graduating top of his class, high school, college, the Academy. Oh, and here he is meeting the woman of his dreams, heading to Denver to be the man in a new Violent Crimes Task Force, and . . . uh-oh, hold on a minute, he's been dumped, and uh-oh, he didn't get that job after all. Now what? Who's Colin Grabien now?'

Colin took a step toward her. Ren stared him down.

'So, get rid of Taber Grace,' said Ren, 'maybe you could step in like a knight in shining armor, show Gary the mistake he'd made not taking you on, well, that would be even better than getting the job in the first place. And, who knows, maybe you'd get the girl back,' said Ren. 'But whatever the hell happened, your big move to Denver wouldn't be such a public humiliation.'

'I'm not listening to this shit,' said Colin.

'Why would you?' said Ren.

'Get out of my face,' said Colin.

'No.'

'You're a fucking nut job,' said Colin.

'You're a sociopath. A textbook fucking sociopath.'

'You need to read some new textbooks.' Colin walked out the door, and Ren followed him into the sub-zero night.

'Stop,' she said. Her breath caught in the icy air.

Colin kept walking.

'How can you live with yourself?' said Ren. 'You *stole* your job from someone, you ruined his life, his family's life. And he knew you did it, that's the worst part. And he didn't take it any further. He just walked away.'

Colin shrugged.

I want to kill you. 'I can't believe you're not even—'

Colin turned around and stabbed a finger at her as he spoke. 'You should listen to yourself some time. You are so messed up. You're in there trying to make sense of a kid who nearly fucking raped you? Are you out of your mind?'

Ren's heart was pounding. 'What the—'

Colin stuck his head right up in her face. 'Ren? You are one crazy motherfucking bitch.'

Ren punched him. The second punch caught his chin, and sent him staggering backwards. The boot slammed against his kneecap brought him to the ground. The sound of his right elbow breaking, and the cry that followed, was drowned out by the slam of the door, as Gary Dettling got out of his car.

68

Ren stood at the sink in the Safe Streets ladies room running cold water over her hand. Her knuckles were flaming. Her nose was red from the cold, her eyes were streaming. Cliff had driven Colin to the hospital. The official story was that he slipped on the ice. The unofficial story was what Ren was now working on as the water numbed her hand, and the pain of the cold traveled up her arm. Gary was waiting for this story. *For this work of fiction.*

Gary hammered on the door. Ren jumped and hit her hand on the faucet.

'Ren, get out here. Don't pull the ladies room bullshit. I'm coming in.'

'No,' said Ren. 'Don't. I'll be right there.'

She heard him walk away. Huge angry strides.

Shit. Shit. Shit. Shit. Shit.

She walked down the hallway. Her head felt vaporous. And so did her story.

Which shade of asshole can I paint Colin Grabien that Gary will buy? What could Colin have said to make me snap? What could be worse than the shit Gary has already heard Colin say to me that hasn't made me snap? Ren kept walking. *I can't do the not-telling-of-the-truth. But I have no proof. And Gary is the man who always needs proof. Watertight, black and white proof. That I can't provide unless I admit sneaking into an old box of personnel files in the creepy haunted basement of Safe Streets.*

Ren flexed the fingers of her red right hand.

Gary Dettling sat at his desk, staring at the door. He continued to stare at the door after Ren had sat down in front of him.

Then he fixed his eyes on her. 'Colin Grabien has offered his resignation.'

What. The. Fuck?

'Ren, I'm not going to dress this up for you: you are manic. You have been manic for the past month at least.'

There are two coffee stains on this carpet. I hope I'm not responsible for them. I bring coffee in here a lot . . .

'Ren!' said Gary. 'This can't go on. You are going to have to go back on medication—'

'What?' said Ren.

'You heard me,' said Gary.

'No,' said Ren, 'I don't think I did. You're telling me, after everything this case brought up—'

'Ren, you've been on mood stabilizers before and they work for you. I'm not asking you to take a drug that hasn't been trialed or is making people psychotic. I'm asking you to take a drug that has worked for you in the past, and that hasn't caused you any side effects.'

'But—'

'What's your solution?' said Gary. 'What do you think you should do? What do you think I should do?'

'I'll go and see Dr Lone.'

'Ren! That's a given. And on its own, talking hasn't

worked for you, because you either stonewall these psychiatrists or sidestep them. Therapy works if you talk, it won't if you don't. But before you even begin to start doing that, you need medication to get you back on an even keel. I could list all the things you've done, and all the things that have happened to you, but you know what they are. You scared the crap out of me. What happened with Cameron Temple was . . .' He took in a breath. 'Ren, I don't ever want to get a phone call like that again.'

Do not cry. Do not cry.

'Do you get that I get sucked into your bullshit?' said Gary. 'It is like I am on that rollercoaster with you, Ren, and believe me, I cannot afford to take that ride. I cannot keep up. No man could. Even you can't. It has to end here.'

Do not cry. Do not cry.

'Now, get out of my office,' said Gary.

Ren stood up. *Just 'get out of my office'? Or 'get out of the building' or 'you are fired' . . .?*

Ren's hands shook as she opened the door.

This was Gary Dettling. You did what he said. You got out of his office when he said 'get out of my office'.

And you awaited further instructions.

Just say it. While it's all laid out. Get it over with while you can.

'Gary, I'm seeing Ben Rader.'

Gary didn't look up. 'He's a good guy,' he said.

'He is,' said Ren. She hovered for a minute. 'Thank you,' she said.

'Ren?' said Gary.

'Yes?'

'Let him look after you.'

OK.

Ren closed the door gently behind her.

*   *   *

She went in to Cliff and sat at the edge of his desk.

'How's my girl?' he said patting her leg.

'Not good,' said Ren.

'I don't like to hear that,' said Cliff.

'I'm scarred,' said Ren. 'I know too much.' She shook her head.

'About what?' said Cliff.

'Everything,' said Ren. 'How does it all work? Everyone getting diagnosed with shit, more drugs taken, more people messed up?'

'Meds work for a lot of people,' said Cliff.

'I'm not saying they don't,' said Ren. 'But there is something very, very wrong if the most successful drugs in a country are antipsychotics. And the people making them are being sued, left and right. That's what I'm saying. And giving kids psychotropic drugs? That's a whole pile of wrong. Children being diagnosed bipolar aged two? Just for wanting to jump around, and laugh and sing and dance, and – God forbid – not be compliant?'

'Our neighbor's an elementary school teacher,' said Cliff. 'She has nine certified hyperactive children in her class. And she says if you open their lunchboxes, you might as well have a pound of sugar in there.'

'Well, great!' said Ren, 'those kids will be ready for weight-loss drugs further down the line, maybe some diabetes drugs . . . Look at Joshua Merritt – he'd obviously gained weight if his little stepsister's calling him a fat freak, he's losing it . . .' She let out a breath. 'Maybe Henry Gadsden's dream is coming through – these companies really will be able to sell to everyone.'

Ren could feel it again, that brief shift inside, that spike of rage. It was useful for work. It got results. It felt so scary, it felt good. When she was aware of it – rarely while it was happening, mostly in hindsight – she called it the bad side of mania. She had said it to Matt once.

'Hate to break it to you, Ren – mania is one big bad side.'

'You've been to paradise, but you haven't been to me . . .' she had said. Matt didn't laugh with her.

'Ren. Please,' he had said, 'you know this. The fallout is never worth it—'

Reminiscence over.

There are two sides, Matt. And you'll never understand that soaring high. It is worth it, it always is. Every time.

Her anger toward Matt flared. She could feel her raised heart beat, her narrowed eyes, her frown.

The bad side, if it took hold, brought with it a strange, roaming anger. It moved like the sea, rolling up on an unsuspecting shore, crashing down, retreating, leaving in its wake an altered landscape. From a distance, it was something beautiful, clear, and alive. But, underneath, it was raging. And then it would strike, tearing at the shore, carrying away broken parts.

Dr Leonard Lone opened his door with a smile.

You are a billionaire.

'Ren,' said Dr Lone. 'Welcome. Come in, take a seat.'

'Thank you.'

A candle was burning on the windowsill, and classical music played from a Bose stereo.

'How have you been?' said Dr Lone, sitting back in his chair.

You are a billionaire. 'I'm good,' said Ren. 'Great.' *You are a billionaire.*

Dr Lone nodded.

'I've been very busy with work,' said Ren. *You are a billionaire.* 'It's been very intense. But, the outcome was positive. We took out a few of your friends in the pharmaceutical industry.'

He smiled. 'I saw that in the newspaper. Well done. That must have been very satisfying.'

'It was,' said Ren. 'It was amazing. We all put in a lot of hard work.'

I slept with two men. I crashed a car. I punched my colleague. You are a billionaire.

'And how are you feeling after all that?' said Dr Lone.

'Great,' said Ren. 'Great.' She started to cry.

EPILOGUE

Taber Grace poured maple syrup over a plate of pancakes. He put down the jug. Melissa Grace was smiling at him.

'I love you,' she said.

'I love you too,' said Taber.

'I don't know how,' said Melissa.

'Because you were the built-in software that came with my heart.'

They both laughed.

'Because,' he said. 'You are responsible for this – for me sitting here, for me meeting up with a life that I thought was running parallel, out of my reach. And here I am, eating pancakes with my wife, while our son is upstairs sleeping like a baby.' He put his hands on her waist and pulled her gently toward him.

'I'm sorry you got dragged in to the case,' said Taber.

'I know that,' said Melissa. She hugged him. 'I know. We're here now. It wasn't for long. They didn't lay a finger on us. TJ and I – we had each other. And . . . we have you now. We have you.'

Taber pulled back and held her face in his hands.

'I never ever stopped thinking of you as my wife, Melissa Eileen Grace.'

She laughed.

'I'd say that in six years, I called you my ex-wife about four times,' said Taber. 'And every time, I would choke on that "ex". Four times, Missy. And I talked about you a hell of a lot more than that . . . I would usually call you my wife . . . to see if anyone would notice, just to make them think "hey, maybe he still loves her after all", so it would give me permission to think, "hey, maybe I still love her after all". Only problem was? I knew all along that I still loved you. Nothing ever changed that. I guess I just didn't love the circumstances we found ourselves in.'

'Me neither,' said Missy.

'Well, those circumstances are gone now. It's just us. You, me and Taber Jr.'

Ren walked into Annie's living room. Ben Rader had fallen asleep on the sofa. He was wearing just jeans, lying on his stomach, his face turned toward her.

I am in a relationship with a Vanity Fair *spread.*

Ren knelt down in front of him and ran her hand down his bare back. Ben smiled, but he was still sleeping.

You are beautiful. You will leave me.

Ren leaned down and kissed his cheek, then his lips. He kissed her more.

'Hey,' he said. 'What time is it?' He rolled onto his back.

'Midnight,' said Ren.

'Why did you let me sleep?'

'Why wouldn't I?' said Ren. 'I'm not your mom.'

Ben sat up. 'I don't know what my mom has to do with it, but come over here.'

Ren sat down beside him and he pulled her legs onto his lap. He looked across at the bookshelves.

'I don't read,' he said. 'I'd say I've read one piece of fiction in my entire life. But I would love to lie on this sofa with you on a Sunday morning, with your legs like this, and your head back, while you're reading your book. Or else you're naked. Your call.'

'We could alternate . . .' said Ren.

'One Sunday on, one Sunday off?'

'One hour on, one hour off.'

Ben squeezed her legs. 'Do you know something?' he said. 'When I was sixteen years old, my father sat me down, and he told me never, ever to settle for anyone. Never to think that my mother or him expected me to marry, and have kids, or do anything by any age. My father was forty-five years old when he met my mother. He saw her walking down the street, and he stopped her right there and then, and asked her out. He said he knew that she was the woman he was going to marry. His friends had teenage children at that stage of their lives, he was the only single one, but he knew he wouldn't settle for less than the best. He is eighty years old, my mom is seventy-three, and I swear to God, they look into each other's eyes like they were still on that sidewalk thirty-five years ago.'

He looked at Ren. 'You just added forty-five and thirty-five together, didn't you?'

'I did,' said Ren. 'You got me.'

'That's because it was easier than thinking about what I was saying.'

'Really?' said Ren.

'Absolutely,' said Ben.

Ren laughed. 'I like you, Ben Rader. I like you a lot.'

'That's good,' said Ben. 'If you keep going like that, in

about ten years, you might catch up with how I feel about you.'

'How did you *ever* work undercover?' said Ren. 'Saying shit like that?'

'Wait 'til we're married . . .'

Ren laughed. 'You are nuts.'

'Is that a yes?'

'You're only joking about it because you don't mean it.'

'Exactly . . . I don't mean it. At all. I'd hate that. It would be a nightmare.'

'OK, seriously. Stop.'

'You stop.'

'You really are eighteen, aren't you?' said Ren.

'Yup. Old enough to marry without my parents' consent.' He paused. 'But they would totally consent to you.'

'I punched my colleague in the face. I regularly flirt with unemployment. None of that is good.' *I am also nuts. And on drugs.*

'And Ben and Ren would look cool on the wedding invitations.'

'I have a major problem dating someone with a name that rhymes with mine.'

'And what about marrying him?'

ACKNOWLEDGEMENTS

To my agent, Darley Anderson, thank you for being wonderful, witty and wise. To everyone at the Darley Anderson Agency, you are brilliant.

Thank you to my discerning, thoughtful, and serene editor, Sarah Hodgson. I am very lucky to benefit from your talents.

Thank you to Kate Elton and to everyone at the amazing HarperCollins.

To Lynne Drew, thank you, always, for your encouragement.

To the mighty Moira Reilly and the tenacious Tony Purdue, thank you for your tireless work. And fabulousness.

Thank you to Joy Chamberlain for her sharp copy-editing ways.

For her editorial advice in the early stages of the book, many thanks to Kate Burke.

Thank you to SSA Phil Niedringhaus from The Rocky Mountain Safe Streets Task Force; you are always informative, patient and generous, despite knowing that one question is never one question.

For *Blood Loss*, I created fake drug companies, fake drugs, and fake lawsuits. And, yes, truth is stranger than fiction . . .

For their fascinating, thought-provoking, and inspiring insight into the realities of the pharmaceutical industry, I recommend the following books, and their expert authors: *The Truth About The Drug Companies* by Marcia Angell, M.D.; *Selling Sickness* by Ray Moynihan and Alan Cassels; *The Emperor's New Drugs* by Irving Kirsch; *Anatomy of an Epidemic* by Robert Whitaker.

Thank you, also, to Marcia Angell to whom I attribute Dr Leonard Lone's clarifying line on the chemical imbalance theory: *'One could argue that fevers are caused by too little aspirin . . .'*

Special thanks to Robert Whitaker for his time, and further plot-specific enlightenment.

To Phil Walter, Special Agent, FBI (retired), thank you so much for sharing your time and knowledge.

Thank you to the always-entertaining Andy and Niki from The Fireside Inn in Breckenridge.

Mauser, you are a marvel.

A mysterious thank you to Cliffy.

To the exceptional Sue Booth-Forbes, and the magical world of Anam Cara.

To all my family and friends, you are what life is all about.

Thank you to the ever-smiling Paul, whose support and kindness are boundless.